THE LURE OF THE DUTCHMAN

CRACKING THE MYSTERY OF THE LOST MINE

Thomas A. Geldermann

ISBN Number   1-57087-523-5
Library of Congress Catalog   00-131664

Professional Press
PO Box 4371
Chapel Hill, NC 27515-4371

Manufactured in the United States of America
04 03 02 01 00   10 9 8 7 6 5 4 3 2

*To my wife, children and grandchildren
whom I love individually and collectively.*

FOREWORD

In 1846, a German adventurer named Jacob Waltz emigrated to the United States. Eighteen years later, he arrived in Arizona. He was 56 years old and the year was 1864. He prospected in the Prescott area and then moved to Phoenix to look for gold in and around the Superstition Mountains, a chain of rugged peaks some 25 miles east-northeast of the center of the city. In the spring of 1878, he found it. Waltz either discovered a mine by himself or was shown it by a Spaniard named Peralta, a native of Sonora, Mexico. Waltz had saved Peralta during a barroom brawl which ensued after Peralta had been stabbed in a gambling dispute. Waltz never disclosed the whereabouts of the mine.

Jacob Waltz was never a congenial man and after he discovered gold, he became downright ornery. He was thought to have killed several men and would threaten anyone who tried to learn the location of his mine. By 1884, he was seen selling small quantities of gold in

1

Mesa City and the richness of his mine began to grow in the minds of other prospectors. The more the fame of his mine grew, the more reclusive and protective Jacob Waltz became. And the more reclusive and protective Jacob Waltz became, the more the fame of his mine grew.

They tried to follow him. They tried to trick him. They searched and searched but they couldn't find the mine. In February 1891, Jacob Waltz contracted pneumonia and on October 25th of that same year, he died. He was 83 years old. He had lived his life in seclusion, coming to town to drink and gamble each time he sold some gold. He was mean and unloved. He died in the home of one Julia Thomas, a baker and perhaps his only friend.

The rumors began immediately. Waltz, known as the Dutchman because of his heritage, had drawn a map. He had given the location of the mine to someone on his deathbed. Maps appeared and were sold as genuine. Amateurs and professionals alike began to search for the mine in earnest. The Superstition Mountains were almost overrun with prospectors. Without a vengeful Jacob Waltz to stop them, the mine was fair game for the first one to find it.

They came, they searched and they died. Over the next 100 years, sixty-eight people lost their lives trying to find the Lost Dutchman Mine. Some perished in the desert climate of the Superstition Mountains, some fell to their deaths from perilous heights, some became victims of the denizens of the desert and some met their maker by violence and murder. But the mine kept

Waltz's secret.

Every year, first timers and veterans alike take up the hunt not even sure that the mine ever really existed. They search and fail. They search again and fail again.

The treasure has become the excitement of the hunt rather than the gold itself.

CHAPTER ONE

In the Southwestern Sonoran desert in the Superstition Mountains, a dent-ridden, rust-marked pickup truck drew to a stop. Two men emerged. They wore jeans, wool shirts, work boots and weathered western hats. They circled the truck from opposite directions, arriving at the back at the same time. The driver lowered the tailgate and the passenger scrambled into the truck bed. He handed a ventilated crate to the other man, who dropped it roughly to the ground.

"Hey! Be a little careful! Will ya, Butch!" the man in the truck bed said.

"What's the matter, Charlie? 'Fraid I'm goin' to hurt 'em?" Butch laughed. "Maybe you'd like to get 'em ready this time. I'm sure you'd be gentle. Har! Har!"

"Cut the crap, Butch," Charlie said. "Let's just get it over with. You know I don't like this part."

With that Charlie dropped from the truck bed beside the crate. Each man grabbed a rope handle, lifted the crate and walked in a straight line away from the truck. After about three hundred yards, they deposited their load on the ground and stepped back.

"All right," Butch said. "I'll do it. You just hand 'em to me and make sure that none get away."

With a small sigh of relief, Charlie opened a wire door on the top of the crate, reached in and extracted a soft bundle of shivering fur. He handed the cottontail to Butch, who grabbed the rabbit by the scruff of the neck and walked another 50 yards into the desert. There he tied a thin cord around a docile rear foot. The other end was attached to a nearby brittle bush. Butch then stood up and withdrew a hunting knife from the scabbard attached to his waist. He bent down, lifted the rabbit by the loose fur above the shoulders and drew the razor-sharp blade across its trembling chest. Blood appeared immediately and streaked the front of the animal. The wound was serious but the rabbit would not die from it. That would come later. Butch placed the animal on the ground, gave it a pat on the head and said, "Bye-bye, bunny!"

He turned just as Charlie was approaching with another rabbit. Butch grabbed the quaking animal and proceeded to perform the same routine. He tethered this rabbit to another bush. Soon he had seven rabbits tied down in a circle about twenty feet in diameter.

"Well, that's that," he said to Charlie. "Let's get comfortable. It's starting to get dark."

They returned to the truck and unloaded a large duffel bag. Charlie drove the pickup away from the stakeout into a small depression. Butch grabbed the duffel and lugged it to a crude blind some twenty-five yards from the circle of rabbits. He had just unzipped the bag when Charlie dropped down beside him.

"Looks like a good night," he said. "Half-moon gives just the right amount of light and no wind to speak of."

"Yeah!" Butch returned. "Just do yer job and let's get outta here."

They had a long wait and they knew it. It was now just past eight o'clock and it would be nearer eleven before anything started. Charlie checked his gear while Butch settled in. First, he assembled the gas-propulsion rifle. This weapon could propel a dart 100 yards with a drop of only eight inches. In the 25 to 30 yards that their projectiles would be traveling, the trajectory would be deflected by less than an inch. Charlie then pulled out a black leather tube and extracted the infra-red telescopic sight. He mounted it on the rifle and sighted it on a nearby palo verde tree.

"Good," he breathed. Next he attached a hose to the bottom of the gun stock and connected the other end to a nitrogen pressure tank. He checked the pressure gauge and inserted a dart into the chamber of the rifle. Now, he activated the night scope and sighted on the crotch of another tree that was located just beyond the rabbit circle. He was in a prone position completely hidden by desert foliage. He squeezed the trigger. There was an almost inaudible hiss as the dart flew to its mark. It hit the tree a half an inch below and three-quarters of an inch to the right of where Charlie had aimed. He made two adjustments on the sight, loaded another round and fired. This time the dart hit the mark dead center. Charlie laid the gun down.

"Ready!" he said.

"Bout time," Butch replied.

It was exactly eighteen minutes after eleven when they heard the first sound. It was just a single low note. It seemed to go unanswered. Then it sounded again. Was it the same or had it come from another direction? It was difficult to be sure. At the first sound, Butch had awakened from a seemingly deep sleep and nudged Charlie. Charlie had been on a nervous watch the whole time and didn't need any prodding. He glanced at Butch and placed a forefinger to his lips. The second note sounded. Both men slid forward. Charlie to his rifle and Butch to a vantage point on his right side. Between them was a rectangular wooden box. Charlie reached over and raised the lid exposing two rows of six darts, each with the point downward. He took the first one from the first row and carefully inserted it into the firing chamber of the gun. He placed the stock to his shoulder, his right eye to the infra-red scope and waited.

The sounds in the night were now double-pitched and more frequent. They seemed to be coming from all quadrants. The rabbits were completely still, only betrayed by their uncontrollable shaking. Then, off to the right of the circle of tethered animals a pair of yellow beads reflected in the light of the half-moon. Another pair appeared on the left and still another behind. The rabbits were trying to become invisible but sensed that they were hopeless and doomed. The beads moved closer and the moonlight unveiled their true identity, the eyes of the hunter. What Charlie had been able to detect through his infrared night scope became visible to Butch as well, as his eyes had become adjusted to the darkness. Butch scanned the area.

"I make out six of 'em," he whispered.

"I get eight," Charlie corrected.

"Good," Butch answered.

The coyotes had completely surrounded the helpless cottontails and were silent, watching, waiting. Then as if on a prearranged signal, they began a high-pitched, blood-chilling yapping. The rabbits froze in terror, unable to move. The shrieks continued until the prey was completely immobilized. Then it stopped as suddenly as it had begun. Steel jaws clamped on soft fur. It was over quickly and perhaps mercifully.

As the feeding began, Charlie sighted on the rear quarters of one of the coyotes nearest the fringe. He squeezed off a dart. The coyote turned in annoyance and then slowly slumped to the ground. Charlie reloaded and downed another and another. The largest of the pack, possibly the leader, sensed that something was wrong. He turned to look at his fallen brothers just as a dart slammed into his hip. He tried to warn the remaining few but his voice was nothing but a gush of air as his legs gave way and his eyes fogged over. Charlie was working rapidly and efficiently. In less than a minutes time he had fired eight darts and eight coyotes lay unconscious on the ground.

"That's it!" Butch said. "Let's pack up and get outta here!"

Charlie had already disconnected the hose at both ends and was busy taking down the scope and rifle. He quickly packed the gear and headed for the truck. Butch had moved out of the blind and was approaching the coyotes, gun in hand. He made sure that each one was completely inert and then began to hog tie and muzzle them. By the time Charlie arrived with the pickup, he had completed his job and was untethering the mangled rabbits. One he found that was still breathing. He crushed its head under the heal of his boot with a final, "Bye-bye, bunny."

Charlie was now by his side. He turned his head in revulsion and said, "Let's get these critters in the truck. We've only got about four hours until they start to wake up and I don't want to be around if they're not in their cages."

"Gottcha!" Butch agreed.

Charlie produced eight bags from the truck. Each coyote was zippered into a bag and laid in the bed of the pickup. A tarp was then secured over the entire cargo area. Butch jumped into the driver's seat.

"Let's go!" he said.

Charlie was only too glad to let Butch drive the final leg. He took one last look around. Satisfied, he climbed into the right side, slammed the door and said, "Okay," as he settled in for the two-hour bone-jarring ride over the rocky off-road terrain that lay ahead of them.

CHAPTER TWO

Bill Dickson took a deep breath as he stood before the imposing door. Even though he had stood in this very spot many times, he still felt the butterflies in his stomach as he raised his fist to knock. Behind the door sat one of the most powerful and intimidating men in the world. Dickson swallowed hard and exhaled as his knuckles struck the solid oak door of the Oval Office.

"Enter," announced the speaker next to Dickson's head.

Bill pushed open the heavy door and stepped inside.

"The Secretaries are assembled in the Cabinet room, Mr. President," Dickson said.

"I'll be just a few minutes, Bill. Tell them that I'll be right in," the President ordered.

Bill backed out, closed the door and went to the Cabinet Room. Inside the Oval Office, Branden David Jefferson, rose from his desk and collected his thoughts.

"Getting here was relatively easy," he mused. "But now I've got to prove myself and it's going to be tough."

Two years ago, he had been elected in a landslide. The campaign issues had been handed to him on a silver platter. Inefficiencies in the old administration and their inability to cope with rising food prices made it easy to place the blame and promise solutions. Now, in the middle of his first, and perhaps his only term, he had been unable to deliver. He moved thoughtfully across the room and opened the door that separated the Oval Office from the Cabinet Room. Small groups stopped talking and hurried to their respective places as the President moved through the room. He walked completely around the huge table, shaking hands and greeting each cabinet member by his or her first name. He came to the center of the table, extended a warm salutation to the vice-president and took his seat. The members of the Cabinet followed his example and the room settled down for business. The table was occupied by the President and the Cabinet Secretaries but the perimeter of the room was filled with high-ranking staff members of each cabinet department. President Jefferson cleared his throat and the room became absolutely still. He addressed the gathering.

"Ladies and gentlemen," he began. "Does anyone not know why we're here?"

Silence!

"Good," he continued. "Now I'm going to remind you of a few facts."

Jefferson slowly looked around the table, catching

the eyes of each of the Secretaries as he traversed the assembly. None of them were able to hold his gaze without lowering their eyes as he went to the next person. The Vice-president, the Attorney General, the Secretaries of State, Treasury, Defense, Interior, Agriculture, Commerce, Labor, Health and Human Services, Housing and Urban Development, Transportation, Education, Energy, and Veterans Affairs all succumbed to his intense stare. When he was certain that he was in complete control, he paused, leaned back in his chair and proceeded.

"Five years ago, a meat shortage began to develop. At the time, no one gave it too much thought. Prices began to rise as is natural in a free market society. The next year the trend continued and it was soon evident that breeding was off in cattle, hogs and sheep. The past administration took a personal interest and publicly resolved to correct the situation. That was a big mistake on their part. They not only failed, but conditions steadily worsened. By election time, meat prices had doubled and had driven other food prices higher. We capitalized on their troubles and made food costs, especially meat prices, a major campaign issue. We won in a landslide and every appointment that I made was predicated on a knowledge of or an access to the livestock industry.

"Now here we are, two years later, and the problem is worse than when I took office. What in the hell is happening and why haven't we been able to correct or alleviate the situation?"

The President looked directly at the Secretary of

Agriculture. "George," he said. "Let's have a report and you'd better have some answers."

George Harkens was from the panhandle section of Texas. He had been appointed Secretary of Agriculture because of his personal cattle interests. He controlled over 100,000 acres of range land and fed 250,000 head of cattle in his and other feedlots. He had a doctorate in animal husbandry from Texas A & M University. He was a self-made man and had built a medium-sized fortune from his chosen career in the cattle business. He was well respected in the industry and had access to every university and research facility in the country. Secretary Harkens pulled a large file of papers in front of him, arranged them in some private order and began.

"Mr. President," he nervously started. "We've made some progress but we still have a long way to go. The universities are all cooperating and their research departments are exchanging information. The Meat Institute has coordinated the research facilities of all the major meat-packing companies and the Cattleman's Association is doing what they can to combine the efforts of the ranchers. The Department of Agriculture has established a central command room where all the information gathered from these sources is combined and fed into a computer. The results are then distributed to all of the participants. We have established a communications network that allows for the immediate exchange of information. And—"

"Yes, yes!" the President interrupted. "We're well aware of all of this, but what have they discovered?"

"I was getting to that, Mr. President," the Secretary continued. "The only thing that we're sure of, right now, is that a virus is infecting the animals and affecting their ability to breed. It looks like the virus is airborne. They're still trying to isolate it in order to develop a serum. So far only warm-blooded, four-legged animals seem to be affected. It appears that wildlife numbers are down proportionately."

"What about that, Bill?" the President directed his question to William Denner, the Secretary of the Interior.

"That's right, Mr. President," the Secretary of the Interior replied. "We've been getting calls from all of the environmental groups demanding to know what's going on. So far we've been able to stall them. But, I'm afraid that they won't keep still much longer."

The President returned his attention to the Secretary of Agriculture.

"We're frantically looking for the host so that we can contain the spread of the virus, but, frankly we've drawn a blank so far. The entire continental forty-eight states seem to be infected, and parts of Canada and Mexico as well."

Marion Townsend Kerstner, the Secretary of Housing and Urban Development, half-raised her hand and interjected, "Well, you'd better get to the bottom of this soon or we're going to have full-scale rioting in the cities."

The President leaned forward intensely, urging her to continue.

"Every major city is experiencing the same thing,"

she obliged. "The inner core is boiling. They're being fed a line and they're devouring it like a bunch of starving hyenas. It appears as if it's being orchestrated, but we haven't been able to find a common denominator. The high price of beef is the main target, followed closely by the other meats, then it's all the rest of the grocery list. And guess who's getting the blame? First, the elusive speculators, then the profiteering cattlemen and the meat packers, grocery stores, the right-wing extremists and, of course, the oppressive rich. In any event, the poor and underprivileged of the inner city are up in arms and they're convinced that the government is withholding something. In my opinion, if we don't come up with something fast, we're going to witness the worst rioting in the history of the country."

The room became deathly silent as the Secretary of Housing and Urban Development sat back in her chair, indicating that she was through for now.

"Any other good news?" the President asked. He looked around the table and settled on Margaret Milfore, the Secretary of State. She had an uneasy look about her and was visibly fidgeting with her notes, the reason, perhaps, that she had been selected.

"Well," she began. "I've been getting serious reports from our neighbors to the south and north. They are experiencing drops in their meat production and they know about our problem. It's certainly no secret. They're talking about quarantines, inspections and restricting our exports, although we haven't been exporting meats or meat products for over two years now. There's a real stigma on our meats. It's worse than the Mad Cow Disease. Nobody will have anything to do with us. The whole world is waiting to see what we do to solve the problem. Our very stature as a world leader is in jeopardy. I can not overemphasize how serious our position is. We absolutely must come up with a total and final resolution."

Once again the President looked around the room, this time taking in not only those seated at the cabinet table but also everyone around the perimeter of the room.

"Ladies and gentlemen," he said. "If any one of you had reservations about the seriousness of the situation, I hope that they have been dispelled. Tomorrow I am going before Congress and ask for a virtual blank check for research, both field and laboratory. But money alone will not solve the problem. Each and every one in this room must take a personal interest in both the solution and speed in which a solution is achieved."

He paused for effect and put on his most serious face.

"This meeting is over. Now get to work! The world is waiting and watching!"

CHAPTER THREE

Brian Nichols was driving his pickup north on Arizona Highway 88. He was past Apache Junction, a blossoming suburb of Phoenix and heading toward Tortilla Flat. The road was known as the Apache Trail and was deserted. The Apache Trail wasn't a heavily traveled route under normal conditions. It turned into an unpaved road just past Tortilla Flat, but at 5:30 in the morning it was almost devoid of cars. In fact, Brian hadn't seen another vehicle for the past fifteen minutes. This was the third Saturday in a row that he had made this trip. Brian lived on the northwest side of Phoenix. The trip to Tortilla Flat, which was nothing more than a restaurant and an abandoned hotel, took well over an hour. It was a lonely hour for Brian.

He tuned his radio to a country-western station and let his mind drift to the vagaries of the music. The program was interrupted occasionally by weather and news. He wasn't concentrating on anything in particular so he barely heard the commentator announce the top story of the day, a story that had been increasingly in the news over the past months. It concerned the rising cost of living fueled by increases in the price of food. Most food items had been rising at about the annual inflationary rate, but meat, particularly beef, had outstripped other staples by a huge margin.

Meat futures on the Chicago Mercantile Exchange had been up the permissible limit for the last two days and had closed at all-time highs. It looked as if the trend would continue into the foreseeable future. Cattle numbers were down to the extent that a congressional probe was under way and the President was going to address the nation on Sunday night. There was a certain amount of panic in the commentator's voice as he tried to capture the attention of the early morning audience. He failed on Brian, not only because Brian's mind was elsewhere, but also because Brian was beginning to lose the signal as he entered the mountainous territory of the Apache Trail.

As in the previous two trips, the humming of the pickup's wheels on the lonely blacktop caused Brian to reflect on his life. He had been born in Chicago. His parents had died early in his life and he had been raised by his older sister Janette. Janette and Jim Stewart had been blessed by a son, Kevin. Kevin was their only child and he had arrived when Brian was ten years old. Brian and Kevin were more like brothers than uncle and nephew. Brian doted on Kevin and took great pride in teaching him the things that he enjoyed. Brian was always an outdoors man and was pleased to find that Kevin took after him. As they grew older, they became inseparable. They hunted and fished whenever they could. Brian finished high school and went to work in the construction industry. He became a carpenter and found that he had a natural talent for woodworking. It wasn't long before he was a finishing carpenter and was doing on-the-job cabinetry. While Brian was learning his trade, Kevin was completing high school where he lettered in wrestling all four years. After high school, Kevin went on to college but lasted only two years. After his sophomore year, he decided to join the army and left in the fall.

Brian made a decision. The construction boom was winding down in the Chicago area but was just beginning in the Southwest, so he headed for Phoenix. It was a good move. There was a shortage of expert tradesmen and Brian had no trouble finding work at premium wages.

He quickly fell in love with the desert southwest. The skies were clear during the day and star-filled at night. Even the scorching summer heat didn't discourage him. The construction crews began early in the morning before the temperatures got into the 110s and 120s and quit just as the heat was becoming unbearable. September through May were delightful months and work continued uninterrupted.

He moved into an apartment complex when he first arrived, but after a year he knew that Arizona was going to be his permanent home. Brian was a confirmed bachelor and felt a need for space. When he decided that this was where he was going to live, he began to look for inexpensive acreage. He found it in northwestern Maricopa County. He bought five acres and over a two-year period built a three-bedroom territorial-style ranch house. One bedroom became his den, office and exercise room, and the other was reserved for Kevin. The two corresponded regularly and Kevin spent most of his furlough time with Brian.

It was shortly after Brian had finished his home that he started to look for things to do in his spare time. He had five acres and was in horse country. He fenced an acre, built a barn and bought a horse, a beautiful light-brown Morgan mare. He called her Tilly for no more reason than the horse seemed to answer to the name. Six months later he bought another Morgan mare. This one he let Kevin name. Kevin called her Sweetstuff because she was so even-tempered and gentle. Brian and Kevin would ride out from Brian's house—he now called it his ranch—for day trips or they would trailer the horses to the Tonto National Forest and spend a day or two camping.

Brian was never sure what had caused him to become interested in flying. It was a combination of things. The clear air. The blue sky. The surrounding mountains. The pure adventure. The great feeling that he had when he was in the air. They all contributed to it and he was never sorry that he had become a pilot. Kevin shared his love of aviation and when they weren't hunting, fishing, riding or camping they were flying over the desert and the mountains.

Like everything else he did, when Brian became

involved in aviation he didn't stop with just his pilot's license. He worked for and attained his commercial pilot's certificate and then upgraded his aircraft type until he could fly almost any single-engine airplane. The requirements of his commercial rating exacted a special skill and Brian was soon a near expert in aerial maneuvers and special types of landings and takeoffs.

Like many private pilots, Brian soon discovered that the fun in flying was in the learning. Once he finished his training, he found that he had nowhere to go. His trade didn't require trips and, though Arizona had many places of special interest, he could fly anywhere in the state and return the same day. Fly-ins didn't interest him because he just wasn't a social person. He was approaching 500 hours in total time and he found that his interest was beginning to wane.

Brian was sitting alone in his home, cleaning his shotgun, when his eye caught the cover of an issue of *Arizona Highways* magazine. It featured a story about aviation in Arizona. He began to leaf through the magazine to find the article when he stopped and stared at the lead picture of another story.

The picture was a composite. It showed a weather-beaten map superimposed over the features of an equally weather-beaten face. Brian studied the map and soon realized that it was a diagram of the location of a gold mine. It looked a lot like a pirate treasure map. However, there was no mistaking the sun-dried face of the man. It definitely belonged to a prospector. The article was entitled, "The Mysterious Lost Mine of the Dutchman." Brian was fascinated. He read the entire article , then read it again.

Finally, he remembered the feature article from the front cover. He thumbed through the magazine until he came to it. He began to scan the article and toward the end, he came to a photograph that made him think that fate may have had a hand in his evening. It was a picture of an airplane that he had heard about but had never given serious thought of flying.

A bump in the road brought Brian back to reality. He crossed a rise in the road and noticed a light in the breaking dawn. That was probably his first glimpse of Tortilla Flat, which consisted of a restaurant and a general store at the end of the paved section of the Apache Trail. The half light of the early morning allowed Brian to check on the load that he was pulling behind his Dodge Ram. He glanced at the rear and side-view mirrors and could see that the eight-foot-long by five-foot-wide by five-foot-tall aluminum box, mounted on a two wheel trailer frame, was traveling effortlessly behind the pickup. By tilting the driver's side mirror up and in, he could see that the eighteen-foot-long, twenty-inch-diameter aluminum tube attached to the top of the trailer was also riding well.

Brian pulled into the parking area in front of the Tortilla Flat restaurant. A couple of lights illuminated the inside and Brian could see that full service was not going to be available yet. He ignored the parking stripes and left his rig parallel to the road. He tried the front door and found it unlocked. He headed for a saddle that served as a stool at the bar and straddled it. A sleepy-eyed, unshaven man wearing a cook's apron appeared.

"What'll it be?"

"Just a sinker and some black coffee," Brian replied.

The man turned and placed Brian's order in front of him.

"That'll be $2.50," he said and left for the mysteries of the kitchen.

Brian finished his breakfast, left $3.00 on the counter and walked out the door. The coffee made him feel a bit edgy. He wondered if he really needed it, as hyped up as he already was with the prospect of his upcoming adventure.

"Well, too late now!" he thought as he put the pickup in gear and pulled away from the restaurant. The headlights were almost a redundancy as they barely lit up the road in competition with the brightening day. He drove about three miles out of town on the dirt road. The terrain was flattening out and Brian easily found the little turnoff that he had discovered last weekend. After a little more than a quarter of a mile of bumpy four-wheeling, he stopped and parked next to a stunted palo verde tree.

It seemed like yesterday, when he had first noticed those articles in Arizona Highways. Now, he was about to begin the adventure that those articles had stimulated. "The Mysterious Lost Mine of the Dutchman" had grabbed his attention immediately. He began to study all the reports, articles and books that he could find on the Lost Dutchman Mine. He was hooked. He knew that someday he would be counted among the people who had spent a disproportionate amount of time and money chasing the Dutchman.

The other article probably accounted for most of the delay in the start of Brian's quest. It was entitled "The Ultralights of Arizona." It described a small group of airmen who flew aircraft known as ultralights. Basically a flying wing, they were very similar to a hang glider. The wing was attached to the pylon of a tubular structure known as a trike, a three-wheeled fuselage with the single wheel in front and the two main wheels on either side to the rear. The pilot sat just above the three wheels, his feet resting on a bar that controlled the steerable nosewheel. A passenger could sit behind and slightly above the pilot. The power plant was mounted directly behind the passenger seat and thrust was generated by a pusher-type propeller. The pilot controlled the aircraft by means of a bar that tilted the wing, side to side and up and down. There was no yaw control as tipping the wing to one side provided a coordinated turn in that direction. Pushing the bar forward tilted the wing upward and slowed the speed, while pulling the bar tipped the wing downward and increased the speed. Climb and descent were controlled by the throttle.

He found an airport seven miles to the northwest of his house that had a fixed-base operator specializing in ultralights. It wasn't long before Brian found himself hanging out in the ozone, suspended in the student seat of a trike. It was thrilling and Brian knew that his love of flying had been rekindled.

The mastering of ultralight flying was harder than

Brian had guessed. The controls reacted just the opposite to the conventional wheel and rudder that he was used to. Brian was a patient man and he took his time because he had lots of it. He spent the better part of four years becoming an expert ultralight pilot and an authority on the Lost Dutchman Mine. As his flying skills increased, he was developing a theory about Jacob Waltz and his gold.

Most, if not all, of the prospectors had concentrated on the area of the Superstition Mountains that lay within easy reach of Apache Junction. They had gone east and south. They scavenged Weaver's Needle and surrounding territory and found nothing. It seemed that each failure encouraged the next group of adventurers to search the same ground. Brian reasoned that Waltz probably came from a greater distance to cash his gold than most people thought.

Tortilla Flat was no more than an outpost in the late 1800s and hadn't grown much since. It once had a population of 125, but after the new hotel burned down, people began to leave, and now the inhabitants of Tortilla Flat numbered only six. Brian decided to search in that region. He would look to the east and north of Tortilla Flat.

Chapter Four

Brian subscribed to the theory that the reward was in the searching and not in the finding. His personal adventure was going to be even greater because he would be searching by air and in his own ultralight. He had been ultralight flying for about two years when he decided that he must have his own personal machine. He ordered a beautiful red, two-place Air Creation XP Twin 582 SL. Four months later, the ultralight arrived in kit form. He enjoyed putting it together. Working with his hands and studying plans were second nature to him. The instructions manual suggested that it would take about forty hours to assemble, but Brian took a hundred, enjoying every minute of it. He built it in his garage, leaving his pickup outside for five and a half months. He inspected each and every nut, bolt, washer and part before he committed it to the aircraft. When he finally stood back and admired the bright red trike, he knew that he had constructed a machine that would be both fun and safe to fly.

The trailer took another two weeks to build. When it was finished, the completed ultralight, snugly stored in the trailer, would fit in one stall of his two-car garage. Brian was ready to fly. He trailed the trike to the airport and put it together. He could have the aircraft ready for flight in less than thirty minutes but he always allowed forty-five. The first flight was a dream. The ultralight handled beautifully and Brian felt like he was a part of rather than the pilot of the craft.

Now, parked in the desert north of Tortilla Flat, Brian repeated the assembly procedure that had become almost routine. Once the ultralight was ready for flight, it needed only the preflight inspection before Brian was ready to take off. He was as thorough with this routine as he was with everything else. He circled the wing checking all the pins, bolts, struts, edges and coverings. He found everything in order. He did the same thing with the fuselage, the engine and the emergency parachute. He then checked the fuel and filled the tanks. He was ready.

It was a bit chilly, as the sun hadn't had a chance to warm the atmosphere, so Brian donned a lightweight jumpsuit, put on a pair of gloves, a helmet and goggles and made one last stop at his pickup. Here he took the last two items that he needed for his prospecting flight, a topographical map and a GPS. The map was secured by two plastic plates, one on top and the other on the bottom. The bottom plate was then strapped to Brian's right thigh. From his sitting position in the ultralight, Brian could read the map and check his location. He could also use a highlighter to trace his course and mark anything significant. The GPS (Gobal Postitioning System), his latest purchase, was strapped to his left leg. The GPS could locate Brian's position within fifty feet. It used latitudinal and longitudinal coordinates to display positions. The GPS homed in on five satellites, any three of which could pinpoint his position. If he could acquire a fourth or fifth satellite, the GPS would also give him his altitude above sea level. This particular GPS had an additional feature. Brian could enter as many as twenty waypoints and then recall them from memory. The waypoints could be entered either manually, by keying in the coordinates, or automatically, by simply pushing the waypoint key and pressing enter. The automatic method would then store his present position as waypoint number 1, 2 or 3, up to the twenty-waypoint limit.

Brian settled into the open seat, fastened the shoulder and seat harnesses and turned the ignition switch. The Rotax 582 SL jumped to life. He released the parking brake, pushed lightly on the throttle, and began to taxi.

The area Brian had selected as his home base could best be described as a 1,000 foot circle around nothing. And that's what it was. A 1,000 foot diameter of gravel and short brush. There was nothing over two feet tall within the circle and those bushes were frail at best. Inside the circle consisted of sand and gravel with an occasional small rock. It was perfect. Brian could take off and land in any direction, which insured him of always heading directly into the wind. Under normal circumstances the wind in the desert was extremely light and it followed the sun. In the morning, the wind would blow gently out of the east. By afternoon, it would increase in strength and blow out of the south. The setting sun would see the wind reduce itself to a zephyr and come out of the west. The exceptions were storms or high and low pressure ridges moving through the area. Brian was at the west end of the circle. He taxied a few yards, turned the ultralight to the East and applied full power. The airplane accelerated as the wheels crunched over the desert floor. After about 200 feet, Brian pushed the control bar forward and suddenly felt himself lifted free of the ground and into the morning air. It was exhilarating. The air was undisturbed and Brian rose quickly to his desired altitude of 200 feet. He trimmed the throttle and wing to cruise and headed toward the Superstitions.

The Superstition Mountains around the Tortilla Flat region weren't mountains in the truest sense of the word. They were more a series of very rugged terrain, consisting of 700-foot cliffs, rolling gullies, jagged outcroppings and rocky upheavals. There were no peaks but the topography rose and fell over 1,000 feet in continuous waves. It was over this treacherous terrain that Brian would conduct his search.

Brian had a plan. He had laid out his search areas in patches. Each patch was about ten miles in length and five miles in width. Brian would fly a back-and-forth pattern, slowly covering the entire patch, much like a crop duster's pattern. He carried three hours of fuel which, when figuring a half an hour to and from the search area, would allow him an hour and a half for aerial prospecting. That worked out perfectly for him as he intended to be on the ground before the ten o'clock winds began to increase in velocity.

Brian had already outlined his work area for the day in blue marker on his plastic map cover. He began to trace his movements with the yellow highlighter once he was within the blue outline. The first time that he reached the extremes of his search area he would enter a waypoint on his GPS. That way when he went to the next area he wouldn't overlap. His first area was the farthest to the southwest.

Brian followed his plan meticulously. The ultralight flew slow enough that he was able to follow the contours of the mountainous terrain and still maintain his altitude and separation. His intent was to trace his route on the plastic map cover with the yellow highlighter. The beauty and the awesome savagery of the ground beneath almost took Brian's breath away. He realized that an engine failure would be disastrous. The glide ratio of the ultralight offered little hope of anything but a controlled crash. Any flat spots beneath him were covered with rocks, cacti and desert foliage that was unfriendly at best. The thrill of the search was beyond Brian's expectations.

He soon discovered that flying the plane didn't leave him the luxury of continuous charting. He compromised by placing a yellow dot on the plastic whenever he made a turn or saw something significant. He would connect the dots later, when he was on the ground. He reserved the GPS waypoints for places that he would revisit on horseback.

By the time he was halfway through his first rectangular patch, his hour and a half was up and he reluctantly headed back to his base. He marked his departure point with the GPS, noting the altitude as well as the coordinates. He had no trouble finding the base as the aluminum trailer reflected the sun from several miles away. He landed easily, taxied to the trailer, shut down the engine, and relaxed. It had been a great day.

An hour later, Brian was heading back to Tortilla Flat, his ultralight riding behind. He pulled into the parking lot at the restaurant-bar. There were a few more cars and trucks in the lot, so he had to park with a bit more care than he had earlier. A few minutes later, he was seated at a table, waiting for a vegetable taco, fries and Diet Coke.

He really wanted a hamburger but when he saw the price, $22.50, and realized that the meat would be paper thin, he opted for a sensible non-meat lunch. While he waited for his order, he studied his map and began to connect the yellow dots. He would then transpose the yellow markings directly on the paper map when he got home.

Brian had just finished connecting the dots when the waitress brought his food to the table. Brian pushed his map aside to make room for his order. He didn't see the two men come into the room and head for the bar. The first man passed Brian just as he was taking his first bite of the taco. The second man almost passed but stopped short and said to Brian, "Hey, man! Is that your rig out there?"

Brian took a sip of Coke, looked up, saw a clean-shaven man about 6 feet 2 inches tall, lean with neatly parted auburn hair, and a face spoiled only by a slightly receding chin.

"What rig is that?" Brian asked.

"The one behind the Dodge pickup. The aluminum box and tube."

"Yeah, that's mine," Brian said. "What about it?"

"Just wondered what it was. That's all. It's kind of strange looking."

"Oh, yeah, I guess it is at that," Brian continued. "I've got my ultralight in it."

"Ultralight?" the man said. "What's an ultralight?"

"An ultralight is a small airplane that can be rigged and unrigged anywhere. It can carry about 600 pounds and has at top speed of 85 miles per hour," Brian explained.

"Hey, that's real interesting. Mind if we join you?"

Brian answered with a shrug.

"Thanks," the man said and then, "Butch! Over here, you got to hear this."

Butch came to the table. He was an intimidating sight, 5 feet 10 inches tall and 225 pounds, all muscle, and a face hidden behind a two-day growth of black stubble.

"This is Butch and I'm Charlie," Charlie said. No last names were offered.

"Brian," Brian said. "Have a seat."

"Thanks," Butch and Charlie sat down and motioned for the waitress.

"Butch," Charlie said. "Brian here's got a thing he pulls around behind his pickup and sets it up wherever he wants and goes flying. He calls it an ultralight. Right, Brian?"

"Well, that's pretty close, Charlie," Brian smiled. "It's not quite that simple. I have to find a spot that I can land and takeoff from and there aren't too many of them around here."

"Yeah, there's gotta be a lot better places than this," Butch drawled. "What ya'll want to be flying around here for anyway?"

"Well," Brian said, taking note of Butch's pugilistic nose. "You'll think I'm crazy, but I kinda got hooked on this Lost Dutchman thing and I'm flying around looking for it."

"You're crazy, all right," Butch said. "Nobody's ever looked way up here. Ever'body knows the Dutchman's way down by Weaver's."

"You're right about that, Butch," Brian said. "All the searchin's been done around Weaver's Needle because that's where all the books say the mine is. I figure different. I figure to look where the lookin's been a little lighter. Besides, 'round here's about the only place I can set up. I suppose if I don't find anything, I'll be as lucky as them that's searched the Needle."

"I guess that's about right," Charlie said.

Brian finished his food, paid his check and stood to leave.

"Well fellas, thanks for the company," Brian said. "I gotta get goin'. See you around."

"You'll be coming back?" Charlie asked.

"Oh, yeah," Brian answered. "I got a lot more searchin' to do."

He turned, left the restaurant, fired up his rig and headed for home. Inside Charlie and Butch finished their lunch, paid their bill and walked to their car. They watched Brian drive off. Their eyes followed him until he rounded the first hairpin turn.

"What do you think?" Butch asked.

"I think we better make a call," Charlie said.

CHAPTER FIVE

The next day, Sunday, Brian was back in Tortilla Flat. His routine was the same, but he was in the air fifteen minutes earlier than the previous day. He flew by GPS heading to the spot that ended yesterday's search and began today's adventure. The terrain became even more rugged as he soared back and forth. He thought about the danger as well as the beauty of his position. The colors and shapes below were fantastic and awe-inspiring but left little in the way of safe options in the event of engine failure. The two-cycle Rotax had never even sputtered but Brian knew that if it did, he would have to make a fast decision. He would either have to crash land or pull the red lever on the side of the fuselage which deployed the safety parachute, designed to lower the ultralight and its pilot to a survivable encounter with the earth below. Since the safety device was attached to the rear of the airplane, Brian would be facing almost straight down at the moment of impact. This caused Brian to search for places where he could survive a landing, even if the ultralight didn't. Brian didn't know the color of his parachute and wasn't anxious to find out.

Even with this constant concern, Brian was able to conduct a reasonable search for the Lost Dutchman Mine. After his second day of exploration, although unsuccessful, he had a feeling of satisfaction and relief. He was famished when he sat down at a table at the Tortilla Flat Restaurant. As he was studying the menu, someone called his name. "Brian! Any luck today?"

It was Charlie, with Butch right behind him. They sat down without invitation and Butch said, "Hey, Amy! Bring us a couple of menus."

"So, how'd it go?" Charlie asked again. Brian ignored him as Amy brought menus and setups. They ordered and as Amy disappeared to the kitchen, Charlie called after her.

"Hey, Amy," he said. "Put it all on my tab, ya hear?"

Brian held up his hand in protest but Charlie would have none of it.

"Thanks," Brian muttered, feeling somewhat puzzled and beholden to Charlie, and a bit disappointed that he hadn't ordered a hamburger.

"Well, how was your day?" Charlie persisted.

Brian could see no way of avoiding the question so he said, "Just about like yesterday. The scenery was breathtaking, the flying was great but the results were disappointing."

"You're just wasting your time," Butch advised. "Whyn't ya go back down by the Needle where ya should be anyway?"

"I got more time than sense, I guess," Brian replied. "I reckon that I'll just stick to my plan and play out my string right here. Besides, I'd miss your pretty faces. By the way, what do you guys do, anyway?"

"A little of this and a little of that," Butch answered, giving Charlie a wink.

"Yeah, right now we're on a contract. Right Butch," Charlie sort of laughed. Butch joined him.

Inside joke, Brian thought. "What's that mean?" he said.

"Can't tell ya," Charlie said.

"It's like classified information," Butch chimed in and they both guffawed, punching each others arms.

"Yeah, it's secret stuff," Charlie agreed. "What about you, Brian? Whatta you do?"

"Me? I'm a carpenter. Been workin' in the valley for years." Brian disclosed. The conversation dwindled as the three finished their lunches. Charlie picked up the check and Brian headed for the door.

"Thanks," Brian said as he closed the door behind him. Quite a pair, Brian thought, glad to be alone and in the open air. I wonder how they ever got together. Charlie looks and dresses like he's had some education but Butch, he's scary. He looks like he grew up on the streets and dresses like he sleeps in his clothes. Quite a pair!

*

Butch Crosswell had been christened Butch and that should have been fair warning. Butch grew up in a trailer park outside of Kingman, Arizona. He was one of six children. Two older sisters and three younger brothers comprised the dysfunctional family. Butch's mother found little to fill her days. A few bottles of beer and some soap operas occupied most of her time. Elma Crosswell had a good week if she didn't receive a beating from her husband, Jeff.

Big Jeff Crosswell's neck was as red as anyone in the Kingman area. What he did for a living no one knew, not even Big Jeff. He was always around trouble. His buddies joked that Jeff had a cell with a revolving door at the local jail. His services, whatever they were, were used by various unsavory elements of Laughlin, Arizona, and Las Vegas, Nevada. He drew welfare checks from any agency that would issue them. He parceled money out with a grudging hand. His kids received no allowance and his wife had to account for every penny. He drove an old pickup, drank enough beer to irrigate a cotton field and beat up his family whenever it pleased him.

Butch took it until he was big enough to do something about it. That happened during his second year in high school. He had been held back once in grammar school and once in high school, so he was seventeen years old. His baby fat had disappeared and his muscles were well developed.

Big Jeff hadn't noticed the change in his son and one night when he came home drunk, demanded dinner by punching Elma in the nose, slapped his youngest son for no reason and raised his fist to Butch, he found himself looking into a pair of steel-gray defiant eyes.

He laughed once as he started to deliver the blow. His fist never found its target. He felt his arm blocked as his nose exploded into a bloody pulp. The force of the blow staggered but didn't fell Big Jeff. He stood dumbfounded as Butch calmly stepped back and kicked his father full force in the crotch. Big Jeff collapsed on the floor in a pool of his own blood. Butch walked to the back door and returned with a baseball bat. He broke both of Big Jeff's arms, one leg, as many ribs as he could and then fractured his skull.

Butch made himself a sandwich, took a soft drink from the refrigerator, put the bat back where he had found it and left without a word to anyone. He never looked or came back. He didn't know whether he had killed his father or not and didn't care. He hadn't. After a long recovery, Big Jeff returned home to vent his rage on what was left of his family. He was greeted by three women and three young men, each armed with a baseball bat of their own. Big Jeff got the message. He got into his pickup and left.

Butch, meanwhile, roamed northwestern Arizona finding work whenever he could and living off the land when he couldn't. Two years after his bout with his father, Butch was camping on the outskirts of Prescott, Arizona, when he noticed a light in the distance. He decided to investigate and as he was approaching the farm house, he found himself looking down the barrels of an over-and-under shotgun. He was marched into the farm house and confronted and interrogated by a group of rough, tough individuals. He had stumbled into the headquarters of the Arizona branch of the

New Revolutionary Militia. He had heard bits and pieces about these malcontents. They were anarchists and espoused the overthrow of any form of structured government. The philosophy appealed to Butch. He joined the New Revolutionary Militia and over the years advanced in the loose organization of the brotherhood. Now after years of arson, riots, bombings, murder and every other terrorist activity imaginable, Butch found himself in Tortilla Flat. He knew that something big was happening. He had no idea what it was but he was happy to be part of anything that produced chaos.

Charlie Whitfield had been raised on the opposite end of the spectrum from Butch Crosswell. His parents were both teachers at a small private college in the San Francisco Bay area. Thomas Victor Whitfield and Maryann Plummer taught political science and history at Bayside College. They were married when JFK became president and Charles arrived the year he was assassinated. During the Vietnam war they burned draft cards, bras, flags and anything else that was flammable.

Charles, as his parents insisted he be called, was raised to hate any authority other than parental. He barely made it through grammar and high schools. His grades were acceptable but his deportment was so bad that he was constantly on detention. Maryann, who kept her maiden name, and Thomas argued politics morning, noon and night, brainwashing Charles. He became convinced that the government was evil and must be destroyed. He went to college and lasted two years. He dropped out during the Christmas break of his junior year. He didn't go home. Instead, he moved in with a girl he had met during a protest rally. A month later she took him to an underground meeting of the New Revolutionary Militia. He was recruited and joined. Charlie was moved around the country to various militia groups. He became an organizer and contact man. He reported directly to headquarters. Charlie knew what was going on and what his job was to facilitate it and was beginning to get the big picture. He had been given specific instructions and was promised that when the time came, he would be completely briefed.

Charlie was the head of the local operation and, as such, was Butch's boss. One of his main tasks was to keep Butch and others like him under control until it was time to turn them loose. It wasn't easy. For even if their goals were the same, Butch's methods were entirely different than Charlie's. Charlie felt that he had to lower himself to Butch's level and he resented it. But he fully understood that, without people like Butch, the dream of bringing the United States Government to its knees could not be accomplished.

*

On the way home that day, Brian had the distinct feeling that he wasn't really welcome in Tortilla Flat. The feeling continued until Brian got busy connecting the yellow dots on his plastic map cover and studying the terrain for the next weekend. Brian was halfway through his microwave meal, when the President of the United States interrupted the local programming. He was trying to calm the nation, stating the situation was under control. Brian was only half listening when that feeling returned.

Who were these two guys, anyway? Why were they always in Tortilla Flat when he was? Charlie and Butch weren't even particularly likable, but they seemed to have a way of getting him to talk and that was one of the things that made him uneasy. He didn't know anything about them, not even their last names, but he felt that they knew about him. And why did they buy his lunch? Maybe he was just being paranoid. Besides there wasn't anything he could do about it. It was a free country. Maybe they wouldn't be there next Saturday. He decided to dismiss the whole thing as a coincidence. He shouldn't have.

CHAPTER SIX

The next Saturday, Brian flew his prescribed course and Butch and Charlie were there to greet him at Tortilla Flat. They sat down again with him at lunch, but Brian found himself reluctant to answer the prying questions. He was definitely on his guard and he thought that it showed. It did! After Brian left the restaurant, Charlie and Butch had a short session.

"I think that we're pushin' Brian a little hard," Charlie said.

"Whatta ya mean!" Butch retorted. "We been usin' kid gloves on the creep. I think that we oughtta rough him up and tell him to keep the hell outta here."

"Wait a minute, Butch," Charlie reminded. "We got orders and we're supposed to find out what he's doin' and what he knows and report back. Don't forget that!"

"Okay! Okay!" Butch acknowledged. "I'll take it easy on him. But I still say that some day we're goin' to have to get tough."

Sunday found Brian flying another dry run. He was tempted to drive through Tortilla Flat without stopping, but thought better of the idea. He was almost finished with lunch and hadn't had any company. Charlie walked by and didn't sit down.

"How'd it go?" he asked.

"Same," Brian replied.

"Keep at it," Charlie said and kept on going.

Brian almost felt slighted. He paid his check and drove home convinced that his imagination had been working overtime.

The next weekend was a replay in both eating and searching. Brian relaxed and concentrated on the job at hand. It was the following Sunday that he found it. Actually it was on Saturday, but Brian didn't know it then. He was just finishing his last pattern of the day when he saw a road or a pair of jeep tracks or a trail in the desert. It seemed to meander from the direction of Route 88 to the east. It looked to Brian that it was invisible from the ground because of the desert foliage all around it. Even from the air, it was hard to see since it disappeared and reappeared through the harsh terrain.

Brian decided to follow it for awhile. He had enough fuel to spend at least another half an hour before he would be forced to return. He punched a waypoint into the GPS and headed east. He began to suspect that the road was not as unused as he had first believed and his interest increased. He checked his watch. He had been into his reserve time about ten minutes. He was about to mark his position as another waypoint so he could start in the same place tomorrow, when he noticed what seemed to be a fork off the main path.

The fork, no more than a wildlife trail, went to the right or south, climbed a small saddle between two steep ridges and disappeared down the next gully. He flew over the saddle and came upon a vista the like of which he had never seen. The trail dropped a hundred feet in a steep decline and then bottomed out. He found himself in a huge bowl with sides rising hundreds of feet into the air. The vivid colors were awe-inspiring and the rock formations stunning. A small creek ran along the bottom, its source a waterfall from the far eastern cliffs. The creek vanished into the bottom of the stark walls of granite to the west.

The bowl itself was about a mile in diameter and Brian could see that there were numerous fissures branching off like reptilian fingers into the impenetrable vertical sides of the enclosure. He wanted to stay and explore further but he knew the dangers of overstaying his discovery. He gained some altitude, made a 180-degree turn and departed, thanking the Lord that he was flying an ultralight with a small turning radius. A conventional airplane may not have been able to negotiate an escape from the box canyon. As he crossed the saddle heading out, a pair of eyes followed the ultralight and a mouth spoke into a powerful two-way transceiver.

Brian made it back to his base with plenty of fuel to spare. He almost lamented the fact that he hadn't extended his time in the rock bowl, as he had begun to think of it. He knew that tomorrow, he would fly directly to the bowl and spend most of his time exploring the natural wonder.

Brian was so excited that he decided to skip lunch and head directly home. As he passed the restaurant at Tortilla Flat, Charlie watched him go by from the driver's seat of his pickup. His face bore a grim scowl as he picked up a transceiver and spoke quickly into the mouthpiece. After a short conversation, he extended a long antenna and dialed long distance on his cell phone. That conversation lasted about ten minutes and when Charlie finally hung up he had a very unpleasant taste in his mouth.

The next day, Brian woke earlier than usual. His sleep had been sound but he had woken several times to check the alarm clock. He knew that he wasn't going to be late, but the excitement kept building in him. He reached Tortilla Flat before the sun was up so he decided to stop for breakfast. There was another truck in the parking lot and it looked a bit familiar. Brian opened the door to the diner and immediately knew who owned the other pickup. Charlie and Butch were seated at the first table sipping coffee.

"Hey, Brian," Butch greeted. "How about that, Charlie? Brian's here."

"Hi, fellas," Brian returned, a bit startled and uncomfortable to see them.

"Sit down," Charlie directed. Brian had little choice. He pulled back a chair and sat down, calling for a menu as he did so.

"I'm a little early," Brian confessed. "But I still don't

have enough time for a big breakfast. I'll just have a roll and some coffee. Sun'll be up soon and I want to get flyin' as soon as possible."

"Must be onto somethin'," Butch said. "That right, Brian?"

"Probably not," Brian answered. "But I found a beautiful boxed canyon and I just can't wait to check it out."

"Someday, maybe, you'd like to fly with me and see it?" Brian asked to either of them. Charlie and Butch looked at each other and responded in unison, "Not me! No sir! Them things are just too darn dangerous."

"I don't want to get any higher than the back of my horse," Butch exclaimed. "I don't know how you can do it. My hat's off to you and any other that's fool enough to leave the ground in one of them contraptions."

"Aw! You just have to get used to it," Brian said. "It's a little scary at first but after awhile it's just like driving a car."

"Well you can do it all you want," Charlie said. "I'm stayin' on the ground."

And that ended the discussion. By then it was time to go and Brian stood to leave.

"Go ahead," Butch grinned. "I'll get your breakfast. You can pick up lunch."

"I'll just do that," Brian called back over his shoulder. "I owe you one anyway."

The sun was rising as Brian left the diner and a hour later he was in the air heading for the last way-point on his GPS. He flew directly to the coordinates and quickly followed the trail over the saddle and into the canyon. The air was unusually calm and Brian was able to trace his movements on the plastic map cover easier than on any other flight. He decided to turn right once inside the canyon and then fly a counterclockwise course around the perimeter. It was exciting and as he got more used to flying inside the stone walls he descended lower and lower into the canyon.

When he came to a fjord, he would climb to the top of the gorge and assess whether or not it was safe to fly into it. He hadn't been able navigate a fjord until he was nearly halfway around the canyon. He turned a corner and came upon a long, wide passageway with sides far enough apart to allow for a 180-degree turn at least half of the way in. Just to be safe, he climbed to the top and made a couple of turns judging the leeway the walls allowed. Then he descended. He was about 100 feet above the floor and the walls towered 600 feet above him when he saw it.

It wouldn't have been noticeable at all if he hadn't had just the right angle, down and forward. He was sure that it was invisible from the ground. It looked like just another boulder, but when seen from Brian's vantage point, the shadow behind the huge stone wasn't a shadow at all. It was an opening in the side of the granite wall and quite a large opening at that. He immediately lost sight of it when his angle shifted as he flew by. He circled again and again. Each flyby revealed more detail of the concealed entrance. Brian flew as close to the canyon wall as he could and, when directly over the guardian rock, entered the location as a waypoint on his GPS.

He then began to inspect the ground around the boulder for signs of activity. There was nothing to be seen since the surface was pure rock. A Sherman tank wouldn't have left a mark. Brian flew in an ever-widening circle covering every square inch of the fjord. When he was satisfied that there were no other possible points of interest, he returned to his discovery for one last look before heading back. He swooped dangerously low on his final pass and could see partway inside the cave guarded by the large granite stone. His imagination saw the initial sculpturing of a gold mine. He was sure that he could see something that looked fairly recent, a few scratches, a polished surface or a disturbed stone. He made his final turn, gained altitude and flew out of the canyon. If he had looked back one more time, he might have caught the momentary reflection of a pair binoculars as they followed his passage out of the fjord.

He was so excited by his discovery that even if he had seen the reflective flash, he would have paid it no attention. He landed, broke down the ultralight and packed it into the trailer and tube, and started home. He had already decided not to stop for lunch, despite the invitation. He wanted to get home and plan his next movements.

He wanted to put a call in to Kevin and invite him on the coming expedition. Kevin was on duty in the Middle East and it took almost a week to get a message to him. Kevin had put in his twenty years and was in the process of deciding whether to re-enlist or not. In any event, he had an extended furlough coming in a month. The timing was perfect. Brian envisioned a pack trip into the Superstitions, perhaps lasting a full week or more. He would be assembling the gear while he waited for Kevin.

His mind was racing so fast that he was in Tortilla Flat before he was aware of it. He slowed down to pass through the short strip that was called town. As he came to the restaurant, he noticed a pickup with its hood up and two men bending into the engine compartment. He slowed even further until he was abreast of the truck. Just then, Charlie raised his head from the pickup and waved Brian down. Brian stopped with a sigh of resignation.

"Havin' some trouble?" he asked.

"Naw," Charlie answered. "I think we just about got it. Pull over and we'll grab some lunch."

"Yeah, remember this one's on you," Butch yelled, his head still buried under the hood.

"Okay," Brian said as he pulled off the road and parked his rig.

Inside the restaurant, they chose a table near the back and Butch volunteered to get the drinks and menus. Brian had his back to the bar and didn't see Butch and Charlie exchange winks as Butch deposited the drinks and menus on the table.

A waitress appeared took their order and meandered toward the kitchen. Charlie and Butch started their questioning immediately.

"How'd it go, today?"

"See anything interesting?"

"Where are you looking?"

Brian tried to be evasive, but slowly the truth came out. By the end of the second beer, Brian knew that his secrets were no longer his alone. They had not only learned of his find but also of his plans to search on horseback. The food came and Butch got three more beers. Brian started to feel a little strange. He felt like he was on a sugar high yet was growing tired and weak at the same time. He wiped some perspiration from his forehead and thought that it was getting very warm and stuffy in the room. He left a substantial part of his lunch on his plate and felt dizzy as he tried to get to his feet.

"Whoa there, partner," Butch said, grabbing him under the arm to steady him. "Feelin' a bit wobbly?"

"I'm okay," Brian stammered. "Too much excitement for one day, I guess."

They helped Brian out the door and into his pickup. As they got Brian belted in, Butch reached across him and flicked the air-conditioning off. Brian didn't notice. Nor did he notice when they rolled up the windows as they closed the doors, making sure that they were unlocked.

"Take yer time. That there's a tricky road," they said as they pointed Brian out to the Apache Trail, heading south.

Brian set out down the empty road. His head felt like it was splitting wide open. Beads of sweat ran down his face. His clothes were drenched. He was developing double vision. He was struggling to have a rational thought. He had a blurred perception of a wide shoulder and managed to pull off the road and park. He fumbled with the ignition and finally was able to turn the key. He tried to open the window, but his hand wouldn't obey his command. He was too weak to fight and too confused to think. He lowered his head to the steering wheel, closed his eyes and saw blackness.

He had barely lost consciousness when a pickup pulled to a stop behind him. Charlie and Butch got out and walked to each side of Brian's truck. Butch was on the driver's side and Charlie on the other. They opened the doors with gloved hands and Charlie removed Brian's plastic-covered map. He studied it for a moment, rubbed out any markings that had to do with Brian's last two flights, redrew them in a different location and then returned it. They did a quick search for any other indications of Brian's recent trips. Finding nothing, they looked at each other and Charlie said,

"Do it!"

Butch's mouth curled into a chilling grin. He pulled out a thin black case, opened it and extracted a hypodermic needle. He bared Brian's left arm, found a vein, expertly inserted the needle, and emptied the contents of the syringe into Brian's blood-stream. Brian never felt the tingling in his arms and legs. He never felt the constrictions across his chest. He never felt the convulsions in his muscles and he never felt the crushing pain in his chest as his heart suffered a massive attack and stopped.

"Bye-bye, Brian," Butch sneered as they closed the doors of Brian's pickup and returned to their own vehicle. They made a U-turn and went back to Tortilla Flat for another beer.

Back on the Apache Trail, automobiles, trucks and buses passed a pickup with a strange-looking rig on its trailer hitch. They glanced at the truck, speculated about the contents and wondered about the sleeping driver. No one knew that they were viewing the sixty-ninth victim of the Lost Dutchman Mine.

CHAPTER SEVEN

It wasn't until dusk that someone finally stopped and discovered that the driver of the Dodge pickup wasn't sleeping. He drove to the top of a ridge and used his cell phone to call the sheriff's office. It took another hour for the police to arrive at the scene. They asked the usual questions, took the usual information, sent the callers on their way, and called the coroner.

While they were awaiting the coroner, another police car pulled up. There was a short conference and the first car left. An hour later the coroner arrived. His name was James Blackwell and he wasn't too happy.

"What in the hell did you call me for, Pete?" he demanded. "It's one hell of a way out here and it's Sunday to boot."

Sheriff Pete Saunders wasn't used to being addressed in that fashion. He demanded respect.

"Jim, you know damned well why I called," Saunders snarled. "I'm just following instructions and you're expected to do the same."

"Don't worry about me," Blackwell retorted. "I'll take care of the body, you take care of the rest."

"When's the meat wagon goin' to get here?" Saunders said.

"Should be along any minute, now," the coroner replied.

"I'm goin' to Tortilla Flat," the sheriff said. "Get that stiff outta here as quick as you can and see that nobody touches anything."

On his way to Tortilla Flat, the sheriff called his headquarters and called for another car with two deputies.

"Tell them to wait by the pickup until I get back," he finished. "I'll need one of them to drive my squad car while I take the truck to the impound."

"Roger," came the reply.

The sheriff parked his car and went into the restaurant at Tortilla Flat. He went directly to the bar and sat next to Charlie and Butch.

"Howdy, boys," he said. "You fellas been here awhile?"

"We got here for breakfast and ain't left yet," Charlie said for both of them.

The sheriff called for a coffee and then said, "You seen anything of a fella, about fifty or so, drivin' a Dodge pickup with a queer-lookin' rig behind?"

"Sounds like ole Brian, don't it, Charlie?" Butch said.

"Yeah, sure does," Charlie agreed. "What's up, sheriff?"

"We just found his truck about a mile or so south of here. It was pulled off on the shoulder and the driver's dead. Looks like a heart attack."

"Well, if that don't beat all," Charlie said. "He was just here havin' lunch with us. He didn't look so good and we helped him to his truck. And now he's dead, is he? I'll be durned. You just never know, do ya?"

Butch was looking into his beer, shaking his head and trying to keep a straight face.

"He's been here every weekend for the last few weeks," he said. "He shore seemed like a nice fella. He's dead, ya say?"

"Sure is! What time did he leave here?"

"He didn't even finish his lunch so it must have been early afternoon," Charlie volunteered.

"Do you guys happen to know what's in the trailer?" the sheriff asked.

"Some fool flyin' machine," Butch grunted. "He's been flyin' 'round here lookin' fer the Dutchman. I told him to look down by Weaver's, but he wouldn't listen."

"Ya happen to know his last name and where he's from?"

"Nope," Charlie said. "He never said and we never asked."

"Well, we'll find out from his belongings or from his registration. Thanks for the help, boys," the sheriff said. "Reckon the coroner's left by now, so I'll be gettin' back to the scene."

The sheriff got up and asked a few questions of the bartender and Amy, the waitress. Just before he got to the door he turned, looked at Charlie and jerked his head toward the outside. Butch was still looking at his beer. Charlie gave him a nudge and said, "Be right back," and went outside.

Outside, Charlie went right up to the sheriff.

"Wadda ya want, Pete?" he said.

"You guys did a good job and if that damned coroner will do his part, this thing should get by without a hitch. Do me a favor, will ya? Call the man and tell him that everything's under control. I oughtta be home by midnight, if he wants to talk."

"Okay," Charlie said.

"By the way, just how much does Butch know?" Saunders asked.

"As little as possible, Pete," Charlie answered. "But he's not dumb and he knows that something big is in the air. I'll have to bring him in soon."

"Ya better wait 'til the man says it's okay. See ya!" Saunders got in his squad car and with a short wave, headed back to Brian's truck.

"What's that all about?" Butch asked when Charlie returned.

"Nothin'," Charlie said. "You know that the sheriff and the coroner both work for the man."

"I figured as much," Butch said. "But what in the hell is goin' on?"

"If I knew, I'd tell ya," Charlie lied. "But I feel that we're gettin' close to something."

"I hope so," Butch said. "I'm gettin' a little tired of just sittin' around. That Brian action is the only thing that's kept me interested."

"Yeah, I know," Charlie agreed. "At least, the pay's

good."

The sheriff returned to Brian's pickup. The coroner had taken the body to the morgue and the car that Pete had ordered was at the scene. Pete directed one of the officers to drive his car to the impound and said that he would meet them there with the truck and trailer. He pulled the registration from the glove compartment and radioed the information to headquarters and drove off. At the impound he checked in the vehicle and asked if they had any information on the owner. They only told him what he already knew, that it belonged to one Brian Nichols whose address was a post office box in rural Maricopa county. Saunders thanked them and took his own squad car back to headquarters. A quick call to the coroner confirmed that the body was safely in the morgue and that an autopsy would be performed in the morning. Saunders signed out and went home.

The next morning Saunders was at headquarters early, despite only a few hours' sleep. He checked his calls, read the night report and called the coroner.

"Coroner's office," was the greeting as the phone was answered.

"Lemme talk to the boss," Saunders ordered.

"One moment, sir. I'll see if he's in. Who shall I say is calling?"

"Tell him it's the sheriff."

A few minutes later, which seemed like forever, she was back on the line.

"I'm sorry, Sheriff, he can't be disturbed. He's in the middle of an autopsy."

"Have him call as soon as he's done," Pete ordered and then added, "Ya got that!"

"Yes, Sheriff Saunders."

It was almost noon before the call came in.

"Sheriff," Saunders answered the ring.

"Pete! It's Jim," Blackwell said.

"What in the hell took you so long?"

"Listen! I got more to do than to return your phone calls!"

"Yeah, well listen up," Saunders snarled. "I hope that was the Nichols guy you were working on and I hope you didn't screw it up."

"Yes, it was and no I didn't!" the coroner said, obviously irritated by the sheriff's implications. "I know what I'm doing and I hope you do, too."

"Don't worry about me," the sheriff retorted. "I been working all morning to find a next of kin. I finally located a sister in Chicago and she's on her way down. What's the autopsy gonna say?"

"Heart attack! What else?"

"Yeah, lucky he didn't roll over the edge or cross the line and kill somebody," Saunders chortled. "What about the blood samples?"

"You think I'm an amateur?" Blackwell answered. "I always have a spare or two to send in when needed."

"Well, just make sure that the report is completed before the dame gets here. I want this thing wrapped up nice and tidy-like and as soon as possible."

Blackwell breathed a "Yeah" into the phone and hung up without another word. It was tough working with the likes of Pete Saunders, but once he had accepted the bribe he was in for the whole nine yards. He wished that he had never started. The only thing that kept him going was the money that continued to flow. He hoped that it would soon be over and that he could return to a normal life and enjoy the money that he had been able to accumulate. This dream would soon become a nightmare.

CHAPTER EIGHT

Janette Stewart arrived at the sheriff's office at four o'clock the following afternoon. She was dressed in a black business suit and her face made her look older than the 65 years that she actually was. Her gray hair was partially hidden under a small black hat and her eyes were red from crying. Her trim figure was concealed beneath mourning attire but she carried herself erect despite the burden she bore. She clutched a small black purse, along with a wet handkerchief in her left hand. She presented herself to the policewoman sitting at the reception desk. She was asked to be seated while the policewoman withdrew behind a door marked private.

A few minutes later, Sheriff Saunders appeared, accompanied by the policewoman, who pointed to Janette and then resumed her position behind the desk.

"Mrs. Stewart," he said. "I'm sorry that you had to come all this way on such a sad occasion."

She took his extended hand as she rose to greet him. She was 5 feet 7 inches tall and was used to looking up when addressing most men, but she found herself looking directly into the sheriff's chest. His eyes seemed to be a full foot above hers. Actually, he stood 6 feet 5 inches tall and weighed 265 pounds. He was powerfully built but was beginning to show the signs of long hours behind a desk or in a squad car. He was rather handsome with a full head of hair. His clean-shaven face revealed a straight jaw-line and sharp features. Dark eyes shifted restlessly as he spoke.

"You were the only relative that we were able to find, and we need positive identification before we can release the body," he continued.

"I understand, sheriff," Janette said. "It's just so hard to believe that Brian's gone. Do you have any idea what happened?"

"There's really nothing to tell, ma'am. We found him alongside the road up near Tortilla Flat. He was dead behind the wheel. The coroner says that it was a heart attack."

"Brian was in such good shape and he never complained of anything. He told me that he had a complete physical six months ago and they didn't find anything wrong with him," Janette said, trying to control herself.

"Yes, ma'am," Pete said consolingly. "I know it's tough and it's very sudden. Feel free to talk it over with the coroner if you wish. I'll make sure that he's at the morgue when you go there to identify your brother."

"Thank you, sheriff. I'd like to talk to him if I may."

"No problem at all. I'll call him and then drive you

over myself."

"You're very kind," Janette said, beginning to feel a bit rushed.

The sheriff made a call and then drove Janette to the morgue. They entered and found the coroner waiting for them at the door.

"I'm Dr. James Blackwell," the coroner said. "And you must be Janette Stewart."

"Yes," the sheriff interjected. "She's here to identify her brother, Brian Nichols."

"If I may," Janette said, removing a handkerchief from her purse.

"Please follow me," he said, taking Janette by the arm and leading her to the elevator. They descended to the basement level and proceeded to the cold-storage room.

There was no one else in the room and the coroner did the honors himself. He opened a stainless steel door and pulled out a drawer. He paused a moment and drew back the covering sheet exposing just the face of the body.

"Do you recognize him?" he asked Janette directly.

"Yes! That's Brian," she sobbed, turning away immediately.

The coroner replaced the sheet, pushed the drawer back into place and closed the door.

"I'm sorry," he said, touching Janette's shoulder. "But I think that he died quickly and without pain, if that's any consolation."

"Yes, it is. Thank you."

"Now if you will come to my office, there's a bit of paperwork to complete," the coroner continued. He placed a few documents in front of her and handed her a pen. As Janette reached the last page, Blackwell said, "That's for the disposition of the body. Have you made any arrangements yet?"

"I came directly here," Janette explained. "I'm staying at Brian's house until my son gets back from the Middle East. Then he and my husband will join me They were almost like brothers, Brian and my son, Kevin. I tried to call him before I left but I couldn't get through. I left a message, but there's no way of telling how long it'll take to get to him. I haven't even placed an obituary notice in the local paper yet. Kevin may not be able to get here for a week or two. Oh!, I'm beginning to ramble," she said, obviously a bit confused.

"It seems like there's so much to do," the coroner consoled. "Don't let it get you down. Maybe I can be of some service."

"Look," he continued, "your brother looks pretty good right now but he may not after a week or two. There's only so much that the morticians can do, you know. Have you considered cremation? It's become quite popular, especially among outdoor people. They prefer to have their ashes scattered over areas that they loved."

As the coroner finished, he looked over to the sheriff and received a nod of approval.

"As a matter of fact, I can make all of the arrangements for you, if you'd like," he urged.

"I don't know. It all seems to be happening so fast," Janette said.

"I think that it's the wise thing to do," the Sheriff

advised. "That way when your son returns you can have a nice service and scatter the ashes over the desert that I'm sure your brother loved.

"Well, if you both think so, I suppose that that's the thing to do," Janette said.

"Just sign here and I'll do the rest!"

CHAPTER NINE

In northwestern Saudi Arabia, about sixty-five kilometers southeast of Mount Lawz, is the vast Hisma Plateau. Gouged out of this plateau is a huge crater nearly 500 feet deep. Protruding into the crater from the northeast is a keyhole-shaped peninsula of solid rock. The top of this rock is almost mirror flat and has an area of two hectares. The sides of the peninsula are almost vertical and range in height from 150 feet where it meets the plateau to 450 feet at the far end of the keyhole. It is probably one of the most inaccessible and easily defended spots in the Middle East.

In the middle of the rounded end of the peninsula, a tent had been erected. A plain blue flag flew from its center post. Inside the tent, Colonel James McDougal sat at a field table studying a map, a telephone to his right.

"I don't understand it," he muttered aloud. "Three

days and nothing. Not an attack, not a probe, not even a shelling, nothing, absolutely nothing."

"It's too quiet. Just too damn quiet," Captain Ted Grossman agreed.

"Well, the good thing is that we only have twenty hours left and this goddamn exercise will be over," the colonel said.

"Yeah! I can't wait to get off this rock," Grossman said. "I wonder what bright-ass dreamed this up, anyway. Infiltrate this position and take the plastic scorpion out of this box. Who are they trying to kid? It'd be impossible to get on this giant flagstone, much less get in and out of this tent."

"Don't get complacent! Let's go over our defenses again. I'm getting nervous."

"Okay," Grossman conceded, thinking, I don't think that they've changed much in the last hour.

The blue team, U.S. Army Special Forces, had a complement of twenty men. McDougal and Grossman were the only officers. Master Sergeant George Standish was the ranking enlisted man. Reporting to him were Roper and Fisher. Roper was in charge of communications and Fisher executed the defense orders. Of the remaining fifteen, three were stationed along the neck of the keyhole, two were outside of the tent, five guarded the perimeter and five were off duty but on ready alert. The shifts were eight hours on and four hours off. The rotation units consisted of five men each and they moved from one position to another at every watch change.

McDougal and Grossman studied the defense plan

in silence for about a quarter of an hour. Colonel McDougal broke the quiet.

"Any suggestions?" he asked.

"Well, sir, if I may?" the captain answered. "It occurred to me that with less than twenty hours left and the fact that it will be dark in a few hours that this will be our last night. The exercise will end before sunset tomorrow. This will be the last chance for the red team to strike unless they plan to move in daylight. I think that we should put all the men on station."

"Good observation, Captain," the colonel said. "Get Standish in here."

Thirty minutes after Sgt. Standish entered the command tent, a decision had been reached and orders issued. The next watch came on duty in two hours. The squad coming off duty would be allowed two hours off, then all three squads would remain on watch for the rest of the exercise.

*

On the southwest side of the keyhole, almost directly opposite the narrow peninsular entrance, was a nearly perfect chimney that had been formed by an earthquake millions of years ago. The chimney was hidden at the top by an outcropping that had failed to fall when the funnel was formed. It was as if a giant carpenter had left a ten-foot tenon at the top and then ran a golden three-foot chisel down the entire length of the solid granite wall. The recess was completely hidden from all directions except from the very bottom.

Two-thirds of the way up the chimney there appeared to be piece of solid rock, but it was moving and moving upward. The pace was slow and deliberate, inching toward the top. Only four hours earlier it had been at the bottom and, at the present pace, it would reach the outcropping at the top just before sunset.

In reality, the rock was a man, camouflaged in clothes that blended perfectly with the colors of the surrounding stone. His back was pressed against one wall and his feet against the other. A pack dangled five feet below him, secured to his waist by a thin line. His average vertical speed was about one foot per minute and he should reach the outcropping in just under a half an hour. This was a free climb and he knew that the real test would come ten feet from the top. He paused for a moment to check the time and the remaining daylight. Satisfied, he pushed against the solid stone that kept him from view and also blocked his path.

He wedged himself in and took stock of his position. A mere ten feet separated him from the top of the stone peninsula. He looked for handholds, cracks and crevices and found what he wanted. He pulled up his pack and found a wedge. He inserted the wedge in a crack and set it in place. Then he pulled a line through the wedge and secured it. It looked like the crack in the stone went alongside the outcropping all the way to the top. He settled in to wait. He would need time to hear the movement of the patrol above and to estimate the interval between passes.

Darkness settled in. He checked his watch for the

last time. He heard the sound of the passing patrol and swung out into space 360 feet above nothing but a hard stone floor and certain death. He placed one wedge after another, clipped his lifeline to the newest, released from the last and made his way around and up. Soon he found that the crack did indeed extend to the top. He was able to use his hands as wedges and quickly pulled himself over the edge. He lay prone and still, his eyes already accustomed to the darkness. He saw the guard walking away, about fifteen yards distant. Noiselessly, he covered the ground in cat-like quickness. He clamped his right hand over the guard's mouth, shutting off any warning that might be emitted. His right foot kicked his victim's feet out from under him as he lowered him to the ground. His mouth was in the guard's left ear.

"You're dead," he whispered.

He rolled the man over and drew a red cross over his chest. Putting his index finger to his lips, he then dragged the soldier into a depression, picked up his pack and disappeared toward the tent. He crouched behind the tent, pulled a radio from his pocket, opened the cover and pressed the number one.

Four hundred yards from the neck of the keyhole, Major Curt Collins saw the number one light up on his handheld receiver. He nudged the man next to him.

"Sarge," he whispered. "He's in place. Let's go!"

Sergeant Billy Ray Taggert gave a hand signal to the two men next to him and they moved down a line of mortars, perhaps thirty in all. The major pulled the cord on the mortar next to him and a parachute flare was sent into the air.

The sky over the tent was suddenly noontime bright. The man behind the tent unsheathed a Bowie knife. The colonel and captain looked at each other and rushed outside.

"Sergeant!" Grossman shouted.

The Bowie knife slit down the rear seam of the tent.

Taggert dropped his arm and his men began to fire the mortars.

The sky above them began to explode, not with deadly shells but with a fireworks display that would put any Fourth of July celebration to shame. There were multi-colored bursts. There were streamers, squealers, squigglers and bangers. There was virtually no pause from one burst of color to the next. The blue team looked for a point of attack from the assault forces. There was none.

The man entered through the slit in the tent, removed the plastic scorpion from the box and replaced it with another object. It took five seconds. The fireworks display took twenty. Outside the tent, the scorpion was placed in a canister, the canister was shoved down the mouth of a retractable tube and fired to the northeast. The canister flew unnoticed through the barrage of rockets, beyond the attacking mortars and exploded. A small parachute drifted downward and landed 100 feet beyond Major Collins. The major gave a shrill whistle and he and his men retreated with the canister.

As the canister was leaving the barrel of the tube, the man threw the tube aside, strapped on his backpack and dashed for the edge of the peninsula. A perimeter guard had recovered from the first shock of the fireworks and had seen the body of his comrade lying in the gully. He rose from one knee just as the man came into view.

"Halt!" he shouted, training his rifle on the running figure.

He was greeted by a splotch of red paint on his chest.

"You're dead, too!" he heard as the man sprinted by and dove over the edge of the precipice. Seconds later, the plop of an opening paravane was heard. The wing was guided away from the peninsula and landed near the opposite wall. Gathering the paravane, the man extracted the radio from his pocket and punched in the number two. Seconds later the whump-whump of a helicopter was heard above the rim. The pilot guided his craft via GPS to coordinates that the radio message had supplied. The landing, pick up and takeoff was accomplished in less than thirty seconds. The copilot turned in his seat and looked back to the passenger compartment.

"Great work, Sarge," he said.

"Thanks!" came the reply. "Did they get the canister?"

"You bet, they did! You dropped it almost on top of them."

The man in the passenger compartment sat back and smiled. He wished that he could have been in the tent when the blue team opened the box and found his trademark instead of the plastic scorpion. He wondered if they even knew what the three-inch metal replica of an Arizona roadrunner was. Then he noted the arrow on the directional compass and the destination coordinates on the GPS.

"Where are we going?" he asked.

"You're being debriefed in Tabuk and then you're heading stateside."

"What's up?"

"Don't know for sure. I think there was a message from your mother."

"Oh!"

The rest of the trip was flown in silence. The helicopter landed in Tabuk and was immediately met by a jeep with command flags on the fenders. The man deplaned and went to the jeep. Salutes were exchanged as he settled into the back seat. A hand was extended backwards.

"Welcome back, Kevin,"

CHAPTER TEN

That night Janette spent her first night in the desert. Brian's house was remote and the sounds after dark made her nervous. She was in a strange house in a strange part of the country. She jumped at almost every sound. She finally dozed off at well after midnight. At three o'clock the phone rang. Her heart nearly stopped. She fumbled in the semi-darkness of a night light until she found the receiver.

"Hello," she mumbled.

"Hi! Mom!" came a voice on the other end. "It's me, Kevin."

"Oh, my goodness, Kevin. You scared me half to death."

"Sorry, Mom. We just got in from maneuvers and your message was waiting for me. I thought I'd better call right away. What time is it there, anyway? And how come you're in Arizona? I called home first and Dad said that you were at Brian's house."

"It's ten after three in the morning," she was beginning to relax a bit.

"What's up?" he asked.

"I don't know how to tell you this," she stammered. "It's Brian."

"Brian! What about Brian? Is he sick?"

"No, I wish it were just that! He's dead, Kevin! Brian's dead!"

"Dead! You've got to be kidding! He can't be!"

"It's true. I just saw him in the morgue."

"The morgue? What morgue? What happened?"

"I know you must be very upset," she answered. "It seems that he was driving back from a place called Tortilla Flat. He had been flying his airplane in the area looking for some lost mine or something, I'm not sure."

"I know all about it," Kevin interrupted. "Brian wrote me. I was going to go with him when I got back."

"Well, it seems that he got sick at the restaurant and started back and then had a heart attack and just died. He was able to pull his truck off the road so no one else was hurt, thank goodness."

"It just doesn't make any sense," Kevin said. "Brian was in good shape and never complained of any problems."

"I know, I know."

"Look, I'll be home as soon as I can. I think that he would like to buried in Arizona. Have you made any arrangements, yet?"

There was a moment of silence and then Janette whispered, "He's going to be cremated. The sheriff and the coroner both suggested it."

"What!" Kevin yelled. "You mean that he'll be gone before I get back! I really wanted to say a proper good-bye."

"Oh, dear," Janette sobbed. "Maybe I shouldn't have signed that paper so quickly."

"Look, Mom. Call them first thing in the morning and tell them that you've changed your mind. Then make arrangements with a local funeral home for a visitation and funeral. We can always decide on cremation later if we want to."

"All right, Kevin. I'll call tomorrow morning. I'm sorry that I acted so fast. I'm sure it'll be all right."

"Okay. Look, I gotta go. I think that I can get a flight to Fort Benning in the morning. I'll call you from there," Kevin ended.

"Good-bye, dear. I love you," Janette said.

"Love you, too. Bye," After hanging up the phone, Kevin left the communication center and went directly to his bunk. He pulled out his duffel and searched through it until he found a packet of rubberband-bound papers. He sat down and began to reread Brian's last few letters.

Master Sergeant Kevin Stewart wasn't used to feeling wetness in his eyes. He had seen men die and had been the cause of some of those deaths. But now he couldn't hold back the tears as he thought of life without Brian. He'd go to Arizona, lay Brian to rest and then sign up for another hitch. Maybe he could sort things out and get a new direction in his life after another four years in the army.

CHAPTER ELEVEN

On the top floor of a high-rise office building in Dallas, Texas, three men sat around a cocktail table. Each had a short glass of whiskey. The chairs were upholstered in full grain leather. The office itself bespoke of money and power—thirty by thirty feet in dimension, a ten-foot ceiling, exterior walls of sheet glass, interior walls of oak, and a thick pile carpet. A huge mahogany desk dominated the outside corner of the room, while a wet bar occupied an inside wall. Aside from a few bookshelves, the rest of the wall space was almost hidden by pictures.

The men were as richly turned out as the room they occupied. All three wore western hand-tooled boots. Four of the six boots rested comfortably on the low oval table they sat around. The pants that covered the boots were hand tailored and shaped. They were held in place by a finely tooled leather belts coupled by massive sterling silver buckles. Three tailor-made jackets hung on an antlered coat rack. The western-style silk shirts were pinched at the neck by bolo ties fastened with bejeweled clips that matched the cufflinks on the French cuffs. Completing the look of each man was the hat on his head. Impeccably cleaned and blocked, the hats never left the heads of their owners. The hatband set each hat and its owner apart from the others, reflecting their individual personalities.

Ed Murphy's hat sported a band of thin leather set with perfectly matched turquoise stones. Ed had acquired his wealth the old-fashioned way. He began as a cowhand and worked his way into a position of ownership. Fifteen years of hard work left him as the sole owner of one of the largest spreads in Texas. He renamed it the BAR-4-LEAF.

Little Jim Plover's hat was banded in solid silver. He got his ranch the easy way—he inherited it. His father, Big Jim, had fought everyone in sight for every inch and every acre. He finally made it big in the '73 bull market by speculating in soybeans and silver. Unlike most of his fellow speculators, Big Jim never gave it back. In fact he never entered the market again. Instead, he concentrated on the cattle business and grew his ranch, the O DOUBLE X, into a fabled operation.

Harry "Slick" Burleson's hat band was made of genuine hand-cured rattlesnake skin. Burleson's holdings rivaled the other two. The cattle business was only one of his interests, but it was one of his favorites. He liked to think of himself as a Texas highroller and one of the boys. He fitted the first category but couldn't get into the second. He acquired his wealth by every crooked means and scam in the books. Intimidation, foreclosure and fraud gave him title to vast acreage. Rustling and hustling on the range and at the card table stocked it. His holdings, although not contiguous, totaled enough to place him among the legends of the cattle industry. He kept his many ranches separate and accumulated a number and variety of cattle brands.

Now, Burleson took a long pull at his whiskey.

"Man!" he said. "We are making money hand over fist. Who'd a thunk that crazy old professor could pull this off?"

"Yeah!" echoed Plover. "Big Jim would sure be proud of me."

"We're making money all right," Murphy agreed. "But things are getting a bit out of hand."

"Whatta ya mean?" The other two asked. "Don't money agree with ya?"

"Oh! I like money as much as the next guy," Murphy answered. "But I think that we're missing the big picture."

"The big picture!" Burleson said. "Why don't you tell us about the big picture?"

"Don't be a smartass, Slick," Murphy growled. "You know damn well what I mean. When we started this operation, live cattle were worth $55 a hundredweight and we were all starving. Yesterday, they were going for over $300. That's one hell of a price. It's getting so that no one can afford to eat meat anymore. We're pricing ourselves out of the market. If we're not careful we're going to shoot ourselves in the foot. Some of our neighbors are having a tough time. Their numbers are way down and they can't replace anything that they market."

"Yer breaking my heart!" Burleson interrupted. "I just picked up ten thousand acres near the Okey border for a song. I'll be producing beef up there by next year and lots of it."

Plover put his half-empty glass on the table and said, "I don't get it. I thought that this is what we all wanted. Just 'cause it's better than we expected, what are we supposed to do? Let everyone in on it and ruin it for ourselves?"

"No! I don't want to let everyone in on it! I don't want to let anyone in on it!" Murphy yelled. "In fact we can't let anyone in on it, unless we want to end up in the joint. Don't you guys see? We've got to ease out of this and I think that now's the time to start."

"Well, I don't," countered Burleson. "I've got my eye on a couple of ranches that are about to go belly-up and, get this, I may have a shot at a packing plant. No! I don't think that I want to turn this off yet."

Both men looked at Plover.

"I'm with Slick," he said. "This things too good to stop. Besides, we got enough clout to beat any rap, if we have to."

"Gentlemen, I hope you know what you're doing," Murphy resigned. "Cattle prices aren't our only problem. I've got a real uneasy feeling about our partners down in Arizona."

"Whattaya mean?" said a defensive Burleson. "I've

known Pete Saunders for over twenty years. If you've got a gripe with him, you better air it out now!"

"It ain't him so much," Murphy said, getting up to refill his whiskey. "Pete seems okay and so does Jim Blackwell. It's those other guys that he's got us hooked up with that I don't trust. To tell you the truth, I think we've got some mavericks on the range and I think we've lost control over them!"

"You're gettin' skittish, Ed," Burleson countered. "You just leave them fellers to me and Pete. When the time comes we'll pay 'em off and they'll disappear. You'll see."

Murphy put his glass to his lips, took a swig and said, "Well, we'd better have a plan and a time to shut this thing off. Give it some thought and meet back here next week."

Plover and Burleson nodded, drained their glasses, got their coats, and left. In the hall, Burleson pulled Plover over and whispered, "We better keep a close eye on ol' Ed, I think he's starting to get a dose of Christianity."

Plover shook his head in agreement.

CHAPTER TWELVE

merican Airlines Flight 587 touched down at Phoenix's Sky Harbor Airport at 3:57 pm. United Airlines Flight 362 had arrived in Phoenix an hour earlier and Janette Stewart had met it to welcome her husband. Together they stood at Gate 15 in Terminal 3 to meet Kevin. The arrival of American Airlines Flight 587 was announced, the entry doors opened and passengers began to deplane.

"Look! There he is! There he is!" screamed Janette as a group emerged through the double doors.

Kevin separated himself from the other passengers and immediately found himself in the embrace of his parents.

"It's good to be back," Kevin said.

"We're glad to have you," his parents chorused.

"Any change in the arrangements?" Kevin asked, as they walked to baggage claim.

"No," Janette confirmed. "It's just like I told you

when you called from Fort Benning. There will be a memorial service tomorrow. The obituary has been in the papers for about a week. We don't expect a large crowd. Brian was a very private person, you know."

"Yeah, I know," Kevin said. "I can't believe that you couldn't stop the cremation. That's going to make for a very cold ceremony."

"I know, dear," his mother said. "I feel really bad about that. I got to the sheriff as soon as I could and he told me that he'd call the coroner and stop it. But then he called back and told me that it was too late. I don't understand why they acted so quickly."

"Well, what's done is done," Kevin said. "We'll make the best of it and I'll scatter Brian's ashes next week."

"I'll get the car and meet you outside," His father said as they arrived at the baggage carousal.

"Okay, I've only got one bag, so it won't take long," Kevin said.

Kevin and Janette stood by the carousel watching luggage pass by. Kevin drew looks from many of the other waiting passengers, especially the younger ones. He was an impressive soldier in his dress khaki uniform, special service beret on his head, hash marks on his arm, chevron on his sleeve, and service ribbons on his chest. The uniform only served to enhance the figure under it. A muscular chest and massive shoulders and arms were outlined by the jacket, and it took little imagination to visualize the athletic legs that were clothed by the khaki pants. Kevin stood 5 feet 11 inches tall and weighed in at 205 pounds. He stood erect with the ease and readiness of a professional basketball player. A smile creased his lips as he spotted his duffel.

"Here it is," he said. He reached over the carousel rim and easily swung his bag over his shoulder.

"Let's go!" he said to his mother as he headed toward the door.

The car was waiting at the curb, trunk popped, and his father at the wheel. Kevin threw his bag into the trunk, slammed the lid and slid into the rear seat. The car pulled into traffic and Kevin settled in for the ride out to Brian's house. He removed his special service beret revealing short-cropped light-brown hair. His eyes were a deeper shade of brown. They were deepset and seemed to be in constant motion. His clean-shaven face revealed softly chiseled features. He had a mouth that seemed to be compressed but easily broke into a wide smile. It was a face that meant business.

*

"Kevin! Kevin! Wake up! Breakfast is ready!"

"Coming, Mom!"

Kevin was used to travel and wasn't usually affected by jet lag but, perhaps because of the solemnity of the occasion, he was still in bed when the wake-up call came. He threw on a pair of fatigues and headed for the kitchen.

"Good morning, Lazybones," his mother said.

"Where's Dad?" Kevin asked.

"He decided to dress before breakfast, but you've got plenty of time. The service is at eleven o'clock. We'll be leaving at about a quarter to."

Kevin ate quietly as he savored the bacon, eggs, hash browns, toast and juice that were laid before him. His mind was elsewhere. He was reliving the years that he had spent with Brian and considering what life would be like without him.

"You certainly look serious this morning," his mother said.

"Yeah," Kevin conceded. "I was just thinking about what I'll be doing after the funeral. My hitch is up and I was kicking re-enlistment around. Now, with Brian gone, I'll probably sign up for another four."

"What's going on?" Jim Stewart said as he seated himself at the head of the table.

"We're just talking," his wife answered. "Kevin thinks that he'll sign up again after he gets back to his base."

"That's probably a good idea," his father said. "Your career has been the army, your friends are there and it's most likely the place to get your life in order after Brian's loss."

They arrived at the Church of the Divine Christ at five minutes before eleven o'clock.

"Look at the cars in the parking lot," Janette exclaimed. "Do you think that there's another service going on?"

"Probably," Stewart said. "We'd better get inside. We're almost late."

They were at the bottom of the five-step stairway when the entrance door opened and the pastor emerged.

"Welcome to God's house," he said. "Please come in!

You must be the Stewarts. I'm Reverend Phillips, the pastor here at Divine Christ."

He extended his arm in such a way that he blessed each of them as he took their hand. He then embraced them as he drew them into a circle.

"Brian talked about you often," he said. "Please come inside."

He directed them toward the door and addressed Janette as he did so.

"I've taken a bit of liberty and I hope that you don't mind. It's our custom at Divine Christ's to invite the friends of the deceased to a modest reception in the church hall immediately after the service. I've ordered in some food, soft drinks and coffee, and I'll be happy to invite everyone if you agree."

"That's very kind of you," Janette said. "I should have thought of it myself, but it didn't occur to me, Brian not having very many friends and all."

They followed him in, the door closed behind them, and they stood in shock as they viewed the inside of the Church of the Divine Christ. Except for the roped-off first pew, the church was full. The pastor took Janette by the arm and escorted her down the center aisle. Jim and Kevin followed in stunned procession. They were seated in the first pew and Reverend Phillips ascended the three steps into the sanctuary. He paused to attach a microphone to his outer robe and then turned to face the congregation.

"Brothers and Sisters," he began. "We are gathered here to remember Brian Nichols. Brian was a quiet man. He was also a giving man. He gave to others in the spirit of true giving. He once confided in me that he felt if giving were recognized it no longer was a gift for then it became a trade, and true giving must be without identification or reward. A truly remarkable thought.

"Brian wasn't a rich man, but still he did what he could financially. His main charitable activities consisted in using the talents that God had given him for the benefit of others. If you look around this church you can see the results of Brian's handicraft. The hand-hewn beams above, the carved doors and the precisely tooled trim are all examples of Brian's fine work. And he didn't limit his giving to the church. Many of you can attest to his gracious neighborliness as he gave of his time, energy and talents."

Reverend Phillips could see that his sermon was hitting home and jumped in with both feet. By the time he crescendoed and eased into a conclusion, a full forty minutes had passed. He dropped his arms to his sides, looked at the congregation and then extended a hand to the Stewarts in an invitation to speak if anyone so desired. The Stewarts looked at each other and Kevin got to his feet and slowly walked to the altar. He shook hands with Reverend Phillips, refused the use of the clip-on mike and turned to the congregation.

"My name is Kevin Stewart," he began. "I'm Brian's nephew, though, I've always considered him my older brother. First, let me thank all of you for taking the time and making the effort to attend this memorial to Brian." He paused for a slow, deep breath.

"Brian taught me much of what I hold dear. He

taught me how to hunt, fish and to enjoy the great outdoors. But more importantly, he taught me to respect
nature and the environment. The greatest days of my
life have been those spent with Brian. I can't believe
that he's gone."

Tears began to well up in Kevin's eyes as he struggled to continue. "I got up to talk about Brian and what
a great guy he is—ah—was. But the fact that all of you
are here says more than I ever could. So, I'll just say,
Brian I'll—we'll, miss you."

Kevin lowered his eyes and returned to the pew. The
church was perfectly silent as the anguish of the
moment swept through the crowd. Finally, Reverend
Phillips returned to the altar.

"Brian Nichols was, indeed, a remarkable man," he
said.

He then recited a few stock requiem prayers and
indicated that the service was concluded. He ended by
saying that the Stewarts had prepared a reception in
the church hall for all who wished to attend. He
descended to the first pew and escorted Janette
Stewart from the church. Her husband and son followed.

CHAPTER THIRTEEN

She sat in the rear corner of the church hall, obviously alone. She had gone through the receiving line, stopped at the buffet table for a coffee and a couple of chocolate chip cookies, and retreated to the chair in which she was still seated. Dressed in a black suit, she had gone unnoticed. But now, an hour and a half later with the crowd thinned down to the minister and one or two others, Janette became aware of her presence. Janette walked to the back of the room and extended her hand in greeting as the pretty young woman with auburn hair rose to meet her.

"I'm Janette Stewart," she said. "Brian's sister. I met you briefly in the receiving line, but I'm afraid that I've forgotten your name."

"Lauri Beth McCartney."

"I didn't know that Brian had any close lady friends," Janette said. "He was such a confirmed bachelor, you know. I can't believe that he never mentioned you to me."

"I never knew Brian," Lauri Beth confessed. "But I wanted to talk to someone about his death and, after attending the memorial service, I think that it should be Kevin. Could you introduce me to him? I'd feel much better if you did, rather than just barging in on him at a time like this."

"Certainly," Janette obliged. She led Lauri Beth over to Kevin, wondering what it might be about.

"Kevin," Janette began. "I'd like you to meet Lauri Beth Mc—."

"McCartney," Lauri Beth finished.

"Yes," Janette continued. "McCartney. She'd like to talk to you about Brian."

Kevin and Lauri Beth shook hands as Janette excused herself to look for Jim.

"Do you mind if we sit down?" Lauri Beth asked.

"Not at all," Kevin said as he pointed to two upholstered chairs flanking a small coffee table. They sat not quite facing each other. Lauri Beth leaned forward in a clandestine manner. Kevin thought that he best follow her lead. Their heads were little more than a foot apart.

"I really don't know how to begin," Lauri Beth said. "Maybe I shouldn't be here at all."

"Oh!"

"You see, I never knew Brian."

"Really?" Kevin said. "I didn't think that Brian had any close girl friends. At least, he never mentioned any to me."

"Like I said. I didn't know Brian. And that's the reason I'm here," Lauri Beth continued. "Look! I'll get right to the point. I work in the coroner's office. I started seven years ago. I'm a lab technician and I assist at autopsies. I was on duty when Brian was brought in. The coroner, Dr. Blackwell, came in and insisted on performing the post-mortem. This is very unusual because he rarely does the work himself unless it's an important death or a sensational one. I was the assistant. For some reason, I began to watch him very closely. Everything appeared to be normal until he took the blood samples. Usually the samples are just handed to the assistant to label and prepare for lab analysis. He wouldn't let me near the tubes. In fact, he took them into his private office and returned to the corpse saying that he would finish lab preparations later. That made me suspicious, so while he was in his office, I took some blood myself. I had to wait a few days until I could be in the lab by myself. But when I finally was able to analyze the blood samples, I found some interesting things."

Kevin was completely absorbed by her story. So much so that when she stopped talking to catch her breath, he found that he was only inches from her head and nearly collided with her as he turned to ask what she had discovered.

"There was just a trace of alcohol," she continued, a bit more at ease now that she had broken the ice. "He probably had a beer for lunch. There was also evidence that he had taken a sedative, and more than just a trace. The chemical that I found when mixed with any amount of alcohol would cause a blackout in most people in a matter of minutes. But Brian appeared to be in top physical condition and the drug didn't work on him as fast as it would on most people his age."

"Could that have caused his death?" Kevin asked.

"Not unless he drove off the road or crashed into another vehicle."

"Could it have caused a heart attack, then?"

"It's possible, if he already had a severe heart condition."

"But he'd had a physical and they found nothing wrong with his heart!"

"Brian didn't die of a heart attack! He died from an injection of metacorathrombusatate, a drug that literally stops the heart by contracting its muscular functions."

"You said injection?"

"Yes!"

"I don't understand," Kevin whispered. "The coroner's report said heart attack and didn't mention any of the things that you found. What's going on here?"

"That's why I'm here," Lauri Beth said. "I don't understand any of it, either. I thought that by coming here and meeting Brian's family I could get some idea as to his background and to whether or not he was into anything illegal."

"Listen! Brian was a straight arrow all the way. You heard what they said in church."

"Look! I'm convinced that his death wasn't natural and that the cremation was part of the cover-up. The coroner's office has nothing to do with the disposition of bodies."

Kevin got up and took a few steps. He thought for just a moment and then returned to Lauri Beth.

"Don't say anything to anyone, including my parents," he said. "I've got some thinking to do. Is there anything else?"

Lauri Beth hesitated and then said, "I've been with the coroner's office for seven years. I went to work there after I graduated from ASU. When I first started, Dr. Blackwell, the coroner, was just as nice as he could be. But, then about three years ago, he started to change. He became very short tempered and critical of everybody's work.

"Not only that but Pete Saunders, the sheriff, was seen with Dr. Blackwell on many occasions. Saunders has a reputation on living on the edge. He's been investigated as much as he's investigated others. He's never been indicted, but there have been a couple of concerted efforts to get him out of office. And the people that he hangs around with would make your skin crawl."

"Are you saying that Brian's death was part of some sort of conspiracy?"

"I really don't know what I'm trying to say," Lauri Beth said. "I just have this feeling that something terrible has happened and I can't do anything about it."

"Look, Lauri Beth," Kevin said as he scribbled his telephone number on a piece of scrap paper. "I'm going to stay around for a bit. Why don't you give me your phone number and I'll get in touch with you. There's a couple of things that I want to check out in light of what you've told me. And don't worry about the coroner and the sheriff, that kind always get what's coming to them."

"You're right, Kevin," Lauri Beth said as she prepared to leave.

Kevin started to say something but, instead, just watched Lauri Beth leave the room. He could still smell her perfume as the door closed behind her.

CHAPTER FOURTEEN

In a remote part of Idaho, not far from the wilderness area, a conference of sorts was just getting under way. Outside of the log hunting cabin a generator hummed away. Inside eleven men were seated on rough planks that flanked tables made of abandoned doors. The doors, as well as the planks, were supported by concrete blocks. Two bare light bulbs provided illumination. In one corner, wired directly to lines from the generator was a powerful computer. Cell phones of every variety sat in front of the participants.

A heavily bearded man occupied the head position. He took a long drink from a can of beer and said, "Well, boys, I reckon that this is it!"

The others nodded. A few banged their fists on the tables. Words of agreement such as, "'Bout time," "Ah'm ready," and "Let's get on with it," were uttered.

General Harry "Dan'l" Boone—a self-styled rank within the militia—drawled, "Well, Ah'm glad to hear that ya'll 're ready. Now ah'm goin' around the table and each one of ya are gonna tell me about what yer gonna do when ya get the signal. This'll probably be the last time that we're all in the same room."

Boone was dressed in combat fatigues, complete with a Castro-type hat. A heavy belt held a holstered forty-five automatic pistol and four clips of ammunition. As he scanned the group in front of him, he saw similarly clad men. Some wore hats, some didn't. The uniforms were of various military and hunting styles, some khaki, others camouflage. All wore sidearms of one sort or another. A few had bandoliers slung over their shoulders or across their chests. Some faces were clean shaven, others held a two- or three-day growth, still others wore facial hair in various stages of trim. All had a determined expression and their bodies sat upright with military rigidity.

Boone had a stack of papers in front of him. He picked up the first one and said,

"Holtsville, New York!"

A man on the left side of the table, two places down, jumped to his feet, saluted and shouted, "Sir! Yes, sir!"

"Status report!" Boone demanded.

"Yes, sir! We have infiltrated the facility. The plan is in place. A simple diversion will pull personnel out of the computer room. Five minutes later, all memory and most of the programs will be destroyed. We have an escape route that has been tested at various times of the day. We should be able to pull it off without a hitch."

"Without a hitch is mandatory! There is no room for

failure and it will not be accepted," Boone bellowed. "Now, what about the backup facilities?"

"They're covered, sir!" the man reported, slightly admonished. "We have exactly the same plan in place with infiltration completed. There will be no failure, sir! Holtsville will be without computers as soon as we get the go ahead."

"Excellent! Andover, Massachusetts!" Dan'l ordered.

Another militiaman stood, saluted and gave his report. It was much the same as the previous one.

"Atlanta, Georgia!"

"Sir! Yes, sir!" Another report accepted.

"Cincinnati, Ohio!"

"Sir! Yes, sir!"

"Austin, Texas!"

"Sir! Yes, sir!"

"Ogden, Utah!"

"Sir! Yes, sir!"

Fresno, California!"

"Sir! Yes, sir!"

"Kansas City, Missouri!"

"Sir! Yes, sir!"

"Memphis, Tennessee!"

"Sir! Yes, sir!'

"Philadelphia, Pennsylvania!"

"Sir! Yes, sir!"

The reporting was over and Boone was beaming.

"Great! great!" he boomed. "All reports received and accepted. Good work, men! Now, here's the situation. We're primed and ready, but we have to wait for phase one to kick in. I expect that to be sometime in the middle of summer. It'll come quickly. Look for a prolonged heat spell. Tempers will be short and our men in the inner cities should be able to promote unrest, especially with these high meat and food prices." He chuckled slightly and continued, "This will be a coordinated effort and you will be kept advised. You must be ready at all times. Keep your weapons primed and your powder dry. Any questions?"

There were none and the meeting began to break up. Small groups formed and wished each other luck. Then they began to drift to the door in pairs. They picked up their rifles, carbines and ammunition that had been stacked nearby and departed in four-wheel drive vehicles. They would be back in place in three or four days. The meeting had lasted for over four hours and had been a good one.

The cabin became quiet, and Boone walked to the rear and tapped on the only other door in the room. The door opened and a tall, lean man entered. Major Jimmy Ray Wheeler was Boone's aide and computer expert. He went straight to the computer and took the papers that Boone handed him.

"I'll have these on the computer in no time," Wheeler said. "What do you want me to do after that?"

"We'll be arranging for the next meeting," he said. "We'll be calling in all the phase-one guys and this place won't hold them all. That old mining camp restaurant ten miles down the road will do just fine. Hasn't been anybody in there for over ten years but the building will hold up a mite longer."

"When do you plan on havin' that?" Wheeler asked.

"As soon as we can get hold of everyone. How long will that take?"

"Hm," Wheeler speculated. "Let's see. We got people in the twenty-five largest cities in the country and you probably want the top two officers from each location. We'll be cramped in that old building, but we can do it. We gotta give them some lead time. I think that we can put it together in three weeks, maybe a few days under. How's that?"

"It'll do. Get started as soon as you finish with the stuff from this meeting. Then make sure that Charlie Whitfield is briefed and get me a full status report on the Arizona operation. This whole thing is gonna require coordination. We'll be closin' down as soon as the boys in phase two complete their job.

Boone turned, pulled a cigar from his breast pocket, bit off the end, spit the piece on the floor and left the cabin to enjoy his smoke outside. He strolled down toward the little creek that somehow always kept running. He could hear the water washing gently over some rocks. He felt really, really good.

It was just ten years ago that he started the New Revolutionary Militia with a few of the other backwoods boys. It was more like a little club when it first began and nobody, especially Boone, had expected it to grow to anything like it was today. Why, he reckoned that they had over five hundred members right now and, with all those active sympathizers, the total could be near three thousand. Boone was no dummy. In fact, if he had a little more education and a little less radicalism, if would qualify to head up any number of large corporations. He was a good organizer and a good delegator and he was a very good persuader. He could sell soot in Pittsburgh, ice to the Eskimos, and hate to the discontented. And since there were far more discontented people in the world than satisfied ones, his little band grew rapidly.

All followers of the New Revolutionary Militia had two things in common, love and hate. To a man and woman they loved the United States of America and they loved it with a passion. They would defend it with their lives and would sacrifice anything for its survival. They loved the mountains, the prairies, the rivers, the forests, the lakes and oceans, the shores, the croplands, the treasures below, and the skies above.

With all this love, one wouldn't think that there was any room left for hate. There was. They hated the government of the United States of America with equal intensity. They didn't hate the President or the Congress or the judicial branch or the army or the navy or the air corps or the individuals that comprised them. They hated the government, that undefined thing that infringed on their lives and liberties and they hated it with the same fervor that they loved their country.

Over the years the members of the New Revolutionary Militia had tried to focus their hatred and had found it difficult to find a single target in the structure of the federal government. Boone's hatred had carried them for the first five years, but then they found their victim, a target so logical that they wondered why it had eluded them for so long. The Internal

Revenue Service had few if any friends even among those who loved the United States of America and its government.

The IRS was easy to hate. They infringed on everyone's freedom and found their way into everyone's life. Most Americans had a deduction on every paycheck as a reminder that there was someone out there that they didn't like. It fit like a glove. Boone had hated the IRS all of his life—he just never realized how deeply this hatred was seated. Once the IRS became the main target of the New Revolutionary Militia, Boone felt that he had been reborn. The concept was easy to sell and he sold it well. He was amazed that those who expressed their hatred toward the IRS the most were the ones who paid the smallest amount in taxes.

For the most part, his army was comprised of people with little education or means. They were the loyal malcontents. Boone himself had graduated from the University of California, Berkeley, with a major in political science. He received his degree and his revolutionary training from the same institution. He modeled his army after the military and the upper echelon was well educated. The people in the field were organized in the communist cell configuration. In fact, some workers were not aware that they were part of an organization, but rather felt that they were an isolated group working for an ideal. All of which suited him very well and made it almost impossible to trace disruptive or illegal activities to a central source.

Boone took one last long drag on his stogie, flipped it into the creek and started back to the cabin.

"By God!" he thought. "The goddam government will soon know there's somebody out there. It won't be a killer punch, but it might bring the bastards to their knees for a spell."

CHAPTER FIFTEEN

The day after Brian's memorial service, Janette and Jim headed back to Chicago. Kevin told them that he would stay in Arizona long enough to settle Brian's estate. He would put the house up for sale, see that the horses were taken care of, sell the truck and the ultralight, and take care anything else that had to be done. Actually, he had no intention of doing anything of the sort.

Janette had asked him about Lauri Beth after seeing them huddled in close conversation. Kevin explained her away. He would be heading back to Fort Benning to re-enlist when he was finished in Arizona. He'd keep in touch.

Kevin dropped his parents at the airport and headed back to Brian's house. He was eager to follow up on some ideas that had been bugging him ever since his conversation with Lauri Beth. He couldn't believe that he had been so lax and stupid as not to have realized what he hadn't found in Brian's belongings. He parked the car and almost ran into the house. Once inside, he went straight to Brian's room and stared at the bed. Anything of any value that Brian possessed had been piled on the bed. Kevin began to rummage through the papers, trying to remember where his mother had said she'd put the rest of Brian's belongings.

"The hall closet! That's it!"

Kevin rushed through the living room and opened the door to the closet next to the front entry. He got down on his hands and knees and reached under some coats to the rear of the closet. His fingers touched a box. He pulled the box out of the closet and slid it into the living room. Still kneeling, he tore open the cross-folded top and spilled the contents onto the carpet. He quickly threw aside the owner's manual for the Dodge Ram, along with the registration and insurance card, and picked up what was left.

Kevin slowly turned over the map sandwiched between two plastic sheets. He felt the strap attached to the bottom half and then looked at the face of the map. He knew exactly what he had. Brian had described his plotting device in numerous letters to him. He examined the Magic Marker lines on the top piece of plastic. He could see where some erasures had been made. This was to be expected, as Brian had explained that after each flight he transferred the markings on the plastic to the actual map, cleaned the plate and began fresh the next flight. He separated the plates and removed the map. After unfolding the map, he placed the top plate over the last line drawn on it.

It didn't make any sense. The current markings on the plastic didn't match up with any of the other lines. It was as if Brian had abandoned all of his previous searches and gone off on an entirely new tangent. Something, indeed, was wrong. Kevin sat for a minute or two, got up, went into the bedroom, found his pack, and withdrew all of Brian's letters. He began reading from the most recent. He flipped through letter after letter until he came to the one where Brian outlined his plans for his search for the Lost Dutchman Mine.

He hadn't even finished the first page, when he lowered the letter and stared at the wall. Of course! What had he been thinking or not thinking! It had been there all the time! The key to Brian's search. The GPS! Where was it? Why hadn't it been returned with Brian's other possessions?

He ran back to the living room and turned the box over. Nothing! He started to search the house, beginning with Brian's bedroom.

Wait a minute! It wouldn't be in the house. Brian never got back here. The truck! or the ultralight!

Kevin dashed outside and made a hurried inspection of the truck. The glove box. Nothing! Under the seat. Nothing! Behind the seat. Nothing! He slammed the door in frustration and went to the ultralight trailer. He opened the rear doors and the sunlight streamed in. He scoured the inside of the trailer with his eyes and found nothing. He climbed in and began to inspect the ultralight itself. There wasn't much to it and there weren't too many places to hide anything. Kevin slowly backed out of the trailer and sat down on the trailer floor. He put his head in his hands and began to think.

Think it through! Think it through! Lauri Beth said that she found a sedative and a deadly chemical in Brian's blood. He couldn't have flown with either and he must have had the sedative first. He lands the plane, packs it away and heads back. He stops at Tortilla Flat for a bite to eat. That's where he got the sedative. It has to be. He only gets a mile or two from the restaurant when he pulls off the road, so he must have been feeling bad when he left. Okay! So, maybe he suspects something. He stops the truck and sees the plastic map and the GPS, probably on the front seat. He wants to hide them. The map is too big and he's not thinking clearly, anyway. He grabs the GPS. It's only about the size of a cell phone. It's got a Velcro strap on the back. He winds the Velcro around the GPS and now he's got a small package. Where to hide it? He's running out of time. Where? Where?

Kevin got up and went back to the truck. He sat in the driver's seat and closed the door. He took out his wallet and held it in his right hand. He let his hand slip to the floor and let his head sag forward. He moved his hand and flexed his arm. His hand hit the panel under the dashboard. He felt the end of the panel. It was open above. Kevin opened the door and lay on his back so he could search above the panel. The space was tight and he was cramped. He got his fingers up and over the edge of the panel and began to probe. He touched something that moved. He tried to grip it and failed. He was able to touch it with his index finger. He gave it a shove to the side and felt it slide forward. He was able to pinch it between his thumb and forefinger. He pulled it out. He slid to the ground and held the object up to the light. The GPS! Brian must have given it a final flick and got it up into the dash panel just before he blacked out.

Kevin closed up the truck and trailer and returned to the house. He sat a full five minutes just looking at the GPS. He had operated them before, but each one was programmed slightly different and he want to make sure that he didn't delete anything accidentally. He pulled his chair up to the coffee table, opened up the map to its full width and turned on the GPS. The screen was blank. He pushed the waypoint key. "Long" and "Lat" appeared. He reasoned that he could either enter a longitude and latitude and store it as a way-point or he could push enter and record his present position as a waypoint. He did neither. Instead he pushed the recall button. "Name" appeared. Brian probably didn't name his waypoints. He must just have used the numbers preassigned by the system.

Kevin entered 20 and pushed enter. The screen came up blank. He redid the steps and tried 19. Another blank screen. He tried 18 then 17. At 16 a pair of coor-dinates appeared along with a direction and distance. Kevin plotted the waypoint on the map and then recalled number 15. He plotted 15 as well. Then 14. When he plotted 13, he found that he was covering an already plotted waypoint on the map.

Well, whatta ya know! I think I've found where Brian flew his last search pattern, or maybe his last two. Anyway, it must have started where the two points agree on the map and it must have ended on waypoint number 16.

Kevin sat back and let the realization of his discovery sink in. This meant that someone had deliberately tampered with Brian's chart and that his death surely was no accident. It also meant the he would not be returning to Fort Benning as soon as he had expected. A telephone call was all that was needed to extend his furlough indefinitely. Kevin picked up the phone and made that call. He was now fully committed and determined that he would find the answer to Brian's tragic end.

He decided that he wouldn't alarm his parents. He would just make some excuse for his delayed departure. It wouldn't be difficult with the closing of Brian's affairs, he could think of any number of things that would require his presence a little longer. Now, he needed a plan and a very carefully thought-out one. If it were true that Brian was murdered—he paused at the thought—then he would be involved with some desperate and dangerous people. He needed to think every step of the way through to the end. His investigation had to appear innocent and innocuous.

Let's see. Where to begin? I'll have to trace Brian's steps and discover if his search for the Lost Dutchman had turned up anything. I'll have to find out all that I can about Tortilla Flat and that restaurant and I'll have to figure out what part the coroner and the sheriff might have played. I'm gonna need some help, some help that I can trust.

Kevin had known all along where he was heading. Lauri Beth! He wanted to see her again and desperately hoped that he wasn't letting his heart lead his head. He spent a long while mulling over his options.

I've got to trust someone. Why not Lauri Beth? How could she possible be involved? True, she had come to him unsolicited. But what could anyone hope to gain by having her open that door? If she hadn't shown up at the memorial service, I'd be on my way back to Georgia, none the wiser. No! She had to be on her own. I've really got no alternative. She's the only one who can find out about the coroner and the sheriff without arousing any suspicion. Okay, she's in! But I'd better watch her closely until I'm perfectly sure.

Kevin did what he knew he was going to do all along. He picked up the phone and dialed Lauri Beth McCartney's home number. It rang four times and he heard the click of an answering machine.

"I can't come to the phone right now," the machine said. "Please leave your number and a short message and I'll get back to you."

Kevin stammered for a moment and then said, "This is Kevin Stewart, Brian Nichols' nephew. Please give me a call." He added his number as a quick afterthought and hung up. At eight o'clock that night his phone rang.

"Hello."

"I'd like to speak with Kevin Stewart, please."

"Speaking."

"Oh! Hi! This is Lauri Beth McCartney, returning your call."

"Thanks! Look, Lauri Beth, I've discovered some things that I'd like to talk over with you. About Brian. Is there someplace we could meet?"

"Sure."

"How about dinner?

"Er...okay."

"Great! Where do you live?"

"I'm in Tempe. Near the university. You're way out northwest aren't you?"

"Yeah, I'm in Peoria. Why don't you pick a place and I'll meet you there? Is tomorrow night okay? And make it close to you. I'm not working and you are, so I've got plenty of time."

"Well, there's a real good fish house on Scottsdale Road just south of Camelback on the east side of the street. It's called Famous something. I'll be there at seven. Okay?"

"Great! See you tomorrow."

Kevin hung up the phone and slid down in his chair. "Phew!" he breathed. He was surprised at how nervous he had been during the short call to Lauri Beth.

"It's been a long time since I really wanted to see a girl," he thought. "You better be careful. She's young and very pretty."

CHAPTER SIXTEEN

Little Jim Plover and Slick Burleson sat in Ed Murphy's reception room waiting for the pretty girl behind the large desk to let them by.

"What the hell is this all about, anyway?" Plover asked. "I thought we weren't supposed to meet until next week and here it is just two days since we were here last."

"It better not be what I think it is!" snarled Burleson. "Who the fuck does he think he is? Callin' us in like we work for him and then makin' us wait out here like some goddam salesmen."

"Gentlemen, Mr. Murphy will see you now," the receptionist cooed.

The door opened and Murphy ushered them in, shaking each by the hand as he did so.

"Sit down, boys," he offered. "Whiskey?"

"Yeah," they both replied.

Murphy set a glass in front of each man and put a

bottle on the table in front of them. A pitcher of branch water was already in place.

"Well," Burleson said, a full glass already in his hand. "What's this all about, Ed?"

Each man sat upright in his chair, feet on the floor, eyes set hard.

"Boys," Murphy responded. "I know that we were supposed to meet next week, but I didn't want to wait that long. I been doin' some thinkin' and I thought that we better have a talk right now."

"Yeah!" Burleson said. "I been doin' some thinkin', too! Let's hear what you been thinkin' about!"

"Well," Murphy began. "I been thinkin' about this here whole damn deal. I think that it's been going on about long enough. I been thinkin' that it's time to quit and ah'm gettin' out right now."

"Well, maybe me and Jim ain't ready to quit and maybe me and Jim ain't ready to get out just yet," Burleson said. "Have you thought about that?"

"Don't make no difference. My mind's made up and that's that!"

"Wait a minute!" Plover said, addressing Burleson. "Just because Ed's gonna stop, that don't mean we have to, does it?"

"Yeah, well I don't think that Ed means just to stop and let his herd stop producing and start to dwindle and get in line like them other assholes!" Burleson said. "Does it Ed?"

"I guess not," Murphy answered. "I reckon what I mean is that when I stop the game is over and we turn the stuff over to the government. It'll still take a couple of years for production to get back to normal. That ought to be enough for you boys, don't ya think?"

Plover and Burleson looked at each other.

"I guess it don't matter much what we think, does it, Ed?" Burleson replied. "And would ya mind tellin' us just how you plan to get the stuff to the government without us all goin' to jail?"

"That's what I been thinkin' about for this last two days," Murphy confessed. "I think I got a plan that'll work. Look! Nobody knows where we get this stuff and nobody knows how it's made or what's in it. Slick, you just tell 'em that we're through and I'll do the rest."

"And just what might that be?" the other two asked together.

"Well, I plan to but a bottle of the stuff in a locker in Dulles Airport. Then I'm gonna mail the key to a guy in the Department of Agriculture. That's all! No note! No nothin'."

"That's it?" Plover asked.

"Yeah! That's it," Murphy said. "They'll pick up the stuff and analyze it and figure it out and start to use it on livestock and the crisis will be over and they'll never know who sent it or how the virus got spread or anything else."

"And what if they're too dumb to figure it out? What then?" Burleson demanded.

"Well, in that case they'll get a phone call from a pay phone in Kansas City or someplace and I'll explain it to them."

"And how long might that take?" Slick asked.

"I'd give about a month and if there hadn't been an

announcement, I'd call."

"So, that's it!" Burleson almost yelled. "We got about a month and we're through! That's it?"

"It'll take another two years to get the cattle numbers back up."

"Bullshit! The minute they make the announcement, prices will hit the fan. I been leveraging most of what I bought. This could ruin me. If I don't get another two or three years, I could go under! You can't do it! For God's sake, don't do it!"

"Sorry, boys. My mind's made up. I got to go to D.C. in ten days and that'll be the end of it," Murphy declared.

"We'll see about that! We'll just see about that!" Burleson shouted. He picked up his whiskey glass, drained it and threw it against the brick of the fireplace. He was already at the door when the last pieces hit the floor. Plover put his glass on the table, turned and followed Burleson out the door. Neither said a word and neither looked back.

Burleson got on the express elevator and was out of the building in less than two minutes. He hailed a cab and wasn't even aware that Plover had gotten in with him. Burleson gave the driver directions, still uttering obscenities under his breath. Ten minutes later, he was in his own plush office. After leaving instructions that he was not to be disturbed and wasn't taking calls, he sat down at his desk and for the first time noticed that Plover was standing in front of him.

"Sit down, goddam it!" he snarled. "Just sit down. I gotta think! That son of a bitch ain't gonna get away with this! You can bet your sweet ass on that!"

Plover was agreeing with Burleson by mutely nodding his head. He wasn't all that upset about closing the operation down. Unlike his colleague, he had banked all his gains and wasn't in any financial danger if the meat industry returned to normal. In fact, deep down, he was getting nervous and was looking for a way out. But he knew one thing for sure. And that was that Slick Burleson was a dangerous man, and it wasn't a good idea to be on the wrong side of him.

Burleson had pulled the phone closer to him and was now dialing. He pulled the handset so close that Plover could scarcely hear him.

"Gimme the sheriff," he whispered into the mouthpiece. "Pete, it's me. We got a problem."

"Yeah! That's right! I said WE!" he said after a slight pause. "That goddam Ed Murphy's turnin' chicken. He wants to call off the whole damn thing. You heard me! He's ready to pull the plug and we got less than a week!"

Another pause as he listened to the sheriff.

"All right, you go ahead and make your fuckin' call. I'll get back to you tomorrow morning and you better have some answers!" Burleson slammed the receiver into its cradle.

*

Sheriff Pete Saunders replaced the receiver somewhat gentler than did his counterpart. He immediately picked it up and dialed a number in Idaho.

"Dan'l, this is Pete. Listen, I need some direction here."

He explained the situation in Dallas in as much detail as he could and then listened. It didn't take much time for Boone to give Saunders his orders—he was a man of few words and quick decisions.

"Okay! I got it!" Saunders said. "Ah'll get it done as soon as possible and ah'll get the stuff as well. Don't worry, Dan'l, none of that stuff will get out of Texas."

Another call. This time to Tortilla Flat.

"Lemme talk to Charlie Whitfield."

"Charlie, it's Pete. You and Butch get down here as quick as you can, and I mean now."

Pete put down the phone and did a little serious thinking. He made a decision and dialed a local number.

"Dr. Blackwell," he said.

The coroner came on the line.

"Coroner Blackwell."

"Jim, it's me, Pete," the sheriff said. "Something's come up that needs fixin'. I got Charlie and Butch comin' in this afternoon. Can you come over?"

"I'm in the middle of an autopsy and it's going to take the rest of the day," the coroner explained.

"All right," Saunders said. "When the boys get here, we'll come over there. I want you in on this."

"But—" Dr. Blackwell said, but the line had already gone dead.

The Sheriff pushed away from his desk, put his hands behind his head, and raised his feet so that the heels of his boots were resting on the desktop.

*

At three-thirty that afternoon Sheriff Saunders, Charlie Whitfield and Butch Crosswell were ushered into the coroner's private office. On their way they passed a young technician carrying a tray full of blood vials to the forensics lab. Lauri Beth recognized the sheriff but the other two were strangers and she involuntarily shuttered as she continued on her way.

Blackwell entered the room at exactly four o'clock. Saunders was in his chair and Charlie and Butch were lounging on the couch, their feet on the coffee table.

"Lock the door!" Saunders instructed.

The coroner obeyed, started for his desk, then looked for a place to sit, as it became evident that the sheriff wasn't going to move.

"What's this all about?" he demanded.

"Just sit down and listen," Saunders ordered. "Boys, we got a problem with one of them rich Texans." He turned to address Charlie and Butch. "How soon can you two get to Dallas?"

"We could leave in an hour," Charlie said for both of them.

"You'll be driving both ways," Saunders said.

"Okay with me," Butch said. "Ah'm gettin' fed up with the damn Superstitions."

"What's the deal?" Charlie asked.

"There's three bigshots down in Dallas that's been financin' this whole thing," the Sheriff explained. "Now one of them wants out and the other two don't. It's pretty simple. You gotta take care of the guy that wants out. His name's Ed Murphy. You two head for

Dallas and check in with me every day. Once you get there, you'll call a guy by the name of Harry Burleson. Here's his number. He's also known as "Slick." I don't want either of you to see him in person. Telephone only! Got that?"

Charlie and Butch nodded. Blackwell sat with his eyes bulging.

"Once Slick gives you the details, it's up to you as to how and when," Pete continued. "It's got to look like an accident or a mugging and it's got to be done before he leaves for Washington. There's one more thing. Murphy's got a bottle of the vaccine. You gotta get it and bring it back. Any questions?"

Charlie had been taking notes. He looked at Butch. They both shook their heads and got up to leave.

"Remember," Saunders cautioned, "once you get hold of Burleson, you don't talk to me until you get back. And don't let him see you!"

Charlie and Butch got up, nodded and headed to the door. Handshakes were not offered or given. As Butch opened the door, both he and Charlie took one good hard look at the coroner.

"My God!" Blackwell cried. "You can't mean what I just heard. You're not going to kill a man in cold blood. You can't! I won't have it! I'm not going to be a part of any such thing! It was bad enough with that Brian Nichols, but that was done on the spur of the moment. This is premeditated. I'm out! I want nothing to do with this anymore. I don't know why I got involved in the first place."

"Listen!" Saunders said. "You're in, and you're in

until I say so. Get it! You were happy enough to take the money when there was nothin' to it. Now you're goin' to earn it. You hear me! And you're goin' to behave yourself and do just exactly as I say. The only reason you were brought in, in the first place, was just in case something like that Brian guy happened. Well, it happened and now you're in as deep as the rest of us. You got shit up to your elbows and don't think that you can wipe it off without askin' me first. Got it?"

Blackwell slumped in his chair as the sheriff walked past him and out the door. Pete went out to his car. As he drove out of the parking lot, he thought there might be another job for Charlie and Butch when they got back, this time closer to home.

CHAPTER SEVENTEEN

Kevin was at the Arizona Famous Fish House at 6:30 p.m. He hadn't realized how easy it was to travel through the greater Phoenix area. Actually, he was early because he was eager to see Lauri Beth again and compare her to the image he carried in his mind. He remembered her as about 5 foot 7 inches tall with an athletic figure—not muscular, just strong and fit. Her hair, he recalled, was shoulder length and a warm reddish-brown, but he couldn't remember the color of her eyes. He was seated at the bar nursing a beer when she walked into the restaurant. She spotted him and picked her way through the cocktail tables to the bar. He watched her all the way and was happy with what he saw. When she smiled she was even more beautiful than he had remembered. Her hair was a little bit more on the reddish side of auburn, and her face wasn't tanned. It was freckled and softly carved in high-cheeked Irish. She was dressed in a light sweater and slacks. She wore low-heeled shoes and carried a tan cloth purse slung over her shoulder with a leather strap. She worked her way through the maze of tables with a certain athletic grace. Her dark hair hung shoulder length and was pinned so that her ears were revealed. She wore pendant Navaho earrings that swung gently as she walked. A matching Navaho necklace encircled her neck. She presented an impressive image, and others in the bar turned to look at her. Kevin rose and offered her a drink at the bar. She declined and a moment later they were seated at their table. Lauri Beth ordered a Chardonnay and Kevin a fresh beer. They buried themselves in the menus until their drinks arrived. They ordered and the protection of the menus disappeared and Kevin saw her eyes. They were green—green as the Emerald Isle from which they surely must have come.

"Nice to see you again, Lauri Beth," Kevin said.

"You, too, Kevin," Lauri Beth answered. "Isn't this weather just horrible. I can't remember it ever being so hot."

"I thought that it was like this all the time in the desert," Kevin responded.

"I guess it isn't too unusual," she confessed. "But I hear that the whole country is experiencing above-normal temperatures. I can't imagine how bad it must be in places where the humidity is the same as the temperature. People must be biting each other's heads off."

"I wouldn't be surprised," Kevin agreed. "At least it's

comfortable in here. Did you notice that not many people are eating outside?"

"I guess that's right. I hadn't noticed," Lauri Beth said after looking through the front windows to the outside dining area. "But I'm sure you didn't invite me here just to talk about the weather."

"That's true," Kevin said. "I do have something to tell you, but I would have asked you to dinner even if I didn't."

Lauri Beth flushed just a bit and turned her eyes to the table as Kevin continued.

"I've been thinking of almost nothing else since you told me what you found in Brian's blood. I finally convinced myself that Brian didn't die of natural causes. Once I accepted that fact, I began to reason more clearly. I pulled all of Brian's old letters out of my duffel and reread them very carefully, looking for something that I had missed or forgotten. I found both.

"You probably didn't know, but Brian had become fascinated with the Lost Dutchman Mine, almost to the point of addiction. He read every book and article that he could on the subject and I think that he had become almost an authority."

"The Lost Dutchman," Lauri Beth said. "I wonder how many people have lost their lives pursuing that dream over the last hundred years."

"Quite a few," Kevin said. "But I don't think Brian was killed because he was looking for the mine but because he found or was about to find something else. He was searching from the air, flying his own ultralight airplane."

Lauri Beth raised her eyebrows in question at the mention of the ultraliight. Kevin spent the next ten minutes explaining the aircraft, how it's flown and how it can be trailered about. By the time he was finished, the entrees had arrived. They had to settle for small talk, each enjoying the food and the company but wishing that they could finish and change the conversation to a more serious topic. Coffee finally arrived and Lauri Beth looked at Kevin, encouraging him to return to his dialogue.

"As I was saying, before I was rudely interrupted by that delicious red snapper," Kevin joked. "I went through Brian's letters. He described in detail his method of searching for the Lost Mine. I had seen his chart but hadn't paid that much attention to it. I took another and better look. Someone had altered the route for the last flight and when I tried to piece it together I couldn't make much sense of it. Then I remembered the GPS."

"I've heard of that," Lauri Beth interrupted. "Let's see, it means Global Position Situation or something like that. I hear it's very accurate and can find your place to within a couple of hundred yards."

"That's pretty close. Actually it's called Global Positioning System," Kevin corrected. "And it can find your position to within about fifty feet. It'll also give you your altitude above sea level if you can hook on to at least four satellites. Brian had a very good handheld GPS. I had forgotten about it and it hadn't shown up with Brian's things. I searched his truck and found it hidden above the plastic piece that hangs down below the instrument panel. Brian must have been able to put it there just before he died."

Lauri Beth was completely captivated.

"Anyhow," Kevin continued. "I was able to piece together Brian's last flight or two and I was able to join the lines on his charts. I know where Brian was and I can find it within about fifty feet."

"That's fantastic," Lauri Beth said. "But what are you going to do about it and why are you telling me?"

"I guess I'm going to try to find out exactly what happened to Brian and who's responsible," Kevin answered. "And as for telling you, you already suspect that something's wrong and I can't think of any ulterior motive that you might have had in telling me. Furthermore, I'm going to need some help and this could lead back to your office and besides, I wanted to see you again, anyway."

"Thanks," Lauri Beth said, smiling "I'm glad you did and I'd be more than happy to help in any way that I can. Besides I was hoping that you'd call. Now, do you have a plan?"

"I've got the beginning of one," Kevin said. "Obviously, the first thing that we've got to do is find out what Brian had discovered or was about to discover."

He was surprised how easily that he had slipped into the plural and how easily she had accepted it.

"You know that the GPS works equally well on land or in the air. I thought that we should check out the location by air first. I can rent a Cessna 182 at the Scottsdale airport but they'll want me to check out in it a few times before they'll let me take it alone. I'm also going to have to find an aerial camera. I figure that they may have one at the airport. I think that I can be ready by next weekend. Do you have any days off?"

"I'm usually free on weekends," Lauri Beth said. "I carry a beeper in case of emergencies, so it's possible that I'd have to cancel at the last minute, but that's really rare."

"Okay, is it a date then?" he asked.

"Sure," Lauri Beth smiled. "Will you give me a call on Friday?"

"You bet! Now, have you seen anything suspicious? I'm pretty sure that the coroner was in on whatever it was and maybe the sheriff, too."

"Strange that you should ask," Lauri Beth said. "Just this afternoon, I saw the sheriff and two guys that would make your skin crawl barge into Dr. Blackwell's office. After they left, he didn't come out until it was time to go home and then he really looked terrible."

"Has Dr. Blackwell changed his lifestyle lately?" Kevin asked as the check arrived and they prepared to leave.

"Well, over the last few years he's been dressing in really expensive suits. I know that he moved into a kind of posh neighborhood and he just started driving a Mercedes," Lauri Beth answered.

"Well, unless he's gotten a raise or won the lottery, I'd say that could be meaningful."

"I think that he joined a country club last year, as well," she said.

"It certainly looks like our friend Dr. Blackwell has come into some kind of fortune lately," he said.

CHAPTER EIGHTEEN

Butch was at the wheel as they pulled into a parking garage in downtown Dallas. They had driven straight through from Phoenix and neither was feeling very hospitable.

"Whyn't ya get yer ass out of the car and call that Slick fella," Butch grumbled. "Then maybe we can find a motel somewhere and catch some shuteye and a shower."

"Okay! Okay!" Charlie said. "Just gimme a minute to stretch my bones. That was one hell of a ride."

Butch slumped behind the wheel and closed his eyes. Charlie finally got out of the car, slammed the door hard and made his way to a pay phone in the office, working the stiffness out of his knees as he walked. He fished a slip of paper out of his shirt pocket and dialed.

"Mr. Burleson," he said.

"One moment please, may I say who's calling?"

"No!" Charlie returned. "He's expecting me." He could feel the chill on the other end of the line, although nothing was said.

"I can connect you now, SIR!"

"Harry Burleson."

"It's us!" Charlie said.

"Who the hell is US?"

"You better goddam well know who US is!" Charlie yelled. "We're from Pete!"

"Okay, I know who you are. What's your name?"

"Never mind what my name is!" Charlie growled as he pulled out a note pad and pencil. "Just tell me what I got to know about this Ed Murphy guy and forget this call."

"All right! All right! Ed's a pretty big guy, about six-foot-four and weighs about 250 pounds. He's in pretty good shape, so don't underestimate his strength. He's got dark hair and looks like an ex-prize fighter. He always wears a dark suit, western boots and a cowman's hat. He ought to be easy to spot. He lives in the Sky Ranch, a downtown high-rise and keeps his car in the building garage. He drives himself wherever he goes so I'm sure that he'll drive to the airport next Tuesday. He drives a black Cadillac STS and the license plate says ROUNDUP. He's going to Washington D.C. Tuesday morning and plans to be back the same day, so he'll only be carrying a briefcase or maybe one other bag. He'll be packing almost a half gallon of serum and that probably won't fit in his brief-case. You know about the serum, don't you?"

"That's why we're here, asshole!" Charlie answered.

"Now gimme his flight number and I'll call you back if I need anything else."

"American 1532, Tuesday morning 7 a.m., Dallas - Washington Dulles. He's returning on flight number 1534 out of Washington National."

"He ain't returning because he ain't gonna get there!"

"You'll call me when it's over?"

"Read about in the papers or watch television!"

"Listen to me—" Burleson realized that he was holding a dead phone.

Charlie got into the car and pulled the door shut as hard as he could. He failed to rouse Butch. He gave him a shoulder shove and Butch responded by turning his head and giving Charlie a chilling stare.

"Ya got the info?" Butch asked.

Charlie tapped his shirt pocket and nodded. "Let's go," he said.

"Where to?"

"There was a little motel that we passed on the way in. Looked like a place that wouldn't ask questions or take much notice."

"Yea, I remember," Butch said. "I think I can find it."

*

They checked in as Jones and Smith, paid cash for three nights and settled in. Neither said a word. They lay on top of the covers fully clothed and slept for six hours. Butch was the first to regain consciousness. He sat up, leaned over the aisle between the two beds and gave Charlie a punch on the arm. Charlie bolted upright.

"What in the hell did you do that for?" he asked.

"I was lonesome," Butch returned.

"Yeah, I bet!" Charlie said, deciding to let the matter drop.

Charlie sat up on the bed and let his legs hang over the edge of the mattress. He waited several minutes for his mind to clear and to annoy Butch.

"Well, here's the way it is," he finally said. "I got Murphy's address and flight numbers. We've got three days before he heads for DC. First thing tomorrow we'll case out his building. He's got a seven o'clock flight and he always drives himself, so he'll be leaving about five in the morning. We should be inside by four. Then we'll check out the mark and make sure that we know where he parks his car. Got it?"

"Yeah! I got it. Let's get some chow and then hit the hay."

They turned in at ten forty-five. Charlie tossed and turned all night. Butch slept like a baby.

At ten the next morning, Charlie and Butch cruised past the Sky Ranch. It loomed thirty-five stories tall and covered half of a city block.

"Fancy place," Butch drawled as the passed the entrance, complete with doorman.

"What did ya expect?" Charlie returned. "Now, let's see if you can find the garage."

"Think that could be it?" Butch asked as they turned a corner and saw a cavernous opening with a large GARAGE sign above it.

"Good work," Charlie satirized as they slowed down to get a good look at the facility.

"I don't think that we'll be using the front entrance," Butch said. "It's got a guard during the day and steel doors at night. Did you spot the edge of the doors hanging down?"

"Missed 'em," Charlie admitted. "We better look for another way."

They parked a block away and circled the building. A steel door facing the rear street gave way to their push.

"This won't always be open," Butch remarked as they entered the building.

"You're right. Let's get into the garage and check it out."

Ten minutes later they were in the garage. It was a three-story basement structure with a ramp at each end and a stairway-elevator complex in the middle.

"You take that side and I'll take this," Charlie said. "See if you can spot his car and look for a place to hide. Okay?"

An hour and a half later, they met on the top level.

"Any luck?" Charlie asked.

"I found his car," Butch replied. "It's on the middle floor near the elevators."

"I think that I may have found a place to hole up," Charlie said. "There's restrooms on each floor and it looks like there's a large air return in each one. We'll need a slot screwdriver. Why don't you go out to the car and get one."

Butch left and Charlie went down to check out Murphy's car. They met a half an hour later.

"I'm pretty sure that door we found is going to be

locked at night," Butch said. "It looks like we'll be spending tomorrow night here."

"We'll do what we have to do," Charlie said. "Now let's see if we can fit in that air vent."

At three o'clock the next night, the return air vent in the men's room on the second level of the Sky Ranch garage was silently opened and Butch lowered himself to the floor. Charlie followed moments later. The vent was replaced and the men quietly assumed their places a few cars on either side of the black Cadillac STS that bore the ego plates of ROUNDUP. They had studied their parts well. They had allowed an hour to drive to the airport and another for the required passenger check-in time. They expected to see Ed Murphy about 5 a.m.

At 4:54 a.m. the elevator stopped at the second level and the doors slid open. A man emerged carrying a briefcase and a carry-on bag. He was dressed in a business suit and wore both western boots and hat. He fit the description that Charlie had received from Slick Burleson. He was at the rear end of his car when Charlie stood up from behind the automobile that was shielding him and said, "Mr. Murphy?"

Murphy squinted in the dim light of the garage.

"Who's that?" he said.

"Mr. Murphy?" Charlie repeated as he closed the distance between them.

"Yeah?". The man was only a few yards from him and he felt uneasy. He suddenly sensed a presence behind him and knew that he was in trouble. He dropped his briefcase to the ground and swung the carry-on at the figure now only three feet in front of him. The bag hit Charlie full on the side of his face and sent him reeling. Murphy quickly turned to face the assailant from behind. As he did so, he threw his right elbow in a blind trajectory toward his unseen foe. He felt the elbow crash into bone and flesh and at the same time felt an agonizing pain in his stomach. Murphy's elbow had connected with Butch's right temple just as he completed his thrust with the knife. He was aiming at Murphy's right side but the unexpected turn had exposed his belly and that's where Butch had buried the blade. Butch was partially stunned but hung on to the knife handle. Murphy now sensed what had happened, dropped the bag and clenched Butch's throat in a death grip. Butch pulled the knife out and plunged it back into Murphy's body, trying for the heart. Charlie recovered and ran to where the two men lay locked in mortal combat. Butch saw Charlie and his eyes said, "Do something! Goddam it! Do something!" Charlie jumped amid the struggling men and swung his foot between Murphy's outstretched arms. The blow forced one of Murphy's hands from Butch's throat. Butch quickly rolled out of the grasp of the other, reached behind his back, pulled out a semi-automatic and fired two shots into Murphy's head.

The gunshots reverberated through the garage like two thunder claps.

"Jesus Christ!" Charlie yelled. "What did you do that for."

"He was chokin' me, asshole!" Butch screamed. "Let's get the hell outta here!"

"Right!" Charlie said as he started to leave.

"Just a minute," Butch said as he restrained Charlie. "Aren't you forgettin' somethin'?"

"The serum!" Charlie exclaimed. "The goddam serum! I'll find it."

They returned to the body. Charlie snatched the carry-on bag. He opened the bag and looked inside.

"Is it there?" Butch asked.

"Yeah, it's here all right, but one of the bottles is broken. It must have happened when he dropped the bag on the concrete."

"Or when he hit your cement head," Butch laughed. "Let's get going."

Charlie closed the carry-on bag and followed Butch to the stairs and then out the door. The carry-on bag was already wet from the broken bottle of serum and neither noticed the slight stain on the concrete next to Ed Murphy's body.

CHAPTER NINETEEN

The next day Kevin was at the Scottsdale airport. He checked in with the local FBO and had a check ride in a Cessna 182. He did well, but the instructor wanted him to put in a full hour of practicing solo takeoffs and landings before he would let him take the aircraft on a cross-country flight. The plane was booked for the rest of the day, so Kevin scheduled time the next day and asked about an aerial camera. He was in luck. They had just purchased a state-of-the-art camera that could be attached to the wing strut and operated from inside the aircraft. It was an electronic camera that allowed the operator to get an image on a video screen, rotate and actuate the camera from either seat. The resulting picture could be printed and enlarged if so desired. The use of the camera was more expensive than the rental charged for the Cessna, but it suited Kevin's needs perfectly.

Lauri Beth arrived at the Scottsdale Airport at 10:30

Saturday morning. Kevin was waiting. The camera had been attached to the Cessna 182 and Kevin had just received a full briefing on its operation.

"Good morning, Laurie Beth," Kevin said, offering a warm smile.

Lauri Beth took his hand, pulled Kevin toward her and brushed her lips against his cheek.

"Good morning," she replied. "It's a beautiful day. I can't wait!"

"Yeah, it should be a great flight. Arizona is one of the best places in the country for private aviation. The weather is so good. Have you been in a light plane before?"

"Nothing quite this small," Lauri Beth answered. "I did some skydiving up at Rimrock, but their planes were bigger."

"Oh!" Kevin said, asking for more information.

"We had a club when I was at ASU," she explained. "We'd go almost every week-end. It was great. I haven't done it since graduation. I think that I'd like to try it again, but I just don't seem to have the time anymore and I've lost contact with my old diving buddies."

"I've had a few jumps myself. Maybe we could go sometime."

"That'd be fun," Lauri Beth said. "But how about today? Don't you think that we'd better get going?"

"Right!" Kevin answered. "I've already preflighted the plane, so we can get in and get under way."

"Just like that," Lauri Beth said. "Just like getting in a car and pulling out of the driveway?"

"No!" Kevin explained. "Not just like a car. Get in

and I'll explain."

Kevin opened the passenger side door for Lauri Beth and helped her in. He handed her the seat belt and made sure that it was fastened, including the shoulder harness.

"My God!" Lauri Beth exclaimed. "This looks complicated and what about the controls on my side? Could I touch something and make us crash?"

"Not unless you knock me out first," Kevin laughed. "I'll explain as we go. Okay?"

Lauri Beth nodded in agreement. Kevin started the engine and throttled back.

"Put this head set on," he said. "We have both intercom and radio communication available automatically. The intercom is voice activated and I control the microphone with a button on my control column. The communications are a push to talk system. In other words, I can't talk and listen at the same time, but the voice activated intercom will work any time. So, please don't talk if I'm on the radio. Now, say something so that I can tell how my side of the intercom is working."

Laurie Beth gave him a nod and a look that said, "What'll I say?" and said, "What'll I say?"

"That's good enough."

Kevin spoke into the mike.

"This is Cessna 2373 Charlie," he said. "We're at Desert Air Services. We'll be VFR departing to the southeast."

"Roger, 73 Charlie," came the reply. "Contact tower on 119.9 when you're ready."

"Roger," Kevin said as he pushed the throttle in and

taxied to runway 21.

During the taxi, the radio was awash with conversation from the tower and other aircraft.

"My God!" Lauri Beth said. "I hope you know what you're doing. I couldn't understand a word of what was going on."

Kevin smiled at her and said into the mike, "73 Charlie ready to go on 21."

"73 Charlie cleared for take off. Understand you're VFR southeast bound."

"Affirmative, 73 Charlie," Kevin replied as he turned onto runway 21 and pushed the throttle to the wall.

Kevin leveled the Cessna at 7500 feet above sea level, turned left to a heading of 90 degrees, and put on the autopilot.

"Well, here we are! Are you all set?" he said to Lauri Beth as he reached into his duffel bag and extracted Brian's GPS.

"I guess so," Lauri Beth answered. "This is very exciting. What are you doing now? And shouldn't you be flying the airplane?"

"Oh! I've turned on the autopilot and I'm getting ready to track Brian's last flight," Kevin explained as he turned on the GPS and brought up Brian's last waypoint.

"See here!" he continued. The last waypoint on the GPS is North 33 degrees 36.5 minutes and West 111 degrees 30.6 minutes. That's almost due east of our present position and only about twenty miles away. I'm going to slow down so that we have plenty of time to set up. I only want to make one pass to avoid any suspicion in case there's something or someone down there that we're not supposed to see."

"Okay, then," Lauri Beth said. "you'd better go over the camera with me one more time."

"All right! There I've got it turned on. It's electronic, so you can see what the camera is pointing at by viewing the screen in front of you. You focus and adjust the telescopic lens by turning the two knobs at the bottom of the screen. The camera angle is controlled by the two knobs next to those cross hairs. If they're centered, then the camera is pointing straight down. I've already centered it so you shouldn't have to touch those. You actuate the camera by pressing that green button on the end of this cable. I'd like you to start when I say "go" and then take another picture each time the image at the top of the screen reaches the middle. That way we'll have an overlap of 50% and should get complete coverage. I don't want you to zoom in too close. We'll try to cover as much width as possible and enlarge later. Any questions?"

"No! Let's go for it!"

Kevin gave her a thumbs up, disengaged the autopilot and concentrated on flying the airplane directly over the target. The terrain below was rapidly rising and would crest at an uneven 7,000 feet. Kevin pushed the throttle in and increased the RPM, as he began his climb to 9,500 feet.

When he reached 9,500 feet, he trimmed the airplane for level flight and concentrated on the GPS. The GPS indicated that they were eight miles from the waypoint and that a heading of 87 degrees would take them directly over it. Kevin turned slightly left until he had acquired the desired heading. He planned to descend from 9500 to 8500 and then cruise over the waypoint as slowly as possible. The GPS indicated that he was five miles out and on course. He began his descent and told Lauri Beth to be ready. She gave him an okay sign and focused on the monitor in front of her.

He was level at 8500. The GPS showed one mile from the waypoint and on course. He nudged Lauri Beth and said, "Go!" She hit the shutter button and the screen froze momentarily. She continued to take pictures at the rate of one every five or six seconds. By the time Kevin signaled her to stop, she had taken a dozen photos and they were a mile past the waypoint.

"Did you see the terrain down there?" Kevin exclaimed. "It was stupendous. When we were directly overhead, it was like something from a lost world. We were over a huge bowl and the colors were magnificent."

"I didn't get a chance to view it directly," she said. "But even on the screen it looked like something special. I can't wait to see the photos."

"Me, too!" Kevin said as he gave her hand a squeeze.

He applied a bit more power and resumed normal cruise speed.

"How about a little sightseeing?" he asked.

"Love to!" she said.

Kevin banked the Cessna to the left and headed toward Four Peaks. He planned to skirt the mountain to the east, fly over Roosevelt Lake and then up to Payson, land, have lunch and return to Scottsdale airport from the northeast. It would cap off a very enjoyable and, he hoped, fruitful day.

*

When 2373 Charlie was completely out of sight and sound, the camouflaged sentry withdrew from his post and handed his camera to his boss.

"Probably don't mount to nothin'," he said. "But a plane flew over a while ago goin' from west to east. I took a picture. Maybe you want to look at it?"

CHAPTER TWENTY

The Dallas newspapers carried the story for three days. It disappeared after it reached the third page. The Dallas local television stations milked it for a full week. The national networks had it as a feature the day the story broke and a week later as a possible connection to the food price problem. Ed Murphy was buried a week after his murder and any association with soaring meat prices would have been buried with him, if it hadn't been for a skinny, thick-lensed forensic lab worker in the Dallas police department.

Harold Spivey liked his work. He spent ten or more hours each and every day, including weekends, in the lab. He wasn't married and forensic investigation was his only love. The autopsy on one Edward Murphy had gone well, considering all of the pressure associated with the murder of a prominent citizen. Harold was in assistance to the coroner, who performed the actual

143 THE LURE OF THE DUTCHMAN

autopsy himself. Publicity brings duty out of the closet and into the limelight.. The coroner did a creditable job, considering the fact that it was his first actual appearance at the table in over two years. It was difficult to determine whether Murphy had died of knife wounds to the body or gunshot wounds to the head. The report read that the first wounds were made by the knife and that the gunshots to the head were inflicted either just before or just after death. It was evident that Murphy had put up a struggle and abrasions on the inside of his right arm suggested that he may have received a kick during the fight. There were traces of flesh under his fingernails. These samples were removed and coded for DNA. The gunshots were fired at close range and the evidence strongly implied that there was more than one assailant.

When the ambulance brought Murphy to the morgue, the homicide detectives dropped off the evidence that they had collected at the scene of the murder. After it was properly logged in and tagged, it was placed on a shelf in the police evidence cage at the forensics lab, awaiting further examination by the scientists. The publicity of the case pushed its priority to the head of the line. Spivey was assigned to examine the various articles that Homicide had brought in from the scene, analyze the autopsy and compile a report.

Spivey had the key in the lock and was just starting to turn it when he heard the telephone ring. The sound startled him and he inadvertently turned the key counterclockwise and disengaged it from the key slot. He tried to turn it again but it wasn't completely in the slot and it wouldn't budge. He experienced mild panic as he fumbled, juggled and turned the key. Finally, the key turned and he heard the lock click open. By the time he opened the door, and half stumbled across the room to the telephone, he was panting wildly. He lifted the receiver on its seventh ring and almost screamed, "Hello!"

"Spivey?"

"Yes, sir!". Spivey thought that just about everyone was his superior and would have answered "sir" to any voice on the other end of the line.

"Listen up, Spivey! This is Lieutenant Bledsoe of Homicide! I'm heading up the Murphy investigation."

"Yes, sir?"

"I'll be at your office at ten tomorrow morning. I want to see everything that you've got, starting with the autopsy report and I want you to lead me through the entire report. Got it?"

"But, sir!" Spivey stammered. "All I've got is the autopsy report at the moment. I won't start analyzing the other items until tomorrow."

"Well, then, you can show me what you've got and we'll go from there."

The phone went dead in Spivey's ear and he assumed that Lt. Bledsoe had hung up. The next day, Spivey was in his office at 6 a.m. He immediately got the autopsy report out and reread it twice. He then proceeded to the forensics lockup and checked out all of the items connected to the Murphy homicide. He laid each item out on the long table in the middle of the lab and began to study them. He wasn't one to be rushed. He had barely finished scrutinizing the clothing when he was interrupted by a noise in the other room. He looked up and found that he was confronted by a very large man in plain clothes.

"Lieutenant?" he ventured.

"Yeah, yeah! It's me, Bledsoe!" the lieutenant said as he strode up to the table. "Let's see what you got."

"Yes, sir!" Spivey said. "Maybe we should start with the autopsy. Have you read it, yet?"

"Yeah! I've read it. Forwards and backwards. Twice."

"And?"

"And I don't see anything different than the original report. Death by multiple knife wounds and/or bullet wounds inflicted by one or more assailants. Looks like a robbery gone wrong."

"That's true," Spivey agreed. "But there's some other things that might give you second thoughts."

Spivey waited for the obvious question. When it didn't come, he continued. "Look! I haven't gone through all of the items connected with this homicide. In fact, I've only examined the clothing up to this point. Murphy's wallet and cash appear to be undisturbed and they were easily accessible. I don't think that the perps were after cash and credit cards. There was an airline ticket in his inside suit coat pocket. Murphy was on his way to the airport. He was scheduled to take an early flight to Washington, D.C. and return the same day."

"Must have been a short meeting. That goes on all the time in D.C."

"I know. I'm not completely stupid. But you might

find it unusual for someone to fly into Dulles and then return from National."

"Into Dulles and out of National!" Bledsoe mused. "That is strange."

"And there's another thing. It's just a short sentence in the autopsy report, but I think it means something."

"What's that?"

"The report mentions that there was a very small trace of oil on Murphy's hands. Oil like you get on your hands from carrying fine leather luggage. There was a briefcase at the scene and that matches the oil on his hands. But you know, a guy usually carries his briefcase in the same hand most of the time. Now the oil on the left hand is the same as the oil on the right and that could be explained by Murphy shifting the briefcase from hand to hand. I don't think that's the case. It looks to me like Murphy was probably carrying two pieces of luggage. One was the briefcase and the other was a matching piece. You know these rich guys have matching pieces of luggage and these cattleman have pieces made from the same hide, sometimes handpicked while the animal is still alive. I think that there were two pieces of luggage and the perps took one and took it on purpose."

"That might put things in a different light," Bledsoe conceded. "Anything else?"

"Not yet," Spivey said. "But I've still got a lot of stuff to analyze."

"Well, you've given me some food for thought," Bledsoe said, obviously softening. "Do me a favor? Keep me informed as you go? Here's my card. Call me any time, day or night."

Spivey nodded in agreement as the lieutenant left the lab. It would take Harold Spivey another two weeks to make his next discovery.

CHAPTER TWENTY-ONE

General Boone sat back in relaxed pleasure. He had just watched the late news on network TV. The anchor had revisited the Edward Murphy murder, speculating that there could have been some connection to profiteering on the skyrocketing meat prices. In the end, he had concluded that there was no evidence to substantiate the premise and that Murphy had merely been the victim of being at the wrong place at the wrong time. The final statement of the program had intimated that the meat shortage was cyclic in nature and would correct itself in time.

Boone switched to the Weather Channel and confirmed that the nation was in the midst of a prolonged heat wave. The heat index was over 90 degrees in most cities and over 100 degrees in the southern half of the country. The prognosis was no better. In fact, in three weeks, the weathermen were forecasting a ten-day heat wave that would set record highs across the country. It couldn't be better.

"Major!" Boone called.

"Yes, sir!" Major Jimmy Ray Wheeler answered.

"How's the meeting coming?"

"Just fine, sir," the major said. "The first ones will be arriving the day after tomorrow and everyone should be here in three days."

"And how are the facilities?"

"We taken over the mining camp, just as you suggested, sir," the major confirmed. "The old restaurant will hold us just fine and the tables have been rearranged as you ordered."

"What about quarters for the men?"

"That's no problem, sir. Most of our people will be driving pickups and campers. Everyone's been instructed to provide for their own sleeping arrangements. If they don't drive their shelter, they'll be bringing tents and sleeping bags."

"We'll be providing the meals," the major said, anticipating the general's next question. "The food will be simple, stew, soup and the like, but there'll be plenty of it."

"Good!"

Wheeler waited for the next remark and, when it didn't come, he returned to his computer screen. The general had asked for the identical information at least twice a day for the last week and, now that the meeting day was almost at hand, the frequency of his requests was increasing. The general was as keyed up as an over-tuned guitar and just as tight. Everything was going so smoothly and the major was so efficient that Boone was finding time on his hands. He wanted to know every detail of the upcoming meeting and his interference was actually holding up progress. He had already planned the agenda and had written the outlines for all of his major speeches. But, both he and the major knew that, when the time came, he would be shooting from the hip, and his heart would take over from his head. Boone was a natural leader and speaker. His fault lay in his inability to close a speech and often he would harangue for a hour when ten minutes would have been sufficient. Nevertheless, his speeches inspired others and, despite the length, his words stirred the emotions of those he addressed.

True to his word, three days later the major reported that forty-six of the expected fifty participants had arrived and the other four would be in before midnight.

"Roll call is at 0800," he informed the general. "The meeting will start at 0830."

Boone nodded in acceptance of the information and headed for his sack. He would sleep deeply and soundly that night.

The next morning the men and women of the conference assembled in the old mining restaurant. There were forty-two men and eight women. The family-style tables had been arranged so that there were two in each row and the rows were six deep. Four chairs were placed behind each table. The last table had a chair on each end, so that it accommodated six people. This arrangement allowed the teams of two from each city to sit together. There was a small pad of note paper and a pencil on the tables in front of each chair.

At five minutes after eight, Major Wheeler walked out of the door that had once led to the kitchen and faced the assembly.

"Good morning," he said.

He was greeted by various responses. He surveyed the group in front of him. All were dressed in some sort of hunting or military clothing. Some were clean shaven, others wore trimmed facial hair, while still others wore their beards in an unkempt style. None of the women wore makeup. A few sat at attention. Most lounged in their chairs, some with their feet on the table in front of them.

"Ladies and gentlemen," the major said. "I hereby declare this special meeting of the New Revolutionary Militia to be in session. The first item of business is the roll call. I will call off the name of the city that is represented here by two people. The leader of that team will stand and identify him or herself. He or she will then identify the second in command for that city. After I have duly recorded their presence, they will be seated. Any questions?"

There were none.

"Atlanta, Georgia!"

A stocky, muscular woman rose.

"Clara Johnson, Commander, Atlanta, Georgia," she said. Then pointing to the slim, dark man next to her, she continued, "Accompanied by Slim Gordon, second in command." Gordon rose slowly and stood next to Johnson. Wheeler checked off their names on the roster in front of him. He studied them for a moment and then nodded for them to sit down.

"Boston, Massachusetts," he continued. A man rose, identified himself and his partner, was recorded and sat down. And so it went, the major patiently went through all twenty-five cities. The operation took thirty-seven minutes. The last team was seated and a quiet fell over the room. The major waited for a full minute, collected his papers and left the room. Five minutes went by. The silence was broken only by the sound of chairs being adjusted and bodies trying for comfort. Tension was rising and everyone could feel it.

Suddenly the door to the kitchen was pushed open. General Boone strode into the room. Everyone snapped to standing attention as the imposing figure walked to the podium. It was an impressive sight. The general looked every bit the revolutionary leader that he was. He was dressed in plain brown khakis, field cap fixed tightly to his head, storm trooper boots resounding on the hard wood floor, his fierce beard flowing over an open shirt collar, and an unlit cigar held in his left hand. He caused a surge of pride and boldness in every heart. Fifty hands snapped a smart salute to fifty brows. The general returned the gesture with a salute of his own. He stood there, looking over his troops, engaging every eye with his own. A minute passed and then another. Finally, he motioned for them to take their seats. The scraping of chair legs on the hard floor and the sounds of fifty people settling themselves soon subsided into rapt attention.

"Today!" Boone boomed. "We begin our mission! Today! We begin our journey that will end in our first blow for freedom! The tyranny of the United States of America will crumble under the bombshell of our attack! The country that we all love will be returned to the people!"

The militiamen and women leaped to their feet and cheered wildly. The general was reveling in the moment. His words were now accompanied by violent gestures. He shook his fists. He banged on the podium. He pointed to the heavens and at the people in front of him. He could barely utter a complete sentence without pausing for the encouragement to abate. He knew that he had them in the palm of his hand and he kept them there for an hour and fifteen minutes. Finally, he concluded,

"Our resolve must not slacken!" he demanded. "We must take it with us when we return to our home cities! We must instill it in all those who follow us! We must be firm! We must succeed! We must believe!"

Boone waited for the applause to subside. He walked to the side of the room and seated himself behind a small desk facing the audience. Wheeler took the podium.

"Thank you, General, for your inspiring words," he said. "The next order of business is the assessment of the readiness of the troops in each of the selected cities. Each team has been instructed to submit a written report. Before those are collected, each team will give an oral report on the same subject. The general wishes that each group be aware of the readiness of the others. That way we will strive to be equal to the best group and therefore attain our highest level of performance. We will again begin with Atlanta. Clara Johnson!"

"Yes, sir!" Johnson said as she rose and turned so that she faced the maximum number of people. She reached down and received a manila envelope from Gordon.

"We have a core group of seventy-five members. These are our most dedicated people. They all are members of the New Revolutionary Militia. They understand the mission and are sworn to complete it. This group is divided into units of five members each. That gives us fifteen groups. Each group has been assigned a section of the city. The entire city is covered, although we are concentrating on the lower income areas and the minority sections. These people are the most dissatisfied and are the easiest to excite to riot and vandalism. Each group of five has solicited twenty-five local residents to recruit the common soldiers. These twenty-five people are equivalent to sergeants. They have a vague idea of what is going on, but their main interest is in causing trouble to the establishment. Their duty for the past six months has been to enlist as many dissidents as possible and to have them ready to riot on a moment's notice These dissidents, or foot soldiers, haven't the slightest inkling as to what is really happening. Their main interest is to riot, vandalize, burn, overturn vehicles and personally profit from the confusion. We have at least two hundred of these people ready to take to the streets. Excuse me, I want to clarify that last remark. I mean that we have at least two hundred of these people for each of our

units. That makes a minimum of three thousand rioters that we can count on. I estimate the actual number
will be three or four times that number when the rioting begins and the word spreads. We can be completely mobilized in less than one hour. We're only waiting
for the word and I hope that it's not too long in coming."

Johnson looked around the room for approval and
then took her seat. Wheeler had been standing during
her report, a clipboard in his hand. He had been making notes and jotting down numbers. He regained the
podium and said, "Thank you, Captain Johnson! The
next report will be from New York City."

That report was substantially the same as the previous one. The numbers were larger because of the size
of the city and the complexity of the boroughs. The
reports continued until all twenty-five cities had been
heard from. It was past one o'clock when the final del-
egate sat down.. The room was slowly filling with
smoke as approximately half of the people had ignited
some form of tobacco. The general took over the podium again.

"Thanks for the fine reports," he said. "We'll break
until three o'clock. Grab yourselves some chow. There's
sandwich makings in the kitchen, behind me, and soft
drinks as well."

There would not be any alcohol served during the
entire two-day meeting. Boone skipped lunch and used
the time to circulate among his troops. He moved from
table to table, calling almost everyone by their first
names. The effect was electrifying.

Wheeler also did not eat. He used his time to tally the results of the first session. The attendees were already in their seats, anxiously waiting for the general to resume the proceedings. There were still fifteen minutes left in the lunch break. Boone and Wheeler were huddled in the corner, poring over Wheeler's figures. The general stood and approached the podium. He carried a fistful of papers.

"Members of the New Revolutionary Militia," he began. "I would like you to know and understand what is going to be asked of you and what your efforts will accomplish. Major Wheeler has just handed me the results of this morning's session. As you know, we have twenty-five units in place, and those units are all represented at this meeting. Each unit has followed our directions in a more or less similar fashion. The outcome is that we now have approximately 750,000 people ready to incite riots across the country. When these riots begin, we fully expect that number to swell by a cautious multiple of four to a more generous number of ten. In other words, when you are given the word, we fully expect somewhere between three and eight million rioters to tear our major cities apart."

Boone paused to let the enormity of his figures take their effect. And take effect they did. Most delegates turned to one another and began whispering in hushed tones. Some just sat back and expelled an awed sigh; others banged on the table in front of them and hooted, "YEAH!"

"You all know the underlying cause is the discontent caused by soaring food prices in general and skyrocketing meat prices in particular," Boone continued as the room was regaining order. "The weather is also on our side. The heat wave that we are in is scheduled to continue. The goddam government is already talking about military interference and mobilizing the national guard."

He leaned over the podium as if he were confiding a deep secret. "Now here's the trick!" he half-whispered as his audience strained to hear his every word. "We've got to promote unrest. We've got to get the people so damned excited that they're a powder keg. But we've got to hold them off until the last moment. Why? Because we want the Feds to be so confused that they won't know which end is up or what hit them. We want them running around putting out brush fires while the forest is burning out of control. Confusion must be rampant! Do I make myself clear? Do I make myself perfectly clear?"

"YES, SIR!!" came the chorus.

"Now you're going to break up into units of five. One unit in each corner and one in the center of the room," he ordered. "You will be exchanging ideas on how best to attain our objective. I've always believed that two heads were better than one and that an idea can always be improved upon. After you've been together for an hour the groups will change and the exchange of ideas will continue. This will continue until everyone has been exposed to every idea. Dinner will be at 2100 hours. You'll sleep on what you've learned and tomorrow morning's session will be a condensing of today's input. We'll break up immediately after I've made my final remarks. You'll get field rations to take along. There will be no lunch tomorrow. Any questions?"

A hand shot up in the middle of the hall. The general nodded and a stocky, bearded man rose to his feet.

"Rocky Manichi, Chicago," he said. "General, I understand what we're supposed to do, but, other than general disorder, just what is it that we're going to accomplish? The riots will last for a little while and then they'll be put down. There'll be a lot of destruction and looting, but just like any other uprising, it'll all be forgotten after a period of time. Don't get me wrong, General, I'm ready and itching to get going and do my part, but I guess I just don't see the big picture."

Rocky sat down amid a number of nods of approvals.

"All right," he said, looking at Wheeler for an instant. "I'll tell you what I can."

Boone took on his most serious face and looked over his audience. The militia men and women were straining forward, not wanting to miss even a syllable.

"All of what you've been trained to do, the rioting, the exciting of discontent, the looting, the burning and everything else has one gigantic purpose: It is to cover up the real operation. I'd tell you what that is, if I could. But you all know that is impossible. If there was any kind of leak, intentional or unintentional, the entire operation would fail. I will not tolerate failure! I will tell you this much. The day after the riots, you will read about it in the newspapers and hear it on television. You will understand completely and you will be proud. You will be proud that you have struck a blow that will change this country forever. You will have been part of the greatest stroke for individual freedom since the Declaration of Independence!"

"Thank you, General," Rocky said in awed reverence. "Rest assured that we will do everything in our power to make the total operation a huge success."

Boone left the podium without another word and retired from the room. There was absolute silence. Wheeler took over the meeting, organized the groups and stood by to be of any assistance that he could.

The next morning the militia reassembled and Major Wheeler conducted the session. The general made his final remarks, as promised. His speech was a combination of his previous remarks. He adjourned the meeting on a note of frenzied encouragement. His teams were ready, and so was he.

CHAPTER TWENTY-TWO

Kevin Stewart was leaning over the dining room table poring over an assortment of enlarged photographs when he heard the front doorbell. He opened the door to a radiant Lauri Beth McCartney.

"Hi! Kevin!" she smiled, giving him a kiss on the cheek as she passed him in the doorway.

"Hi! Lauri Beth!" Kevin returned. He caught up to her in the living room, spun her around and kissed her full on the lips. The kiss lingered as she returned it. They hesitated and then reluctantly broke apart.

"Over here, in the living room," he said, taking her by the hand and leading her to the collage of photographs. "Can I get you something to drink?"

"A diet something would be great," she answered.

Kevin returned with a drink in each hand. He carefully set them down on coasters on the buffet along the long wall behind them.

"Thanks," she said.

"I'm usually not this careful about coasters," Kevin explained. "But I feel that everything here still belongs to Brian."

"I understand," Lauri Beth said compassionately. "These really look good," she continued, studying the photos.

"Yeah! You took nine shots and I've got them laid out from right to left. Number five should be the one over Brian's last coordinates."

"The resolution looks perfect, and look at those beautiful colors!" she exclaimed. "Have you been studying them long?"

"No! As a matter of fact, I haven't really gotten a good look yet."

"Well, then, let's get started."

"Here's a magnifying glass. I've got one for each of us. I suggest that we start with the first photo and work our way slowly through them. I think our course was pretty much down the middle. You did a great job with the camera. See how they fit one over the other, overlapping by just about one quarter of the next picture. It's amazing how good the depth perception is. See here, you can almost feel the undulations and the drop-offs."

"Oh! yes!" she exclaimed. "I think I remember this spot. It's just as beautiful in the photo as it was from the plane. In fact, I think the landscape is more sensational in print because we have more time to study it."

They proceeded slowly from photograph to photograph. They were well into the second hour of investigation when Kevin said, "Look over here, Lauri Beth. Doesn't that look like the ground has been smoothed out or worn? Almost like a path or even a road."

"Let me see," she replied. "Oh! Yes! You have to look really close, but I can see what you mean. The ground is so hard it's almost impossible to see and I'll bet you'd never notice from the ground."

"See here where it crosses a ridge and then seems to descend into this amazing bowl. And you know what? We're approaching ground zero."

"Did you ever see anything like this?" Lauri Beth said. "Look how steep the walls are, and see that waterfall that drops to the bottom and forms a river that goes from one end to the other and then just disappears."

"If I know Brian," Kevin said. "He couldn't resist going in for a closer look. It's just too enticing."

A half an hour later, they were still on the same panel when Lauri Beth made the discovery.

"I think I see something," she said. "It looks like a cave or an opening of some sort in the side of the canyon wall and I think that I can see some sort of rock or bush or something that could be hiding the entrance from the ground."

"Let me see," Kevin said as he moved his magnifying glass into position. "Yeah, you're right. And I think that I see something else. Something that could be very disturbing."

"What's that?" Lauri Beth asked, moving her own glass next to Kevin's.

"Look right here," Kevin directed. "Can you see a little speck of light? Like a reflection or something? It could be a printing flaw, but I don't think so."

"Where? Oh! I think I see what you mean. I don't think that it's a printing flaw. I think that it's a reflection off of something metallic, or maybe a piece of glass."

"We better assume the worst," Kevin said. "I think that someone was watching our flyover. If they took a photo and enlarged it, they may have seen the camera. That means that I'll have to be extra-cautious when I check out the site. I'd better plan on making a call to my old base and getting some special equipment sent over. Just to be on the safe side."

"Wait a minute! Just wait one damn minute! What do you mean 'I'll' have to be cautious. You meant 'we,' didn't you?"

"No! I meant 'me'! I think that this thing could get to be very dangerous and the traveling is going to be rugged."

"Oh! So you think I can't take it, do you, Mr. Tough Guy? Well, let me tell you something. I've been mountaineering since high school. I've got my black belt in Tai Kwan Do and I spent one winter as a guide for Outward Bound. Maybe I haven't killed anyone, but don't think for one minute that I can't keep up with you, and don't think for one minute that you're going to leave me behind, so when you order this special equipment, you better just make it for two sets of whatever it is you're ordering!"

Kevin turned a pale red. He wasn't expecting anything like this, and he hadn't considered taking Lauri

Beth with him.

"Outward Bound, eh? What course did you guide for?"

"Avalanche training and mountaineering out of Leadville, Colorado."

"That's impressive. You must have been pretty young."

"I was twenty-one. I could take care of myself then, and I can take care of myself now."

"Tell me about it," Kevin said, sensing that there was a story behind her simple statement.

Lauri Beth hesitsted for a moment, not certain that she wanted to reveal that part of her private life.

"Go on," he urged.

"Well, it was in the middle of February. We had completed the five-day avalanche training, going up to the fracture line of old releases and setting off charges on dangerous cornices. There was a group of high school seniors, five of them, and the leader was a real smart ass. He probably weighed over two hundred pounds and played on the football team.

"The mountaineering part had gone well. We packed fifty-pound packs and made our way up the Collegiate Range on skis. On the third day, we made igloos and early the next morning scaled Mt. Colgate to its summit. That night, back in the igloos, Mr. Big began to get romantic. I told him to back off, but he kept coming on. His pack was encouraging him. He grabbed me and I got mad. I laid him out."

"That's all? You just laid him out? Come on! There's got to be more to it than that!"

"Well," she said, wishing she hadn't opened the door in the first place. "The Denver papers said that he'd had a fall. We made a travois and brought him down the mountain in it. It was good training for the rest of the group."

"How bad was he hurt?"

"He had three broken ribs, a fractured right arm, and a badly sprained left knee and ankle."

"I'll think about it," Kevin said after a moment of reflection.

"There's nothing to think about. I'm going and that's that." Lauri Beth concluded.

Kevin turned back to the photographs, partly to continue his study but mostly to adjust to the new image of his new friend. The idea of having Lauri Beth with him during the exploration intrigued and pleased him. He began to mentally play down the dangers and by the time they had studied the last photo, he had already accepted the idea of including her. He put off the acceptance of her demand as long as he could. Finally, as he was packing up the film, he said, "Okay, you can go."

She rushed to him, put her arms around him and kissed him hard on the mouth. Kevin knew that he had made the right decision.

CHAPTER TWENTY-THREE

At the end of the week, a large box arrived via UPS. Kevin unpacked it and checked off its contents against a list that he had prepared when he called his unit at Fort Benning. Everything was there and in duplicate. He checked for sizes and it looked as if the package was complete.

Kevin and Lauri Beth had been planning the excursion for over a week, ever since they had made the discovery of the entrance in the cliff. Now all that remained was the checking of equipment, packing and getting under way. The plan was simple. They would load the horses in the trailer and haul them to a spot about ten miles from the target area. They were going to avoid going through Tortilla Flat, which meant that they would have to go all the way up to Payson and then come back down past Roosevelt Lake. After that they would travel the unpaved, torturous Apache Trail southward until they found a place to leave the road.

Once they were off the road and felt that their rig was well hidden, they would saddle up and pack in as near to their objective as they thought safe. Here they would tether the horses, set up camp and proceed on foot, packing essential gear only. The two Morgans, Tilly and Sweetstuff, would serve as both saddle and pack horses. Kevin and Lauri Beth would pack their special equipment in backpacks and shoulder that load themselves. The tent, sleeping bags, cooking equipment and supplies would have to packed behind the saddles. It would be a tough trip, but it would allow them to come in from an unexpected direction.

The alarm broke the silence of the morning darkness. It was 5 a.m. Kevin reached across his body to turn it off and found the his arm was pinned under an unfamiliar weight. As he flexed his muscles to free himself, he heard a soft murmer. He smiled and said, "Wake up, sleepyhead. We want to be on the road by six."

Lauri Beth stirred beneath the covers and rolled towards him.

"I'm way ahead of you," she said.

She was now on top of him and reached over to the nightstand to quiet the buzzing of the clock-radio.

"I'm not so sure," he replied as he felt her body against his.

"Hm!" she whispered as she snuggled even closer. "I feel what you mean."

They made love, exchanging lover's vows and feeling the satisfaction of the early morning physical contact.

It was Friday morning and Lauri Beth had arrived

just before dinner on Thursday afternoon. She was taking a sick day on Friday and had the rest of the weekend free. Kevin had spent the entire day packing and loading the pickup. She had walked in the door wearing jeans, a simple blouse and a large smile. She was carrying a small bag. Kevin had prepared the extra bedroom for her. She walked over to him, kissed him long and hard and without saying a word proceeded to his bedroom and deposited her bag.

Kevin had prepared a simple Italian dinner, complete with Chianti and spumoni. After they had eaten, Kevin brought out a few of his special items that might require fitting. The first were articles of clothing. They all fit Lauri Beth reasonably well, as did the belts and special harnesses. The last thing to try on was an unusual helmet. Kevin took it out of a packing box and held it up.

"What the heck is that?"

"This, my dear, is our security blanket."

He unwrapped it and held it aloft while turning it in his hands. It looked like a fighter pilot's helmet with a baseball cap brim in front. He slipped it on Lauri Beth's head.

"How does it feel?" he asked.

"A little snug and heavy," came the reply.

"Wait 'til I adjust a few things. I'll explain as I do. Okay?"

Kevin worked his fingers inside the helmet alongside Lauri Beth's ears.

"Here, let me adjust the earphones. That feel better?"

"Yep!"

"Now, let me pull the throat mike out and fit it around your neck. There! This is a two-way communication radio. I've got the other set in my helmet. It'll transmit for over a mile and you can talk in a whisper because the mike will pick the vibrations from your voice-box. It works like the intercom in the airplane—you talk, I hear, and vice-versa. It's a secure frequency so we don't have to worry about our conversation being picked up. Okay?"

"Okay! What next?"

"Next, I want to put this small battery pack on the outside of the helmet. It doesn't weigh much and it should balance the helmet a little bit."

"I can feel the difference. The helmet feels lighter and more comfortable already.

"Good. Now there's just this one last item."

Kevin went over to the wall and turned off the lights.

"Now, reach up to the bill above your eyes. That's it. Now, pull down the glasses. They're hinged and they should come down right in front of your eyes. They're infrared night-vision glasses and they activate when you pull them into position. How do they feel?"

"My God," Lauri Beth said. "I can see everything in the room just as clearly as in bright daylight."

"Fine," Kevin said as he made a slight adjustment. "Now push them up and I'll turn on the lights. Protect your eyes—a sudden light will partially blind you for a few minutes and could do serious damage to your eyes if it's bright enough and left on long enough."

"That's really great! Anything else in your bag of tricks?"

"Nothing that needs fitting or explaining right now. Now, I'm going to put my helmet on and we'll check the intercoms."

That done, they packed the remainder of the gear and loaded it into the pickup. The horse trailer was already attached, waiting for its four-legged passengers. It was about nine o'clock when they reentered the house.

"We'd better turn in," Kevin said. "We should be on the road by six tomorrow morning. I've fixed up the extra bedroom for you."

Without a word, Lauri Beth put an index finger to his mouth and, taking his hand in hers, she led him into his bedroom and closed the door.

They had breakfast in Payson and by noon were on the Apache Trail heading south. On the way Kevin had given Lauri Beth her own handheld GPS, and she was busy tracking their position relative to a road map that she had on her lap. Kevin found a wide spot in the road and they pulled over for lunch.

"It looks like we've got about another hour until we should be looking for a place to leave the road," he said. "Do you see anything that looks inviting?"

"We're here, right now. How far will we be an hour from now?"

"We leave the river just up ahead, then it will be tight curves and washboard conditions. We'll be lucky to make twenty-five or thirty miles."

"I've put an 'X' on the map where I think our destination is. Look here, doesn't this look like a jeep trail or something? It goes off to the east and then bends south," she pointed out. "I'd say that it's about ten miles from the 'X' right here and then it turns north again."

"That's where we're going, then," Kevin said.

Two hours later they were on the jeep trail and had reached the point where the trail turned north. Kevin pulled the truck to a stop and surveyed the country.

"We'd better unload here, saddle up and then scout around a bit for a place to hide the rig," he said.

They led Tilly and Sweetstuff out of the trailer, gave them a drink of water and let them stretch before they were saddled and loaded with gear. Kevin was adjusting his cinch when he said, "Wait a sec and I'll give you a leg up."

He turned to see Lauri Beth comfortably astride Sweetstuff.

"Thanks, maybe next time," she laughed. "How about you? Do you want me to dismount and help you up?"

"Sure!" he said, as he swung easily into his saddle. "Let's go."

He gave Tilly a nudge and she started into the high desert landscape. Lauri Beth and Sweetstuff fell in behind. The going was slow because Kevin was careful to guide his mount over hard ground. After an hour of searching, they came upon a depression that was deep enough to hide the truck and trailer and that the truck could negotiate. Another two hours slipped by before the truck was safely hidden.

The sun was still high even though it was a few minutes past six o'clock. It would disappear behind the western mountains at eight-thirty. Kevin was anxious to get going though he was right on his schedule. He punched his present position into his GPS and instructed Lauri Beth to do the same. According to the map, they still had about nine miles to go to the 'X'. He wanted to get as close as possible before bedding down the horses and proceeding on foot. This meant that he needed some daylight to assess the terrain and remain out of sight. They could probably make four miles an hour and still keep their tracks to a minimum. It was 7:55 when Kevin decided to stop. He signaled to Lauri Beth and they dismounted in a depression surrounded by small boulders. They unsaddled and unbridled the horses, gave them some water, food and a quick brushing. They tethered them lightly with hackamores and prepared to set out on foot.

"I'll be just a few minutes," Kevin said.

He opened his pack and removed a quart can. He went out twenty-five or thirty feet and walked a complete circle around the horses.

"What was that all about?" Lauri Beth asked when Kevin returned.

"Oh! I'm sorry," Kevin said. "I just sprinkled a bit of territorial powder around the perimeter of our corral. It'll keep predators and other curious animals away while we're gone."

"Did that come in your CARE package?"

"Yeah!"

"I can't wait to see what comes out next," Lauri Beth

said.

"Who knows?" Kevin joked. "Let's pack up and move out. We've still got over two miles to go."

They shouldered their packs. Kevin's weighed seventy-five pounds and Lauri Beth's weighed fifty. Kevin led the way. They had decided to go single file to keep their tracks to a minimum. The going was easy at first, but quickly got more difficult as the terrain became littered with boulders and rocks. The vegetation grew sparse and their main camouflage became the increasing darkness. There was still enough afterglow to pick their way safely when they came upon a small disturbance on the rock floor. Kevin signaled for Lauri Beth to stop.

"Look at this!" he said. "I kind of remember this little trail from the map and the flight, as well. See how it seems to lead up into that saddle. I think that we're only about a mile from point 'X'.

"Forty-eight hundred feet, according to my GPS," Lauri Beth confirmed. "We had better go on extra stealth mode from here on in."

"I agree," Kevin acknowledged. "It's getting pretty dark. I think it might be a good idea to put on our helmets. It'll give us a chance to check them out and get used to them."

They donned the helmets, shifting the weight from their backpacks to their heads. Lauri Beth felt the transition more than Kevin, who seemed not to notice any change. They quickly checked the communications and infrared goggles. Kevin led the way up to the opening in the saddle.

"Look here," he said. "There's some evidence that there's been some traffic here. See the disturbance between the rocks. Someone or something has been by here."

"How long ago?" Lauri Beth asked.

"It's hard to tell. "Probably since the last major rain."

They moved up to and through the saddle. Once they were well below the high point, they stopped to take note of where they were. In the semi-darkness, they could see the outline of a huge bowl. There appeared to be several fissures that fingered off at various points. They could barely distinguish the multitude of colors that had attracted Brian to fly into the rocky tureen. Lauri Beth was the first to speak.

"I feel that we're someplace special. I would love to see this place in the daylight."

"Someday, maybe!" Kevin said. "But right now, let's keep moving."

They made their way down the steep decline that led to the canyon floor. Making their way slowly, they came to a small, fast-flowing stream They were able to cross it on stepping stones enabling them to keep their feet dry. Kevin signaled Lauri Beth to lower her infrared goggles. The range was just over a hundred yards, but they still were able to pick up the far wall of the canyon. Kevin focused on his GPS and pointed slightly to his left. Their progress became very slow as they began to concentrate more on stealth than on forward movement. Lauri Beth tapped on Kevin's arm.

"Look over there," she whispered as she pointed further left. "What's that large shadow?"

Kevin led the way to where Lauri Beth had directed. He stopped about twenty-five yards short.

"It's not a shadow," he said. "It appears to be an opening in the rocks. Let's move closer. Be very careful."

They crept forward until they were only ten yards from the opening. They were hidden behind some very large rocks and some unusually dense foliage. Kevin motioned Lauri Beth to stop and crouch down behind the largest rock. As she knelt down her knee touched a good-sized boulder. She was startled when the boulder easily moved under her weight. Lauri Beth reached down and felt the rock. She pushed against it. It rolled to one side. She put her hands on each side, bent her knees and prepared to lift it. She almost let out a cry as the stone offered no resistance to her. Catching herself before she tumbled over backwards, she held the "boulder" in her hands. It measured about two feet in diameter. She easily turned it over several times, inspecting it from all angles.

"Kevin, look at this!" she exclaimed.

He turned in amazement as he saw her holding a two-foot boulder at arm's length. He indicated that she should return the stone to its original position. He moved to a giant rock, perhaps ten feet in diameter. He caressed it with his hands. Then he put his shoulder to one side of it and gently applied pressure. He backed off immediately.

"I could push this rock with just a little effort. I think this whole area has been strewn with ultra-light rock. It's probably lava rock or something equivalent."

"That's not all," said Lauri Beth. "Look over here at this palo verde tree. I think it's made of plastic."

Kevin moved over to where she was examining the tree. He touched the leaves and then the trunk.

"Yep!" he said. "It looks like this whole area has been covered with artificial rocks and foliage. Let's go see what they're hiding."

They had raised their infrared goggles to examine the imitation stones and vegetation. Now they lowered them again, and keeping as low as possible, crept under and around the artificial camouflage. They finally came to a vantage point that kept them completely concealed yet gave them a full view of the wall in front of them. A mere twenty feet separated them from the vertical stone face.

"Oh!" Lauri Beth breathed. "I think we've found it. I really do."

They were staring at a solid rock wall that rose several hundred feet. At the bottom was a cavernous opening that measured more than twenty feet across and possibly fifteen feet in height. Even with the help of their special glasses, they couldn't see the end of the tunnel beyond the opening.

"You might be right," Kevin admitted. This has been here for some time, like over a hundred years, I'd guess. It looks to me like the entrance to an old mine."

"Do you think that it could possibly be—?" Lauri Beth asked.

"That would be something, wouldn't it?" Kevin said. "But I think that's somewhat unrealistic. This is pret-

ty far from the commonly thought of location of the
Lost Dutchman."

Suddenly, Kevin stiffened. He held up his hand for
Lauri Beth to see.

"Wait! Something or someone moved just inside of
the entrance."

CHAPTER TWENTY-FOUR

Harold Spivey had been working very diligently, almost day and night. It was the way he liked it. The problem was that he was being inundated by a large number of cases and it was becoming difficult for him to focus on one case the way he preferred. Lt. Bledsoe had been on his back from the beginning and he wasn't letting up as the days progressed.

It was ten o'clock at night and Spivey had just hung up the phone after another session with Bledsoe. He was still at the lab and it looked like he would be there for at least another two hours. He was nearing the end of the Ed Murphy investigation. The circumstances still pointed to a crime of random violence, but Spivey had a lingering suspicion that wouldn't go away. This feeling had transmitted itself to the lieutenant and made him even more difficult to deal with. Spivey was determined to make his final report and lay the matter to rest, despite his own misgivings. A few hours earlier he had finished his examination of the last piece of evidence that the police had deposited with the forensics lab. Now, he sat at his table with everything spread out in front of him. He picked up each article and turned it over in his hands, hoping that something would transmit itself through his touch. Nothing came to him and he was just getting to admit to himself that his suspicions were probably unfounded when he realized that something was missing.

"Where is that little envelope that the cop handed me?" he half-thought and half-said. "The one with the stain sample."

Spivey rose from the table and went back to the locker. He carried a step stool with him. Standing on the stool, he leaned into the locker. There at the far rear, wedged between the wire mesh and the shelf floor, he felt a piece of paper. He pulled hard and finally freed it.

"That's it!" he said aloud as he extricated himself from the locker.

He returned to his examining table and opened the envelope. Inside was a plastic bag containing a smear of some liquid. Harold quickly made a slide and put it under the microscope.

"Strange substance," he murmured. "Very strange, indeed."

Spivey took the smear to his testing station and began a long and exhaustive process. It was well after midnight, when he found Bledsoe's card and dialed his nighttime number. A weary voice answered on the third ring.

"Yeah?"

"Lieutenant, it's me, Harold Spivey, from the forensics lab."

"Whatta ya want? It better be good!"

"Well, I was just beginning to write my final report on the Murphy case, when I remembered a scraping from the scene that a cop gave me. Somehow it got stuck in the back of the evidence locker and I just found it a couple of hours ago. I've been analyzing it and it appears to be some sort of serum or antitoxin. It's quite strong, probably used on large animals. I haven't discovered the exact purpose yet, but I thought that I'd better let you know right away. I think that it confirms my theory that there were two pieces of luggage involved and that the murderers took one of them."

"How long before you can be more specific?" Bledsoe asked.

"I plan to work straight through," Spivey said. "I might know a lot more in the morning."

"I'll see you at seven. And, Spivey,—thanks for the call."

Chapter Twenty-five

Kevin and Lauri Beth huddled behind a huge imitation rock not more than twenty feet from the large hole in the rock face. They activated their night-vision lenses and peered into the cavern in front of them. They slowly were able to make out the details of the interior.

"It looks like an old abandoned mine," Kevin whispered into his throat mike. "See the timbers near the entrance and, if you look closely, you can see more, further down the tunnel."

"I agree. I can see a good hundred feet inside and there appear to be timbers shoring up the walls and ceiling all the way back. I think I can see some openings that branch off to either side as well."

"I'm sure there are tunnels all over the inside, left and right and up and down." Kevin agreed. "Those old miners followed the veins until they ran out and then went back to find another. There's no telling how extensive the excavations are. We could be seeing most of the mine or this could be only the beginning."

"Do you see anything moving?" Lauri Beth asked.

"About halfway back," he said. "I thought that I noticed something. It could be a guard sleeping or just another rock, but I thought that it moved a little. Look behind the first upright timber on the right. Doesn't that look like a folded-up chair?"

"I'll bet that's the guard's station during the day," Lauri Beth speculated. "They probably relax their surveillance at night. What do you think?"

"I think that it's time I found out."

"There you go, again. Using that damned 'I' again."

"And this time I mean it. This could be very dangerous. Besides, I don't want both of us to be discovered at the same time. I want you to wait here. I'm going in. If I decide it's safe and there's good cover, I'll call you in. Remember, we're not armed."

Kevin didn't wait for Lauri Beth's argument or answer. He took off his backpack, removed a few items from it and was suddenly gone. Lauri Beth's eyes followed him for about ten feet and then he simply disappeared. Even with her night-vision goggles, she could only pick out an indefinite shadow. She resigned herself to Kevin's orders and hid behind the rock that had provided cover for them. She was beginning to settle in, when Kevin's voice sounded in her headset.

"Lauri Beth!"

"I hear you loud and clear," she responded.

"I'm about thirty feet inside the mine on the left side, just by the second upright. I've got good cover and there is no one at the entrance. It's okay for you to come in. Leave your pack with mine. Be prepared for a drastic change in temperature. It's cold and gets colder with every step inside."

"Roger." Lauri Beth answered. "Be right with you."

In less than a minute, Lauri Beth crawled to where Kevin was situated. He pointed ahead, indicating his next position.

"Wait here until I make sure it's okay to follow."

Kevin proceeded deeper into the mine. Lauri Beth was able to follow his movements easier this time, but she still had to concentrate lest she lose him in the darkness. She could see him move ahead. He would stop each time he reached another vertical timber or and indentation in the rock wall.

"Stay where you are and don't move," Kevin whispered. "There's another tunnel off to the right and I think it's where the guards bunk."

Kevin moved across the main tunnel and disappeared into the darkness on the right side of the excavation. He cautiously approached three still forms on the ground. He removed a canister from his belt and crept to the first sleeping bag. He quickly sprayed a small amount of substance into the face of the sleeping guard. He moved to the next man and repeated the process. The third sleeping bag moved slightly as its occupant turned over in his sleep. Kevin froze for an instant. He determined that the last guard was still breathing regularly and administered another dose of spray. He then crept deeper into the chamber. It was about fifty feet in depth and the ceiling tapered down to meet the floor at the end. He quickly searched the rock-walled room and returned to the three guards. He checked each one and then took a plastic container from under his shirt. He poured a small amount of liquid onto a cloth and covered each man's nose and mouth for a moment. He knelt next to the comatose men and summoned Lauri Beth.

"Lauri Beth. You can follow me into the opening on the right but be careful. I found three guards in here and there may be others about."

"Roger that," Lauri Beth answered as she left her location.

She knelt beside Kevin and asked, "Is it safe? What did you do to them?"

"They're okay," Kevin said. "They'll stay asleep for a couple of hours and then they'll have a slight headache when they get up in the morning. Let's move on."

Kevin got up to leave and Lauri Beth moved to get a better look at the guards. She reached over and grabbed Kevin by the arm.

"Wait!" she said. "I've seen this one before."

"Are you sure? Where?"

"Let me think. Just a minute! I recognize this one, too! And I know where I saw them. It was at the coroner's office. They were going into a room and the sheriff was there, too."

"We'd better think about that later," Kevin said. "Right now we ought to continue looking through this mine."

Kevin and Lauri Beth moved out of the small cavern back into the main tunnel. They turned right and proceeded about twenty yards when the passageway made a sharp bend to the left. Kevin cautioned Lauri Beth to remain a bit behind him and stiffened against the rock wall. He peered around the corner and detected a soft glow emanating from a recession a hundred feet down the shaft. It was on the left side, so he ventured forward. Lauri Beth moved up to where Kevin had been and remained there. He crept to the opening, took a cautious look inside and disappeared around the corner. Lauri Beth was getting nervous when Kevin hadn't reappeared in fifteen minutes. Suddenly her headset crackled.

"Come on down here," Kevin said. "You won't believe this."

Lauri Beth was at Kevin's side in less than a minute. She stared dumbfounded as Kevin explained.

"There must be about twenty cages," he said. "Twelve of them have a coyote in them. The animals appeared to be drugged or sedated because they haven't woken to our presence. This table looks like an operating bench. The little refrigerator contains vials of fluid and hypodermic needles. That cabinet above the frig is stocked with rubber gloves and masks. And, see, over in the corner, there's a chemical waste disposal unit. I suppose that's used to get rid of the animal urine and feces. Can you feel the air moving? There's also a ventilation system. It probably runs throughout the mine but it seems to be stronger in here. That means that there's also a generator someplace, probably outside the mine and well hidden. We could trace the wires and find it, if we had the time."

"My God!" Lauri Beth exclaimed. "What do you make

of it all?"

"No time to figure it out now," Kevin replied. "We better finish our tour and get out of here before the guards wake up."

They left the room and continued down the main passage. Suddenly Kevin pulled up short, causing Lauri Beth to collide with him. He pushed back so hard that she almost fell over backward.

"Whoa, there! Big guy," she said. "Take it easy. You almost knocked me down."

"And you almost pushed me into an open shaft," he retorted.

Lauri Beth looked around Kevin and saw a gaping hole in the floor. It was nearly a dozen feet in diameter and practically invisible, even with the infrared goggles.

"Whoops!" she said. "That was close."

Kevin had untied a coil of rope from his belt and was securing one end of it to a solid timber.

"What are you doing?" Lauri Beth asked.

"I'm going to take a quick look," Kevin said. "I've got a hundred and fifty feet of super-thin line here. I'll drop down and be back up in a matter of minutes."

He coiled the rope around his body in rappelling fashion and was over the side before Lauri Beth could object. True to his word, Kevin scampered back over the edge in less than five minutes.

"Well?" Lauri Beth asked as he was coiling the rope, retying it to his belt.

"I went down about a hundred and twenty feet," Kevin said. "There are a couple of shafts going off in different directions. I think that the main shaft could be three hundred feet deep. It doesn't look like our friends are using anything but the main floor."

"How did you get down and back up so fast?"

Kevin produced a pair of handheld grips that ratchet on the line, showed them to her and then stowed them in a side pocket.

"Jumars," she said.

"Yeah. You've got a pair in your climbing gear. I guess I didn't show them to you back at the house."

"I'll check it out later," Lauri Beth said. "Right now, we'd better finish up and get out of here."

They continued down the main tunnel another seventy-five feet until Kevin came to a deep niche on the right. He signaled Lauri Beth to stay put and ventured around the corner. He pulled up short as he sighted another guard. This guard was awake and apparently on active duty. He had his back to Kevin. It was a mistake he wouldn't repeat. He never even sensed Kevin's presence as darkness enveloped him and he sank into unconsciousness.

Kevin proceeded into the large abyss. He was into what appeared to be a well-stocked laboratory. There were tables supporting various scientific apparatus and cabinets housing supplies and other equipment. Bunsen burners, beakers and distilling coils were abundant. As Kevin went deeper into the lab, he discovered yet another room connected to it.

He peered around the entrance. No guard was in evidence. He stepped forward into a rough living quarters. A simple study occupied the main section with dining and sleeping facilities in two of the corners. Water was stored in a large overhead tank and a portable chemical toilet was next to a cot. Kevin slipped into the cavern. The bed was occupied. Kevin crept to the bed, his spray can at the ready. He was about to apply a quick sedation, when the sleeping figure stirred just enough to reveal his face.

The features were obscured by a full white beard. Kevin could see that the man was well advanced in years, probably into his seventies. He decided that a simple sedation could prove lethal in the case of one so elderly and possibly in poor physical condition. He quickly surveyed the room in more detail and went back to the lab. He called Lauri Beth on the intercom and told her that it was all right for her to enter. He met her in the lab.

"What's all this?" she asked.

"I'm not quite sure," Kevin answered. "But it wouldn't surprise me if it was connected to the coyotes in the other room."

"What are we going to do?"

"Why don't you look around. You've got a medical and scientific background and can make more of it than I can. I'm going to take some pictures and see if I can find any documents that can give us a hint," Kevin said as he pulled a pocket-sized spy camera from a pocket.

Lauri Beth gave him a quizzical look.

"Infrared," Kevin said, answering the unasked question.

They spent another fifteen minutes in the lab, Lauri

Beth examining all of the scientific paraphernalia, and Kevin photographing anything of interest, including some apparent schedules on the wall. Kevin touched Lauri Beth on the arm, indicating that it was time to move on.

They continued down the main passage until it ran out. At the very end an air shaft ran vertically upward. Electric cables shared the space with an exhaust fan.

"The generator is probably on the ground near the top of the shaft," he said. This fan keeps the air circulating in the mine. I thought that I felt a movement of air ever since we came in."

"We've been here for well over an hour." Lauri Beth said. "How long did you say that the guards would be out?"

"You're right, it's time to go. I think that we've seen enough for now. Be careful of that big opening in the floor. It would be a thrill and a half if we dropped into that."

The guards were still sleeping soundly as Kevin and Lauri Beth passed them on their way out. The trip back to the horses was just as tedious and time-consuming as the journey in. The horses were restless and sensitive to the slightest sound as Kevin and Lauri Beth approached. They quickly calmed and saddled the horses. They reached the truck a few hours before daylight and decided to wait until sunup to drive out. Bed rolls were laid out. Kevin and Lauri Beth snuggled into them.

CHAPTER TWENTY-SIX

Lieutenant John Bledsoe was greeted by a bleary-eyed Harold Spivey. It was five minutes after seven o'clock and the lieutenant had shown himself into the forensics lab and had entered Spivey's office without ceremony.

"You know any more than you did last night?" he demanded.

"I'm not sure exactly what I told you," Spivey answered. "It appears that my suspicions were correct. The fluid that was scraped from the garage floor is definitely a serum, one used to counteract some sort of virus. I think I mentioned it was high in potency and was probably formulated for use on large animals. Ed Murphy was a cattleman, so I guess that it's safe to assume that it was administered to cattle. Maybe it was experimental or something. I guess that everyone's trying to find out what's keeping cattle production down."

"You're doing a lot of guessing, Spivey," Bledsoe said as he lowered himself into the chair behind the researcher's desk. "Let's see if we can make some sense out of what you found."

Spivey took the chair in front of the desk.

"Let's say that you're correct in your assumptions," Bledsoe said. "That means that either the serum is working and that Murphy's cattle are immune to whatever is causing the calving problem or that he was just experimenting and that the serum isn't proven as yet."

"It could also mean that the serum works but it's still too early to know just how effective it is."

"Yeah, that's true," Bledsoe agreed. "But, unless the serum is a total failure, we may have a motive!"

"A motive for murder?" Spivey asked.

"Yeah! A motive for murder!" Bledsoe sneered. "What did you think I meant, a motive for petty larceny! I'm investigating a homicide. That's murder, in case you may have forgot."

Spivey flushed at the rebuke and remained silent as Bledsoe continued.

"Okay! I'm going on the theory that Murphy was murdered for the serum. I've got some digging to do. We've received notice from the Department of Agriculture that we're to report anything remotely associated with the cattle shortage to Washington, immediately. Here's a copy of the notice. Give 'em a call. I'll contact you tomorrow. I'll want to know what the department said and I'll want to know if you've come up with anything else. Good work, Spivey! I'm outta here!"

Bledsoe rose and headed for the door. As he passed Spivey, he gave him a congratulatory punch on the shoulder. It took fifteen minutes of constant rubbing for the pain to subside.

Spivey was finally able to feel enough strength return to his arm to pick up the receiver of the telephone. He pulled the notice in front of him and dialed the number highlighted toward the bottom of the page.

"Department of Agriculture," an electronic voice answered. Spivey was presented with a list of menu items that led to another list that led to another list that led to still another list. Finally, he was connected to a live voice.

"How may I direct your call?" it asked.

"I'm calling regarding the meat shortage," Harold said. "I have some information that may be very important."

"One moment, please." A long pause ensued. Finally a connection was made.

"Paul Stockton, special assistant to the Secretary."

"My name is Harold Spivey. I'm with the Dallas, Texas, Police Department Forensics Lab. We've come across something that may be of significance to the meat-shortage problem, Mr. Stockton. Maybe I should be talking to the Secretary himself."

"I'm special liaison to the Secretary in all matters concerning the meat shortage, Mr. Spivey. Why don't you tell me what you've got and I'll decide whether or not the Secretary should be personally involved."

"All right. As I said, I'm with the Forensics Division of

the Dallas Police Department. A few weeks ago, we had a homicide that looked like a random crime of violence. A prominent cattleman was murdered in his parking garage. He was on his way to Washington. We don't know what he was going there for or who he was going to see. We do know that he was flying into Dulles and leaving from National, which seemed a bit strange on the surface. We now believe that he was carrying two pieces of luggage, one of which was found at the crime scene. The other hasn't shown up yet. One of the officers at the scene took a smear of a liquid substance from the concrete floor of the garage near the body. I have just finished examining that smear. It appears to be a serum or antitoxin. It would be administered to protect against a virus of some sort. The strength was such that led me to believe that it was intended for large animals. Since Mr. Murphy was a cattleman, it suggests that the serum was to be used on cattle.

"I'm working with a Lieutenant Bledsoe on the case. When I informed him of my hypothesis this morning, he showed me your bulletin and instructed me to call you."

"Yes, thank you very much," Stockton said. "This could be extremely useful. I'll get it to the Secretary immediately. He may want to contact you personally. Please give your name again and your telephone number and, oh, your fax and e-mail, if you have them."

Spivey complied and the conversation was over. On the other end of the line it was just beginning. Stockton dropped the receiver into its cradle and hurried across the hall to the office of the Secretary of

Agriculture. As he passed his secretary, he ordered, "Alice! Bring me a tape of that telephone conversation, immediately. I'll be in Mr. Harkens' office."

He paused briefly at the reception desk in the Secretary's outer office to explain his mission. He was promptly ushered into the inner sanctum.

"Mr. Secretary!" he blurted out before realizing that Secretary Harkens was on the telephone.

George Harkens completed his conversation, replaced the receiver on its base and said, "Hello, Paul! What is it? Is the building on fire, or what?"

"No, sir!" Stockton explained. "But I may have something of a breakthrough!"

"Go on!" the Secretary directed.

"Well, sir. I just received a call from—," Stockton looked at the notes he had taken during his telephone conversation. "—a Harold Spivey with the Dallas Police Forensics Division. He's come across something during a routine investigation."

He was interrupted by a knock at the door.

"Come in!" the Secretary directed.

The receptionist entered with a small cartridge in her hand.

"Alice said you wanted this," she said to Stockton. She handed it to him and left the room.

"It's all on here, Mr. Secretary," he said as he handed over the cassette.

Five minutes later, Secretary Harkens was on the phone to the President of the United States.

"Yes, sir, Mr. President!" he concluded as he hung up the phone and turned to his assistant.

"Paul," he said. "This is top priority. We have complete authorization to involve the FBI and anyone else that can help. You are to assemble a team, stat, and get down to Dallas. I'll expect to hear from you tomorrow morning."

"YES, SIR!" Stockton replied as he turned on his heel and left the room in true military fashion.

An hour later, Spivey answered the telephone.

"Paul Stockton here!" he heard before he could say a word. "Listen, Spivey, I'll be in Dallas tonight with my investigating team. We'll be at your place at six a.m. sharp. Okay? And have that lieutenant there, too!"

The phone went dead before Spivey could say "Hello" or "Good-bye."

*

Lt. Bledsoe hadn't been idle. By the time his beeper pulsated, he had uncovered some interesting facts. He had left the forensics lab and gone directly to the office of the late Edward Murphy. He entered the reception area and could see in a moment that a pall still hung in the air.

"I'm Lt. Bledsoe," he said to the mourning-clad receptionist. He produced his identification as he spoke.

"I'm sorry to have to bother you at a time like this," he continued, "but there are some routine questions that I'd like to ask."

"Yes, of course," she whispered.

"Could we go into Mr. Murphy's office?"

"I guess that it would be all right," she said. "I'll

have to get someone to cover for me. I'll just be a minute." She disappeared behind a door and returned shortly with a girl in tow.

"I won't be long," she said to her replacement as she looked to Bledsoe for confirmation. He nodded. She led him into Murphy's private office.

"And you are?" Bledsoe asked.

"June Travis," she answered. "I've been with Mr. Murphy for over ten years. Isn't this just awful?"

"Yes, ma'am, it certainly is," he said. "I'll try to be as brief as possible. First, do you know of anyone who was threatening Mr. Murphy or gave you cause to be uneasy?"

"No, to the first part," she said. "But there have been a couple of his friends that I don't feel at home with."

"And who might they be?" Bledsoe asked.

"Mr. Plover and Mr. Burleson," she replied. "They started coming around here about three years ago. I just never felt comfortable when they were here."

"Were they ranchers?" He asked.

"Yes, but not real cowboy types. You know what I mean?" she said. "Oh, Mr. Plover was okay, I guess. But he was loud and bragging all the time. You know what I mean? But that Mr. Burleson, he gave me the creeps. He could look right through you and make you feel undressed. He was really scary. You know what I mean?"

"Yeah, I know what you mean," Bledsoe agreed. "Now this Mr. Plover. What was he bragging about all the time?"

"You know, the regular things," she answered. "How

rich he was and how smart he was and how this new scam was the best of all. Oh, and whenever he mentioned anything about this new thing, Mr. Burleson would get very upset and tell him to shut up. Sometimes I thought that Mr. Burleson would hit Mr. Plover, but, of course, it never came to that."

"That's real interesting," Bledsoe encouraged. "Do you have any idea what this scam was that Mr. Plover liked so much?"

"Not really," June said. "But if I had to guess, I'd say that it had something to do with the high price of meat. They were always talking about meat prices and laughing every time the newspaper headlines talked about it."

Bledsoe finished jotting down some notes on his pocket pad. He purposefully put the pad back into his jacket pocket and said, "Now, I'd like to look at the books."

"Oh, I don't know, Lieutenant. I'm certainly not authorized to do anything like that."

"Well get me someone who is!" Bledsoe ordered.

Travis went to her phone, dialed and returned to the inner office.

"Mr. Honore will be right in," she said.

A long five minutes later, a slender young man with light tan skin and a thin mustache sauntered into the room. Travis did the introductions.

"Lieutenant Bledsoe, this is Jose Honore, our chief accountant."

They shook hands. Bledsoe noted a firm grip and a certain hostility by the accountant.

"I'd like to see the books of the cattle company," he said. "Especially the last three years, and I'd like you to include the number of cattle shipped to market and to which markets they were shipped."

"Well, I'm afraid that's impossible," Honore said, setting himself firmly in front of the lieutenant. "You see, that's privileged information and I can't release it."

"Let me put this in a way that you can understand," Bledsoe said with just a bit of an edge to his voice. "You can show me now, here in this office, or you can lug all of your records downtown and spend a few days explaining everything to our accountants. They're not too bright and it may actually take a week or two before they're able to grasp the intricacies of your books."

Honore's skin turned a few shades paler as the request became less of an option and more of an order.

"I'll see what I can do," he said as he started to leave the room.

"Just a minute, young man," Bledsoe ordered. "Let's just go over to Mr. Murphy's computer. I'm sure that you can provide all the information I need on the screen."

Honore seated himself in front of the computer and Bledsoe pulled a chair alongside.

"Now show me the profit and loss statements for the last three years," Bledsoe charged. Numbers began to appear on the screen.

"These are the P & Ls in short form," Honore explained. "You can see that profits are down even though cattle prices have risen. That's because our numbers have fallen faster than prices have gone up. It's the same all over the country."

Bledsoe noted a slight tremor in Honore's voice. He watched the accountant's hands on the keyboard and detected some nervousness.

"Let me see the marketing figures," Bledsoe said. "I mean the actual cattle shipped and the source and destination."

"I-I-I don't have those," Honore stammered.

"Well, where are they?" Bledsoe demanded.

"All those records are kept at the individual ranches and feed lots," he said. "All I ever get are the sales and cost figures. Everything else was sent to Mr. Murphy over a private network."

"Well, you must have the names and addresses of the ranches, feed lots, processing plants and terminals," Bledsoe countered. "Get me them and get them fast!"

Honore disappeared for a few moments and returned with a small ledger.

"Here," he said. "This is all I've got."

Bledsoe grabbed the ledger and scanned the contents.

"Now listen, Mr. Honore," he said. "There'll be at least ten accountants from the Dallas Police Department arriving as soon as I make a telephone call, and you had better be cooperative or you'll be held as an accessory to grand larceny and perhaps murder. Get it!"

Bledsoe sat down at Murphy's large ornate desk, picked up the telephone and dialed.

"Let me talk to Casper," he said as he identified himself. A few minutes later Bledsoe's assistant was on the line. "Casper! Bledsoe here."

"Yes, Lieutenant. What is it?"

"This is in connection with the Edward Murphy homicide," Bledsoe began. "Forensics had come up with something interesting and I'm following up on it."

"Yes! Go on."

"I'm calling from Murphy's office and I'm in need of some technical assistance. I need a team of accountants and auditors here first thing in the morning."

"Okay! Would you mind telling me exactly what they'll be looking for?"

"I need verification of the financial activities for the company for the last three years. I'm also looking for the physical numbers of their stock, where the cattle came from and where they went. I want any connection, whatsoever, to two other cattle men, Jim Plover and Harry Burleson."

"Is that it?"

"No!" Bledsoe continued. "I want you to make a thorough canvass of all the cattle markets and processing plants within three hundred miles of any of Murphy's or Plover's or Burleson's ranches or feed lots. I want to know if any new brands have appeared or if these destinations have received cattle from any new shippers over the same period. You'll have to solicit the help of police departments all over the state and probably New Mexico and Oklahoma, as well."

"Anything else, Lieutenant?" Casper droned.

"Yeah!" Bledsoe ordered. "I want a complete file on

Murphy, Plover and Burleson on my desk by noon tomorrow."

"Could you give a hint as to what's going on?" Casper pleaded.

"I can tell you this much," Bledsoe confided. "This may not be a simple crime of a mugging gone wrong. It may be a crime of national proportions!"

CHAPTER TWENTY-SEVEN

Kevin and Lauri Beth pulled into the driveway of Brian's house a little after noon on Sunday. Kevin parked back by the corral. They unloaded the horses and, after combing them out, set them loose inside the fence with water in the trough and feed in the bunker. Kevin hauled the equipment inside while Lauri Beth made a couple of sandwiches for lunch.

"Well, what now?" Lauri Beth asked.

"First, we'd better check out our gear," Kevin said. "As soon as we finish eating. I'm starved."

They finished in silence and cleaned up the kitchen together. After lunch they began unpacking the backpacks and other bags. They laid all the paraphernalia out and performed a rigid inspection.

"Look's like everything's in good working order," Kevin noted as they began repacking the bags.

"Good," Lauri Beth said. "What's next?"

"Next, I'm going to develop the film and make some prints then we'll go over our experience and make some decisions," he said. "Then you'd better head for home, get some sleep and get ready for work tomorrow."

"Sounds like a plan," Lauri Beth said. "Except for the part about me going home and going to work."

Kevin gave her a puzzled look.

"That's right," she continued. "I'm not going home just yet. I'll call in tomorrow and arrange for a vacation week. I've got three coming and I'm sure they can cover for me."

Kevin could see that there was no sense arguing with her, so he simply said, "Okay."

An hour later, Kevin emerged from the bathroom that he had converted into a darkroom holding a handful of prints. He laid them out on the dining room table and called Lauri Beth.

"Let's see what we've got," he said as she joined him and began poring over the photos.

"Wow!" Lauri Beth exclaimed. "Those shots of the schedules are so clear you can read them just like they printed on standard paper."

"Yeah," Kevin said. "That camera is a real work of art. I don't know how much it cost but I do know I couldn't afford one."

"Look at this one," he pointed out to her. "It's the one I took of the lab entrance. The guard is already asleep, but see which way his chair is facing."

"It's facing into the lab," Lauri Beth said. "What does that mean?"

"I think it means he was guarding against anyone leaving rather than anyone entering," Kevin said. "I think the old guy was being held some sort of prisoner."

"I think you're right," she agreed. "And look at these schedules. There appears to be two distinct sets. This first set seems to be a shipping schedule for various parts of the country. It's headed 'Wileys out.' This one over here is like a count on a per-week basis and it says 'Wileys in.' I wonder what a Wiley is?" Then this other set is another shipping chart, but everything goes to Dallas. There are three different drop points: Murphy, Burleson and Plover. But look here, Burleson's and Plover's are current, but Murphy's stops a couple of weeks ago."

"Wiley, wiley—why does that sound so familiar?" Kevin asked.

"I got it!" Lauri Beth shouted. "Remember that old cartoon show? You can still see the reruns. It was called the 'Roadrunner'. Remember? Well, the road-runner was always being chased by a coyote and the coyote was named, Wiley, though it was spelled Wile, E. as an initial, Coyote."

"You've got to be right," Kevin said excitedly. "These are log-ins of the coyotes in the cages and then they must do something to them and send them out."

"I'll bet that's where the old guy fits in," Lauri Beth reasoned. "I'll bet he's some kind of doctor or scientist or something."

"That would explain all the lab equipment," Kevin said. "I wonder what they're up to?"

"I've got an idea on where we can start," Lauri Beth suggested. "We could find out who those three guys are who are receiving the shipments from the lab."

"Let's see," he said. "They're all from Dallas. Maybe we could start with long distance information. What were those names, again?"

"It's on this photo," Lauri Beth said. "Murphy, Burleson and Plover."

"There's probably a million Murphys," Kevin observed. "Try the other two first."

Lauri Beth went into the kitchen to use the phone. Ten minutes later, she returned.

"There were only a few Burlesons and Plovers, but get this, there was a cattle company or feed lot in each of their names. So, I asked information to check on a Murphy cattle company, feed lot, ranch or anything like that. Sure enough, there's a Murphy Ranches, Inc. listed."

"Great!" Kevin said. "We'll start calling first thing in the morning. That'll give us time to think up a strategy."

"We can start early," Lauri Beth reminded him. "During Daylight Savings Time, Dallas is two hours ahead of us."

"We'd better turn in," Kevin said. "But before we do, tell me again about those two guys that you recognized."

"Like I said, I'll never forget that one guy," Lauri Beth shuddered. "His face was the meanest that I've ever seen and the way he walked and looked right through you scared me to death. I only remember the other one because he was with the first guy. They both seemed to be buddy-buddy with the sheriff and I had the feeling that they controlled the coroner, since the three of them were walking together and my boss was bringing up the rear."

"That sort of leaves us in a tough spot," Kevin noted. "If we uncover something wrong, where do we go with it?"

"I guess we better figure that out tomorrow," Lauri Beth suggested. "Right now, I think you had the right idea a minute ago. Let's go to bed."

*

The next morning, daylight poured into the room despite the closed curtains. The subdued glare woke them both at almost the same instant. Lauri Beth snuggled up to Kevin and soon felt his gentle hands on her body.

Forty-five minutes later, they broke their embrace and rose to meet the day.

"Well," Lauri Beth said. "It's eight o'clock. That makes it ten in Dallas. It's as good a time to call as any. What are we going to say?"

"I've been thinking about that," Kevin answered. "I guess we'd better try to find out if there's a connection between the Dallas guys and the mine. Suppose we call and say we're from the sheriff's or coroner's office and see what happens. Which do you think would be better?"

"You know," she said. "They might have caller ID. I don't think that we should call from here. Why don't I go back to the office? I've got a couple of things to finish up and I could make the calls from there, using the generic number."

"Sounds like a good idea," Kevin said. "Do you have two phones in your office? You could place the call and I'll be the coroner. All we have to find out is if there's any name recognition."

"I think it'll work," Lauri Beth agreed.

An hour and a half later, Kevin and Lauri Beth were in her office. Lauri Beth got out the reports that needed attention and placed them on her desk. Kevin was seated at a small table in the corner of the office. The only thing on the table was an extension phone to Lauri Beth's line. Lauri Beth looked at Kevin, took a deep breath and dialed Dallas.

"I have a call for Mr. Plover," she said after the connection had been made.

"Yes," she continued in answer to a question. "Dr. James Blackwell calling from Apache Junction, Arizona."

Lauri Beth pointed to the instrument in front of Kevin and indicated that he should pick it up.

"Hello," he said. Then waited until a voice came on the line.

"Yes, that's right, this is Dr. Blackwell," Lauri Beth heard him say. "I was just calling to see if everything's all right on your end."

"Yes, I understand, sorry," he finished and hung up the phone.

"Wow!" he said to a wondering Lauri Beth. "I think that they know each other. I was told, politely but firmly, that I was never to call him in person and that any-thing that he had to say I could find out from the sher-iff after the sheriff talked to Harry. He hung up on me while I was still apologizing."

"Harry," Lauri Beth wondered. "Let's see, Harry must refer to Mr. Burleson...yeah, here it is, on my phone list. Harry Burleson."

"No need to call him," Kevin said. "Let's try Murphy."

They got ready for the next call. Lauri Beth dialed and Kevin was at the ready by the other phone.

"Hello," she said again. "I have a call for Mr. Murphy."

She listened intently for almost a minute, then sig-naled to Kevin that he needn't pick up his receiver.

"What's up?" he said.

"You won't believe this!" she exclaimed. "Mr. Murphy is dead! Murdered! The investigation is still going on! He was killed in a robbery attempt in his apartment garage!"

"Man," Kevin said. "If there's any connection between his murder and what's going on at the mine, we're onto something big. Now if we're right about the old guy being held some sort prisoner, we could see the outline of a puzzle falling into place."

"What's that supposed to mean?" Lauri Beth asked.

"It means that we're going back to the mine," Kevin said.

CHAPTER TWENTY-EIGHT

Charlie Whitfield rolled over in his sleeping bag. He checked his watch. The luminous dial read 3:30 in the morning. It was pitch black and the inside of his head wasn't any brighter. Charlie raised up on one elbow. He thought his head was splitting in two. He tried to reach over to Butch but the pain in his head only allowed him to roll on his back and lie still, hoping that the throbbing would subside. An hour passed and Charlie felt confident enough to try another move. This time the pain was only the severity of an ordinary morning after. He stood in the darkness and looked at his two companions. Butch wasn't pleasant to waken even on his best days, and this wasn't likely to be one of them, so Charlie opted for the other man.

"Jasper, Jasper," he whispered as he nudged the inert sleeping bag. "It's your turn to stand watch."

The sleeping bag moved and a man groaned.

"Leave me be! Just leave me be!" Jasper pleaded. "If

I'm not already dead, shoot me! I got the grand-daddy of all hangovers. God! My head feels like it was used as a battering ram by Attila the Hun and my mouth feels like he's still in there!"

"Take it easy, Jasper!" Charlie instructed. "Just lay still for a while. You'll feel better in about an hour. I'll take your watch."

"Thanks, Charlie," Jasper managed to utter as he rolled back into silence.

"Damn, that leaves Butch," Charlie thought. Charlie crossed to Butch's sleeping bag and nudged it as gently as he could. Nothing! He found Butch's shoulder and gave it a small push. He moved his face to the opening at the top of the bag and was about to whisper. Suddenly, he was on his back on the mine floor, Butch was on top of him and a knife was at his throat.

"Butch! Butch!" Charlie screamed. "It's me! Goddam it! It's me! Relax! For God's sake, relax!"

Butch blinked his eyes, but the knife didn't move. Charlie could see the pain in Butch's face and prayed that reason would take over before the agony in his head caused a impulsive reaction. Slowly, Butch relaxed his hold on Charlie's throat. The knife moved a fraction of an inch. But it moved away from Charlie's face.

"Butch," Charlie said. "It's okay. It's okay."

Butch withdrew the knife and slid it under his belt. He rolled off of Charlie into a sitting position and placed his forehead against his knees.

"Who the fuck sapped me?" he said. "I'll get the son of a bitch if it's the last thing I do!"

"Nobody hit you," Charlie explained. "I woke up with the same headache, so did Jasper. We didn't have that much beer. It must be something else, unless the beer was bad."

"The beer was fine," Jasper said. "We had some out of the same case night before last and we were okay. Must be something else."

"Man, my head's splittin' open," Butch said.

"It'll ease up in a bit," Charlie consoled. "We better check on Bubba. You guys feel up to it?"

"Yeah," Jasper said.

"Maybe," Butch said.

"Jasper and I'll take care of it, Butch," Charlie said. "You wait here. We'll be back in a minute."

Charlie and Jasper left the entrance and walked through the main tunnel.

"Watch out for the shaft!" Charlie warned. Jasper was lagging and the distance was lengthening.

"Thanks," Jasper said. "I'm not too steady. Wouldn't wanna fall down that baby."

"It'd cure your headache for sure," Charlie joked.

Charlie arrived at the lab well before Jasper. The watchman's chair was in place but unoccupied. A figure lay sprawled in front of it. Charlie rushed up to the prone figure and began shaking it.

"Bubba! Bubba! Are you okay?" he yelled. "What in the hell happened?"

Jasper arrived at the scene, took a quick look and said, "How's Bubba? What happened here, anyway?"

"Don't know, yet!" Charlie answered. "I think he's okay. Stay with him. I'm going to check on the professor."

Charlie disappeared into the lab and connecting living quarters. He went to the old man's cot and shook him awake.

"Hey! Professor!" Charlie called. "Wake up!"

The old man rubbed his sleep-laden eyes and peered at his intruder.

"What? What?" he mumbled.

"How you feeling?" Charlie asked.

"I'm okay, I guess. That all you want to know?"

"How's your head?"

"Okay!"

"No headache?"

"Nope!"

"Go back to sleep. I'll see you in the morning."

Charlie returned to Jasper and Bubba. Bubba was sitting up and holding his head.

"Bubba got the miseries!" Jasper said. "Same as the rest of us."

"I'm gonna check back with Butch," Charlie said, implying that Jasper should remain with Bubba.

Fifteen minutes later, Charlie and Butch joined the other two and asked, "How's everyone feeling?"

The reply was mixed. Butch and Jasper were on the road to recovery, Bubba was just experiencing the first painful throes, and Charlie was almost back to normal.

"We better wait 'til daylight when you all are feeling a mite better," Charlie said. "Then we'll try to sort this out."

There weren't any objections. Charlie went back to the mine entrance. The others curled up where they were and waited for the morning and better, clearer heads.

Daylight filtered through the mine entrance and slowly into Charlie's brain. He was awake but not fully functional. He shook his head and discovered that the expected pain wasn't there. The inside of the mine wasn't going to be affected by the sunrise, so Charlie made his way back to the main light junction box. He opened the panel door and activated every circuit. The entire main level of the mine was flooded with light. Charlie backtracked to the lab entrance. He found Butch, Jasper and Bubba in various positions, rubbing their eyes. All seemed to be free of any earlier pain. Charlie addressed his little group.

"I don't think that last night's pain was caused by anything that we ate or drank," he said. "In my mind that only leaves a couple of possibilities."

"Oh, yeah!" Butch growled. "And what might they be?"

"Well, for one, I can think that maybe there's something wrong with the ventilation system, and for another, it's possible that we were infiltrated and knocked out by some sort of chemical," he ventured.

"The ventilation system is still running," Jasper observed. "I can hear the fans. Doesn't that mean that we'd still be sick if it was the blowers?"

"All right, we'll rule that out for now," Charlie conceded. "That leaves us with an intruder. We're going over this mine with a fine-toothed comb. I want to know if anything has been disturbed, and I mean anything. Butch! You and Jasper start at the entrance and work your way back to the coyote pens. Bubba and I will do the lab and the professor's quarters and then we'll check out the generator and ventilator, just to be sure. Okay?"

"Come on, Jasper," Butch said as he headed toward the front of the mine. "Let's get this over with."

"Tell me, again, about last night," Charlie said to Bubba after the others had gone.

"Well, it like I said," Bubba answered. I was sittin', facin' in and, all of a sudden, I get so tired that I'm fightin' to stay awake. Next thing I know, you're standing over me."

"You feel or hear or smell anything unusual?"

"Come to think about it," Bubba wondered. "I seem to remember a slight breeze and then a smell like some kind of a flower or perfume or something. As a matter of fact, I think that I remember a sort of chemical smell when you woke me up."

"Yeah! Yeah! I might have smelled something when I woke up," Charlie said. "Let's check out the lab. You check the professor's digs and I'll do the lab. See if the old guy remembers anything strange."

Charlie started his search of the lab. He wasn't sure what he was looking for—a telltale mark, a broken piece of apparatus, or something out of place. He began at the corner of the entrance and worked his way around the room in a clockwise direction. Having covered the perimeter of the lab, he inspected the tables and equipment. After an hour, he sat in a chair in the middle of the cell and began to think. He was certain that there was something out of order, but he couldn't put his finger on it. It wasn't any hard evidence, like a footprint or something broken. It was something else.

Bubba came out of the living quarters and shrugged his shoulders, indicating that he had found nothing out of the ordinary.

"What'd the old man say?" Charlie asked.

"Nothin'," Bubba said. "He said that he had a dream about someone coming to rescue him. He thinks that it was his guardian angel. He's nuttier than a fruitcake!"

"Yeah! He's queer, all right. But don't forget that he's got an IQ that's higher than the altitude of this mine," Charlie said. "He might have dreamed it or he might just have felt that somebody was in the room with him. I got a feeling that someone was here. I just can't prove it yet."

"Well, everything looks okay to me," Bubba offered.

"Looks ain't everything, Bubba," Charlie returned. "Say, who got the last shipment of serum? You recall?"

"Nope! But I can check the list in the drawer. We have to initial it every time something goes out, and it says what it was and who got it," Bubba answered.

"Yeah! Here it is," Charlie said as he took a pad of paper out of the desk drawer. "Let's see now. It says here that we sent a load of serum to Burleson last week. Now why does that seem strange to me? Hand me those individual sheets from that clipboard on the wall over there. Will ya, Bubba?"

Bubba handed him the clipboard.

"Well! Well! Well!" Charlie exclaimed. "Would you look at this! I think this is very interesting."

Bubba was straining to see, but obviously didn't see

what Charlie was seeing.

"If I'm not mistaken," Charlie continued, "our procedure is to mark any shipment on these individual sheets and then record it on the master sheet in the drawer."

"That's right," Bubba confirmed. "What about it? Both sheets agree, don't they?"

"Yeah, they agree, but that's where it ends," Charlie explained. "We always put the most recent shipment at the bottom of the pile when we're finished recording it. So, how come Burleson's is still on top? Now look at the master sheet, Bubba. Who was the previous shipment to. I mean the one before Burleson's?"

"It was Murphy," Bubba said.

"That means that the next one on the list should be Plover, doesn't it?" Charlie said as he looked at the next sheet. "Then how come it's Murphy?"

"Dunno!" Bubba answered, not quite grasping the significance of the discovery.

"I'll tell you what it means, Bubba," Charlie exhilarated. "It means that someone was here and read these reports and didn't put them back in proper order. It means that our headaches were the result of someone slippin' us a mickey and it means that we got some serious thinkin' to do. Get the other guys in here. Now!"

Bubba took off like a shot and was back in less than five minutes with Butch and Jasper in tow.

"What's up?" Butch asked.

"You guys find anything?" Charlie countered.

"Nothin' conclusive," Butch said. "Some suspicious

marks around the entrance and some disturbances around the shaft."

"Well, those marks may be more meaningful when you hear this," Charlie said. "Look over here!"

Charlie produced the clipboard and repeated his discovery.

"I get it!" Jasper exclaimed. "We haven't mixed those reports up since this operation started. It's got to mean that someone else was in here last night."

"Yeah!" Butch agreed. "And if I ever find the son of a bitch, he'll be history! And you can make book that he'll feel a whole lot worse than we did this morning!"

"That's all well and good," Charlie said. "But we've got more important things to do first."

Three sets of eyes bore down on Charlie, waiting for him to explain.

"First, we better tighten security around here. No more sleep watches. Butch make up a watch schedule. Rotate the entrance and the interior duties. Four on and four off. Second, I've got to inform the general. That'll put me outta here for about eight hours. Cover my watches for me and I'll make it up when I get back."

"I thought that we weren't supposed to have any direct contact with the general," Butch said. "How you gonna get to him?"

"I got ways," Charlie said. "Take my word for it. Right now I gotta go."

Charlie packed a few supplies into a backpack and left the mine. Two hours later he was in Tortilla Flat. He grabbed a bite to eat and drove his pickup toward

Apache Junction. Once he was sure that he was out of the mountainous terrain and had good cellular reception, he pulled off the road and made a call to Idaho. His call was answered by an answering machine. Charlie spoke three numbers and hung up. Forty-five minutes later, his cellular phone rang.

"Oh-four," Charlie spoke into the mouthpiece.

"Four minus three," came the reply.

"General Boone," Charlie said, the identification complete. "It's good to hear your voice. I wouldn't be calling, but I think that something happened that you should know."

"Go ahead," the general ordered. "But keep it brief. I don't want this line open any longer that necessary."

"Yes, sir!" Charlie said. "I think that the mine has been compromised. We have evidence that someone was reading the shipment sheets and we think that all of us were rendered unconscious during our watches. We woke up with unexplained severe headaches."

"That's serious," the general said. "We can't take any chances at this point. We're almost ready to launch the main operations."

"Yes, sir! That's why I called right away."

"This could change a lot of things. I need a little time to think," the general said. "Stay where you are. I'll get back to you within the hour."

The phone went dead.

CHAPTER TWENTY-NINE

Little Jim Plover put the telephone receiver back into its cradle. He slid deeper in his chair. Beads of perspiration appeared on his forehead. He placed his fingers under his chin and remained in that position for the next fifteen minutes.

What the hell was that all about? he thought. This damn Murphy thing must have unnerved that wimpy coroner. Now, what the fuck am I supposed to do?

It was obvious to him that he had to call Slick Burleson. He dreaded the call. He had seen Slick react to bad news on other occasions and it hadn't been pretty. He finally decided on a plan of attack and dialed. It took a few minutes to get through the several layers of insulation the shielded Burleson from the outside world. Finally, Plover heard the awesome voice.

"Yeah!"

"Plover here,"

"Make it quick!"

"I gotta see you."

"Why?"

"I don't think that I should say over the phone. How about lunch?"

"Okay! The Branding Iron at noon tomorrow!"

The phone went dead before Plover could say another word.

*

Plover was ushered into the dark private recesses of the Branding Iron at exactly twelve o'clock. He had to look hard to see who was sitting in the corner booth.

"Where the hell ya been?" Burleson greeted him.

Plover slid into the booth opposite him without answering. They both ordered steak, rare, bourbon and branch water. They were on their second drink when the food arrived. They ate in silence. Burleson pushed his half-finished steak to the edge of the table and pulled out a cigar.

"Well, what's so all-fired important?" he said as he moistened the end of the Cuban.

"Late yesterday morning, I got a call," Plover said. pushing his empty plate to where it would be picked up by a busboy. He reached in his breast pocket and extracted a cigarette and a lighter. As he flipped the lighter open he felt a restraining hand on his arm.

"Sorry, sir, but this is a non-smoking restaurant."

He looked across the table at Burleson, who was rolling his cigar around his mouth. He extracted it and displayed a chewed end. He held the wet and mangled cigar up for Plover to see and gave a small shrug of his shoulders. Plover returned his lighter to his pocket while depositing the unused cigarette in the leftovers on his plate.

"As I was saying," he continued. "Yesterday morning, I got a call that I think you'll be interested in."

"Yeah? Tell me about it."

"It was from Dr. James Blackwell, the coroner."

"I know who he is!" Burleson derided. "What the fuck was he calling you about?"

"I never found out. I just chewed his ass out for calling and hung up."

"Are you sure it was him?"

"I never met him or talked to him in my life," Plover said. "How would I know if it was him or not? The call came from his office. I checked my caller ID. And my secretary said that his secretary placed the call."

"Okay! Okay! Let's get this straight. Blackwell calls you and doesn't say anything and you hang up on him?"

"I didn't say that he didn't say anything," Plover corrected. "Yeah, he said something. Let me think. He said something like, 'How's everything on your end?'"

"How's everything on your end? What the fuck is that supposed to mean?" Burleson exploded. "I think that the son of a bitch has flipped. That dumb bastard of a sheriff might be right. He told me that he thought that Blackwell was going off the deep end and losing what little nerve he had in the first place."

"Well, what should we do, now?"

"You don't do nothin'. I'll take care of it!" Burleson stood up without another word and left the restaurant and the check.

Back in his office, Burleson wasted no time in dialing Sheriff Saunders in Apache Junction. The sheriff listened intently as the situation was explained to him.

"Ya'll just forget all about it," he said. "I'll take care of the whole thing."

The sheriff hung up the phone, waited for less than a minute and dialed an unlisted number in Idaho. The conversation was short and concise. Saunders replaced the receiver, sat back and reflected on his instructions. I'm not surprised, he mused. That Blackwell was beginnin' to get on my nerves, anyhow.

CHAPTER THIRTY

L auri Beth was up early. She had the coffee brewing and was in the first stages of preparing poached eggs, waffles and sausages. While she was opening the frozen waffle package, she reached over the counter and switched on the TV. The local news was just coming on. In Arizona all news was considered local. The beginning of World War Three would take a back seat to the opening of a strip mall. The weather lady was predicting another day in the low 120s. The teaser to keep viewers interested through a series of commercials was being announced.

"Local official found dead in his home. Suicide suspected," the anchor said. "Right after this."

"Kevin!" she called. "Breakfast on the table in a couple of minutes."

By the time Kevin entered the room, Lauri Beth was placing the waffles on their plates, pouring orange juice and coffee and waiting for the eggs and sausages to finish cooking. As she finished serving, the TV screen switched to the morning commentators. The man announced a few trivial news items and turned to watch his partner deliver the next story.

"In a late-breaking story," she said, her face taking on the visage of a carrier of important news. "Dr. James Blackwell was found dead in his home this morning. He lived in a luxurious home located in the foothills of the Superstition Mountains. He was found by Sheriff Peter Saunders early this morning when he failed to answer the door in response to the sheriff's continued efforts to rouse him for a scheduled meeting."

Two forks simultaneously bounced off the breakfast table an landed on the floor. Kevin and Lauri Beth looked at each other with blank stares.

"My God!" Lauri Beth said.

The commentator continued to describe the coroner's death. The sheriff appeared on the screen with a mike at his chest held by the interviewer.

"First indications point to a heart attack," Pete Saunders said. "There was no sign of violence. It appears that the good doctor was distraught over personal matters. I've known him for a long time and I can testify to the fact that, of late, he has been extremely nervous and edgy. The people have lost a valued servant."

An unseen party asked a question.

"No, we haven't definitely established the cause of death, the investigation is still under way and will probably be concluded after the autopsy," the sheriff responded.

A few questions later, and after a panoramic view of the late coroner's estate, the news changed to another subject promising to return if anything further broke.

"I just can't believe it!" Lauri Beth said. "I was talking to him just last week. I have to admit that he seemed nervous and I think that he's lost some weight. But this! I'd never have thought! I'd better call in." She looked at her watch. "At about nine o'clock," she concluded.

"Well, well, well," Kevin said. "First, you think something's wrong with Brian's death. Then, we find the mine and figure that something illegal or at least highly suspicious is going on. Then, we find that one of the people connected with the mine has been murdered. Now, after we fake a call from the coroner to another guy associated with the mine, the coroner turns up dead. Very, very strange!"

"And don't forget that those two guys that I saw with the coroner and the sheriff were in the mine," Lauri Beth added.

"No question that we have to get back in there," Kevin said. "I've got to figure a way to talk to that old guy. Maybe he can shed some light on this whole thing."

"Do you have the feeling that there's much more to this than we think?" Lauri Beth asked. "Like maybe we're only seeing the tip of the iceberg?"

"Yeah! I got that same feeling," Kevin agreed.

It was approaching 8:45 and Lauri Beth couldn't wait any longer. She picked up the phone and called the office.

"Hello. This is Lauri Beth. Yes, I know. Isn't it awful? Could you put me through to Doctor Riggles?"

"He's the assistant coroner and will be taking over for a while, I suppose," she whispered to Kevin as she waited for her call to be transferred.

"Doctor, it's me, Lauri Beth."

"Yes, I just saw it on television."

"Yes, yes, I see!"

"Of course, I understand."

"Will this afternoon be all right?"

Lauri Beth gently replaced the receiver.

"They want me to come back to work until things settle down," she said. "I won't be able to get free until the weekend."

"You gotta do what you gotta do!" Kevin said. "I should be able to do what I have to do at the mine while you're at work. See what you can find out. I've got a sneaking suspicion that your boss didn't die of natural causes."

"I was kind of thinking the same thing," she said.

Lauri Beth wasn't feeling too enthusiastic about going back to work and Kevin wasn't feeling too good about going to the mine without her. They both were beginning to sense that they were a good team.

"I'll take Tilly," Kevin said, referring to the Morgan mare. "I plan on leaving tomorrow and I should be gone for only two or three days. Do you think that you can be here on Saturday and Sunday?"

"It would take a team of wild horses to keep me away. Turn the answering machine on when you go and I'll leave a message on it when I'm sure."

"Okay, I'll see you in a couple of days," he said.

They kissed hard and long. She let her hand drag along his arm and linger momentarily on his fingers as she reached the door.

Lauri Beth drove her car, a little foreign 4X4, to the coroner's office in sort of a daze. The latest turn of events had overwhelmed her and she was barely returning to reality when she parked her car and entered the office. A chorus of "Hi's" and "Good to see you's" greeted her as she went to her office.

Nobody seems to be as upset as I feel, she thought. Is it just me or did they have time to talk about it and get used to it?

A tall, good-looking, clean-shaven man in a green working smock was waiting for her as she entered her office.

"Good afternoon, Lauri Beth," he said.

"Good afternoon, Dr. Riggles," she returned. "Sorry I wasn't here when all this happened. What do you want me to do?"

"Get your working clothes on," he ordered. "We've got an autopsy to perform and I've got some special instructions from Sheriff Saunders."

"Oh?"

"Yeah, get this," Riggles continued. "Everything has to go through the sheriff, not the sheriff's office, but the sheriff personally. Not only that, but we're to do all lab work in house, nothing goes out to an independent facility. And he wants a rush on the whole procedure."

"That's weird. What's his reason?"

"He claims that the coroner was a close friend of his and he wants to be sure that everything is done properly," he said.

"Well, let's get started, then," Lauri Beth said.

The autopsy took three hours. When it was over Dr. Riggles started to clean up.

"Please get the report done as soon as possible," he said. "I don't want Saunders breathing down my neck."

"Me neither," Lauri Beth agreed.

Riggles left the room to change clothes and Lauri Beth went to her desk and began writing the report. It would show death due to coronary failure. She heard the outer door close and went directly to the specimen locker. She pulled a small vial from her pocket and put a dab of Dr. Blackwell's blood in it. The vial went to the bottom of her purse and she went back to the lab.

The autopsy report was on Dr. Riggles' desk when he arrived the next morning. He read it over carefully and called the sheriff. He confirmed the findings and arranged for a copy to be hand-delivered to the sheriff's office.

Sheriff Saunders personally signed for the coroner's report. He sat down at his desk and read the entire findings. Satisfied with the contents, he filed the report in his desk drawer and returned to the work in front of him. His desk was covered with records from US West, the local telephone company. He was particularly interested in one phone call that was made from the coroner's office to Dallas.

"Well, I reckon that this is it," he said to himself. "It's the right day and looks to be about the right time. Let's see, here, it was placed on the general number but their system still charges any outgoing long distance call to a particular instrument. Number 0317! Now who could that be?"

Saunders checked a list of about fifty numbers.

Number 0317. Here it is. Ms. L. McCartney. I guess I'd better find out a little about Ms. McCartney. Good place to start is right here. Lemme see. I can get a printout of all the numbers that she's called over the last month. Maybe that'll tell me something.

A few minutes later, Saunders had his printout. It didn't take him long to find a number that recurred with some frequency. He placed a call, identified himself and received the answer to his question.

"Brian Nichols! Now where have I heard that name before?" he pondered. "And this address is way the hell out in the northwest part of the county."

He sat perfectly still, letting his thoughts and memory have a free rein. Suddenly, he bolted upright in his chair.

"I got it!" he cried aloud. "I got it!" Brian Nichols was that guy that was flying around the mine, he recalled. The guy that Charlie and Butch took care of. Looks like I got some serious work ahead of me.

CHAPTER THIRTY-ONE

Kevin watched Lauri Beth pull away in her car. He was half-hoping that she would stop and come back, even though he knew she wouldn't. When her car had been out of sight for almost a minute, he turned and began preparations for tomorrow's trip to the mine. All of his equipment had to be check and double checked. Packing for this trip required less equipment than for the previous one because Kevin knew exactly what was needed. He was able to lighten the pack by almost twenty pounds, even after adding certain things that he hadn't carried the first time. He took as much time as he felt that he needed. It was mid-afternoon when he completed his packing. He still had Tilly and her trailer to get ready. He felt ready just before dinner time. After a microwaved meal, he picked up the phone and dialed Lauri Beth. No answer. He left a message to call him and turned in. He set the alarm for four o'clock in the morning and let sleep envelop him.

Two hours later he was jolted into consciousness by a loud ringing. It took a few moments for him to realize that it was the telephone and not the alarm clock.

"Hi, sweetheart!" Lauri Beth said. "Hope I didn't wake you but I just got in the door."

"It's okay," Kevin said. "I wanted to talk to you anyway. Busy at work?"

"I'll say," she answered. "You wouldn't believe what's going on here. Sheriff Saunders has taken over. He wants everything to go to him and him only. I'm beginning to feel that our call to Dallas might not have been such a good idea."

"Listen!" he said. "That phone call was a great idea. If it had anything to do with Dr. Blackwell's death, we're on to something big. Speaking of that call. Are you sure that it can't be traced to your phone?"

"I didn't think about it at the time, because I was concentrating on the caller ID thing from the Dallas end. But if anyone checked our internal records, they could find out which individual phone the call came from."

"Uh-oh," he warned. "We better assume that we've been made. If anyone asks you about the call, just play dumb. Anybody could have made the call from your phone. Too bad you finished those reports. That puts you in the office at the time the call was made. Let's just hope that we're wrong and the connection hasn't been put together."

"That makes me feel a lot better," Lauri Beth said. "Now listen! One of the reasons I was late is because I took an extra sample of blood and stayed in the lab to analyze it. There's a trace of metacorathrombustate, the same drug that killed Brian."

"Now I'm getting mad," Kevin said. "I don't think that you should call here for a while, at least until we know for sure if we've been made. I'll call you at your house when I get back and we'll compare notes. Don't come by here either. I'm going to take your gear and both horses with me and I'd better secure the pictures as well."

"I'm beginning to get a little bit scared," she confessed. "I'd better let you get back to sleep. Good night, sweetheart!"

"Good night, sweetheart! I'll see you in a couple of days!"

The rest of the night wasn't as restful as the part before Lauri Beth's call. Nevertheless, the alarm caught Kevin asleep. He was about a half an hour behind schedule when he finally pulled out of the driveway. He hadn't counted on packing Lauri Beth's gear, hiding the photographs and sealing the doors of the house with Scotch tape to discover if it had been broken into.

In spite of his late start, Kevin arrived at the turnoff slightly ahead of his planned time.

The second time is always quicker, he thought as he readied Tilly for the overland ride. The sun was dropping behind the mountains as Kevin took up his position outside of the entrance to the mine. He checked his night-vision helmet and pulled a new piece of equipment from his pack. He plugged a very compact audio-focusing unit into his headset and began scanning the opening in front of him. He already was aware that this trip wasn't going to be as easy as the last one. The guard at the entrance was facing directly toward him. He could pick out a cup in his hand, probably coffee. There was no sign of sleeping bags, and an automatic rifle was propped against the stone wall within easy reach of the guard. The demeanor of the guard was professional. He was alert and wary. A pistol was holstered on his right side and the flap had been turned under, allowing for quick extraction.

A movement inside the tunnel alerted Kevin to the approach of another person. He checked his watch. Eight o'clock! A routine changing of the watch! Kevin focused his audio receiver on the guard.

"That you, Bubba?" he heard.

"Yeah, Butch. I'll take the watch," Bubba said. "Your turn with the perfesser."

"Yeah! Yeah! I know, goddam it! I sure wish Charlie would get back. I could use an extra four off," Butch said.

"Me too!" Bubba replied. "I thought that he was due back yesterday. Whatta ya supposed happened?"

"He shouldda been back before that. I don't know. Could be anything. Keep an eye out for him. He wouldn't like it if you plugged him!" Butch joked.

"Ha ha!" Bubba said as Butch disappeared into the interior of the mine.

Kevin had a problem. The mine entrance was fairly spacious but left no room to maneuver when guarded by an alert sentry. He settled in, waiting for an opportunity to present itself. An hour and a half had elapsed and Kevin was beginning to think that he would have to create a small diversion to get past Bubba, when he heard a noise from behind him off to his right side. He turned cautiously and focused in the direction of the sound. His infrared goggles picked up the figure of a man walking along the granite rim of the canyon bowl. Bubba hadn't seen the man as yet, but he sensed something. His body was tense and the carbine was no longer leaning against the wall. Bubba scanned the perimeter of his responsibility until he focused on the movement of the man. He brought the carbine up to his shoulder and shouted, "Who goes there!"

"Charlie Whitfield," came the reply. "Hold your fire!"

"Show yourself!" Bubba ordered.

A flashlight blinked fifty yards from the entrance.

"Advance and be recognized!" Bubba said.

Kevin was impressed by the military aspect of the exchange. It was far different than he had expected from his earlier experience at the mine. He quickly stowed his gear and inched his way closer to the entrance.

The intruder was now less than fifty feet from Bubba. He was shining the flashlight directly in his own face.

"Okay, Charlie," Bubba said. "I can see it's you. Come on in!"

"Thanks!" Charlie said as he advanced.

"Where the hell ya been all this time?" Bubba asked.

"It wasn't my doing," Charlie explained. "All hell is about to break lose. We gotta have a little conference.

Where's Butch and Jasper?"

"Butch's on watch with the perfesser and Jasper got four off," he answered, following Charlie into the mine. They had gone nearly twenty yards in when Charlie suddenly stopped.

"I guess I'll have to brief you one at a time," he said. "You better get back on watch. We can't afford another security breach."

His advice came about thirty seconds too late. By the time Bubba returned to his post, Kevin was well inside and invisible against the rock-and-timber interior of the mine. He stealthily trailed Charlie back to the lab and waited as Charlie addressed Butch. He was close enough that he didn't need his listening device as both men's voices were resonating off the granite walls.

"What kept ya?" Butch asked.

"It was one thing after another ever since I left," Charlie explained. "First I call the general and tell him about somebody maybe being in the mine. He takes it pretty well and tells me to wait for a hour and he'll call me back. I wait for an hour and a half and he finally gets in touch with me. He says that I gotta wait until the next day and he'll call me again. So he does and this time he's really upset. He's cussin' up a storm. He says that the coroner or somebody has called Plover and that it looks like everything is fallin' apart. He tells me to stay where I am and he'll get back. So I wait and I wait. Finally he calls again. He tells me that Blackwell's dead and he's gonna have to start things rollin' whether he wants to or not."

"What the fuck does that mean?" Butch snarled. "We been sittin' in this hole for most of two years and I still don't have clue of what's goin' on. We go out there and get us a bunch of coyotes and the perfesser works on them and then some militia guys come and get them and take them who knows where and then the perfesser make a batch of his goddam joy juice and we send it off to Texas and then we do it all over again. Now you tell me that the goddam general might have to start things rolling and I say, 'What the fuck does that mean?'"

"It means that there's a hell of a lot that you don't know and some that I don't know either," Charlie said. "There's some stuff I can tell you now and some that I can't."

It happened so quickly that Kevin was taken by complete surprise. Charlie was pinned against the stone wall. Butch had him spread-eagled and a double-edged hunting knife was creasing the skin just below Charlie's right ear.

"Now you listen to me!" Butch breathed into Charlie's face. "I ain't spent all this time not to be gettin' something outta it. I want to know what the payoff is and I want to know what my share is gonna be."

The knife pressed a little and the point broke Charlie's skin at his jawline.

"Butch! What's going on here? I thought you knew we were doing this for the cause."

"Fuck the cause!" Butch said. "I don't even know what the cause is anymore. I joined this outfit to screw the goddam government. Now, I want something outta it for number one!"

"I'll tell ya everything I know," Charlie whispered. "Just put that knife down and get away from me."

"I'll think about it!" Butch said as he pulled the knife back far enough to let Charlie's skin straighten out. A trickle of blood ran down Charlie's neck and under his collar. "Start talkin'!"

"Goddam it, Butch! I swear I don't know what's come over you! Just give me some breathin' room and I'll tell you everything I know!"

Butch released his grip on Charlie, but kept the knife a few inches from his face. Charlie pulled back as far as he could. Butch was still restraining him, but he was able to see Butch's eyes. Even in the darkness of the mine, Butch's eyes were those of a demon, wild and demented. Charlie took a deep breath. He had heard that Butch was unstable and violent, but in his two years of being with him, Charlie had only seen small evidence of these traits. Now, he was experiencing the full outer edge of Butch's personality. He was scared and doing his best not to show it.

"Okay! Here's what's been happening!" Charlie began, trying to cover the shakiness that he felt in his voice. "You remember that we took over here at the mine about two years ago?"

Butch nodded.

"Well, this operation started nearly three years before we got here," Charlie continued, still a bit shaky. "We're the third shift. Anyhow, about five years ago the general came across the professor. I'm not sure how they met, but I think Saunders had something to do with it. The professor was working in a lab for some big drug company. He was specializing in genetics and during the course of his experimenting he discovered a serum that caused mice to become sterile. For some reason, the powers in the drug company weren't interest in the discovery. But that didn't stop the professor. He continued his experimenting on his own time and developed it to a point that is was effective on any four-legged animal, large or small.

"Well, Ole Dan'l was real interested in the professor's discovery. He convinced the professor that he could make him rich, but he needed an antidote. So the professor gets busy and develops one. By now, General Boone has got a plan pretty well worked out. He needed a way to distribute the serum on a national basis, and the professor comes up with the idea of turning the serum into a virus. That's all the general needs. His plan is simple. He is in a position to cause a rapid decline in the birth rate of four-legged animals. Saunders contacts the cattlemen in Dallas and shows them how the militia can spread the virus through infected coyotes and how they can inoculate their herds against the virus and profit from skyrocketing meat prices. The Dallas guys go for it and the operation begins.

"At first the goal is just to make a lot of money to finance the militia. The general sends some men down here to collect some coyotes. The general and the professor have decided that coyotes would make the perfect carrier of the virus . They are the only predator increasing in numbers and they are found in all forty-nine of the North American United States, as well as Canada and Mexico. As in many cases, the carrier is immune to the virus he is transporting.

"The first group of militia begins to trap coyotes in the Superstition Mountains. During the course of their work they stumble on this mine. The general decides to make the mine the base of his operations. He sends the professor down and supplies him with everything that he needs. The professor doesn't mind the isolation. He's so wrapped up in his work that he actually likes the seclusion.

"You know how it works. The coyotes are brought in, the professor injects them with the virus, the militia collects them, takes them around the country and releases them. The coyotes travel around the country spreading the virus, meat production goes down and prices go up. The guys in Dallas have immunized their herds. They devise a scheme to market their cattle without calling attention to the fact that their numbers have not been affected. The general is selling them the antidote. It was cheap at first but the price keeps going up. The guys in Dallas start to protest, but they're hooked. They gotta pay whatever the general wants. And he wants plenty."

Kevin heard every word. All the pieces were falling into place. No wonder Brian was murdered. He could have ruined the whole money machine. But what about Murphy? Maybe he was trying to get out and they wouldn't let him. And the coroner?

Butch heard every word, too. But, he wasn't trying to piece anything together. He was thinking of the money that the general had been collecting from the cattlemen.

"Well, that there is a pretty clever scheme the general has cooked up! But when's the payoff and how much is our share?"

"There's more to it than that," Charlie tried to explain. "Ya see, General Boone has another operation going and he's using the money from here to finance it."

"Ya mean he's stealing our dough! Don't ya?" Butch growled. "He ain't gonna get away with that!"

"Hold on, Butch!" Charlie said in a low voice, trying to calm the maniac in front of him. "You still want to screw the United States government, don't ya?"

"Yeah, I guess so, but now I want to be paid for it."

"You'll be paid all right. You got my word on it."

Butch released his hold on Charlie and pushed him away. Charlie began to breathe a little easier. He was thinking that maybe Butch had better be taught a lesson, when he felt a sharp blow on his jaw and sank slowly to the floor.

"That's just so you don't get any funny ideas," Butch said to the unconscious man at his feet. "You can start your watch right here and now. I'm gonna grab some shuteye."

Butch turned and left for his sleeping bag, removing the knife handle from his fist and returning it to its sheath as he left.

Kevin watched him disappear into the darkness before he inched his way to the prostrate figure in the lab entrance. Charlie emitted a low moan just as Kevin sprayed the knockout formula into his face. Charlie settled back into a deep sleep. Kevin stepped over the body and made his way quickly into the professor's quarters. The old man was sleeping peacefully on his cot. Kevin shook him gently on the shoulder and covered his mouth at the same time. It took the old man a few seconds to realize that this wasn't an ordinary wakeup call. His eyes widened and he tried to shout an exclamation. Kevin's hand pressed harder on the old man's mouth as he released the pressure on his shoulder. Kevin placed his index finger in front of his mouth and whispered, "I'm a friend," to the unspoken question.

He could feel the old man's body relax and he cautiously removed his hand from his mouth.

"Wha....who?" the old man stammered as Kevin again signaled for silence.

"My name is Kevin Stewart," Kevin whispered. "I'm a member of the United States Army Special Forces."

Kevin made a quick scan of the person that he was restraining. He saw a frail older man, perhaps in his late sixties, although it was hard to tell because of his beard and unkempt hair. His eyes were sunken and his general physical condition was poor.

"Thank God you've come," the old man murmured. "I've been held prisoner here for almost five years. I'd given up all hope of being free again."

"Who are you?" Kevin asked.

"I'm Dr. Bernard Middlestat," the old man said. "I was working for the American Drug company in the genetic research department when I met General

Harry Boone. He convinced me that a discovery of mine was worth a lot of money commercially. My company wasn't interested, so I threw my lot in with the general. It was a big mistake."

"I guess so. Hasn't anyone been concerned with your absence?"

"I have no family or close friends," the doctor explained. "I also had a reputation of being slightly eccentric. So when I didn't show up for work, it wasn't a cause for any great concern. I suppose the company made some inquiries and then just let the matter drop."

"So you've been held here against your will?" Kevin asked.

"Absolutely! I'm afraid for my life! If I don't keep producing the virus and antidote, or if they could make them without me, I'd be dead right now."

"I'm afraid you're right," Kevin agreed. "There have been three murders or mysterious deaths already. These are desperate people."

"I know that they have been using my formulas to restrict the production of livestock," Dr. Middlestat said. "Can you tell me if it has been effective?"

"I'm afraid that it's been very effective. Meat prices have soared out of the range of the general population and the unrest in the cities has reached serious levels. Riots are a distinct possibility."

"I don't know whether to be happy or sad with that news," the old man said. "It means that my work is successful, but it also means that it has been put to criminal use."

"Can you tell me anything about what the general is planning? I overheard two of the guards talking and it appears that whatever is going to happen could take place very soon."

"I know this much," Dr. Middlestat said. "General Boone and his gang of cut-throats are planning to incite riots across the country as soon as they feel the time is ripe. From what you say, that could be almost any day."

"What do you know about this General Boone? Where is his headquarters and what does he call his outfit?"

"The general is like a will o' the wisp," the old man replied. "You don't find him. He finds you. He hides out somewhere in the northwest—Idaho or Montana. He calls his 'army' the New Revolutionary Militia. All these guys are members and I think that the one known as Charlie is pretty high up in the organization."

"There's a guy named Butch," Kevin said. "What about him?"

Dr. Middlestat pulled back at the mention of Butch's name.

"That one gives me the creeps," he said, shivering at the thought. "I feel that he'd just as soon slit your throat as look at you. He's just a strong arm. I wouldn't trust as far as I could throw him. I have a feeling that Charlie doesn't trust him either."

"Is there anything else?"

"Yes, there is," Dr. Middlestat whispered. "but I can't put my finger on it right now. It's got something to do with the general's big-picture plan. I'll think of it! It's right on the tip of my tongue."

"I don't think that we can wait around until your memory comes back, Doctor. I'd better find a way to get us out of here. Wait right where you are! I'm going to scout deeper in the mine and see if there isn't another way out."

Before Dr. Middlestat could focus on his liberator, Kevin was gone. He could feel an air flow moving toward the rear of the mine. He engaged his infrared goggles and moved with the current. The shape of the mine became more and more irregular as he got deeper into it. Shafts went off to the left and right, but the airstream continued to lure him on. He came to what appeared to be the end of the main tunnel. As he reached the far wall, he could see a cave carved out of the solid stone to his left. He moved cautiously into the shallow indentation. The floor seemed to slope away from him. He took two steps forward and stood perfectly still. He sensed that the next step could be dangerous. He looked down, but the night-vision glasses didn't pick up any sharp distinctions. Still, he hesitated to proceed. Kevin got down on his hands and knees. He could feel the air flowing past him but it seemed to be going downward. He crept forward, feeling with his hands. Suddenly his lead hand fell on empty space. He caught himself before his momentum carried him any further. He peered through his infrared goggles and finally was able to make out the outline of a hole. The sides were cut at such an angle that they were almost invisible and the edges were so sharp that the delineation from the floor was imperceptible. Now that he was aware of the excavation, he could begin to make out its proportions. It appeared to be about five feet in diameter. He peered over the edge and couldn't see the bottom. Scanning the sides of the hole, he began to visualize the shaft. The diameter of the hole was fairly uniform and there were horizontal tunnels dug into the sides at various levels. These tunnels appeared to be of an exploratory nature and were no more than crawl spaces. The miners had apparently followed traces of gold but gave up either because the veins gave out or the ore content was too small.

The air was definitely turning down the shaft. Kevin extracted a small pressure can from his pack, pointed it down the well and pushed the spray top. A wisp of red smoke emerged from the diffuser. The smoke was drawn downward about fifteen feet and then disappeared into one of the lateral openings.

Kevin removed a line and a wedge from his pack. He found a crevice to the rear of the hole and just above the main floor. He secured the wedge and attached one end of the line to it. He stuffed a few items into his pockets and tied the backpack to the other end of the line. He lowered the pack into the hole. The line was fully uncoiled and there was still pressure on it. That meant that the shaft was at least a hundred and fifty feet deep. A few deep breaths later, Kevin was over the side. He dropped to a point just below the horizontal opening that the aerosol had disappeared into. He pulled himself up so that he could reach into the crawl space. He found a handhold and proceeded headfirst into the small tunnel. The dimensions of the passage-way barely allowed him to crawl on his hands and knees. In this position, he was unable to lift his head high enough to see straight forward. He inched ahead using the sixty degrees of vision that was allowed him. His helmet was scraping the top of the tunnel. Suddenly, he felt the pressure release. His head was in some sort of vertical column. He estimated that he had come some fifty feet and that there was another ten feet or so to the end. Kevin squirmed until he was on his back looking directly upward. The chimney appeared to be about three feet in diameter and extended up nearly forty feet. There was a slight glow at the top.

He braced his back against one side and began to climb. At the top, he found a shelf that went laterally some three feet and then the chimney continued. As he wormed his way into the upper section of the chimney, he noted a distinct brightness, so much so that he dis-engaged the infrared goggles. Fifty feet later, Kevin emerged into the fresh desert air.

The moon was three quarters full and bright enough to supply the light that Kevin had seen inside. He sat down, removed his helmet and began to summarize his situation. He estimated that he was about eighty feet above the entrance to the mine. The column that he had ascended was probably dug as a supplemental air shaft. The shelf was either the result of the shaft being dug from both ends or was purposely designed as a rain diverter. From the accumulation of dust and lack of any evidence of recent use, Kevin decided that his hosts were unaware of the excavation.

He reached into a leg pocket and withdrew his cell phone. He realized that both his and Lauri Beth's phones could be tapped but the chance that their cellular phones were being listened to was very remote. He dialed Lauri Beth and waited. It was nearly midnight. He hoped that she had left her phone on. Even if she hadn't, she had US West messaging and Kevin could leave a memo. After what seemed an eternity, the message service came on the line. Kevin mouthed an "Ah nuts!" and collected his thoughts.

"It's almost midnight," he said. "I've found another way out of the mine." He gave the coordinates from his GPS as well as the altitude. "I'm about eighty feet higher than the main tunnel at the top of an air shaft. I got to the old man. See what you can find out about a Dr. Bernard Middlestat. I'm going to try to get him out. I'll call you after I get home. Cell phones only. I love you!"

Kevin replaced the phone and sat down to rest for a minute. He began to consider his message to Lauri Beth. I think I told her that I loved her, he thought. I wonder if that was very smart. Maybe it wasn't such a good idea to leave it as a phone message. She probably would have liked to hear it from me in person, if she wanted to hear it at all. It just kind of came out. I hope I didn't screw up. Oh, well! Back to business.

He rechecked his gear and headed for the airshaft. It didn't take Kevin long to retrace his steps down the shaft, through the crawl space, and back up to the main tunnel. He pulled up his line and removed the backpack. He gently lowered the line back down the shaft. He worked his way to the lab. The entrance was unguarded. He adjusted his infrared goggles and slipped into Dr. Middlestat's quarters. The old man was completely under the covers. Kevin marveled at the professor's ability to sleep when he knew that rescue was imminent. Kevin reached out and gently shook the doctor's shoulder.

The bed exploded in a flurry of covers. Kevin was immediately blinded as a powerful light was trained directly into his eyes. He felt as if a branding iron had been shoved into his face. The pain started at the bridge of his nose and it penetrated to the back of his brain. He felt his helmet being pulled from his head. Then an exterior agony, matching the one already inside his head, erupted into his vanishing consciousness as a blunt object crashed against his skull.

"Har! Har! How do ya like that headache, ya son of a bitch?" was all he heard as darkness replaced the pain.

Chapter Thirty-two

Sheriff Saunders pulled up in front of the modest ranch house and surveyed the situation. He had called three times and received no answer. He had done two drive-bys and had been able to study all four sides of the residence. He called one more time with the same results. He got out of the car, reached into the back seat and removed a black satchel.

The sheriff was dressed in jeans, flannel shirt and western boots. He wore a large-brimmed hat pulled well down over his forehead. The car that he had just left was his personal vehicle, a three year old Chevy. He approached the front door without hesitation and rang the bell. No answer. He rang two more times before he was convinced that the house was unoccupied. He pulled an assortment of burglar's tools from his pocket and had the front door unlocked and open in short order. Once inside, he made a quick search of the interior. Satisfied that he was alone, his search became more thorough. He went through every room, pulling drawers and emptying their contents on the floor. He did the same with the closets. It wasn't until he was vandalizing the kitchen that he found what he was looking for. Hidden under the container that held the everyday eating utensils was a manila envelope. It had fallen to the floor when he had overturned the drawer. Saunders opened the envelope and pulled out the contents. He spread out the photographs on the kitchen counter and smiled. He was right. That girl from the coroner's office and/or her boyfriend had been in the mine and probably knew a lot more than they should. He knew how to take care of that. If he was lucky, he could literally kill two birds with one stone.

Saunders knew what he was going to do long before he had entered the house. He wasn't worried about the mess that he made during his search. The best forensics expert in the world wouldn't be able to tell what the inside was like before the explosion. First, he turned off every pilot light inside the house. Then, he picked up his bag and went to the gas-burning combination oven and range top. Saunders pulled the unit away from the wall and found what he was hoping for, a tee fitting with one end capped. He took a small wrench from his bag and took off the cap. A rush of propane gas hit his nostrils and began to fill the room. He quickly pushed the stove back into place and went to the back door. He placed an ignition device against the bottom of the door. This apparatus was set to create a spark if was moved even slightly. The igniter that he placed on the front door was different from the one on the rear. This one had a long thin wire protruding from the lower edge. Before the sheriff closed the front door, he laid the wire across the threshold. After the door was closed and locked, he pulled the wire until he could feel the instrument seated against the door. One more pull brought the wire under the door and the device was armed. Now it would act just as the one in the rear of the house. Saunders wound the wire into a coil and stuffed it in his pocket. He strolled back to his car with a satisfied smug on his face.

Driving back to his house, Saunders decided that he should check in with the boys at the mine. He dialed a paging service and placed a message on Charlie Whitfield's pager. He was pulling into his driveway when his phone rang.

"Saunders, here," he growled into the cell phone.

"It's Charlie. How's the reception?"

"Good."

"I'm making this call from just outside the entrance," Charlie said. "We got some stuff going on here and I didn't want to go all the way back to Tortilla Flat."

"Yeah! What exactly have you got going on?"

"Well, we caught some guy in the mine. Butch knocked him cold. I think that he was trying to get the professor. You should see this guy. He's camouflaged so good you can hardly see him if you're standing right in front of him. I think he's some sort of special forces guy. You oughtta see the stuff that he's got on him. I'm tellin' you that he came prepared."

"Any idea who he is?"

"No ID! What do ya think we oughtta do with him?"

"Well, I gotta idea who he is! Keep him tied up and under guard. Have you told the general yet?"

"No! It takes too long to get hold of him. I didn't want to be away that long," Charlie said. "Besides, I'm supposed to contact him tomorrow, anyway."

"You stay put," Pete ordered. "I'll talk to the general. I know he'll be interested in this. I'll be out there tomorrow and I think I'll have some special orders that'll include our friend and the whole operation."

"Okay, Pete," Charlie said. "Oh! There's one more thing that you should tell the general."

"What's that?"

"Well, it's Butch. He's been acting real strange lately. He jumped me and I thought he was gonna slit my throat. Then he starts talking about what's in it for him. I think that Butch's outta control."

"Yeah, thanks," Saunders said. "I'll be sure to mention that to the general."

"See ya tomorrow," Charlie said as he broke contact and headed back into the mine.

"Yeah. Tomorrow," Pete answered.

Saunders was well into his house by the time the conversation ended. He turned off the cell phone, pulled a beer from the refrigerator and settled in to do some serious thinking. He had been elevated to his present position when the general got the idea using the virus to control meat production. The fact that the main theater of operations was to be in central Arizona was probably more responsible for his promotion than was his record. He had been a loyal member of the militia since its inception. Even though he was part of the local government, he hated the national bureaucracy and its constant intrusion at the state and county level. He had seized the opportunity that was offered to him and had quickly involved the coroner. It had been a good move and Blackwell had proven a valuable asset when Brian Nichols had stumbled on to their operation but, when the coroner started to panic, Saunders had no compassion or reluctance to carry out his deadly orders. That was the third murder that he had been involved in and he felt no remorse for any of them. Now, things were coming to a head and he intended to see that there were no foul-ups that fell under his command.

Saunders organized his thoughts and began the routine that would bring him in contact with General Boone. Thirty minutes after he made his first connection, the phone rang, precisely on schedule

"Three!" Saunders said.

"Three minus two!" came the reply.

"Glad to hear your voice, General," Saunders began. "We've got a situation down at the mine that you should be aware of."

"I know that the mine could have been compromised and I know that I'm right in the middle of directing the biggest operation in the history of revolutionary antigovernment actions. Make it quick, Pete."

"As quick as I can, General. The mine has not only been compromised, but we've caught the intruder."

"What! You mean that someone actually wandered into the mine?"

"Not wandered!" Saunders emphasized. "Penetrated! This guy looks like a special forces character. Camouflage clothes, face paint, night-vision goggles, the whole works. I don't think we would have got him if Butch hadn't been suspicious of the way the professor was acting and beat him until he talked."

"Any ID on him?"

"Nope! But I gotta pretty good idea who he is!" Saunders bragged. "I did some checkin' on my own, before I heard that Charlie and Butch had captured this guy."

"Yeah...?" the general encouraged.

"Yeah! I got a little suspicious about that phone call from Blackwell to Murphy. I found that it came from a phone in the coroner's office, all right, but it wasn't from Blackwell's own phone. It came from the office of his assistant, a Lauri Beth Mc- somethin'-or-other. Then I did some checkin' on her calls. She's been making a lot of calls out to the house of one Brian Nichols."

"Brian Nichols? That sounds familiar."

"I thought so, too," Saunders said. "Brian Nichols is the guy that Charlie and Butch knocked off. The guy that was flying around the mine lookin' for the Lost Dutchman's diggin's."

"He's dead! What's she calling out there for?"

"I think that she's gotta boyfriend and he's livin' out at the Nichols place. I'd lay odds that this is the guy they've got at the mine."

"Doesn't matter who he is, he's gotta go and so does the dame," the general said. "Lemme think for a minute."

After two minutes of silence, Saunders broke the quiet. "General, pardon me, sir, but there's more."

"What? Okay! Go ahead, Pete, might as well hear everything at once."

"I had a talk with Charlie," Saunders explained. "He's got some problems with Butch. It seems that Butch took a knife to good old Charlie and almost slit his throat. Drew some blood, according to Charlie."

"The boys must be gettin' a little antsy, bein' holed up in that cave for so long," General Boone reasoned.

"It's more than that," Saunders continued. "Butch might be goin' off the deep end. Seems that he's gettin' interested in makin' some money out of this whole thing."

"Now why would he be thinking that?"

"I think that Charlie was on the spot and had to explain a little more of the operation to Butch. He must have told him that you were selling the serum to those guys in Texas and collecting a good price for it. Once Butch heard that money was involved, he wanted his share of it, maybe more. I tell ya, General, that Butch has always been a loose canon, as far as I'm concerned."

Saunders heard a "Hmmmmm" coming from the earpiece as the general considered his options.

"Now listen up good, Pete!" the general ordered. "I've just made a decision. There's only four of us that know the whole picture. That's Major Wheeler, Charlie, me and you. Phase one is gonna start real soon. That'll trigger phase two. We don't need them Texans anymore and that means that we don't need the mine anymore either. Ya get what I'm sayin', Pete?"

"Yeah, I understand, General! What about Charlie, Butch and the boys? And what about the professor and that special service guy and the gal?"

"I need Charlie up here with me. I want you to send him up ASAP. Then I want you to close down the mine. Permanently!"

"Okay!" Saunders said. "I got my orders. I'll need a little time to get hold some dynamite."

"You got about a week! Make sure that the professor stays with the mine, and that army guy, too, and I wouldn't cry my eyes out if Butch met with an accident during the explosion, either."

"What about the other two, Jasper and Bubba?"

"Hell, they're good soldiers. Keep them with you and I'll have something for them when you report the job done."

"Yes, sir! I'm going down there tomorrow. I'll send Charlie up to you and figure out just how I want to blast the mine."

"And, just one more thing, Pete," the General admonished. "If there's any coyotes left down there, set 'em free. I just hate to have animals suffer!"

"Yessir!" Saunders said as he cradled the receiver.

Chapter Thirty-three

Lieutenant John Bledsoe was seated behind his desk sifting through the reports that had just arrived. Casper had worked hard, long and fast. He had an inner feeling that speed was essential in this investigation.

Bledsoe had the reports sorted and laid out on his desk. He had made a quick evaluation and the results were indicative of a pattern. A pattern that involved Murphy, Plover and Burleson. He was just beginning to write the outline of a report when he was interrupted by ring on his intercom line.

"Yeah," he answered. "Okay send them in."

The door opened and Bledsoe's office was immediately filled by bodies that he didn't recognize. At the rear of the intruding group, he spotted Harold Spivey.

"Hey! Spivey!" he called. "What's this all about?"

Spivey made his way to the front of the group.

"Lieutenant," he said. "These gentlemen are from Washington. They arrived last night and were at my office at six this morning. They were expecting you to be there, too. I'm sorry but I couldn't get hold of you last night and your secretary said that you weren't to be interrupted when I called this morning."

"Lieutenant," an authoritative voice broke in. "I'm Paul Stockton, special assistant to the Secretary of Agriculture. I'm in charge of the meat-shortage investigation. I'm here in response to a telephone call from Mr. Spivey. He indicated that he had some substantial information regarding the decrease in cattle production. I have with me two members of the FBI Washington office, agents Robert Mulligan and Clancy Thomas."

The two men stepped forward and offered their hands to Bledsoe. He took them and directed his attention to the other twosome in the background.

"Oh, hi, there Greg," he said to one of them. "I didn't see you at first."

"Hi, John.," Greg responded. "Agent Mulligan brought me in. It's customary to involve the local office. I brought Willard Sponsen with me."

Bledsoe acknowledged Sponsen with a shake of his head while taking Greg Larkins' hand.

"Gentlemen, to what do I owe this honor?" he said.

"I think you already know the answer to that," Stockton said with a bit of irony in his voice. "We expected you to be at the forensics lab this morning. I hope that what you were doing justifies the delay that you're causing us."

"I'm real sorry if I've inconvenienced any of you boys from the government," he returned. "But, guess what?

I've been just a little busy findin' out some stuff that might bail ya'll out."

"And what might that be?" Stockton asked.

Bledsoe waited what seemed an eternity before he responded.

"Well, while Spivey here was calling you, I was over checking out Murphy's office. I found out a couple of things. First, there could be three of them in on whatever is going on. The other two are Little Jim Plover and Harry Burleson. I checked them out. They been thick as thieves for about three years now. The accountant over at Murphy's wasn't too cooperative, so I sent Jerry Casper and some of his boys over to check out his books. I got the preliminary reports right here on my desk. Casper thinks that Murphy was keeping two sets of books. We'll probably find the same for Plover and Burleson. It appears that Murphy has been setting up small ranches and feed lots to ship his cattle from. This explains why he's able to show a decrease in production. I think we'll find that all three have been doing the same thing. They ship their cattle from these sites and the buyers don't know that they're really part of the original herds. Not that they'd care that much in this market. I've got men out in the field right now confirming Casper's findings."

"By the way," he added. "What's the hurry on this thing?"

"Don't you guys in Texas read the papers?" Stockton said as the two FBI agents smiled derisively. "Don't you know that the country is on the verge of civil war? The cities are about to erupt. We've got to get some

positive information to the public to avoid mass rioting. The rumors are that the President is about to call
up the National Guard. He's going on national television tomorrow night. He's either going to placate the
people by telling them that we've discovered the cause
of the food shortage and that supplies and prices will
return to normal in short order, or he's going to declare
martial law."

"Martial law!" the lieutenant said. "Don't you think
that's a little extreme?"

"Dallas must be on another planet!" Mulligan broke
in. "Have you been watching the temperatures and
heat indices across the country? Don't you know that
we've been setting records from Maine to New Mexico?
Haven't you heard that road rage has doubled in the
last six months, that serious crimes, especially armed
robbery, have risen dramatically, that child and spouse
abuse is growing daily, and that general looting is taking place on an alarming basis?" He looked Bledsoe
directly in the eyes and added, "Do you think those are
reasons enough to want some quick answers?"

"All right! All right!" Bledsoe conceded. "You've made
your point. Yeah, things have gotten worse in Dallas
but I had no idea that they were so bad nationally."

"Well, you know now," Mulligan said.

"Let's get down to business," Stockton ordered, making sure that he was still in control. "I've got to get
back to the President with a report that will explain
what's been going on and how we're going to stop it.
And I've got to do it fast!"

"Okay, here's what we've got so far," Bledsoe said,

---

taking center stage. "We know, or strongly suspect, that these three cattlemen have entered into a conspiracy, with person or persons unknown at this time, to affect the breeding of large four-legged animals, specifically cattle, in such a way as to cause a sharp decline in cattle numbers. They have also developed an antitoxin that protects their own herds. Furthermore, they have created small marketing units to disguise the fact that their operations haven't been affected. The financial gains must have been incredible. We think that Murphy might have wanted out and that he may have been going to Washington to somehow inform the government."

"Wait a minute," broke in Larkins, the head of the Dallas FBI office. "Didn't you say that Murphy had a ticket to Dulles and was leaving out of National?"

Bledsoe nodded.

"Well, since he had a return ticket, that could mean that he wasn't intending to turn himself in," Larkins postulated. "If he was carrying a supply of this serum, it could mean that he was planning to turn this over to someone, maybe the Department of Agriculture, in such a way that he wouldn't be implicated."

"That would explain the motive for the robbery and the murder," Thomas, Mulligan's assistant, offered. "Whoever's behind this couldn't afford to let this serum get into the hands of the government and they knew that Murphy had become a loose cannon and had to be silenced."

"Who are *they*?" Sponsen from the local FBI office asked. "And where did this virus come from that is the cause of the breeding problem in the first place?"

"If we knew the answers to those questions, we'd have this thing solved and we wouldn't even be here," Stockton said.

"Let's start by arresting Plover and Burleson," he continued, directing his remarks to agent Mulligan.

"On what charge?" Mulligan joked. "Being associated with a murdered cattleman or giving his secretary the creeps?"

"The best we can do is to bring them in for questioning," he continued. "But if they've got any kind of legal representation, we won't have them for long and all we'll accomplish is putting them on alert that we have them under suspicion."

"What about the serum?" Stockton asked, focusing on Harold Spivey. "How quickly can we produce enough to inoculate all the cattle in the country?"

Spivey was lingering at the rear of the group and was surprised by the question as all eyes turned toward him.

"Ah," he stammered, "we don't even have a complete breakdown, yet. The small smear that we do have has only allowed us to determine some of the ingredients. The exact composition, including percentages, is going to take a little while. As far as production on a commercial scale is concerned, that's a bit out of my field, but I would guess that it won't be overnight."

"Great!" Stockton moaned. "So all I've got to take back to the President is a couple of theories and a microscopic slide of something or other."

"That's about it," Bledsoe said. "But on the bright

side, our guys in the field should have some answers in the next few days. I'm going to put the word out that I want blood samples from any cattle that have originated from any of these new sources. Spivey, here, will make a quick analysis to determine if they're carrying the antidote. If that's the case and we can prove that these are, in fact, cattle from the herds of Plover and Burleson, I think we'll have cause for some arrests."

"I don't think that possessing the serum and not sharing it is a crime, Lieutenant," Mulligan observed. "Although, we should be able to bring them in for questioning. And I think the FBI should take over at this point."

"Not that the Dallas police aren't capable," he continued, addressing Bledsoe's objections before he made them, "but, I think the FBI can be more intimidating. You will be present, of course."

Bledsoe wasn't happy but he saw the wisdom in the proposal and kept quiet.

"I guess that I can't get anymore information than I already have," Stockton complained. "So, I'm outta here. Maybe the President can calm the people enough to get through the weekend without calling up the Guard. I sure as hell wish we knew more about this virus and how it gets around."

With that comment, Paul Stockton, special assistant to the Secretary of Agriculture in charge of the meat shortage, packed his briefcase and left for the airport.

CHAPTER THIRTY-FOUR

Kevin's head felt like it had exploded. His chest was constricted by the constant pressure of having his hands tied behind his back. He lay on his right side, his face against cold stone. He didn't move a muscle or open his eyes. He kept perfectly still, allowing consciousness to creep back into his mind. As his awareness increased, so did his memory. He remembered the blinding light that pierced his brain and the sharp pain the followed. He slowly pieced together the events preceding his blackout. He recalled entering the mine and finding the airshaft. He wasn't sure but he thought that he might have called Lauri Beth before he came back down. He recalled that he had decided to take the old man out with him and that he was trying to waken him. But it ended there.

He mentally retraced his steps of the immediate past. The fight between Charlie and Butch came into focus and he remembered leaving his rope dangling into the deep shaft toward the rear of the mine. His thoughts were interrupted by some voices in the distance that seemed to be getting louder. He remained still. He knew that his chances of survival depended on how much he could learn before his captors discovered that he was awake.

Bubba and Jasper took up positions about five yards from where Kevin lay.

"That damn Butch is startin' to act as if he owned the place," Jasper said.

"Yeah," Bubba agreed. "You'd think we didn't know it was our watch back here, the way he ordered us around. I'm gettin' tired of all his bullshit. Now, we got this guy to watch along with the professor and the lab. Whatta do ya think's goin' on?"

"Dunno, for sure," Jasper said. "But we oughtta find out something pretty soon. I heard the sheriff's on his way out."

The pain of not moving had become too much for Kevin and he emitted a low moan.

"Hey! I think that guy is finally waking up," Bubba said. "Better get Charlie. I'll watch him and the professor."

Jasper disappeared and was back a few minutes later with Charlie. Charlie rolled Kevin over to get a better look at him. Kevin allowed his eyes to open slowly.

"Well, it looks like naptime's over," Charlie said.

*

Sheriff Saunders arrived at the mine completely out

of breath and physically drained. That damned two-hour hike would be the death of him. Thank God he wouldn't have to do that many more times. He provided identification to the newly alerted sentry at the mine's entrance and proceeded inside.

"Hey! Charlie!" he yelled. "It's me! Pete! I gotta talk to you."

"Over here, Pete," Charlie answered. "Be right with you."

Saunders took the time to put on a jacket, thankful that he had remembered how cold the inside of the mine was. Charlie appeared out of the semidarkness.

"Hi, Pete," he said. "What's up?"

"A lot. I just finished up a long talk with the general. We're closing down this operation. Pack your gear. You're headed for Idaho."

"I about figured as much," Charlie said. "Can't come soon enough for me. What about the other guys?"

"I got orders for them, too," Saunders said. "But, first, I'd like a peek at this guy you got collared."

"Follow me," Charlie directed and started back deeper into the mine.

When they arrived at the professor's quarters, Kevin was sitting up against the rock wall, his hands still secured behind him. Jasper was warily standing guard as if Kevin could overpower him at a moment's notice.

"So this is the tough guy," Saunders said. "Anyone ever see him before?"

Jasper shrugged. "Nope. For all we know, he just might have stumbled in here by accident. It's the damn suit and equipment that makes me suspicious. Take a look at his helmet. Looks like a damn fighter pilot's."

"Thanks, Jasper," he said. "We'll watch him for a while. You can take a break."

"This his stuff over here?" Saunders asked Charlie, as Jasper disappeared around a corner. "Looks like SWAT-team gear, only more sophisticated. He done any talkin' yet?"

Saunders picked up the helmet and examined the inside all the while emitting several "Hmmms."

"He just woke up a couple of hours ago," Charlie said. "We tried to question him but we couldn't get anything outta him."

"Don't really matter none," Saunders said. "We're closing this place down and him with it. The general is gonna start phase one on Saturday and phase two will be done early Sunday morning. That's why you're heading up to headquarters. He wants you and Wheeler with him when it all starts."

"Phase two, also," Charlie mused out loud. "All ten cities? There won't be too big a diversion up in Holtsville or Andover. We can't afford to have anything go wrong anywhere."

"Quit worrying, Charlie! It's gonna go just fine. The US Government won't know what hit it. When our guys finish in the big cities, it'll make Watts look like a kindergarten playground."

"What about the old guy?"

"He's gonna stay in the mine, too. And, get this, Ole Dan'l wants the coyotes set free. He don't want anything to happen to them."

"That won't set too well with Butch. He's been

countin' on havin' a little sport with them. You know, movin' targets and all."

"Speaking of Butch," Saunders said, moving closer to Charlie. "How do Jasper and Bubba get along with him?"

"Nobody gets along with Butch and the longer you're around him the less you like him. Why?"

"The general doesn't trust Butch too much. In fact, Butch worries him, especially since Butch started gettin' money happy. The general wouldn't be too unhappy if Butch had an accident and stayed in the mine with the other two."

"Just between you and me," Charlie whispered, "it wouldn't make me too unhappy, either."

"Well, get your gear and we'll split. You better give Butch instructions and tell him that I'll be back with the dynamite and when I do, I'll have further orders for him. Just make sure that he knows that he's in charge for now but that I'll be the boss when I get back and he'll be responsible if anything goes wrong."

Saunders was still firing questions at Kevin and getting no response when Charlie returned and announced that he was ready to leave.

"I guess that you're gonna die with your mouth closed, smart guy," Saunders said to Kevin. "Won't make any difference to us, you'll be just as dead."

He gave Kevin a brutal kick in the ribs as a parting shot. Kevin rolled onto his side and averted most of the force of the blow. He watched the two militiamen leave the cavern. Jasper returned to finish his stint of guard duty.

"Hey! You!" Kevin said. "Gimme a hand, will ya? I can't get myself back up after that son of a bitch knocked me over."

"Yeah! Yeah!" Jasper said. "I guess you might as well be comfortable. You ain't goin' anywhere, anyhow."

He reached over, grabbed Kevin by the shirt collar and pulled him into a sitting position. As he did so, Kevin slid his buttocks to his right, positioning himself at the edge of the opening to the main tunnel. His instincts told him that this was a more favorable spot to be, even though he had no real plan of escape. Kevin had been working against his bonds, but had made no progress in freeing his hands. He was resigned to hoping that his captors would have to loosen the straps before they moved him. It was at this point that he would have to make his move. If he couldn't escape, he was determined to take one or more of them with him.

An hour went by and then another. Jasper had just been relieved by Bubba, when Kevin felt something on the hair of his left wrist. He froze. A scorpion? No! The sensation increased in pressure. A small animal, perhaps a pack rat. He felt his bound wrists being moved gently forwards and back. Then, he felt the touch of cold steel against his skin. He moved his wrists back as far as he could and held his fists firmly against the rock floor. The pressure on his wrists increased and he felt the sawing object penetrate lower and lower. Then his hands were free.

He didn't move any part of his body, afraid that he might somehow give away his new-found freedom. He needed time for the circulation to return to his hands, arms and shoulders. He waited and waited. Now, the time had come.

"Hey, guard!" he said. "Could you loosen my collar button? I feel like I'm choking to death!"

"Well, we wouldn't want that to happen. Would we?" Bubba snickered.

He crossed the few yards that separated them and leaned over to check Kevin's shirt.

"What the hell are you talkin' about, boy?" he said. "Your shirt ain't even buttoned."

Bubba suddenly felt a pair of clamps on his shoulders. His head was drawn down against his will and his nose exploded as it collided with Kevin's forehead. The dizziness that followed was accompanied by vision blurred with blood. He felt himself being rolled to one side. Before he hit the ground, Bubba was aware of a pinching of the artery in his neck. Darkness descended and the pain disappeared.

Kevin swung his knees one hundred eighty degrees and extended his feet. A pair of hands came out of the darkness holding a Bowie knife. The knife slashed the bindings around his feet in one fluid motion. He got to his feet and stumbled as the circulation began to return to his legs. He turned his back to the wall and leaned against it. As he bent over to massage his ankles, a figure brushed past and knelt over the fallen guard. Bubba let out a low moan as he tried to rise. Abruptly, he collapsed and his breathing became the steady rhythm of the unconscious.

Kevin felt a steady pressure on his elbow as he was led into the darkness of the main tunnel. He turned to get a glimpse of his rescuer but saw nothing. He was given a more forceful shove and pressed on. As he was guided deeper into the mine, he slowly began to recover from the blow he had administered to Bubba. Without warning, the guiding hand on his arm became a restraining one. He felt a signal to kneel and got down on his hands and knees. A hand then closed over his own and moved it forward. The hand forced his downward and he felt nothing. He knew where he was—at the edge of the pit that led to the rear airshaft. He started to whisper something but a hand closed over his mouth and another handed him the line he had secured when he first discovered the escape route. He swung himself over the edge and descended to the tunnel that connected to the ventilating chimney. He moved into the tunnel as a body tumbled in beside him. Again he was pushed deeper into the tunnel. This time he needed no urging. He found the vertical shaft, scaled the chimney to the shelf, wiggled his way to the continuation of the chimney and soon emerged into the desert darkness. A few seconds later a figure was sitting beside him. Hands reached up and removed its helmet. Lauri Beth rubbed her eyes, shook out her hair and said, "Did you really mean it when you said, 'I love you'?"

CHAPTER THIRTY-FIVE

Harry Burleson was sitting in the middle of the room surrounded by four FBI agents, two from the local office and two from Washington, D.C. He knew who was from which office but had missed the names as they had introduced themselves. The only one he could remember was standing directly in front of him, the one from Washington who was obviously in charge, Special Agent Robert Mulligan. He found it amusing that they addressed each other as Agent This or Agent That. They never used first names and Mulligan was always responded to as Sir. He recognized the guy in the far corner as a local cop. He'd seen him before, Lt. or Sgt. Bledsoe.

As far as Burleson was concerned, they were all cops and they were all assholes. He'd figured them out immediately. They were just fishing around. If they had anything at all, he wouldn't be in an office. He'd be in an interrogation room and his lawyer would be beside him. No, he had nothing to worry about. He'd let them have their fun and he'd lead them on a couple of wild goose chases, but in the end, he'd tell them nothing and he'd be on his way.

What Burleson didn't know was that Little Jim Plover had been in the same chair a couple of hours earlier and hadn't been quite as cool or as perceptive as Burleson. The cops hadn't learned a whole lot from Plover, but he had been very nervous during his entire visit and his shirt was noticeably wet from perspiration when he left. Now, as Burleson concluded his questioning period, some obvious discrepancies appeared in the two stories.

"Well, what do you think?" Mulligan said, after Burleson had left the room.

"That's one smooth cookie," someone observed.

"Yeah, but I think the other one will crack if we can get something solid against them," another agent said.

They were busy rearranging the chairs into their normal configuration when the telephone rang. Agent Greg Larkins circled his desk and picked up the phone.

"Yeah, he's here," he spoke to the handset as he proffered it to Bledsoe.

"Bledsoe!" the lieutenant said, then waited as the secretary on the other end of the line explained the nature of the call.

"Okay, put him through," he said. Bledsoe listened and the others in the room could sense his intense interest in the call as he interspersed various "yesses," "go aheads," and "I sees" into the conversation. Finally, he lowered the handset and looked at the others.

"I'm going to put this call on the speakerphone and ask the caller to repeat what he just told me," he said. "I've been talking to Kevin Stewart. He's calling from somewhere in Arizona called the Superstition Mountains. I think that he's on a cell phone and he must be in one of the few remaining areas in the country that doesn't have 100 percent coverage."

Bledsoe switched on the speakerphone. "Kevin," he said. "I've got you on the speakerphone and I'm going to ask you to repeat what you just told me. In the room with me are Special Agents Robert Mulligan and Clancy Thomas of the Washington D.C. FBI office, and Agents Greg Larkins and Willard Sponsen of the Dallas FBI office." Everyone muttered introductions into the speakerphone.

"Gentlemen," Bledsoe continued. "I have Kevin Stewart on the line, calling from somewhere in the Superstition Mountains. He's been investigating the death of his uncle and has uncovered some very interesting facts concerning the Edward Murphy homicide and the current meat shortage. Go ahead, Kevin."

"As I told Lieutenant Bledsoe, my uncle, Brian Nichols was flying his ultralight around the Superstitions, looking for the Lost Dutchman mine."

"The what?" Special Agent Mulligan interrupted.

"The Lost Dutchman Gold Mine," Kevin explained. "It's a gold mine in the Superstition Mountains, north of Apache Junction, in the Phoenix area. A guy found it in the 1800s and when he died the location died with him. People have been searching for it ever since."

Kevin went on to explain how Brian had died, how Lauri Beth had become suspicious and how they had decided to investigate his death. Then he answered questions about the sheriff and the coroner and explained why he didn't feel safe going to the local authorities.

"We found the mine and were able to get inside, where we found some very curious things." He detailed their exploration, including the coyotes, the professor and the photographs they had taken.

Following another barrage of questions, Kevin described how they had called Plover's and Murphy's offices and discovered that Murphy had been murdered. He continued with his reasoning for contacting the Dallas police and how that call had been directed to Bledsoe.

"We've just emerged from our second visit to the mine," Kevin went on, electing to omit the part about his capture and rescue by Lauri Beth. He did, however, explain what he had learned while in the mine, concluding with their intent to reenter the mine and save the professor.

"You'd better let us handle that," Special Agent Mulligan said. "Give me those coordinates that you mentioned and I'll have a team down there in the morning."

"That'll probably be too late," Kevin said. "I think that they're planning to abandon the operation, destroy the mine and kill Dr. Middlestat. There's something else. There's a militia group involved, they could be behind everything, and they're planning to incite riots across the country over the weekend. The riots are to cover up a strike in ten cities. I didn't get what they're planning to attack, but I do know that two of the special cities are Andover, Massachusetts and Holtsville, New York. That mean anything to anyone?"

The remark drew blank looks around the room.

"Clancy," Mulligan said. "Get that information to Washington. Maybe they can figure it out. And then get me Paul Stockton."

"Mr. Stewart, is there anything else?"

"Probably," Kevin replied. "But I can't think of it right now. And, by the way, it's Sergeant Stewart, U.S. Army, special forces."

Mulligan snapped his fingers and pointed a finger at Larkins, who interpreted the signal perfectly. He left the room and found another phone line. He was back a moment later, holding his right hand in the air, thumb and forefinger forming a circle and the other three fingers pointing vertically.

"Sergeant," Bledsoe asked the speakerphone. "How can we reach you?"

Kevin rattled off his cell phone number and said, "You probably won't be able to reach me once I'm back underground. I'll shut off my ringer and leave the phone on vibration. I sure as hell don't want anyone calling me while we're penetrating mine security."

"Reinforcements should be there tomorrow," Mulligan said. "I'm turning you over to Agent Larkins. Please brief him on location and entry of the mine. And Sergeant—."

"Yes?"

"Good luck to you and Ms. McCartney!"

Mulligan looked around the room for further comments. Receiving none, he signaled for everyone except Larkins to leave the room. Larkins turned off the speakerphone, settled behind his desk and began taking notes as Kevin explained the intricacies of finding the mine.

Kevin turned off the cell phone, leaned back on his elbows and sighed.

"Well?" Lauri Beth asked.

"You heard everything, didn't you? Do you think that I left anything out?

"Not that I can think off, but I couldn't hear what they said to you."

"They're sending help, but they won't get here until tomorrow. That Saunders guy is probably on his way back with the dynamite by now. We don't have any time to spare. We'll rest for an hour and then head back down. I sure wish I had my headgear."

"Sshh," Lauri Beth whispered as she settled into Kevin's arms and pushed him gently back onto the rough ground.

CHAPTER THIRTY-SIX

Paul Stockton arrived at Washington National Airport at three o'clock in the morning. It was Friday and the President was scheduled to address the nation at seven o'clock in the evening. Stockton figured that he had enough time to get home, shower, change clothes and get back for his scheduled breakfast with the Secretary of Agriculture. He wished that he had more to report.

Stockton arrived at the Department of Agriculture at precisely six o'clock. He was quickly escorted to the Secretary's private dining room. A large table had been set with three places at one end. Secretary Harkens was seated at the head of the table. He motioned Stockton to the empty place on his right.

"Paul, this is Bill Dickson, special assistant to the President," he said, indicating the brown-haired, forty-ish man seated on his left. Paul circled the table to shake hands with Dickson.

"I'm Paul Stockton," he said. Dickson half rose to

accept the handshake and nodded to acknowledge the introduction.

Stockton sat at the place he had been assigned by the Secretary. By the time he had his napkin in place, a plate of scrambled eggs and bacon was in front of him and coffee had been poured. The Secretary allowed him a few minutes to begin his breakfast and then said to Dickson, "Paul has just returned from Dallas. The police down there have been investigating a homicide that could be connected to the cattle situation."

The Secretary and Dickson both directed their attention toward Stockton. He finished the food that he had just shoveled into his mouth, took a swig of coffee to wash it down, and directed his comments to Secretary Harkens.

"As you know, Mr. Secretary," he said. "I traveled down to Dallas in the company of two FBI agents from the Washington office. As soon as we arrived, we hooked up with two local FBI agents. The five of us met at the forensics lab of the Dallas police force. We met with a forensics expert, Harold Spivey. Spivey is a real Milquetoast kind of guy, but he knows his stuff. A Lt. John Bledsoe was supposed to be there, but didn't show up. Bledsoe is heading up the murder investigation of a cattleman, one Edward Murphy. Murphy was murdered in his parking garage. It was considered a case of random violence until it was discovered that he was heading to D.C. and that a piece of luggage he was carrying was missing. On top of that, the police discovered a smear on the concrete near the body. Spivey analyzed it as a serum or antitoxin that could fight a virus in large animals.

"That was enough to get us interested. Spivey confirmed his findings but couldn't provide us with a complete breakdown of the chemicals involved. He's personally convinced that this is the solution to the cattle problem. He also believes that it will take some time to manufacture the serum in any quantity and get it distributed.

"That was all that we could get from the forensics lab, so we took Spivey with us to Bledsoe's office. Bledsoe hadn't been idle. He had gone to Murphy's office and made the connection between Murphy and two other cattlemen, James Plover and Harry Burleson. He had also discovered some discrepancies in Murphy's books. He immediately called in accountants from the DPD and instructed field agents to look into any unusual activity relating to cattle sales or delivery. The original findings led him to conclude that Murphy, Plover and Burleson had set up dummy ranches and feed lots for the purpose of shipping cattle. The purpose was to conceal the fact that their cattle numbers hadn't been affected by the virus that was sweeping the country. Bledsoe fully expects that the investigations will confirm his suspicions. And, by the way, so does the FBI and so do I."

Stockton sat back, took a big gulp of his coffee and waited for reactions from his breakfast companions. Secretary Harkens was the first to respond.

"That's more than I expected after talking to you on your return flight," he said, glancing at Dickson, who was still engrossed in taking notes.

Dickson put down his solid gold Mount Blanc ball-point, pushed his yellow legal pad a few inches further onto the table, raised his eyes to the ceiling, and expelled a long slow breath of air. Suddenly, he bolted upright in his chair as if struck by lightning. He fixed his eyes directly on those of Secretary Harkens. His hands were on the table and he was leaning forward in strained intensity.

"By, God!" he said. "I think that we can run with that! Yes! I'm sure of it!"

Harkens and Stockton exchanged astonished looks and then focused on the President's special assistant.

"Don't you see?" he continued. "The President can claim that substantial breakthroughs have been made in the meat-shortage crisis and that supplies should be increasing and prices coming down in the very near future. He can state that, in his opinion, there is no need for calling up the National Guard. He can calm the country. He can allude to some heinous, subversive activity that he has uncovered and swear that the perpetrators will be brought to justice and punished. He can reverse the rating polls in one fifteen-minute speech. He can—"

"Don't you think that you're stretching things just a bit?" Stockton interrupted. "Most of what we've told you is conjecture. If we're proved incorrect, this could come back to bite you."

"I guess you guys never watched the President's speech writers at work," Dickson smirked. "When they get through, you won't recognize the story, the President will be hailed as the savior of the situation and won't be accountable for anything he said."

"Yes," Secretary Harkens said as he pushed his chair away from the table. "I've seen the government speech-writers at work. In fact, I've lost some sleep editing some of the things that they've written for me."

"Don't worry! We'll edit it down and the President's legal staff will make sure that he doesn't say anything that could be laid on his doorstep the next day," Dickson countered. "I'll be tied up the rest of the day with the President and his staff. President Jefferson will want at least three hours to prepare himself for the telecast."

It was approaching 9 a.m. when the meeting adjourned. Dickson left for the White House. Harkens motioned for Stockton to remain.

"I'd like you to go over that with me one more time," he said. "And I'd feel more comfortable if we had the FBI present. Do you mind?"

"Not at all," Stockton said. "The more the merrier."

"Meet me back here in an hour," Harkens said.

Stockton returned to his office to wait out the hour when his telephone rang.

"I have a Lieutenant Bledsoe from the Dallas Police Department on the line."

"Put him through."

"Paul," Bledsoe said before Stockton could even acknowledge the call. "Thank God, I've finally gotten through to you. I've been trying since early this morning. Didn't you get any messages to return my calls?"

"No! I've been in meetings all day! What's up?"

"Plenty!" Bledsoe said. "Just after you left, you were

probably on the plane, I got a call from some guy named Kevin Stewart. He was calling from the top of some mountain in Arizona and he told me a story that sounds like a sci-fi movie."

Bledsoe went on to unveil the entire episode that Kevin had related to him.

"Just a minute," Stockton said after Bledsoe had been on the phone for over an hour. "You mean to tell me that we may have solved the meat problem? How soon can we close down that operation?"

"The FBI was in my office when Stewart called," Bledsoe said. "They're in the process of sending a squad to Arizona as we speak. They should have everything under control by tomorrow or at least the day after. However, there may be a couple of problems."

"Problems? Like what?"

"Like maybe the mine is going to be destroyed and Dr. Middlestat murdered before the FBI squad can get there and maybe this whole meat thing is part of a much bigger plot to incite riots across the country and cause diversions for even more destructive acts."

"Acts? What kind of acts? And where?"

"We don't know what they're planning, but we do know that ten cities are involved and the two of them are Andover, Massachusetts and Holtsville, New York."

"And who the hell are *they*?"

"They appear to be some sort of militia group and they appear to be pretty well financed. It's possible that some of the rewards from the meat shortage have been filtered back into the militia treasury. We don't have a name or location for them, yet," Bledsoe explained. "But Stewart is going back in the mine in an attempt to rescue Dr. Middlestat before it's blown up. He doesn't think that the FBI can get there in time."

"Anything else?" Stockton said. "This is terrific stuff. Oh my God! I'm late for a meeting with the Secretary and the FBI is supposed to be there. Thanks, again! I'll be in touch!"

Stockton burst into the private office of the Secretary of Agriculture and was greeted by the disapproving looks of the Secretary and the five men seated around his desk.

"Where have you—," Secretary Harkens began.

"Mr. Secretary!" Stockton cried. "This thing has broken wide open! I'm sorry I'm late but I was tied up on the telephone. I spent the last hour and fifteen minutes on a call from Lt. Bledsoe of the Dallas Police. You won't believe what I've just learned."

"Try us!" a dark blue suit challenged.

"Paul, these men are from the Washington Bureau," Secretary Harkens said as he motioned to the five dark-blue suits surrounding his desk. No further introductions were offered, so Stockton began his story.

An hour later, he was no more than half-way through. The questions from the Bureau bordered on the ridiculous. They were obviously skeptical and becoming downright derisive.

"You believe this shit?"

"Who is this Stewart, anyway?"

"Coyotes infecting cattle across the entire country, give me a break!"

"And how many murders was that, again?"

"This whole thing sounds like a fairy tale, or maybe a hoax!"

"Gentlemen! It may be just that," Stockton said, containing his irritation. "But we're treating it as fact and so are other members of the FBI. So, please, let me finish!"

"Please, go ahead, Paul," Secretary Harkens said, ending the discussion.

Another hour elapsed before Stockton finished. This time, however, the questions were concise and to the point. The blue suits had gotten the message.

"Paul," Harkens said. "We've got to get this to the President before he goes on television."

"I'll tell you what!" the head blue suit said. "You go ahead and do that. The boys and I will do a little checkin'. If the story checks out, the President will be very grateful. If not, well..."

"Get me the White House," Harkens spoke to his intercom.

After a few minutes, the intercom declared, "I'm sorry, Mr. Harkens, but the President can not be disturbed."

"Then get me Bill Dickson. And make sure that he knows that it's me and that it's very important."

Five minutes later, he heard, "Mr. Secretary. It's Bill Dickson."

"Bill, we've just come across some information that's vital to the President's address tonight."

"Mr. Secretary, the speech has been put to bed an hour ago. The President's working on his delivery. He does not want to be interrupted. He's goes on the air in two hours."

"Bill I haven't got time to give you all of the details, so listen carefully."

Fifteen minutes later, Bill Dickson contacted security and arranged clearance for the Secretary of Agriculture and his special assistant to enter the White House. Then he made his way to the Oval Office and knocked on the door.

CHAPTER THIRTY-SEVEN

The only sound breaking the pristine silence of the Idaho forest was the soft hum of a small generator. The sun was still at a forty-five-degree angle, tilting to the west, producing long shadows but not giving any relief to the unusual heat wave that was encompassing the country. The small rustic mining cabin that stood next to the generator was as open to the surrounding air as possible. Both the front and rear doors had been propped open though neither had screen protection. Every window had been opened. Even the flue to the stone fireplace had been opened with the hope of providing a draft for the heated air to escape.

The two men inside were stripped down to their shorts and T-shirts. They only wore boots to protect their feet from the rough-cut wooden flooring.

"Man," General Boone said, addressing Major Wheeler. "Have you ever known it to be this hot up here in the north woods?"

"No, sir! I sure haven't. I believe that this is some sort of a record," the major responded. "The woods are so dry that the least spark could set off a fire big enough to burn the whole state."

"I believe you're right, Jimmy Ray," the general chuckled. "But just imagine what it's like down in the cities. Those poor slobs must be burning alive. We couldn't have asked for it to come at a better time."

"And not a drop of rain forecast for the entire weekend. The farmers must be pulling their hair out by the roots," the major laughed as he joined in the joke.

"Ya better fire up the tube, Jimmy Ray," Boone advised. "We wouldn't want to miss that asshole President's speech."

"Ya think he'll call out the Guard?" Wheeler said as he turned on the TV set that was powered by the generator and received signals from the small dish antenna pointing skyward in a clearing.

"Don't matter none," the general explained as he seated himself on a plank bench and leaned back against the table. "He's fucked if he does and he's fucked if he doesn't."

Wheeler gave him a quizzical look as he handed the general a beer, twisted the top off of his own and sat at the other end of the bench.

Boone twisted the top off his bottle, took a long swig and threw the cap out the open door.

"Don't you see?" he said. "If he doesn't call them up, the local police won't be able to handle the riots and he'll get the blame for not acting and if he does, the confrontation will make the riots even worse, and he'll be blamed for inflaming the situation. We got him both ways. I kinda hope that he does call up the Guard and even declares martial law. That'll make World War II look like a high school pep rally!"

Both men turned to the television set. The presidential address to the nation was about to begin. The usual predictions by various news analysts had been boring the early listeners for over an hour. The announcer suddenly became very serious, lowered his voice to its gravest tone and introduced, "The President of the United States."

The cameras were already in place, as was the President. He was seated behind his desk in the Oval Office. The Seal of the United States of America was emblazoned on the front panel of the desk and the country's flag was proudly displayed on a flagstand behind it.

"My fellow Americans," he began. "Several years ago, our great country was beset by a problem that seemed an impossibility to preceding generations. We began to fail in our ability to produce adequate food to supply our people. We had always been an exporter. We were known as the breadbasket for the world. Our inadequacy was focused in our declining herds of animals.

"When I was elected to the highest office of the land, I made you a promise. I promised to find out what was causing the deterioration of our livestock and to correct it. I am here to tell you that that promise will be kept."

During the ensuing pause, the two men in the rough cabin in Idaho leaned forward in rapt attention.

"The task force that I appointed has just informed me that they have identified the virus that has been causing the decrease in production. Furthermore, I have been advised that a serum, an antidote, has been discovered that will reverse the disease in the afflicted animals. In other words, I am announcing that meat prices will be coming down and that all foods will be affordable to all Americans.."

The President paused to let his statement receive its full reward. He sat a bit straighter and his chin protruded just a little. He wanted the world to know that he was the man of the hour. The pause was timed to the microsecond. The President erased whatever pleasure might have shown on his face and took on a most somber look as he continued.

"There is another situation facing us that causes me great alarm. It has been caused partly by skyrocketing food costs, which I am certain are going to be brought into control, and partly by the uncommon weather that we have experienced across the nation. I am referring to the general unrest that has taken hold in our population centers. We have seen a rise in all crimes associated with passion and irritability. Violent crimes are up in every city of this great country. Our police forces have been taxed to the extreme. We are in danger of destroying the very fiber of our nation. We are at a very serious crossroads. I have informed you that the danger of food shortages and high prices will soon be a thing of the past, thanks to the diligent efforts of my task force. The terrible and unusual weather will be with us into the near foreseeable future, but we have eliminated one source of tension. I ask you to be tolerant about the other. I promise you that this, too, will pass.

"Just this very afternoon, as I was working on this speach, I was informed that there might be an organized effort to provoke normally peaceful citizens into doing things that they would usually despise. Before learning of this possibility, I was convinced that, once you learned of our successful resolution to the food shortage, the weekend would pass without civil disruptions. I felt sure that the local authorities could handle any problem that arose.

"Now, after receiving this alarming information, I have second thoughts. I feel that I would be derelict in my duties as your president if I did not take steps to insure the safety of our citizens. Therefore, I have placed the armed forces and the National Guard on active duty. They will not be dispersed unless absolutely necessary. The use of these forces will be at the discretion of the local governments. I pray to God that they do not have to be used. That part is up to you.

"Now, let me say this. If it should turn out that there is an organized group behind any unrest, riot or destruction, I will not rest until that organization is discovered, brought to justice and punished. I am confident that all of our citizens will act in a manner befitting our great country and that the resolution of the food crisis will be accompanied by the resolution of many of our differences.

"Thank you. God bless you and good night."

The network anchorman jumped in immediately and

announced that there would be a short question-and-answer period beginning in two minutes. He took those two minutes to expound on the President's address, trying to convince his audience that his opinion was relevant.

Major Wheeler turned to the general.

"What do you think, sir?" he said. "It sounds like they may have made us."

"Are you crazy?" the general countered. "They got shit! We got so many layers between us and the man on the street that they couldn't prove anything even if found out who we were. Only the people that were here know who we are and they won't talk."

"What about the army and the National Guard?"

"Couldn't be better for us. All they'll do is make the situation worse. Just imagine how the looters and rioters will close ranks if they're faced by brown uniforms. Wait a minute! He's coming back on for the questions. This oughtta be good!"

"Are you declaring martial law?" the first reporter asked.

"Certainly not. We're merely taking reasonable precautions in the event that the local police can't control the situation."

"Then you expect that rioting will occur in the cities?" another joined in.

"We are expecting a peaceful weekend, but we're not going to be caught flatfooted if we're wrong."

"What about the meat shortage?" another asked. "How long before supplies return to normal?"

There was a distinct hesitation before the answer

came.

"You know that you can't produce a full-grown steer overnight. It'll be about two years from the time of vaccination until a steer can be brought to market."

"And what about the vaccine? How long before that becomes readily available?"

"We should be able to have the vaccine into the hands of all growers within twelve months."

A feeling of apprehension sweep through the room, into the cameras and then into the living rooms across the country.

"Do you mean that it will take up to three years before prices come down and the average person can purchase meat again?"

The President merely nodded his head in admission. An aide came to his side and whispered something in his ear.

"I'm sorry, but that's all I have time for this evening."

With that, Branden David Jefferson, President of the United States, rose from his desk and left the Oval Office.

"Whatta ya think now?" Boone said as he punched Wheeler lightly on the shoulder.

"Well, I guess we don't have to worry about meat prices tomorrow or anytime in the foreseeable future," Wheeler said, rubbing his shoulder and slipping slightly out of range. The old man still packed a punch.

"You bet your ass, we don't!" the general said. "And what about the way he positioned the army and the National Guard. I couldn't have done it better myself. Once we get them looters and rioters goin', there'll be no stoppin' them. Just wait 'til they see some brown uniforms. They'll go crazy!"

"Guess you're right, General," Wheeler agreed. "I can't wait 'til tomorrow."

*

Bill Dickson was waiting just outside the Oval Office. He motioned the President aside.

"I've got some real news, a breakthrough!" he said. The President arched his eyebrows and let his features ask the question.

"Remember those two cities, Holtsville and Andover? Well, we've figured out their significance. It was one of those things that was so obvious that nobody put it together. Holtsville and Andover are IRS centers. The other eight cities are..." he paused to extract a scrap of paper and read from it, "Atlanta, Cincinnati, Austin, Ogden, Fresno, Kansas City, Memphis and Philadelphia."

"Order increased protection around the IRS buildings in those cities. We couldn't take another Oklahoma City.

"It's already been done, sir." Dickson said. "A fly couldn't get within a hundred yards of any one of them."

*

The two militiamen were ready to turn in for the night, when they heard the sound of gravel being displaced by off-road tires.

"Must be Charlie," Wheeler said. "He made real good time."

Charlie pulled his rented four-wheeler to a stop outside of the cabin, slung a small duffel over his shoulder and strode to the door.

"Hey! It's me! Charlie! Don't shoot!" he said as he stepped through the opening.

"Come on in, Charlie," the general welcomed. "Man, you sure didn't waste any time gettin' here."

"I was lucky. I caught the shuttle from Phoenix to Boise and they had a car waiting for me. What did the President say?"

"You'll love this," Wheeler said and then went on to describe the President's address in detail.

"If they suspect that the riots may be orchestrated, do you think that they might have heard about phase two and the ten special cities?" Charlie asked.

"Don't matter if they've figured it out or not," the General answered. "Our guys are already in place inside the buildings. Nothing's going to stop them. Tell me, Charlie, did Saunders seal up the mine?"

"Not yet, sir," Charlie answered. "I left as soon as he told me that I was needed up here. But he told me that he wouldn't have the dynamite until tomorrow. You don't have to worry, General. The mine will be sealed forever and there will be three bodies buried inside, the professor, the special service guy and Butch Crosswell."

CHAPTER THIRTY-EIGHT

B utch was in his glory. He had been left in command. His contingent consisted of only two people, but that didn't make any difference. He put Bubba in charge of the rear of the mine and Jasper in charge of the entrance. Then he patrolled the mine like a drill sergeant. After a couple of rounds, he retired to plan the rest of his tenure. He decided that he should rotate his men and their duties.

He approached Jasper and said, "I want you to relieve Bubba. Go back there and take over his position. Tell him to report to me here at the entrance."

"Yessir!" Jasper said, acknowledging his orders with a mock salute and an expression that said, "Who died and made you boss?"

"On the double!" Butch shouted after him, adding insult to injury.

Ten minutes later, Jasper was back at the mine entrance.

"What the hell are you doin' back here?" Butch roared. "I thought I told you to switch places with Bubba."

"If I did that, I'd have to be lying down and unconscious. You better get back there."

Security broke down completely, as Jasper followed Butch into the interior of the mine, leaving the entrance completely unguarded. Even before they arrived, Butch knew what he would see in the dim light of the low-intensity bulbs.

"Shit! Shit! Shit!" he repeated as he stopped beside Bubba's inert form.

"What the fuck happened? Where's the goddam prisoner?" Butch screamed.

Bubba moaned and started to move. Butch reached down, grabbed him by the shirt and pulled him into a sitting position.

"Well! Well!" he demanded. "Answer me, goddam it!"

Bubba's eyes were still glazed over. The best he could manage was, "Wha...?"

It was then that Butch lost it. He stepped back and delivered a full swinging kick to Bubba's ribs. The blow knocked Bubba back down to the floor.

"Fuck! Fuck! Fuck!" Butch repeated as he continued to kick the inert body.

Jasper tried to restrain him. It was a bad mistake. Butch backhanded him across the face and knocked him against the wall. Jasper covered his face with his forearms and felt a fist enter his solar plexus. He doubled over and sank to the ground. A kick hit him on the shoulder as he drew himself into a ball. He felt a glancing blow to his head and a solid kick to his buttocks. He waited for the next punishing jolt. It didn't come.

Butch's rage disappeared as quickly as it had begun. When Jasper finally ventured a look, he found Butch bent over Bubba trying to administer to him.

"Gimme a hand over here," he said.

Jasper managed to crawl to where Bubba lay.

"Get me some water," Butch ordered.

Jasper struggled to his feet and returned with a pail full of cold water. Butch grabbed the pail and emptied it on Bubba's head. He handed the pail back to Jasper and indicated with a nod of his head that he wanted a refill. Twenty minutes of intensive first aid resulted in Bubba sitting up and fully conscious.

"He asked me to undo his collar button. I leaned over and that's all I remember," Bubba said in answer to Butch's questioning.

"He musta had a little saw hidden somewhere. Look at the way the ropes have been cut," Jasper observed.

"Well, he didn't come out the front door, so he must still be in here somewhere," Butch reasoned. "Jasper, get your ass back to the entrance. I don't want him sneakin' out while we're back here."

"I'm gonna take a look around. I know that son of a bitch is still here," he concluded. "Bubba, do you think that you can watch the professor without screwin' it up?"

Bubba was only able to let out an affirmative groan as he began to crawl back to the lab.

"Now where's that fuckin' helmet! Maybe I can use it," Butch mumbled to himself as he picked up Kevin's helmet and tried it on.

"Well, it fits okay. Now, let's see if I can figure it out. What's this eye shield?"

Butch pulled down the infrared glasses.

"Now, lookie here. Ain't that somethin'? I can see almost as good as day. Okay, smart guy. You can hide but you can't escape."

Butch took a swing toward the lab, but he soon discovered that the effectiveness of the goggles diminished rapidly as the light grew brighter. He left the lab wing and turned into the main tunnel proceeding deeper into the mine. He made his way cautiously, inspecting every nook and cranny along the way. He knew he couldn't afford to let his quarry get behind him. The deeper he got into the mine the more nervous he became. By the time he reached the rear shaft, he had his sidearm unholstered and gripped in his right hand.

He warily approached the gaping hole in the floor. Getting down on his hands and knees, he peered into the abyss. Straight down and no bottom in sight. He scanned the side walls as far as his infrared vision would allow. He picked up the horizontal shaft that led to the escape vent. Then he saw another about thirty feet lower. He dropped to his belly and thought that he could make out a third tunnel spoking off below him. As he made another sweep of the shaft, he became aware of a thin vertical line. At first he thought that it was a crack in the stone wall, but upon closer inspection, he could tell that it hung out from the side of the excavation and was not imbedded into it. He followed the line up and over the edge of the pit. Butch got to his feet and made his way around the shaft to the point where the line crossed the floor.

"Ah!" he breathed. "So this is where you're hiding. Well, let's see how you like this, you son of a bitch!"

He bent down, unfastened the line from the wedge that secured it and tossed it over the rim. He listened intently for the line to hit the bottom. He never heard a thing.

"Wow! That's one deep mother," he said out loud. Then, he shouted down the shaft, "Have a nice life, fella! Sorry, that it won't be a long one, but at least you'll have a couple of million tons of stone for your marker."

Then, he added as an afterthought, "So long, sucker! The next sound you hear will be twenty sticks of dynamite collapsing the mine. Sleep tight!"

Convinced that he had solved the problem of the mysterious intruder, Butch headed back to brag to Jasper and Bubba.

*

Kevin rolled over onto his back and felt a small stone between his shoulder blades. It was just enough to bring him to full consciousness. He raised his left arm until he could see the luminous dial on his watch. He nudged Lauri Beth.

"Rise and shine," he whispered. "It's two in the morning. Time to get back down there. I'm afraid that we've already slept an hour longer than we wanted. We must have been really tired."

"I could use a cup of coffee," Lauri Beth joked. You didn't pack any did you?"

"Next best thing," Kevin said as he reached into an inner pocket, pulled out a tube and opened one end. "Try this. It'll wake you, for sure."

Lauri Beth squeezed the tube into her mouth, forced the liquid down her throat and nearly gagged as her eyes popped open and the blood coursed through her veins.

"My God! What is that stuff?"

"It's almost pure caffeine," Kevin said. "How do you feel?"

"Like the top of a snare drum. I don't think I could even close my eyes much less sleep. How long will this stuff last?"

"Six to eight hours," Kevin said as he swallowed some of the jet-black fluid. "Let's see your pack. You'll be leading the way since I don't have my infrareds."

Lauri Beth emptied the contents on the rocky floor. Kevin touched each item before he handed it back to her to repack.

"I'd better take the large flashlight," he suggested. "The small one should be fine for you. I sure hope we can find my helmet and pack. We lose the advantage if they've figured out the night-vision glasses work. They didn't get my boot knife and you're still fully armed. Check your sidearm and make sure your knife is where you can get to it."

Lauri Beth checked the clip to her pistol, shoved it into the handgrip and jammed a round into the chamber. She slid the safety to the on position and holstered the weapon.

"Ready!" she said.

"Let's go!" Kevin responded as he led the way to air shaft.

Lauri Beth slid over the side in an effortless motion and made her way to the shelf. Her smaller build gave her an advantage in the descent. The shaft seemed to fit her perfectly, while Kevin's longer structure gave him less of a purchase against the rock walls. Lauri Beth easily navigated the S turn at the shelf and finished her climb down the lower chute before Kevin had reached the shelf. He wiggled and squirmed his way through the S turn and finally arrived in the tunnel next to Lauri Beth.

The intercom was useless since Kevin was without his helmet. They had agreed on a few simple signs prior to their descent. Kevin pointed down the tunnel and Lauri Beth led the way. Kevin kept a hand on her back and followed her to the edge of the passageway. Lauri Beth lay prone with her head and shoulders extending over the abyss. She rolled on to her back as Kevin pressed her calves to the ground. She looked up and surveyed the rim. Then she inched her way back into the tunnel.

She put her mouth to Kevin's ear and whispered, "All clear! But I couldn't find the rope."

Kevin indicated that they should switch positions. He pushed himself over the edge so that his entire torso hung in space. Lauri Beth was lying across his ankles, providing as much counterweight as she could. Kevin swung his body back and forth while his arms flailed the empty air. He finally signaled that he was coming back and muscled his way on to solid ground.

"It's gone," he whispered in Lauri Beth's ear. He then motioned for Lauri Beth to drop her pack. He reached in and extracted her line which was the duplicate to his. He uncoiled about ten feet of line and began to fashion a climber's halter around his body.

"What do you think you're doing?" Lauri Beth whispered.

Kevin signaled that he was going to free climb to the main level and then pull her up.

"Are you crazy?" she breathed. "Do you think that I'd be able to belay you if you slipped? You'd pull me right out after you and I don't see anything that would afford a good anchor. I'll do the climbing and you can back stop me. Besides I've got the night eyes."

Kevin started to protest but he saw that she was absolutely right. He nodded his head in agreement, untied his halter and retied it around Lauri Beth. Once secure, she gave him a thumbs-up. Kevin wrapped the line around his body so that he could pay it out and still cinch it if needed. He found a small indentation in the floor, just big enough for his heel. He sat down behind it and got his boot wedged as best he could. He held the line firmly but loose enough to pay out as needed and returned her thumbs-up.

Lauri Beth faced the side wall and made her way to the opening. Her right arm extended around the orifice and her hand searched for a hold. Slowly she worked her way closer to the edge. The left side of her body was providing enough friction that she was fifty percent in and fifty percent out. Her right hand felt a small ledge. She picked at it and decided that it would hold. Her left hand moved toward her body until her fingers found the crack that she had seen. She swung her body out until only her left forearm and left foot were still inside the tunnel. Her right foot searched for a ledge and found it. She pulled her left side into the shaft and disappeared from Kevin's view. He slackened the line just a bit and waited to feel the pressure as Lauri Beth began her climb.

The infrared goggles provided a clear view of the walls of the shaft. Lauri Beth could see all the way to the top. She scanned the sheer rise in front of her and planned her ascent. There was a crack that ran the length of the wall. She moved her right hand over until she could get her fingers wedged in the fissure. Her right foot already had a hold, so she pulled herself up and over. She knew where the next hold was for her left hand. She found it easily and raised her left foot to a small ledge. She released her right hand and moved it upward. The crack grew slightly larger as it approached the rim. This time she was able to get her hand into the crack all the way to the knuckles. Her confidence grew with each foot or hand hold.

Lauri Beth was five feet from the top. Her right hand felt secure and her left hand had a finger grip on a small rock. She pushed up on her foot holds and removed her right hand from the crevice. Just at that moment the rock pulverized under the fingers of her left hand.

Kevin had been paying out slack on an as-needed

basis, keeping enough pressure on the line to feel Lauri Beth climb, but not enough to impede her. Suddenly he could feel the line go soft. He braced himself and pulled in as much line as he could. The line that he had retrieved was ripped from his hands and he felt a constriction around his upper body as he absorbed the shock from Lauri Beth's thirty-foot free fall.

Lauri Beth hung suspended in space. The first shock of the once-slack-now-taut line was replaced with a side blow to her body as she was slammed against the rock wall fifteen feet below Kevin. The line that Kevin had retrieved and then had wrenched from him gave a small bit of deceleration to Lauri Beth so she didn't receive the full force of her fall. The harness that Kevin had tied around her distributed the shock between her shoulders and waist. She dangled over the blackness and sucked in her breath as best she could. The jolt at the bottom of her fall had knocked the wind out of her. It took her a bit to recover and by the time she felt strong enough to climb back to the tunnel, she could feel the wall scrape her body as Kevin lifted her, hand over hand.

Lauri Beth reached over the side of the tunnel floor and laid her arm against the stone. The friction allowed Kevin to release his grip on the line and haul Lauri Beth onto solid ground. She sat down, breathing hard as Kevin began to untie her harness.

"What are you doing?" she breathed.

"Getting ready to take your place," he whispered.

"Like hell, you are," she mouthed. "Just because I let

a loose stone screw me up doesn't mean that I'm not going again."

Lauri Beth's lips formed a string of expletives that surprised both of them. She was venting her frustration and anger in a silent string of four-letter words. The ferocity of her quiet demonstration caused Kevin to take a step back.

"Okay! Okay! One more time and then I go!" he mimed, holding his index finger vertically to emphasize the point.

Lauri Beth moved to the edge of the tunnel and felt a tug on her harness as Kevin cautioned her to wait until he had repositioned himself. A moment later, Lauri Beth stepped into space for the second time. A mere six minutes had elapsed when Kevin felt two quick pulls on the safety line, indicating the she had reached her goal and was established on the main level.

She secured the line around a timber, signaled to Kevin, and seconds later was helping him over the edge. They hugged briefly and gave each other a thumbs-up. Kevin released the rope from the stanchion, coiled it and stowed it in Lauri Beth's pack.

Without a word or a signal, Lauri Beth started down the main tunnel with Kevin's hand on her back. The target was the lab. The prize was Kevin's pack with his helmet being a hoped-for bonus. They hugged the passageway wall and moved silently. Unless a person was looking for them with night-vision goggles, they were invisible. Lauri Beth reached the corner of the excavation containing the lab. She stopped and both she and

Kevin strained all of their senses to ascertain their position. A full three minutes elapsed before they felt comfortable enough to peer around the corner. Lauri Beth dropped to her knees and swept the lab with her infrared glasses. A guard was seated at the entrance to Dr. Middlestat's quarters. He was situated so he could view both rooms by looking from side to side. Lauri Beth scanned the lab for Kevin's pack. The pack itself was halfway into the lab and was leaning against a wall. The deflated condition of the bag suggested that it was empty. She continued her search, concentrating on the floor. She began to pick out various items of Kevin's equipment strewn across the floor as if it had been examined and tossed carelessly aside. She found a short piece of rope, one jumar, a battery pack, the GPS, another jumar, a ration kit, and some first aid items, but no weapons and no helmet.

Lauri Beth got off her knees and stood completely erect. She inched her way around the corner until she was fully into the lab. Proceeding a bit further she found a niche that concealed her from the guard's direct line of vision. She was now able to view the lab from a different angle. She began to search the tops of the lab tables. The scientific apparatus hid most of the free space, but on a small desk in the far corner she spied a knife and a pistol. Once again, on her hands and knees, Lauri Beth crawled to the far corner of the cave, using the lab tables as a shield. The going was slow, but she made it to the table without detection. Keeping low, she reached over the edge of the table and groped for the weapons. She felt the cold steel of the knife and the metallic bulk of the handgun. Lauri Beth slid both items to the edge and reached up with her other hand to bring them to the floor. She brought the knife down first and laid it gently on the floor.

As she transferred the gun from one hand to the other, she was caught off guard by the weight of the pistol. It slipped from her grip. Lauri Beth grabbed at the falling gun, but only succeeded in slapping it across the room. She prevented the noise of a direct impact, but the gun made a clatter as it bounced across the floor. It came to rest with a thud in the middle of the lab halfway between Lauri Beth and Kevin. Kevin dropped to his knees and scurried toward the gun.

Jasper turned his head at the sound.

"What's that?" he said loudly with a slight tremor in his voice.

Kevin huddled under the nearest lab table. Lauri Beth froze at the far end of the room.

"It's just me," came a guttural voice from just inside the main tunnel.

"Is that you, Butch?"

"Yeah, it's me! Who the hell did you think it was?"

"What was that noise? Sounded like it came from the lab?"

"Naw! It was just me! I'm trying to get used to these goddam night-vision glasses. I nearly killed myself bumping into the wall."

"What're you doin' back here, anyway?" Jasper asked.

"I'm checkin' out the rear of the mine. You just make sure that the old man doesn't beat the shit out of you and escape."

"Ha ha! Very funny!"

"I'll be back to check and I ain't trying to be funny."

Butch left for the back of the mine and Jasper got up to check his ward. Kevin crawled to the middle of the lab, swept the floor with his hand, found the gun and returned to the main tunnel. Lauri Beth moved from the far end of the lab to the same spot as Kevin.

As they met, Kevin signaled for Lauri Beth to turn toward the mine entrance. She gave him a questioning look and then understood his intentions. With Butch to their rear and with his imminent return to the lab, they had nowhere to go but to the other shaft. She took the lead because the infrared goggles still provided an advantage, even with the dim lights that were strung at forty-foot intervals along the stanchions that lined the main tunnel.

She stopped at the edge of the vertical excavation, her climbing line already out of her pack. Kevin indicated that she should check out the shaft for possible tributaries that would offer shelter while he slipped the line around a timber. Lauri Beth knelt next to Kevin and whispered, "Looks like there's tunnel at about the fifty-foot level but it's on the other side of the shaft."

"I'll hold the line off that far edge," Kevin said. "Once you're in the tunnel secure the line and I'll slide across the shaft to the tunnel."

He carried the doubled line around the open shaft, wrapped it around his body and signaled for Lauri Beth to descend. She went over the edge without a word. She quickly rappelled the fifty feet to the horizontal excavation and pulled twice on the line. Kevin felt the two tugs on the line, moved to the other side of the shaft and waited for the next signal that would tell him that Lauri Beth had the other end of the line secured. Moments later, Kevin hooked his feet around the line and lowered himself hand over hand across the pit.

"Welcome aboard," Lauri Beth murmured.

Kevin acknowledged the greeting with a quick one-armed hug. He then began pulling on one side of the doubled line. The line slid around the timber at the top of the shaft until the end passed through. The end fell into the shaft and was hauled back to the tunnel. As Kevin coiled the line, he looked at Lauri Beth and they both knew that they were in for another hazardous free climb.

"We'd better check out our new home," Kevin suggested. "How're your batteries holding out?"

Lauri Beth consulted the built in power meter.

"I've still got about three-quarters of my power left."

"We'll switch to flashlights as soon as we get deeper into the tunnel. That should be safe and we want to conserve the infrared for later."

CHAPTER THIRTY-NINE

S heriff Saunders arrived at the entrance of the mine at daybreak. Caution was no longer part of his repertoire. He drove his four-wheel drive across the rough high desert, over the saddle and down into the bowl that held the mine. The back end of his vehicle was loaded with wooden crates. The crates all bore a stencil marked, "Danger Explosives."

Sanders pulled up to the entrance and blasted the horn. Bubba limped out to meet him.

"My God!" Saunders said. "What in the hell happened to you?"

"Butch," Bubba said. "And he got Jasper, too."

"That guy got loose and Butch went ape," he continued, seeing Saunders' questioning eyes. "Jasper's not as bad as me. I was still stunned from when I got head-butted."

"So, where's that Stewart guy now?" Saunders demanded.

"Butch thinks that he went down a shaft in the rear of the mine to hide. Butch found a rope tied to a timber and dropped it down the mine shaft. He's back there checkin' now."

"Well, I'll talk to him when he gets back. Meanwhile, help me unload these crates."

"Looks like you got enough dynamite to blow up half the county."

"Could be. I want this mine closed for good when we're finished."

Saunders opened the tailgate and began handing boxes out to Bubba, who carried them into the mine. Butch came out of the darkness just as the last crate was stacked.

"You sure know when to show up," Bubba snarled at Butch, feeling braver with Saunders by his side.

"I'm surprised you didn't blow us up just unloading that stuff," Butch retorted.

They started to face off when Saunders intervened.

"We got some other stuff to do before we leave," he said. "Let's get them coyotes out here and empty the cages. Butch, make yourself useful."

Butch grumbled his way back to the coyote staging area and returned in a few minutes with a caged animal. Bubba and Saunders took the cage out a few yards from the entrance and opened the door. The coyote walked slowly into the open air. When he had traveled a dozen or so feet, he stopped and turned his head toward his former captors. The coyote stared at them for a moment with disdainful eyes, turned away and disappeared into the brush.

Butch dragged the empty cage back into the mine. He threw it into the first shaft and returned with another.

Eleven trips later, he announced,

"Well, that's the last one. Now, what?"

"Now, we'll set these charges and get ready to blow the mine," Saunders said.

The three militiamen pried open the cases and armed the sticks of dynamite. Then, under Saunders' direction they placed the charges into every crack they could find within twenty feet of the entrance. They didn't have the benefit of a drill, so they had to use any natural crevice available. After they had set twenty-five sticks, they attached the detonating wire and spooled it well outside the mine.

"Here," Saunders said, handing a couple of sticks of dynamite to Butch. "Take these back with you. They're fused with slow burners. Maybe you oughtta drop them down the chute where that Stewart guy is. Send Jasper back and take care of the professor anyway you want."

A smile crossed Butch's face. "You got it!" he said. Then his brow furrowed and he added, "You know who this guy is?"

"Yeah," Saunders admitted. "His names Kevin Stewart. He's the nephew of that Nichols guy you offed. Been stayin' out at Nichols' house and he's close with a gal from Blackwell's forensics lab."

"Where'd he come from?" Butch asked.

"Near as I can figure, he's with the army and came back on special leave."

"That explains a lot," Butch said. "It'll be a pleasure to bury that guy. He's been a real pain in the ass."

"Do what ever you want, but do it quick. I want to be

outta here."

Butch accepted the two fused sticks of dynamite and went back into the mine. He skirted the first shaft and made his way to the professor's living quarters.

"Tie the old guy up and then get back to the entrance," he ordered. "Saunders is there with Bubba and he's getting ready to blow this place."

Jasper didn't need any encouragement. He grabbed Dr. Middlestat by the shoulders, spun him around, threw him on the cot, and hog-tied him.

"That oughtta keep him," he muttered. "Sorry, Professor, but orders is orders."

Jasper didn't waste any time getting back to Saunders and Bubba.

Butch reached the last shaft and peered into its depths. He still wore the infrared goggles but he couldn't get a good enough angle to see more than a hundred feet down. He pulled out a cigarette lighter and lit it. He took one of the sticks and applied the flame to the fuse. The fuse was twelve inches in length. The flame caught. The fuse sputtered and started to burn. Three inches disappeared in about the same number of seconds. Butch's eyes widened. He threw the dynamite over the edge and dove for cover. Five seconds later, the ground shook around him and his eardrums were almost split open. He covered his head as rocky debris and dirt flew out of the shaft and descended on his body.

"Son of a bitch!" he yelled. "I thought that was supposed to be a slow burning fuse!"

Kevin and Lauri Beth felt the tremor of the blast

and heard a slight rumble.

Middlestat felt his bed shake, heard the blast, closed his eyes and resigned himself to an underground death.

Butch picked himself up from the mine floor, brushed himself off, thought of pleasure he would have of punching out the sheriff and started for the entrance.

Saunders heard a distant reverberation, let his mouth curve into a grim smile and pushed the plunger.

The sound was deafening. The opening of the mine filled with a dense smoke and seemed to be supported by it. The first cloud emerged as a lethargic billow. Then came the roar of crashing timber and splitting rock as the original murky halo was propelled outward like a smoke ring from a medieval dragon. The entire face of the mountain seemed to hang in suspension and then slowly began to sag like a snow-covered telephone line strung between two rotting poles.

As the smoke and dust cleared, Saunders, Bubba and Jasper loaded themselves into the four-wheeler and drove to the saddle. Saunders parked the vehicle on top and the three men got out and looked back. The destruction was complete. The dust was settling and the slowly brightening sky pierced the obscurity just enough for them to see a giant pile of boulders where the entrance to the mine had once been. Above the granite tomb, the mountain sagged into a bowl.

"That oughtta teach Butch a lesson," Bubba said.

Jasper nodded. Saunders got back in the SUV.

"Let's go," he said. "We've got things to do and places to go."

*

Butch was knocked over backwards by the force of the blast. The air was forced from his lungs as if a giant fist had buried itself in his stomach. His helmet was blown off and his head hit the floor with a resounding thud. Then he lost consciousness.

Middlestat was thrown from his bed and into a corner. A timber crashed down from above and would have crushed him had not one end come to rest against a huge rock that had been dislodged and rolled in front of him. He lay in a fetal position constrained by the ropes that still bound his hands and feet. He took a deep breath and nearly choked on the airborne impurities. He realized that he was still alive, tried to utter a cry for help and passed out from exertion and fright.

Kevin and Lauri Beth were the most protected of those in the mine. They were fifty feet below the main force of the blast and three hundred feet into the secondary tunnel. Even so, the explosion knocked them off their feet. The resultant wind storm was far less severe than that of the main tunnel, but still filled the air with dust and impurities. They were doubled over on their knees, hands held over their faces and breathing with great difficulty as the rumble slowly faded.

Breathing became easier as the dust settled. They got to their feet and looked at each other, silently asking if the other was all right.

"What was that?" Lauri Beth managed to say.

"I think that our friends have left and locked the door behind them."

"What about the smaller noise before the big one?"

"They may have closed the back door, too!"

Kevin scanned the area with his flashlight. The powerful beam lit up the walls of the tunnel. They had just turned a corner, a fact that helped deaden the force of the explosion. The tunnel ended about twenty-five feet further on. Strewn about the floor at the end of the tunnel were various mining tools, apparently left there as the mine played out.

"Let's see if our way to the main tunnel is still clear," Kevin suggested.

Lauri Beth was in complete agreement and led the way around the corner. Kevin ran into her as she stopped dead in her tracks.

"Oh, my God! Look at that!" she cried.

Kevin splayed his flashlight beam on a pile of rubble fifty feet away that completely closed off the tunnel. The end of a timber protruded from the rocks at a weird angle. The heap had a slope of about forty-five degrees and formed a semicircle at the base. Kevin approached the mound with caution and inspected it carefully.

"This could be serious," he understated as he dislodged a stone and threw it backwards.

Lauri Beth was speechless. Her mouth opened but no words came out. Kevin looked at her and gave her shoulders a gentle shake.

"We've got some work to do," he said as if there was nothing wrong that a little hard labor wouldn't cure. "Let's go back and take a look at those tools at the end of the tunnel."

It was like a virtual treasure chest of hardware.

Kevin handed Lauri Beth a couple of hand picks, a large chisel and a maul. He armed himself with a full-sized pickax, a grubax, a spade, a pry bar and a sledge-hammer.

"Let's go," he said.

They deposited their equipment at the foot of the cave-in.

"Where do we start?" Lauri Beth asked.

"Notice how the pile seems to be bigger on the right side?"

"So, we should start on the left?"

"No, I don't think so. It looks to me like it might have collapsed from a weak spot in the right wall. That could mean that another tunnel exists there but was sealed off years ago. Let's start at the bottom of the right side first."

They began by picking up any loose rocks that they could move by hand. These were thrown as far back as they could manage. They soon uncovered a boulder that measured nearly three feet in diameter. They cleared as much debris from it as possible.

"This is where we become miners," Kevin said.

He set the chisel on top of the rock and pounded it with the small sledge. He soon had a depression deep enough to hold the chisel.

"Watch your eyes," he said as he hoisted the large sledge-hammer above his head and delivered a blow. The sledge glanced off the chisel and struck stone instead of metal. The chisel flew out of its seat and car-omed across the tunnel.

"I haven't done this in a while," he said sheepishly.

He reset the chisel and swung the sledge. This time he connected squarely. A small crack opened in the top of the boulder. Two hits later, one third of the great stone rolled on to the floor of the tunnel. Kevin moved it out of his way, reset the chisel and swung again. This time the weakened rock broke into three pieces which were easily moved. Some smaller rocks and gravel quickly filled part of the newly created cavity.

Kevin and Lauri Beth cleared the area by hand and shovel. Kevin grabbed his flashlight, got down on his hands and knees and sent a beam through a small hole that appeared where the back of the rock had been.

"I think that I can see beyond the wall. Maybe it's another tunnel."

A half an hour later they had cleared a twelve-inch area and were able to see into the freshly discovered space.

"It doesn't look very big," Kevin reported. "It's more like a crawl space. Can't be more than four feet high and it appears to curve off to the left about eight feet in."

"Let me see!" Lauri Beth said as she nudged Kevin out of the way.

After five minutes of scrutiny, she turned back to Kevin.

"What are you doing?"

Kevin had removed all of his gear and stripped down to his T-shirt and pants.

"I'm going in to get a good look," he said.

As much as he wiggled and squirmed, Kevin could get no more than his head and one shoulder into the opening.

"Looks like we'll have to do some more digging," he said as he squeezed back out.

"Maybe you will," Lauri Beth said as she moved toward the opening clad only in her blouse and climbing jeans.

She was able to get her torso into the hole but couldn't wiggle her hips through. She backed out, removed her jeans, handed them to Kevin and twisted through the hole pushing his flashlight before her. She was gone for eight or nine minutes. Kevin could hear scraping sounds as she made her way back to the opening. She lay on her back and pushed her head into the hole.

"You're right," she reported. "The passageway curves around to the left but it goes all the way around to the main tunnel. I think that it originally was a large semicircular cut and, when part of it gave way, the rest of the wall caved in on top of it. That's why the debris goes all the way to the ceiling. I pushed with my feet at the other end and I think that we can dig our way out. How much more before you can squeeze through?"

"I could get through right now. I'm going to make it a bit bigger to be able to fit in with all my gear."

"Good! There's another small excavation going in off the middle of this cut. I'm going back and check it out."

Kevin was prying what he hoped would be the last rock out of the now enlarged opening, when he heard the muffled scream. He cleared the area and dropped to his knees in preparation to enter the passageway.

"Lauri Beth!" he yelled. "Are you all right?"

His answer was a beam of light careening off the

interior walls and rapidly approaching him. He stepped back and allowed a breathless Lauri Beth to scramble out of the hole.

"Oh God! Oh God! Oh God!" she cried.

"What? What? What?" Kevin said, shaking her shoulders.

"Th-th-th-there's dead people in there!"

"Where?"

"Back there in the small hollow! There's bones in there! Skeletons! Just sitting there!

"Okay! Okay! Just calm down! They're dead? Right? They can't hurt us. Here, put these on and we'll check it out," Kevin reassured her as he handed Lauri Beth her pants.

"You go first," she insisted as she picked up her gear.

"Stow all your gear. We'll carry the tools with us. We'll need them at the other end," Kevin said.

Kevin led the way with his flashlight. Lauri Beth followed with her infrared goggles providing for her vision. They arrived at the small cut and Kevin poured light into the cavern. He focused on two skeletons, sitting on either side of a pile of melon-sized sandbags. Ragged bits of clothing lay draped over various skeletal remains. Guns, belts and holsters sagged on fleshless pelvic bones. Kevin crawled closer and examined the remains.

"This one was lucky," he said. "There's a bullet hole in the side of his head. I can't find a mark on the other one. He probably starved to death or was shot in the stomach or heart."

Lauri Beth let out an audible shudder followed by a

sharp cry as a pack rat scampered out from under one skeleton and out of the cave. Kevin followed the rat's path with his light beam.

"Good," he said. "Did you see? He ran to the right. That could mean that we can get out that way, too."

"Well, lookie here," he continued. "Each one died with a sand bag between his legs and look at that pile behind them."

Kevin handed Lauri Beth the flashlight and relieved the nearest skeleton of its charge. He sat down next to the bones as if the dead man was an interested spectator.

"It's not light," he said, as he untied the leather string. "Shine your light over here."

Kevin reached into the bag and pulled some of the sandy material out in his palm. Lauri Beth focused the beam on his hand. Kevin set the bag down and began to finger the substance.

"Do you see what I see?" he asked.

"I think so but I'm afraid to guess."

"Go ahead, take a chance!"

"Gold?" she gasped.

"I'd bet a dollar to a donut," he said. "How many would you guess are back there?"

"A lot!" she said, shining the beam past him and his two new friends. "They're stacked wall to wall and floor to ceiling. Remember, it's sort of small but I'd guess about twenty-five and I can't tell how deep they go. I think there's at least two rows. What do think it's worth?"

"Check my math," Kevin said. "Of course, it depends

on the quality. I'd say this bag weighs about fifteen pounds. That's one hundred eighty avoirdupois ounces and at $300 an ounce, that comes to, ah, $54,000 a bag. Fifty bags. Wow! Two and a half million dollars. That probably make us the two richest people to ever be buried alive."

"Except for the two guys guarding it," she countered. "What do you think happened here, anyway?"

"Looks to me like the stories about ol' Jacob Waltz are probably true."

"Who?"

"Jacob Waltz, the Lost Dutchman. My uncle, Brian, was searching for the Lost Dutchman Mine. Wouldn't that be something if this was that very mine? Here's what could have happened. My guess is that these two guys found the mine. Waltz probably shot the one in the head and then killed the second guy with a shot to the abdomen or chest. Then he puts a bag of gold in each one's hands as his little private joke and seals up the chamber. Waltz probably dies shortly thereafter and the secret dies with him until this blast opens up his little cache."

"Wow!" Lauri Beth exclaimed. "Reminds me of the old adage, 'Three people can keep a secret, if two of them are dead!'"

CHAPTER FORTY

Victor Yanich walked into the employees' entrance of the Internal Revenue Service Building. He wore a plain brown service uniform complete with matching baseball cap. Jerry Klinger matched him step for step, dressed in the same clothes. He allowed Yanich to ease in front of him as they approached the single-width door that allowed entrance into the rear of the building.

"Morning, George," they said in unison as they waved their credentials to the guard.

"Morning, boys," George replied as usual.

They had been going through the same routine for over a month. Arrive just before eight o'clock in the morning, busy themselves around the building and end up on the twelfth floor. The twelfth floor housed the computers of the district IRS office. Yanich and Klinger, posing as maintenance men, had slowly become fixtures. They carried ID's that gave them clearance to any office in the building. The tool boxes they toted were filled with sophisticated instruments that intimidated the ordinary person and completed their disguise.

Over the past two weeks they had been bringing their real equipment in by bits and pieces. The parts were stored in the ventilation system on the twelfth floor. They would be retrieved tonight after six, when most of the offices were empty. Until that time, their job was to look busy and blend in.

The security at the building was marginal at best. The guards did a haphazard job of checking people in, and during the mass exodus at quitting time, they did their best to avoid being trampled, so the check out was non-existent. As the last of the white-collar workers disappeared down the elevators, Yanich and Klinger secreted themselves in a supply closet. The room was big enough that they decided not to lock the door, figuring that if anyone should open the door, they could pretend that they were either getting or returning supplies.

At six o'clock they opened the door and strode nonchalantly into the hall. They proceeded to the men's washroom. Jerry placed a sign outside the door which read, "Restroom being cleaned." This time they locked the door. Yanich had a small stepladder under the ventilation grid and was standing on top reaching for the ceiling with a screwdriver in his hand. He lowered the grid to Klinger and said, "Set this off to one side while I hand the stuff down."

He began to transfer about ten pieces of equipment to Klinger.

"Watch this last one," he said. "It's pretty heavy."

He extracted what appeared to be a battery charger but was in fact a powerful transformer that could quadruple the voltage from an ordinary 110v electrical outlet. Klinger carefully positioned the transformer on the floor and handed Yanich the grid for replacement.

"That oughtta do it," Klinger said as he helped Yanich from the ladder. "You got the diagram?"

"Right here," Yanich confirmed as he produced a small pamphlet from his coverall pocket. "I know we've done this a hundred times, but we'd better lay out the parts and follow the instructions to the letter."

"I agree," Klinger said.

The instructions took them through the construction phase just as thoroughly as if they were building a mechanical toy. Thirty minutes later, they stepped back and admired their handiwork. What lay before them resembled a direct television satellite dish. The diameter of the dish was only eight inches and the cone that protruded from it was narrow at the inside and wide at the outer end. Behind the dish, imbedded in a handle were an on-and-off switch, a frequency dial, and two wires that would connect to the transformer. A shoulder harness was attached to the transformer which made the entire rig highly transportable.

The plan was to wait until the disturbances were at their greatest and then proceed into the IRS computer room. They figured that about high noon tomorrow would be the time. On Saturday the facility would be lightly staffed or empty. They settled in for the long wait.

At 10:35, they were aroused by a noise in the hall and

then by a hard rapping on the restroom door.

"Anyone in there?" a deep voice shouted. "We're evacuating the building. Orders from Washington!"

The two looked at each other for guidance. Klinger took the initiative.

"Be right out," he yelled back. "We're just finishing up in here."

"Be quick about it!" came the reply.

The voices faded into the distance as the guardsmen continued on their mission.

"This is a godsend," Yanich said. "Unlock the door and get into one of the stalls. Stand on the seat and make sure the door is ajar."

They had stood on the toilet seats for fifteen minutes when they heard the footsteps in the hall as the guardsmen made their final inspection. The door to the restroom opened and Victor and Jerry froze.

"Look here!" a voice chuckled. "They left in such a hurry that they forgot to take their sign down."

The guardsman put the sign inside the restroom, flashed his light about and left.

Klinger got off the toilet but stayed in the stall.

"We better wait for a while to make sure they don't come back," he said.

They waited for a good hour before they felt safe enough to leave the stalls. Klinger stuck his head into the hallway and motioned for Yanich to approach.

"We're all alone up here! Can you believe it?"

"No lights," Yanich said.

Klinger nodded and ventured into the passageway with Yanich close behind. There was enough ambient light for them to make their way to the IRS computer room. The door was locked. Yanich pulled out a small case and, after a few minutes working on the lock, swung the door open. The light was a little better inside the computer room because of the many red and green warning lights that glowed and flickered. Once their eyes became accustomed to the darkness, they moved about with relative ease.

Klinger was shouldering the transformer and soon found a 110v outlet. He plugged his device into the wall and paid out the cord as he crept to the center of the room. Yanich held the dish by its handle. While Klinger steadied the cords from the transformer, Yanich inserted the ends of the wires from the dish into the sockets. Klinger turned a knob on the transformer and a subdued hum grew louder. He watched the needle on a dial moved from left to right and pegged itself on the stop.

"Full power," he whispered.

Yanich threw the switch on the rear of the dish to the "on" position. He moved a control until a needle was centered in the green zone.

"Ready!" he said.

They had assembled a powerful electromagnet whose force could be concentrated and focused. Yanich inched his way around the computer room directing the magnetic beam at the memory banks, the software programs, and the drives of the Internal Revenue Service's electronic records. Twenty-eight minutes later, he put the dish down in the middle of the room.

"Do you think you got them all?" Klinger asked.

"Yeah, but now let's make sure."

They huddled over the dish. Yanich produced the manual and spread it out on the floor. They traced the instructions with their fingers.

"Got it," Klinger said. It was a statement, not a question.

"Me, too."

With the aid of a small pliers and two screwdrivers, they took the cap off of the cone and spread the sides of it outward until it almost lay against the inside of the dish.

"Set it for full power and let's get the hell outta here," Klinger urged.

Yanich twisted the dial and threw the switch to the "on" position. There was a soft hum emanating from the dish as they left the room. The walked to the stairs, descended twelve floors, left by the rear service entrance and disappeared into the night.

Three blocks away, two men left the rear service entrance of another building. That building housed the backup files of the Holtsville IRS. The scenario was parallel.

In the dark, the stars bore witness to the progression of the magnetic destruction of the Internal Revenue Service's files.

Three hours after the Holtsville raid, four men met in a safe house just outside of Fresno, California.

"How'd it go?" one of them asked.

"Just like clockwork," another replied. "If they all went as smooth, the goddam IRS should be history."

"Let's hit the hay," a third said. "We're supposed to report in tomorrow night."

CHAPTER FORTY-ONE

Sheriff Saunders negotiated the rough terrain back to the Apache Trail and then turned south toward Apache Junction. Once on the blacktop, he began to think. Even though the curving road required concentration, he was able to contemplate his position. By the time he had left the s-curves and switchbacks behind, he had a definite plan.

He had been uneasy about his position for quite some time. Now with the coroner out of the way and the professor and Butch facing certain death in the mine, only Jasper and Bubba remained a threat. True, the general and Charlie could expose his activities, but they were in as deep or deeper than he was. His tracks would be covered if Jasper and Bubba were eliminated

"Boys," he said, addressing Jasper and Bubba. "We got one more job to do before you go on up to head-quarters."

"Yeah? What's that?" Jasper asked while Bubba

became attentive.

"The general wants us to search Nichols' house. That's where this Stewart guy has been hanging out. He wants to make sure that he didn't hide something that might lead to the militia."

"That shouldn't take long," Bubba said. "You know where it is?"

"I think I can find it," Saunders said with a hidden smirk as he passed through Apache Junction and turned toward Phoenix.

The grey of morning was just beginning to show as they pulled up in front of the isolated ranch house that belonged to the late Brian Nichols.

"Here we are, boys," Saunders said as he parked at the end of the long driveway.

"Can't you get us a little closer?" Bubba asked.

"I'm gonna park over by those palo verde trees," Saunders explained. "I don't want to take the chance of anyone seeing a car in the driveway. Besides the walk won't kill you. Go along the side of the house and go in the back door. That way you can take your time working on the door without worrying about being seen.

"Okay," Jasper said.

"I'll be up in a minute. I'm gonna call the general and tell him where we are and what we're doing." Saunders said. "When do you think that you'll be getting up there?"

"My car's back in town," Jasper answered. "I guess we won't get started before noon. Tell him it'll be sometime tomorrow afternoon."

Jasper and Bubba shuffled off to the back of the

house while Saunders put the car in gear, drove a hundred yards further down the road, parked next a small stand of palo verde trees and waited.

As they reached the back of the building, Jasper pulled out his flashlight and, hooding the beam with his hands, proceeded to the rear door. Bubba was close behind. He tapped Jasper on the shoulder.

"You smell anything funny?" he asked.

"Just a bunch of horseshit."

"You don't smell anything like gas, do you?"

Jasper lifted his face skyward and took a deep breath through his nostrils.

"All I get is horseshit."

"Yeah, I guess you're right," Bubba conceded. "I must be gettin' paranoid. Shine your light on the lock and I'll get busy."

Bubba pulled a rolled-up cloth from his pocket. He laid it on the cement walk, unrolled it and chose a couple of lock picks. In less than a minute, he announced that the lock was open and that they could enter the house.

"That was easy," he said. "He must have felt pretty safe livin' way out here in the country."

He stepped back as Jasper turned the knob and pushed the door inward.

The explosion felt to Pete Saunders as if he was situated in the center of an earthquake. His car rocked to a forty-five-degree angle and returned to all four tires with a forceful thud. He crouched on the steering wheel with his hands covering his head. His eardrums felt like they were going to explode. Then the rain began. It wasn't water but small particles of debris that pelted the roof of his vehicle.

The noise subsided and he turned to view the house. He was greeted by a cloud of dust that rose a hundred feet into the air. As the dust settled, he looked for the outline of the structure. There was nothing. Even the chimney had been leveled. A bathtub lay upside down in the driveway and a television set sat in the middle of the lawn facing the street as if waiting for some viewers to sit down in the desert and begin watching. Back where the kitchen had once been, a flame burned from a broken gas pipe resembling an Olympic torch and flickering in tribute to the once dignified building that had occupied the site.

Satisfied that he had eliminated the last connection between himself and the mine, the sheriff started his car and drove back to town. He would place the call to the general from the comfort of his own living room.

CHAPTER FORTY-TWO

"We better think about getting outta here," Kevin said, breaking the trance caused by the discovery of the gold.

"Can't we take some with us?" Lauri Beth asked, touching Kevin's forearm.

"If we're gonna, we better do it now. I don't think we'll have another chance to get back here."

His statement was confirmed by a distant rumble followed by a crash as a timber gave way in some far corner of the mine.

"Let's get out of this place first." He continued moving in the direction taken by the pack rat. He picked up some tools and motioned for Lauri Beth to do the same. Hunched over, they crept to where the cave-in sealed their passage to the tunnel.

"I think you were right about the rubble being thinner at this end," Kevin said.

He pointed his light at the lower corner of the blockage.

"Right here," he said. Kevin pulled a couple of good-sized rocks away from the heap, grabbed the prybar and jammed it into the pile. A few strong pokes later, the steel pole slipped through to his forward hand. It took almost forty-five minutes to clear a hole big enough for them to slip through.

"You go on through," Kevin said to Lauri Beth, "and I'll pass the tools to you."

"What about the gold?" she pleaded.

He handed her a number of the bags, then poked his head through the opening and dragged the rest of his body to the other side to join Lauri Beth.

"That's twenty bags," he said. "Do you think a million dollars is enough? I sure hope we live to spend it."

They carried the tools to the edge of the tunnel and then went back for the gold. Lauri Beth scanned the vertical shaft with her infrared goggles. Kevin did the same with his flashlight.

"That blast did us a real favor. It looks like a huge slab broke loose from this wall. We can almost walk straight up."

"I wouldn't be too sure," Lauri Beth corrected. "I'll bet there are a lot a weak spots now. We better not take any chances. It's still a long way down."

Kevin was busy fashioning another harness for Lauri Beth.

"You go on up. Once you're safely in the main tunnel, I'll tie the tools on the line and you can haul them up one at a time," he said. "I'll do the same with the gold."

Lauri Beth was up and out of the shaft like squirrel up a tree. Once in the main tunnel, she surveyed the damage done by the blast.

"Wait 'til you see this," she called down to Kevin. "The cave in comes halfway to the opening of this shaft. It looks like the whole mountain collapsed."

"I'll bet," he yelled back as he tied a slip-hitch around the T of the pickax. "Haul away."

Lauri Beth pulled the rope up hand over hand until she had the pick resting securely on the floor. She untied the knot and sent the line tumbling back down to Kevin's level. The operation was repeated until all of the tools were safely in the main passageway. Then came the gold. After the last bag was retrieved, Lauri Beth secured the line and Kevin appeared at the edge a moment or two later.

After coiling and storing the line, Kevin surveyed the main tunnel.

"I see what you meant," he said. "There's no way in hell that we're going to get out the main entrance. Let's just hope that the first explosion didn't seal off the rear."

"Maybe we better go check," Lauri Beth said, starting toward the rear of the mine.

"Hold on a minute, Lauri Beth, I think we better check on the professor first. If he survived the blast, he may know another way out of here. "Let's get back to the lab and don't forget the tools. We may need them just to get back there."

They were lucky. The main passageway back to the lab was still intact. Kevin and Lauri Beth shouldered their tools and made their way to the lab to search for Dr. Middlestat. There was plenty of debris strewn about the floor that caused them to either climb over or detour around. Each deviation added time to the journey. Throughout the trip there was a low rumbling from the bowels of the mine, accompanied by the creaking and cracking of timbers that sounded like an eighteenth century square rigger sailing through heavy seas. Miraculously, some of the interior lights still functioned, but they were flickering at increasingly frequent intervals.

They reached the lab and found only one light working. The residential section was completely dark. They made their way through the maze of lab tables and into the professor's quarters.

"Doctor Middlestat!" Kevin yelled. "Can you hear me?"

They listened for a response for what seemed an eternity. Finally, a low groan echoed through the chamber.

"Doctor Middlestat! Is that you?" Kevin shouted again.

The sound grew a little stronger and they made out a faint, "Over here."

"It seems to be coming from that far corner," Lauri Beth ventured.

They moved across the room, Lauri Beth with her infrareds and Kevin with his flashlight.

"My God! This place is a mess," she observed as they stepped over a fallen timber.

"Over here," Kevin said as he directed his beam at a huge boulder that had left a cavity in the ceiling and filled the corner of the room.

He bent over and focused his light between the wall and the bottom of the rock.

"He's in there! I can see his legs," Kevin said.

"Professor! Are you all right?"

"I think so," came the weak reply. "I can't really tell. I'm quite numb."

"Just hold on. We'll have you out in a jiffy," Lauri Beth consoled.

The jiffy lasted for over two hours as they chipped and chiseled away at the granite. At last they loosened a piece big enough for Kevin to reach the professor's legs. The old man was slowly and painfully extracted from his prison. They carried him to what was left of his bed, laid him down, and made him as comfortable as possible.

I don't think that he has any broken bones," Lauri Beth said, as she finished examining him. "Only a few bruises. He should be ready to move after a little rest."

She found some blankets under the bed and began to layer the professor with woolen bedding.

"I can't believe that it's so cold in here, when it's over a hundred outside," she said shivering. "Why don't you bring the bags down here, while I take care of him."

Kevin nodded and began a shuttle. He could carry two bags in each hand. The complete delivery took five trips and consumed the better part of an hour.

"How's he doing?" Kevin asked after he had placed the last bag outside of the lab entrance.

"I feel much better now that I think I'm going to live," Middlestat answered for himself as he shed the covers and began to sit up.

Kevin squatted until he was eye level with the doctor.

"Living may depend on more than just feeling okay, doctor. Do you know of any ways out of the mine other than the front door?"

"I'm afraid that I can't be of any assistance in that matter," he sighed. "They kept me a virtual, no make that an actual, prisoner back here. They allowed me to exercise in the main tunnel, but I never found any other way out, and, believe me, I was looking for one."

"Stay with him, will you, Sweetheart?" I'll scout the back air shaft."

"Just a minute," Dr. Middlestat interrupted. "I just thought of something that might be of help. Maybe you could trace the wires to the generator. I know it's located outside of the mine and it requires regular service. Fuel and the like."

"Thanks, Doctor. That's a good thought," Kevin said as he blew Lauri Beth a kiss and disappeared around the corner.

Kevin picked his way through the obstacle course created by the explosion. Timbers and boulders were strewn about like the gods were playing pickup-sticks and marbles. As he approached the rear shaft, the footing became treacherous with all the loose stones. His beam picked up the outline of the vertical shaft and he crept to the edge. He peered over the rim from a prone position. The previously invisible bottom came into clear focus as he looked down on a cone of rock. The first discharge had loosened the sides and caused them to implode. The wreckage had plummeted to the bottom and piled on top of itself, rising halfway up the shaft. Kevin trained his light on the horizontal tunnel that led to the escape chimney. It was gone.

"Holy shit! Now what?"

He moved the light back and forth, up and down across the shambled walls, looking for any sign of escape. About thirty feet below and twenty degrees to the left of the original opening, he steadied the beam on a slight depression. It was a possibility, but first, he wanted to check out the powerline.

He started back to the lab, cautiously moving the flashlight beam across the floor. The timbers growled and he felt the floor quiver. Then he heard another sound. At first, he thought it was caused by the twisting logs but it lasted far longer than any he had heard before. It came from his right and he moved in that direction. A huge ceiling support had been dislodged from one side and rested obliquely from the top corner to the floor. When it had fallen, much of the tunnel roof had accompanied it so that it acted as a ridge pole for a rocky lean-to. The moan was coming from beneath the pile. He began to pull at the bottom rocks but found them firmly wedged.

"What'd you find?" Lauri Beth asked Kevin as he reentered the lab.

"I'm gonna need some help," he said. "I think someone is buried back there. Doctor, wait here. Lauri Beth, grab some tools and follow me."

The area of the canted log rafter was devoid of light and Kevin noted that the main passageway was losing illumination at a rapid rate as one bulb after another flickered and died.

"Over here," Kevin directed as he pointed his beam at the stone that he had tried to remove.

"This place is a real mess," Lauri Beth commented, handing Kevin the prybar and small pick.

The prybar moved the stubborn rock with relative ease and Lauri Beth pulled it out of the way. Kevin dislodged several other stones and was now working with the pick as Lauri Beth continued to pull the loosened debris out of the way.

"Hold up a minute," she said. "I think that I can get my arm in there now."

She lay prone and put her hand into the opening. She was in up to her elbow when she was suddenly drawn against the rock up to her shoulder. She screamed in pain and surprise. Kevin grabbed the prybar and inserted it into the hole. He pushed it slowly until he was sure that he was past Lauri Beth's hand. Then he rammed it in full force. He felt the tip bury itself into something soft. Lauri Beth yanked her arm out as the grip on her hand was released.

"You son of a bitch," roared from inside the pile as Kevin wrenched the bar free.

"You okay?" Kevin asked Lauri Beth. She nodded rubbing her forearm to get circulation going.

"Butch!" he added leaning his head in the direction of the sound. She answered with a grimace. "That bastard lives mean and is going to die mean. Well, I guess we'll have to get him out. We can't just leave him there, although I've no doubt that he'd leave us if the tables were turned."

"Besides, he might know a way out," Lauri Beth justified.

The rescue took a full hour with Kevin manning the bar and pick and Lauri Beth hauling the debris out of the way. When the hole was two feet in diameter, Kevin called to Butch.

"Can you get out by yourself?" he asked.

"Yeah!" Butch growled back like a bear leaving hibernation.

He emerged with the disposition of that same bear. Lauri Beth stepped back to allow him plenty of room. Kevin, however, bent down to help him to his feet. Butch rose slowly as the pain in his joints subsided. Kevin easily avoided the elbow that Butch threw at his head. He spun Butch around until they were face to face and delivered a blow to his midsection followed by a chop to the base of his neck.

"You're welcome," Kevin said as he forced Butch to his feet and shoved him against the wall.

"Lauri Beth!" he said as he frisked Butch. "If he so much as blinks, shoot the bastard."

"It'll be my pleasure," she said pointing her sidearm at Butch's head.

Kevin finished his body search and returned to the escape hole that they had dug for Butch. He lit the inside of the cave with his flashlight, reached in and retrieved his helmet.

"Thanks for keeping this for me, Butch! I hope you didn't leave any lice." To Lauri Beth, he said "The timber kept the rocks from crushing him. In fact, I don't think that he was pinned down at all. He was probably knocked unconscious by the concussion of the explosion and was just coming to when I heard him."

Kevin donned his helmet and tested the infrared goggles.

"The glasses seem to be working," he announced and then turning on his intercom. "Lauri Beth, how do you read me?"

"Five by five," she confirmed.

"Good, let's get back to the lab," Kevin said as he turned off the intercom and pushed Butch in front of him.

The light in the mine was becoming dimmer by the minute. The night-vision goggles were now a distinct advantage, if not a necessity. Butch stumbled repeatedly as he was pushed forward by Kevin and Lauri Beth. His grumbling was accompanied by wild swings of his arms and streams of profanities. They neared the lab opening and a fallen beam lay across the floor. Butch failed to see it and tripped one more time. The air was filled with blasphemies as he landed face first in a bunch of sandbags.

"What th' fuck!" he cursed. "Where the hell did these things come from? They weren't here when I last checked on the old man!"

"None of your business, Butch," Kevin replied as he yanked Butch to his feet and propelled him into the mouth of the lab.

"Stand up facing that wall," he commanded.

Butch's hands were secured behind his back, his feet were tied and then the two were connected by a rope which drew them together on his backside. Butch lay on his side, hogtied.

"That oughtta hold him," Kevin said as he stepped back to view his handiwork. "Now, I'm goin' to check out the generator wires. Honey, watch him but don't get too close and keep your gun trained on him and keep it hot!"

"How're you doin', Doctor?" he continued.

"I'm feeling better, thank you," Middlestat replied. "Sorry that I can't be of any help."

Kevin gave him a reassuring gesture, not really sure that he could see it in the extremely dim light.

"You're wasting your time, smartass," Butch volunteered.

"Yeah?"

"Yeah! I know where those lines lead. They go back past the back shaft and then straight up for a hundred feet. The hole is only about one foot square. I heard that it was a natural chimney. Pack rats go up and down like it's their private elevator, but you won't even get your shoulder inside. It's a good hour's hike to get to the generator from the front entrance, but I guess you won't be goin' that way."

"I guess I better take a look, anyway," Kevin said as he left for the rear of the mine.

"Hey! Sweetheart!" Butch addressed Lauri Beth as Kevin disappeared. "Tell ole Butch what's in the bags. It won't matter none, we're all gonna die down here, anyhow."

As if to confirm Butch's prediction, a tremendous roar came from deep within the mine accompanied by sounds of breaking timbers and crashing stone. The ground shook under their feet. Lauri Beth was almost thrown to the floor but recovered without losing her balance.

"Maybe so," she said, keeping the gun trained on Butch. "But, remember! What you don't know can't hurt us!"

CHAPTER FORTY-THREE

It began immediately after President Jefferson's address to the nation. First, the news commentators analyzed the speech. Then, interviews with leaders of both parties occupied all of the major networks' air time. Following the interpretations of those comments, the predictors, soothsayers, talkshow hosts and pundits got into the act. To a man and woman, they foretold of dire things to come. They forecast the worst days in the nation's history. Citing the weather and the prolongation of the meat crisis, they forecast the riots and pandemonium that would undoubtedly begin with the rising of tomorrow's sun.

Meanwhile, church and civic leaders, police and fire officials, and national heroes of all varieties appeared on television and spoke on radio pleading with the general public to remain calm and to think of the country first and themselves second.

Saturday arrived on schedule and with it came two

events that would shock the doomsday forecasters. The first was considered a miracle and was one of God's favorites, the weather. A powerful static high pressure area had dominated the climate of the continental United States for the past three weeks. This high, described as a blocking high, had prevented the jet stream from dipping below Hudson Bay, thus barring the cool Canadian air from spilling below the border. The lower circulation pattern of the high brought the warm and moist air from the Gulf of Mexico into the country, creating the heat wave.

During the night of the President's speech, this high had suddenly and inexplicably begun to deteriorate and as the dawn broke on Saturday, cool Canadian air poured past the northern border like the raging waters of a broken dam. This cold phalanx spread out and covered the entire country in a meteorological blitzkrieg. The cold air collided with the stagnant warm air and set off showers and thunderstorms. The weather radar looked like a green blanket covering the nation.

The second event was an economic anomaly. Contrary to all of the forecasts of the country's leading economists, financial analysts, and market strategists, the price of meat, lead by cattle, began to decline and the decline occurred overnight.

The high cost of beef, pork, veal and lamb had driven the vast majority of Americans away from the butcher's counters. The substitute foods that they put into their diets had actually improved the nation's health. Waistlines had shrunk and excess pounds had disappeared as if by magic. It would take time for taste buds to take precedence over well-being.

The price of meat and the President's prediction to the end of the shortages brought sellers out of the woodwork. Some producers had been holding back livestock greedily waiting for yet even higher prices. Others decided that the time was ripe for thinning out depleted herds and upgrading the quality of their stock. But they were too late. The ripple effect had taken place in a few short hours. Somehow, without a formal declaration, the grocery stores knew that they could no longer sell high-priced protein. The wholesalers knew that the grocers would not be ordering and the meat packers knew that their market had disappeared. When the producers called the stockyards on Saturday morning and asked for the current prices for live animals, they received no bids. The market was gone. Just like the tulipomania bubble of the seventeenth century, the meteoric rise of meat prices over the past few years gave way to a precipitous fall. The ensuing charts would look like a mountain with half of its mass sliced off by a giant rotary saw. And in the end it was the market, that nebulous mystic thing that few understood and all feared, that prevailed.

The core of the New Revolutionary Militia took to the streets early on Saturday morning. By the time they reached the first of their new recruits, they were drenched to the skin and their enthusiasm was draining like a deluge into a storm sewer. Instead of thousands pouring into the streets with waving banners and shaking fists, a hundred or so, most of them the nucleus of the militia, huddled under any shelter that was available, shivering from the unexpected cold and the penetrating rain.

The idea of rioting ebbed away as cool air swept into ghetto apartments and public housing developments. The media had deployed thousands of personnel and tons of equipment waiting for the predicted bedlam. Disillusioned by the relatively empty streets, they focused on whatever group they could find, no matter how small. Interviewers tried their best to instigate demonstrations and vandalism. In some cases they were successful and the video cameras began to roll, taping minor incidents that would be blown out of proportion for the evening news.

In Queens, New York, an overturned automobile; in Chicago, a broken pane glass window; and in Los Angeles, a few looters carrying appliances down the street were featured on network news as evidence of the unrest that they considered their duty to report to the American people.

The police had canceled all days off and extra patrols were cruising the streets. Mounted officers and canine units had been placed at strategic locations. The United States Army and the National Guard were in position and heavily armed. Bayonets were fixed and gas masks were at the ready. Central communications, linking all available forces, kept all units apprised of the situation.

It became evident by ten o'clock in the morning that the situation as expected was not going to develop. Soaked by the constant rain, the troops were systematically dismissed. By three o'clock in the afternoon, all army and Guard units had returned to their bases and regular-strength police components patrolled the streets. The stand-down followed the time zones, and by six o'clock eastern time the West Coast was back to normal. The only exception was New Orleans, where the falling temperatures and accompanying rain showers brought half-clad merrymakers into the streets and a riot of a different sort had to be controlled.

The news analysts didn't miss a beat. Their predictions, only a few hours old, were cast aside like old shoes. None admitted to their miscalculations and by the end of most broadcasts, the deep-voiced all-knowing pundits were suggesting that they had forecast just such an outcome.

The weathermen and women were not to be outdone. Charts and maps cluttered the video screens showing in detail how the hotspell had been broken. No reference was made to previous forecasts and, just like their counterparts in the news departments, by the end of their segments bragging rights had been established.

President Branden David Jefferson watched the news until two o'clock in the morning. After he was satisfied that Los Angeles, San Francisco and Seattle had made it through the day with little or no disruption, he telephoned his press secretary and arranged an early morning meeting. There would be news conferences and news releases but they would be conducted by his staff. He would wait until the right political moment to make a full-blown address and take credit for the victory.

*

In the wilderness area of the great State of Idaho, General Boone had his eyes glued to the television screen. He had been motionless, seated three feet in front of the tube, since early morning when the first newscasts began from the East Coast. The only sounds he emitted were profanities as it became clear that the planned riots would not occur. Major Jimmy Ray Wheeler and Charlie Whitfield were seated behind him well out of his reach. Occasionally, one or the other would sneak out for a snack or to use the toilet facilities or to stretch.

It was well after noon when the general stood, stretched his arms, rubbed his rear-end and uttered one last obscenity.

"Goddam it all, anyway!" he stormed. "Who wouldda figured the son-of-a-bitchen weather and the fuckin' market?"

Wheeler and Charlie were looking for shelter when the telephone rang. Charlie made a dive for it and just managed to beat out the major.

"Yeah!" he said and then listened for what seemed an interminable time to the others. "Good! I'll tell the general."

He put the receiver down and faced two demanding scowls.

"That was Homer from Atlanta. He's calling to report that his operation went off without a hitch, both the main office and the backup location. He figured you'd want to know as soon as possible. He thinks that, with all the security goin' on, they won't be back in the building until Monday morning."

"Only good news I've had today," Boone grumbled.

Charlie and Wheeler were starting their second high five when the phone rang again. This time Wheeler picked it up.

"Yeah," he said, mimicking Charlie's earlier response. He continued to listen, his features showing obvious excitement. He put his hand over the mouthpiece and signaled thumbs-up.

"Andover," he whispered.

It went on that way for the rest of the day and into the early evening. Fresno was the last to report. All of the messages were the same. Mission completed. Both locations destroyed. The outside perimeter guards would be in place until Monday so it seemed unlikely that their activities would be detected until after the weekend.

*

In Dallas, Burleson watched the same shows that were being seen by the President and the general. There was no redeeming aspect for him. The authorities had been closing in on his operations and were certain to indict him in a matter of days. His attorneys had assured him that the direct evidence was only circumstantial and that the grand jury would in all likelihood not send him to trial. Unless a direct connection could be established between him and the virus outbreak, he and Little Jim Plover would go free.

These facts gave him some consolation, but not enough to offset the financial disaster that confronted him. He had leveraged his position to the hilt and had paid premium prices for ranches and feed lots. It had all looked good on paper as long as cattle prices remained high, but now, with prices plummeting, his empire was in serious jeopardy. Monday morning would be a hell on earth. His devious mind began churning as he tried to figure a way to lay off his losses on others.

Thank God for that last conversation with Pete Saunders. The destruction of the mine and with it the death of Dr. Middlestat and the other meddlers left him with only his financial crisis to worry about. He doubted he could survive if both catastrophes hit at the same time.

CHAPTER FORTY-FOUR

Ninety minutes after he had disappeared into the darkness, Kevin's shadowy form reentered the lab. He looked at the three occupants and addressed Lauri Beth.

"Is he behaving himself?" he asked, moving his head in Butch's direction.

"So far," she said. "I think he's beginning to mellow just a bit or, at least, the ropes are getting their point across."

"Good! There may be a way out of here after all. I followed the generator wires back some seventy-five feet past the rear shaft and found the chimney that Butch mentioned. The explosion did us a favor. It looks to me like that chimney was formed by two vertical slabs and when the mountain collapsed up front, the slabs pulled apart and now there's a four-foot-square going straight up. I couldn't see any daylight but if the fracture followed the original slab line, there's no reason why it shouldn't go all the way to the top."

"Thank God!" Lauri Beth and Middlestat exclaimed in unison.

"Let's get the hell outta here, then," Butch grunted. "How about gettin' these ropes offa me? I won't give ya any trouble. I figure we're all in this together and if we're gonna ever see daylight again, then we're gonna have to do it together."

"You're right about that, Butch," Kevin said as he leaned over and cut the ropes. "But I still don't trust you. You make one false move and you'll end up just another skeleton guarding this mine."

"What the hell are you talkin' about?" Butch said as he rubbed circulation back into his hands. "I ain't never seen any skeletons."

"I guess you've never been where we've been, then," Lauri Beth said.

Kevin gave her a signal with his forefinger to his lips and she turned to Middlestat.

"How are you feeling, doctor?" she asked. "Are you up to getting out of here?"

"I'm pretty weak, but the thought of getting back to the real world will give me enough strength. I'm sure."

"Doctor," Kevin said. "There are couple of things I need to ask you before we start. First, is there any serum in the lab? And I mean the virus-causing stuff as well as the antitoxin."

"The lab!" said the doctor as he suddenly clarified his thinking. "Of course, the lab. There's about a dozen or so containers of each chemical. They're stored in gallon plastic bottles and they're quite heavy. And then, I'm going to need all of my notes and formulas.

"Well, we 'd best get that stuff together," Kevin said. "The other thing I wanted to know is how much you might have learned about this entire operation."

"Watch what you say, professor!" Butch threatened.

"You don't scare me anymore, Butch! I'll tell Kevin everything that I know, starting with your involvement with the murder of Ed Murphy in Dallas."

Butch made a move toward Middlestat, but Kevin stepped in between. Butch turned around with a menacing look toward both of them. Kevin led Dr. Middlestat into the lab and motioned for Lauri Beth to follow.

"I don't think he'll be going anywhere," he said, referring to Butch. "And I think that you should hear what the good doctor has to say.

As the three unwilling speleologists busied themselves collecting bottles and papers at the direction of Dr. Middlestat, he revealed a tale that bordered on the impossible and the unbelievable.

"It began with my introduction to Little Jim Plover at a Dallas social event. Plover scheduled a meeting with two other cattlemen, Ed Murphy and Harry Burleson. Burleson convinced the others that my discovery of a virus that controlled or retarded the reproductive ability of animals could be put to genetic and financial advantage. Burleson also had a relationship with Sheriff Pete Saunders of Maricopa County, Arizona.

"Saunders was also a member of a group known as the New Revolutionary Militia. This dissident band was headquartered in Idaho and was aggressively recruiting new members. Its leader is a self-styled militarist who calls himself, General Harry Boone. His real name is anybody's guess, but I suspect that Harry was probably the only part of his moniker that he carried since birth.

"The sheriff provided cover for their trapping activities as they secured and injected coyotes to carry the virus around the country. The first trappers stumbled onto this mine and so they set up operations here. The general quickly assumed control and began to plan for a revolutionary strike. He planned to use soaring meat prices to generate cover for a raid of some sort against the establishment. Saunders got his friend, the coroner, involved and the general sent Charlie Whitfield and Butch Crosswell down here to run this end of the business."

Middlestat paused for a long sigh, then continued. "I started to protest, and that's when I became a prisoner. I overheard Butch bragging about how he murdered Ed Murphy and then how Saunders did the same with the coroner. He and Charlie Whitfield also murdered some guy named Brian something or other who just happened to be flying too close to the entrance of the mine."

"That was my uncle, Brian Nichols," Kevin said. "That's how I got involved and how I met Lauri Beth. She worked in the coroner's office and suspected something was irregular with my uncle's death."

"How did you ever find this place?" Middlestat asked.

"That's a long story, too long for now. Do we have everything you need?"

"I guess so, I'm sorry to be such a bother, but I think it's all-important."

"Don't worry about it," Kevin reassured him. "We'll get you and your things out first and then bring up the gold if there's still time."

"Gold?"

"Yes, doctor, Butch guessed it. We came across a cache after the explosion and brought twenty bags with us."

"My goodness!" Middlestat exclaimed. "Who would have thought that there was anything of value in this godforsaken place."

They carried and dragged the bottles and papers to the entrance of the main tunnel. There they found Butch sitting on the bags of gold with an open one on his lap, the leather thong untied, and the fine powder sifting through his fingers. He clutched the open bag by its throat and stood as they approached.

""Well, it looks as if we got ourselves a little reward after all. This'll pay for all my trouble."

Kevin was about to answer when Butch was thrown backwards onto the other bags by a concussive convulsion somewhere in the mine. Lauri Beth dropped the four bottles she was carrying as she was flung to the ground. Middlestat sat unceremoniously on the hard floor, his arms still securely around the accordion folders that held his precious research papers. Kevin managed to keep his grip on the case of serum that he was dragging across the lab, but slammed into a table and was caromed into another.

The noise that accompanied the convulsion was deafening. A combination of crashing rock and splitting timbers was followed by a billowing of dust and debris that filled the mine.

"I hope we're not too late," Kevin panted as he regained his footing. "That one could have closed off our escape route."

It took ten precious minutes for the dust to settle. Even then eyesight was limited to a few feet.

"Follow me," Kevin directed as he hefted a carton of chemicals that weighed close to a hundred pounds. "These goggles still help, but the dust is pretty thick. Doctor, you follow me. Butch, you grab some bottles, take the flashlight and help the professor."

"Fuck you, mister," Butch exploded. "I'm totin' the gold."

Kevin put the carton on a pile of rocks and turned to Butch.

"You so much as touch one of those bags and I'll kill you on the spot. You carry these bottles and papers just like the rest of us and we'll see about the gold later."

"So it is gold!" Butch smiled in triumph. "Just remember, what I carry out is mine and mine alone!"

The trip to the rear of the mine was extremely slow and was hindered further by a rhythmic tremble that dislodged timber and rock alike. It took a full half hour for the party of four to reach its destination. Kevin and Lauri Beth helped the doctor to a relatively comfortable seat among the rocks and inspected the chimney.

"That last big quake closed the gap by about six

inches," Kevin pointed out. "We don't have any time to waste."

The next two trips went considerably faster as the doctor remained by the shaft.

On the last trip Kevin and Lauri Beth each put a hand pick in their belt.

"These might be real handy. That shaft could be smooth in some spots," Kevin said as they headed back to the shaft for the last time.

"It'll be time to go as soon as I scout out the shaft," Kevin said to Middlestat. "Ready?"

"What about my papers?"

"Well, they're not too heavy. Since we're going to be hauling you up anyway, I think that we can tie most of them under your clothes."

He then began to tie a boatswain's chair for the doctor to sit in. Once Middlestat had his legs and arms through the loops and was in a seated position, Kevin made a sack of his shirt and stuffed it with the papers. He was able to load all of the doctor's valuables on his person and then tie them firmly in place with loops around his body.

"There, that ought to do it," he said as he stepped back to inspect his work. "Now let's get out of here. I'll go first and after I've tied off the line, I'll pull Dr. Middlestat up, with Lauri Beth helping from behind. Butch, you can start tying stuff on the end of the line. As soon as we're secure on top, we'll haul out the bottles. If there's any further collapse within the mine, you get out in a hurry. Grab the line, wrap it around your wrist and then just walk up the wall. We'll be hauling from above. Got it?"

"Yeah! I got it! Ole Butch don't count! He can stay until last and, if the fuckin' mine don't cave in around him, then he can come out! That's it! Ain't it?"

"No, Butch that ain't it. You're not a climber and Lauri Beth is. She'll be twice as valuable as you helping from behind. If I had my way, she'd be the first up, you'd be right after Dr. Middlestat and I'd be last. Lauri Beth isn't strong enough to hoist Dr. Middlestat and I want to do the free climb. As a matter of fact, I'd better start that right now."

With that, Kevin tied the coiled line around his waist.

"Lauri Beth, do you have the picks?" he asked, searching the nearby floor.

"We each put one in our belts, remember?"

"Yeah," he replied. "I don't know what I was thinking. Give me yours, please. There's no telling what I'll run into."

The first part was easy and handholds were abundant but as he approached the mid-point, the chimney narrowed and purchase places were scarcer. He was forced to use the pickaxes to widen the minuscule chinks in the almost polished wall. Each handhold was painstakingly achieved and he literally clawed his way upward.

His goggles allowed him to see above only if he strained his neck to tilt his face upwards. There was a small outcropping at the fifty-foot level and negotiating it took all of Kevin's mountaineering skills. As he pulled himself over the ledge, he could see why the sky was invisible from below. The shaft ran at a ten-degree angle from that point to the surface. There were ample finger and handholds along the bottom edge and the slant made for an easier ascent. As he climbed, moisture appeared on the slanting surface and increased until droplets started running down the incline. His feet were feeling the slackening adhesion just as his fingers curled around the upper edge.

Kevin was soon breathing the fresh wet air of a stormy Arizona dawn. He unfastened the line from his waist and took the loose end some twenty feet from the opening. There he looped it around a solitary mesquite tree and tied it off with a full hitch. He put his weight against line and satisfied himself that the tree would hold. He then let the rope slide between his fingers as he proceeded to the open shaft. A large boulder blocked his path and he wrapped the line twice around it with a double clove hitch. Kevin dropped the line down the shaft and watched it slide down the upper chute and over the edge of the outcropping. He grabbed the rope and began to rappel down the shaft . Once over the ledge he slid rapidly to the bottom.

"It's okay," he declared. "There's an outcropping about halfway up that's going to give us some trouble, but otherwise it's okay."

"That's great news," Lauri Beth said. "But what kind of trouble?"

"Nothing serious. It just means that we're going to have to go up in two stages to avoid sawing on the rope. How much line do we have down here at the bottom?"

Kevin was assessing the extra line as he spoke. He peeled off twenty feet from where the line lay on the mine floor and severed it.

"Looks like a least a hundred feet. That should be plenty," he said as he coiled the line and handed it to Lauri Beth. "By the way, it's raining up there!"

"Here's the plan," he continued. "We'll tie the doctor's bos'n's chair to the end of the line and then you and I will go on up. I'll hoist him to the first level while you take this extra line and secure it around a mesquite tree on top. Once I've got him over the ledge, I'll change lines to the chair and come up to join you. After we've got him safely on top, I'll go back down and have Butch tie a carton of serum to the main line. From then on it should go fast. I'll haul up and over the ledge, retie the load to the second line, and you haul it up to the top from there. I'll be lifting the next load and have it ready by the time you've dropped the line back down. Okay?"

Then turning to Butch he began, "You got th—?"

Butch was nowhere in sight.

"Now where in the hell did he disappear to?"

"I think he's gone to fetch the gold," Middlestat said.

The words had no sooner been uttered when Butch appeared half carrying half-dragging four of the bags.

"Goddam it, Butch!" Kevin yelled. "I thought I said we'd leave the gold for last."

"Yeah! I heard ya!" Butch snarled. "It'll be last all right and I'll be bringin' it up."

A low rumble, accompanied by a slight shaking of the earth, interrupted the potential argument.

"Look!" Kevin said, addressing Butch. "We're taking Middlestat up now. Once I drop the line back down, tie on another load and I'll haul it up. We ought to be finished in three or four loads. Then we'll think about the gold."

Kevin turned toward the dangling line, without waiting for an argument or reply. Lauri Beth was halfway up when he grabbed the line and began his ascent. He pulled himself over the outcropping just in time to see her scramble out of the shaft. Kevin found the footing that he was looking for, took some slack out of the line and looped it around his torso to prevent him from being pulled off the ledge. He leaned over the edge and began hauling up his human cargo.

He can't weigh over a hundred pounds, even with all his papers, Kevin thought, thanking the Lord for small blessings.

Suddenly the weight seemed to double as the chimney shook and the walls closed about six inches. The attending crescendo almost caused Kevin to lose his grip on the rope. As it was, the unexpected tremor dropped the doctor about five feet in a free-fall plunge.

"Kevin! Are you all right?" Lauri Beth screamed from above.

"Yeah! That was really a big one," he managed to grunt out a reply.

It took more effort than he had expected to get Middlestat over the ledge and there was no place for him to anchor the doctor while he changed lines.

"Lauri Beth!" he yelled upwards. "This is a little more difficult that I figured."

"Anything I can do?" she answered.

"Okay, I've got the second line on him. You can start pulling him up. Doctor, just turn facing me and crawl right over me and up the wall while Lauri Beth pulls you up."

The doctor obeyed without a word. Kevin could see the fear in his eyes as their faces passed.

"Just hang in there, doctor," he whispered. "You'll be outta here in only a few more feet."

Kevin got a knee and then a foot in his face as Middlestat squirmed past him being pulled steadily upward by Lauri Beth. Once he was sure that Middlestat was past him and safely on his way to the top, Kevin dropped the line down the shaft. He waited patiently for the tug on the rope that would signal the next load ready. Two light jerks on the line indicated that the load had been tied on and Kevin began hauling it toward him. He was expecting a case of serum, but the dead weight of six plastic bottles in a wooden container exceeded sixty pounds. The wooden box swung back and forth as he raised it hand over hand. Finally it appeared at the ledge and with one surge of strength, Kevin hoisted it over. He reached for the second line that Lauri Beth had dropped and for the first time looked into the crate.

"Son of a bitch!" he exclaimed. "That rotten no good son of a bitch!"

"What's wrong?" Lauri Beth called from above.

"That goddam Butch packed the box with four bags of gold and left the serum below."

Before Lauri Beth could comment, Kevin had

pushed the crate over the ledge. He heard it crash on the mine floor and uncoiled the line from his body. It seemed to Butch that only a split-second had elapsed between the time that the box had exploded at his feet and Kevin stood before him.

"Get outta my way," Kevin said, as he shoved Butch in the chest and reached for an unbroken crate.

As he pulled the crate toward him, he sensed a movement from Butch. Kevin instinctively rolled to his right and over a fallen timber just as the point of a pickax buried itself in the wood. He continued his roll and began to rise in a crouched position when he felt his helmet ripped from his head and thrown into the darkness. His head snapped back in resistance to the unexpected force. Butch recovered from his two-handed throw of Kevin's helmet and kicked in blind fury. His foot found its mark just above Kevin's groin. Kevin doubled over in pain as a pile-driver blow descended on his neck. He felt his legs give way as he fell to the rocky floor. He stuck his right hand out to break his fall but just as his fingers felt solid ground, he let his arm collapse and tucked his right shoulder. He collided with the debris-strewn floor with the back of his right shoulder and continued to roll.

He felt a swish of air past his face as Butch aimed another kick but missed to the inside. The force of the kick carried Butch to his right and off balance. By the time he recovered, Kevin's head had cleared and he was back on his feet. Butch sought to keep his advantage by bull-rushing his opponent. He lowered his head and charged Kevin's left side. He was six inches from contact when he felt Kevin's hands on his shoulders. He struck empty air as Kevin pushed downward on his foe and allowed his left leg to swing freely, giving Butch nothing but a brush with his clothing and sending him careening further into the mine.

The only light was supplied by a single fifty-watt bulb that somehow had managed to remain alight and Butch's flashlight, which he had propped against a timber and focused on the pile of gold bags. The shadows cast by the two combatants were Fantasia-like specters as the fight moved across the mine. First from one side of the escape shaft and then to the other, the contest varied from karate chops to wrestling. They were equally matched in strength. Kevin held the advantage in ability, while Butch's street technique and hatred evened the field.

The cobwebs caused by Butch's first attack were rapidly dissipating and Kevin's strength was approaching one hundred percent. Kevin was clearly getting the upper hand and an open palm to Butch's face sent him reeling. He stumbled backwards toward the open shaft that had supplied the first escape route and tripped over a fallen beam. He landed hard on his back and, with a string of profanities, rolled over. As he attempted to regain his footing, a rock gave way and he frantically pumped his legs searching for solid ground. Unfortunately for him, he found it and he propelled himself unwillingly to the edge. As momentum carried his upper body over the empty shaft, he reached back, desperately seeking a handhold. His right hand found a projection and he locked onto it.

The force of his slide swung him over the edge and he dangled over certain death with a single precarious grip. He was unable to pull himself up and, cursing Kevin and every living thing, he resigned himself to his fate.

Kevin reacted quickly and in the only way that he knew. He bent over the edge and grabbed Butch's wrist. He hauled Butch high enough so that he could get a leg over the rim and then dragged him onto solid ground. Butch lay prone, gasping for breath as Kevin backed off making sure that he was out of his reach.

"Had enough?" Kevin asked.

Butch curled his mouth into a snarl and was about to answer when the ground began to quiver to a low but growing rumble. Both men sensed the seriousness of the warnings. Butch got to his feet and pushed past Kevin without a word. They arrived at the chimney amid growing sounds from the belly of the mine. The safety line was swinging to and fro like a reed in the wind and loose rocks were falling from above. Kevin grabbed a bottle of serum and one of the virus, regretting that he didn't have time for more. He turned to Butch and found him frantically tying gold bags to his belt.

"I don't think we've got time for that," he said.

"Fuck you, mister," came the reply. "I'm takin' all I can carry."

Kevin reached into his pack, pulled out his jumars and tossed them to Butch.

"You know how to use these?" he said. "You'll need them to get up with all that gold."

"Yeah!" Butch growled and then mumbled an unintelligible, "Thanks."

Kevin stuffed the two bottles in his pack and reached for the swinging rope. Just before he began his ascent, he took a look back at Butch. He was tying bags of gold together in a makeshift sling. Counting the four bags that he had already secured to his belt and the four in the sling, he would be lugging an extra one hundred twenty pounds.

With a shrug, Kevin placed his feet against a wall of the chimney and began to climb. The mine continued to groan and shake with increased intensity. Rocks and gravel were falling down the chimney, bouncing off the walls and pummeling Kevin about the shoulders. He dreaded the thought of a direct hit on his head and kept it tucked beneath his raised arms.

At the bottom of the rope, Butch had finished his sling and was now tying the remaining twelve bags into two clusters of six each. These he tied to the loose end of the rope, about ten feet apart. The chimney was disgorging rocky vomit at an alarming rate as Butch loaded the sling over his head and engaged the jumars. The strain on his body was overwhelming but his greed fueled his adrenaline and he started to climb the rope. Without the jumars, he wouldn't have made it up the first ten feet, but the clamping handles gave him enough purchase on the line to allow a painful but steady progress.

By the time Butch had begun his ascent, Kevin had already reached the outcropping. He negotiated it easily and found that the raining debris lessened considerably in upper half of the shaft. In less than a minute, he was at the top and into the Lauri Beth's welcoming arms.

"Thank God! Thank God!" she repeated. "I thought the mine would collapse before you got out. What made you go back down, anyway?"

"That fool, Butch, sent up gold instead of serum. I had to go down and load it myself. And he tried to stop me."

"Where is he, anyhow?" Middlestat asked.

"He's down there somewhere. He was loading himself up with enough gold to rival Fort Knox. He'll be lucky to get out alive."

As if to make Kevin's prediction a reality, the ground erupted in a violent shake that knocked all three off their feet and produced a billow of dust from the narrowing shaft. After the smoke had settled, Kevin beamed the flashlight down the shaft. He could make out the rope going over the edge and the tautness of the line indicated that Butch was somewhere below.

"Pull up the goddam rope," Butch yelled. "I'm hangin' here and the fuckin' mine is falling apart all around me."

"Okay!" Kevin yelled back. And then to Lauri Beth and Dr. Middlestat, "Lauri Beth come over here and give me a hand. Doctor, undo that first loop around the rock, then sit behind it with your feet against it and take up any slack as we try to pull him out."

The ground was now in a continual state of flux and the noise from the mine was unceasing. Kevin and Lauri Beth braced themselves as best they could and began tugging on the line. Inch by inch and foot by foot they dragged the rope backwards. They had retrieved about ten feet of line when they ran out of footing.

"Take up the slack now, Doctor," Kevin ordered. Then to Lauri Beth, "This wet line doesn't help any."

Middlestat pulled the rope around the rock and then sat back keeping tension on the line and allowing the boulder to work as a giant winch.

"Okay," he signaled.

Kevin and Lauri Beth released their hold on the line and went back to their original positions. Before grabbing the line, Kevin directed the flashlight beam down the shaft. He saw one hand above the ledge. It held a bag of gold.

"We've almost got him up. One more pull should get him over the ledge."

By now the last twelve bags were suspended above the ground and instead of pulling just two hundred pounds of humanity they were trying to hoist an extra one million dollars in three hundred pounds of gold.

"God, he's heavy," Kevin exclaimed. "All together now, on the count of three. Ready! One! Two! Th—."

It happened in less time than he could say the number three. The ground dropped three feet and a seam appeared two yards to their right. The ensuing detonation split their eardrums and sent a shock wave of pain through their heads. The ground on the far side of the seam slid forward a full yard. It jolted to a stop with a colossal bang. Rocks, boulders and foliage that had been in place for thousands of years were torn from their foundations and deposited in new locations that would be their homes for at least another millennium.

Kevin and Lauri Beth had been anticipating the undelivered count and had maximum pressure on the line as the mine collapsed. They were thrown unceremoniously on their rear ends partly by the movement of the earth and partly by the fact that the rope had parted and they held a line with no resistance on the other end. Middlestat crawled from behind his boulder and joined his stunned companions.

"What was that?" he trembled.

"I think that was the end of the mine and the end of Butch, as well," Kevin answered.

The three crept to the edge of the shaft, only to find the once three-foot-by-three-foot opening had been reduced one tenth of its original size. Kevin poked his flashlight into the hole and reported to the others.

"There's nothing there. The whole shaft is gone. I can only see about five or six feet down and its solid rock. It's like the shaft was being held apart by some gigantic force and when the mine collapsed, it slid together like a piece of machinery with a zero degree of tolerance."

"Butch?" Lauri Beth asked.

"He couldn't have felt a thing," Kevin said. Middlestat nodded in agreement.

The collapse of the mine and rapid closure of the shaft had created a bellows effect that propelled a huge mushroom cloud into the atmosphere. The particles from which were just beginning to settle. Lauri Beth felt it first.

"That's strange," she said.

"What?" the other two said in chorus.

"The texture and the color of this dust," she said. "It's so fine."

Kevin collected some in his palm and rubbed it between his fingers.

"Look at this," he said, showing the stain on his thumb and forefinger to Lauri Beth and Middlestat, who bent over for a closer look.

"It looks like..." he mused.

"Gold," Lauri Beth finished.

"Yep!" Kevin said. "I guess Butch finally got his just reward."

CHAPTER FORTY-FIVE

The three sat back on the still-quivering ground and reflected on their good fortune. "A few minutes difference and we could have suffered the same fate," Middlestat said, tilting his head toward Butch's final resting place.

"What a tragic end to a tragic life," Lauri Beth reflected.

"I'm glad we got out," Kevin said. "Butch would have made it, too, if it hadn't been for his insane greed."

"Thank God, you were able to get at least one bottle of serum and virus," Middlestat said. "You have no idea how that will speed up the manufacture of the antidote. I'm quite hopeful that my findings will eventually lead to a positive contribution to society. At least, I'm going to devote my life to that end."

"Speaking of the future, we've still got to get off this mountain and back to civilization. How's everyone feel?" Kevin said, as he adjusted the bottles in his pack and made room for the Middlestat files.

"No broken bones, but a bit tired and shook up," Middlestat reported.

"I'm okay, too," Lauri Beth said. "How about you, Kevin? You're the one that we should be worried about."

"I'll make it. My shoulders are pretty sore from all those rocks hitting me as I came out, and Butch roughed me up quite a bit during our little argument, but I'm good enough to travel."

"Let's go then," Middlestat said as he got to his feet, determined not to hold the others up.

Lauri Beth extended a hand to Kevin, which he gladly accepted as he got up and shouldered his pack.

"Thanks," he said. "Lauri Beth, would you please pack those two hand picks? We may still have some use for them."

"What's the course, captain?" she said. "It'll be great traveling in daylight for a change. I could just picture the three of us falling down the mountain in the dark."

"Set your GPS for the main entrance to the mine and we'll follow the contours and ridge lines until we know exactly where we are."

"Aye, aye, sir," she answered, giving a mock salute and starting off in the direction indicated by the GPS. Her spirit cheered the other two and Middlestat took the second position while Kevin followed up the rear. The going was slow and wet. Every steep pitch had to be traversed and Middlestat required assistance around the switchbacks and over any sizable boulder. Three hours after they set out, the hikers reached the bowl containing the mine entrance. The only safe way down was a long march along the ridge line that led to the original saddle. Even though the passage was relatively easy, the trip took well over an hour. It was just after high noon when they descended to the saddle.

"Let's rest here before we start for the horses," Kevin suggested.

Kevin and Lauri Beth dropped their packs and helped the doctor find a comfortable spot. Kevin had planned to spend the best part of an hour before they resumed their journey and was beginning to drift off when he heard it. Lauri Beth picked the sound up a few seconds later. It started like the ticking of a wind-up alarm clock and quickly grew to the rhythmic sound of a Persian rug being beaten clean of a ten-year accumulation of dirt. Then it turned into the familiar "whump-whump" of helicopter blades beating a path through the air.

Lauri Beth and Middlestat looked skyward and failed to pick out the aircraft. Kevin recognized the tone of the beats immediately and focused his eyes just above the horizon.

"What a beautiful sight!" he exclaimed as the twin-jet Bell 206 screamed toward the saddle at 120 knots. The pilot gained a few feet of altitude, cleared the saddle and within seconds was hovering at the collapsed entrance to the mine. The sliding side doors were already open and Kevin had noted two pairs of combat boots planted on each of the cradle bars as the chopper roared by. Now those boots became animated. Two men deplaned from each side, followed by two equipment bags which were in turn followed by more men. The eight men deployed as their feet hit the ground. The chopper leaped straight up, made a thunderous left turn and disappeared as quickly as it had come. Six of the eight provided cover while the other two dragged the equipment bags out of the open area. It was almost comical to see eight fully trained and camouflaged men training their automatic weapons on a pile of rocks, for that was what the entrance to the mine had become.

Kevin wasn't about to take any unnecessary chances. He cautioned Lauri Beth and Middlestat to keep out of sight, while he extracted a piece of cloth from his pack and began waving it.

"Up here! Up here!" he yelled.

A pair of binoculars were immediately trained in his direction and the officer in charged gave a series of quick commands. Two of the men left the main body and began leapfrogging toward the saddle. When they got within fifty yards of Kevin's position, they sheltered themselves, and one of them called out, "Drop all weapons and come out with your hands over your heads!"

Kevin nodded to his companions, dropped his pack, raised his hands and slowly showed himself.

"Identify yourself!" the trooper demanded.

"Master Sergeant Kevin Stewart, United States Army, Special Forces," Kevin snapped in return.

"And the others?"

"Lauri Beth McCartney, civilian."

"Doctor Bernard Middlestat, liberated prisoner."

The tension eased visibly, although the guns remained trained on the trio.

"I'm the one that called into the Dallas Police and gave the location," Kevin volunteered.

The first soldier approached while the other spoke into a hand-held radio.

"His name checks out. Get some ID!"

Kevin reached into his pocket with his left hand and produced a plastic sealed card.

"ID's okay," the first soldier confirmed to his partner.

"What goes on here?" he continued, addressing Kevin.

"Mine's been closed," Kevin said. "Dynamited. That used to be the entrance. We got out through a vent shaft in the rear. That's gone now, too. The three that set the blast all got away. A fourth didn't make it out. He got caught when the rear shaft closed."

They were now being escorted down to the other soldiers. One of them left his position and met them halfway.

"Captain Jeremy Scott," he said returning Kevin's salute and extending his hand. "FBI Special Task Force."

Kevin offered a synopsis of their involvement and description of their latest adventures. Scott nodded his understanding.

"That about wraps it up," Kevin concluded.

Scott called his second officer aside and the two conferred for a few minutes. The two separated. Scott returned to Kevin while his second in command spoke into his walkie-talkie.

"I'm going to leave Lieutenant Burns here with the rest of the squad. They'll scout around until dark and we'll pick them up then. Meanwhile,—."

His voice was drowned out by the sound of the returning helicopter. The pilot set the chopper down a few yards from them and let the rotor spin.

"Meanwhile," Scott continued as the noise abated, "we'd better get the three of you out of here."

"Okay," Kevin said. "You can drop Lauri Beth and me off at our horses. We've got a truck and an SUV parked further on down and I'd like to get back to the house before we debrief. Dr. Middlestat's more important at the moment. Your boss will probably want him in Dallas as soon as possible."

"I'll tell you what," Scott decided. "I'll check in as soon as we're airborne and see if headquarters will agree."

They boarded the chopper and as soon as they took off, Scott dialed the second radio to a secure frequency and began talking. The pilot was about to touch down near the horses as the captain turned the radio off.

"The chief wants to see you as soon as possible," he said. "However, he's willing to make one concession. He'll meet you at your house and begin the debriefing immediately. What's the address?"

Kevin supplied the information and shook Middlestat's hand as he stepped out of the chopper.

"Take care, doctor," he said. "You're in good hands, now. Good luck."

He turned to the captain and said, "Just one more thing. Could you get Lauri Beth's car back to her house? I'd like her to ride with me."

"No problem," Scott said. "Just give me the keys and

her address."

Lauri Beth handed over her keys, dictated her address and said, "Just park it on the street and lock the keys inside. I've got another set."

She gave the doctor a hug and whispered encouragement to him as she followed Kevin. They hurried out of the rotor's range in the customary stooped posture. The blades began to speed up as they shielded their eyes and ears from the resulting mini-tornado. The sound disappeared along with the helicopter and they found themselves alone with Tilly and Sweetstuff.

The horses nickered in joyful recognition as Kevin and Lauri Beth stroked their necks and noses in preparation to saddling up. The ride to the truck and 4x4 was uneventful and by the time they came into view the tensions from their escape were beginning to ebb. The horses were loaded into the trailer and the backpacks, tools and other equipment in the truck bed. Kevin started the engine, leaned over and kissed Lauri Beth long and hard. He put the truck in gear and began the rough ride back to the paved road. Lauri Beth sat back, closed her eyes and smiled.

Once the wheels hit the smooth pavement, Lauri Beth said, "Let's stop at that little restaurant in Tortilla Flat. I'm so hungry I could eat everything on the menu."

"Great idea," Kevin agreed. And a few minutes later, he swung the truck off the road and into the parking lot.

They chose a corner table in the rear and were soon inhaling a couple of the daily specials. Each had a beer and finished with a cup of coffee. Kevin called for the check and paid with his credit card.

The waitress was clearing the table after checking her tip. The bartender watched them leave and noted the direction of their departure. He went to the drawer that held the business copy of the charge receipts. He pulled out the last receipt and read the name embossed on it. He replaced the receipt, closed the drawer and went to the end of the bar. There he picked up the telephone and made a call.

Chapter Forty-six

Middlestat grabbed for any handhold available in the stark interior of the military version of the Bell 206 Jet Ranger. He had no idea that a helicopter could travel so fast and produce such a turbulent ride. The only good thing about the trip was that it was short. Middlestat's stomach was pressed against his backbone as the pilot made a steep left turn and settled onto the helipad at Luke Air Force Base just outside of Phoenix. The rotor was still turning as a corporal slid the starboard door open, assisted the passengers to the wet tarmac and stood at attention.

"That jeep is waiting to transport you to your aircraft, sir," he said to Captain Scott. Scott led Middlestat to the jeep and the United States Air Force vehicle took them across the base to a waiting olive drab 727. Once on board, they were greeted by two men and a woman. The inside of the 727 was not luxurious by any stretch of the imagination, but it was practical. Three rows of the regular seats had been removed and the space was occupied by a large table. The seats on either side of the desk were facing it, providing ample seating for four people. Across the aisle, a smaller desk replaced a single row of seats. Scott huddled with the two men and then motioned for Middlestat to join them.

"Doctor, meet Robert Mulligan and Clancy Thomas of the Washington Bureau," he said. "They'll be interviewing you on the way to Dallas, and Cindy Vaughn there will be recording the conversation."

"I imagine you're hungry," he continued. "Please sit down and we'll get you something from the galley."

The engines began to spool up and the aircraft started to move.

"Buckle up," Scott instructed as everyone took their seats. "I'm sorry, doctor, I guess you'll have to wait until we're airborne."

They leveled off at thirty-three thousand feet, well above the solid cloud cover that still covered most of the nation. The seat belt sign went off, Scott left for the galley and Mulligan opened the conversation.

"Doctor, why don't you start at the beginning and just tell us everything that happened. We'll interrupt you if we don't understand anything and Cindy will get it all down on her court reporting machine."

Middlestat took a deep breath and began to tell his story. He began with his academic and scientific accreditations, which were very impressive. He moved to his experiments and his research into animal genetics, concentrating on his work with large four-footed creatures. Next, he told of his chance meeting with Jim Plover and how he was duped into believing that he was benefiting the scientific community with the application of his virus and serum discoveries.

At this point he was interrupted by a series of questions. He took the opportunity to eat his lunch between answers. Feeling rested and stronger after eating, he continued. This time he was continually questioned by his hosts as his story centered around his activities in the mine. The seat belt sign came on and the pilot announced preparation for landing. Agent Mulligan signaled that they were through and picked up the air-to-ground phone. He dialed the bureau in Washington and was connected immediately to the Director. A hurried explanation followed. Then a slight pause as he received instructions. He hung up as the wheels smoked the runway.

"Car should be waiting," he announced.

The automobile pulled up to the jetstairs as the passengers deplaned. Once the car got underway, Mulligan pulled out his cell phone and dialed the local FBI office.

"Greg Larkins!" he ordered. "Greg, this is Agent Mulligan. That's right. The D.C. bureau. We're on our way to your office. Pick up Plover and Burleson and have them there ASAP. Oh! And call that Lieutenant Bledsoe and invite him, but let him know that it's just a courtesy and that it's a Federal case."

"By order of the President of the United States," he added as he flipped his phone off. "This should be an interesting afternoon," he said, addressing the others.

They arrived at the FBI office and found Lieutenant Bledsoe waiting for them. Mulligan did the introductions as they gathered around a table in a small conference room.

"So you're the guy that's behind the meat shortage," Bledsoe said to Middlestat, who squirmed in obvious discomfort.

"Lay off!" Captain Scott said. "Whatever the doctor did, he did under duress. He's been a virtual prisoner for the last five years. We're lucky that he got out alive. He's the one person that can produce the vaccine and turn this thing around."

"Sorry," Bledsoe said. "I guess that I'm not completely filled in."

"Apology accepted," Mulligan said.

Just then, the door burst open and Agent Larkins entered the room.

"We've got Burleson," he said to everyone. "Plover is out of town but we'll have him in an hour or so." Then to Mulligan, "How do you want to run this show?"

"Good!" Mulligan said, glad to have control. "Do you have an isolation room for questioning?"

"Yeah, we've got a room with a one-way mirror for observation."

"All right, take him there. You and I and Agent Thomas will question him while the rest of you watch. Then we'll bring in the good doctor for the coup de grace. When Plover gets here, hold him in the next room. When we're finished with Burleson, we'll start on Plover. Make sure that they pass each other during the switch. But no talking! Okay!"

"Sounds like a plan," Larkins said as they rose to follow him to the interrogation room.

The cross-examining room in the FBI office wasn't the stark, bare light bulb, kitchen chair area depicted in television police shows. It was more like the room reserved for auditors in a giant corporation's headquarters. The room was windowless but comfortable. A good-sized table occupied the center of the room; padded chairs surrounded it. Lighting was provided by recessed fluorescent tubes hidden behind egg-crate coverings. A dark mural adorned one wall and a five-by-three foot mirror occupied the wall opposite. The room was clearly designed with intimidation as its focus.

Mulligan sat himself at the head of the table, with Thomas and Larkins on either side. A single chair opposite Mulligan at the far end of the table was reserved for Burleson. A knock on the door signaled Burleson's arrival. Mulligan waved entrance to Agent Sponsen and Harry "Slick" Burleson was ushered into the room. He was accompanied by a short round man in a blue pinstriped suit and a briefcase in his left hand.

"Who's that?" Mulligan asked.

"Burleson's attorney, Simon Goldstein," Larkins answered. "We picked Burleson up at his home and he told his wife to call Goldstein as we led him out the door."

"Got here pretty quick for a Sunday, didn't he?" Mulligan said. "Has Burleson been read his rights?"

"Did it myself," Larkins confirmed.

"Well, Mirandize him again while his lawyer's here," Mulligan ordered. "We don't want any slip-ups."

Burleson was read his rights as he was seated at the end of the table. Goldstein sat alongside him.

"What's this all about?" Burleson demanded. Goldstein cautioned him with a wave of his hand that indicated to all present that he would do the talking.

"Yes," he said, addressing Mulligan. "What are the charges? Who are you? And what's so damned important that it couldn't have waited until tomorrow morning?"

"The charges are conspiracy to commit fraud and illegal price-fixing—both felonies and subject to the RICO act—endangerment of the general public and accessory to murder. I'm Robert Mulligan, Federal Bureau of Investigation, Washington, D.C. I represent the Justice Department and the Government of the United States of America. This is my assistant Agent Clancy Thomas. And this is Agent Greg Larkins of the Dallas FBI. And the reason that this matter couldn't wait until tomorrow is that we are under the direct order of the President of the United States of America to arrest and convict any and all persons involved in the infamous meat and food crises that has plagued our nation. Does that answer your question?"

Burleson and Goldstein sat speechless as they digested the seriousness of the accusations. Goldstein recovered his composure first.

"Ridiculous," he snorted. "I'll be interested in what proof you think you have."

"That will have to wait until we've finished our question-and-answer period, Mr. Goldstein," Mulligan said.

That period lasted nearly two hours. Mulligan, Thomas, and Larkins interrogated, threatened and cajoled with little results. Goldstein continually advised his client not to answer and Burleson complied. He sat erect, expressionless and apparently oblivious to his surroundings. Inside, he was in turmoil. His cool exterior contrasted with the perspiration that he felt accumulating on his body. He wanted this session to end. He wanted to be alone so that he could plot his strategy and make a decision. By tomorrow he hoped that he would be safe in some obscure country with his funds from a Swiss bank account available and his creditors left holding the bag.

As if reading his mind, Mulligan said, "I wouldn't plan on sleeping at home for a while, Mr. Burleson. We're arraigning you tomorrow and we'll be requesting no bail."

"You must be out of your mind," Goldstein shouted. "You've got nothing but supposition. We'll be on the street in less than an hour."

Thomas stood up and signaled at the mirror. A moment later, the door opened and a wizened gentleman was ushered in by a captain in field dress. Goldstein looked puzzled. Burleson sank back into his chair. Goldstein turned to see his client slumped beside him.

"Who's that?" he asked.

Burleson pulled his lawyer down within whispering

389 • THE LURE OF THE DUTCHMAN

range.

"That's Dr. Middlestat," he breathed. "He was supposed to be—."

He caught himself in mid-sentence, stood up and left the room with Goldstein trailing after him.

"Book him!" Mulligan called after him, directing his comment to Lt. Bledsoe, who was standing in the doorway.

As the trio rounded a corner, they encountered Plover and his entourage. It was almost comical to see the two groups attempt a dignified passage. Burleson did his best to appear unruffled and tried to impart a message to Plover. Plover, on the other hand, was already in a state of disarray and his eyes betrayed a sense of panic that gave little solace to Burleson. Plover and his two companions finally negotiated their way clear of the other group and approached Mulligan, who was standing by the open door of the interrogation room.

"Well, well, well," Mulligan said. "Now, who do we have here?"

"I'm James Plover and these are my counselors, Randall McGuire and Saul Stern."

Mulligan suppressed a smile at the unneeded introduction and ushered his new guests into the room. He indicated the witness end of the table for Plover and his attorneys, exchanged business cards with the lawyers and seated himself at his usual place.

"Read him his rights," he said.

Clancy Thomas produced a small card and performed the ritual leaving the clear impression that it

was for the benefit of the attorneys and that these proceedings were going to be conducted by the book.

"State your name," Mulligan began after Thomas
had completed his task.

"James-er-er-Plover."

It appeared to all that Plover might suffer a heart
attack on the spot. The perspiration on his forehead
was beginning to bead and his hands had a vice-like
grip on the table. Middlestat sat alongside the inquisi-
tors and would confirm or deny Plover's testimony as
he proceeded. After hearing the accusations, Plover's
legal team urged him to cooperate and he couldn't wait
to implicate Burleson and exonerate himself.
Throughout the testimony Captain Scott stood in one
corner. He was neither introduced nor referred to, but
his presence served to further intimidate the witness.
The only interruption was the return of Lt. Bledsoe
and he indicated that Burleson had been booked and
was now in detention. This information had the
desired effect on Plover and he went into overdrive.

In less than an hour, Mulligan and Thomas left the
room, accompanied by Middlestat, Larkins, and Scott.
Bledsoe stayed behind to book Plover, who was
cradling his head on his forearms as he wept openly.
His counselors were busy talking with each other,
oblivious to their client's state of mind.

"I've never seen anyone break down so completely,"
Thomas commented.

"It was something to see," Mulligan agreed. "We'll
have this thing wrapped up once we get our hands on
Saunders and Boone."

"What about Dr. Middlestat?" Scott asked.

"He'll be booked as an unwilling accomplice but not held," Mulligan said. He turned to Thomas.

"I want a twenty-four guard placed on the doctor. And call Washington. I want to talk to Paul Stockton."

"Yes, sir," Larkins said. "What about this Charlie Whitfield that both Dr. Middlestat and Plover mentioned?"

"See what you can find out about him and then we'll pick him up."

Ten minutes later, Thomas announced that Stockton was on the line from Washington, D.C.. He pointed toward Agent Larkins' office, indicating that Mulligan could find more comfort and privacy if he took the call there. Mulligan quickly agreed. He knew that he was in for a long session as he brought Stockton up to date.

"Stockton's on his way down here," Mulligan announced nearly two hours after he had picked up the phone. "Book Dr. Middlestat into a good hotel. Stockton wants to see him first thing in the morning. And put all of his bottles and papers under safekeeping. It sounds like the manufacture and application of the antitoxin is the number-one priority."

"Captain Scott," he continued. "I guess that you can return to Luke anytime now. Thanks for all you did. I'll see that it doesn't go unmentioned."

The two shook hands and Scott left for the airport. Mulligan picked up his coat, turned to Thomas and said, "We better get some shut-eye. I think tomorrow's going to be one busy day. Tell them not to call me unless they've picked up Sheriff Saunders!"

CHAPTER FORTY-SEVEN

Lauri Beth nodded in an uneasy sleep, jarred into semi-consciousness by the rough road and the constant turning as Kevin negotiated the slick switchbacks of the Superstition Mountains. As they approached Apache Junction, the quality of the ride improved, although the ground was still wet and a misty rain coated the windshield. Lauri Beth sank into a fitful stupor.

"Won't be long, now, Sweetheart," Kevin said, mostly to himself. They had cleared the heavy traffic of the Phoenix freeway system and were about to turn onto the dirt road that led to Brian's property. The rutted surface jolted Lauri Beth awake.

"Where are we?" she asked.

"Almost there," Kevin said. "We should be able to see the roof line of Brian's house as we clear that next curve."

Daylight was beginning to settle in the west as

Kevin finished the turn.

"What's the matter," Lauri Beth said, as Kevin stopped the truck and squinted through the windshield.

"I don't exactly know," he responded. "The mist is so thick that it's playing tricks with my eyes. I can't see the house at all and it looks like there are some cars parked where it's supposed to be."

He put the truck back into gear and drove slowly toward the house.

"My God! It's gone!" Lauri Beth whispered. "It's just not there anymore."

They drove on in silence, pulled into the driveway and parked next to a car with government plates. As they got out of the truck, a man approached them.

"Agent Joseph Donovan, FBI, Phoenix," he said.

"Kevin Stewart and Lauri Beth McCartney," Kevin said. "What in the hell happened here?"

"That's what we're trying to find out," Donovan said. "Gas explosion demolished the house and it looks like two people were killed. There's not enough left of them to make an identification. The lab will do the best they can with what we've got. They were literally blown apart when the house exploded. They must have been trying to get in by the back door. At least, that's where we found most of the body parts.

"Hey, Joe! Look at this," a man in blue coveralls said as he approached the trio. He was holding a small object in his extended hand.

"What've you got there, Sam?" Donovan asked.

"It's part of a wallet and there's some ID inside. I

haven't tried to get it out yet."

"Let's see," Donovan said as he produced a pair of surgical gloves and accepted the scorched leather.

"Hmm, the plastic is smoked and the paper behind it is a bit charred, but I can make out part of the first line. J—A—S then a B or F or P then E or F and the last letter appears to be P—no—make that an R."

"Jasper!" Lauri Beth and Kevin shouted together.

"Jasper from the mine," Kevin continued alone. "He was one of the militiamen who was working at the mine. Never did know his last name. The other guy was Bubba. Didn't know his real name either."

"Agent Mulligan gave me a quick phone briefing before we came over. I'm supposed to get your statements concerning the mine and everything that happened there," Dononan said as he produced a notepad and pencil. "You say that there were two of these— militiamen, you called them—working there—."

"Yeah! They were the only two who were there at the end. I'm sure there were others. Jasper and Bubba escaped with Sheriff Saunders after they blew up the entrance and left us for dead. There was also a guy named Charlie something and his partner Butch. Charlie was sent up to militia headquarters earlier and Butch died when the mine collapsed and crushed him."

"So these two guys left with Sheriff Saunders. Now, what would they be doing at your house?"

"It's not my house," Kevin explained. "It belonged to my uncle, Brian Nichols. He was killed out by Tortilla Flat. I was just staying here."

Donovan looked up momentarily and then resumed taking notes as he mused aloud, "Now, how do you suppose they got here? There isn't a car in the wreckage and footprints in the mud lead around to the back. Looks like they were dropped off. Makes me wonder if whoever dropped them off knew that the house was about to explode. They were with Saunders when you last saw them, right?"

"Yeah! They all left and then Butch came back to seal up a shaft in the rear of the mine. Just after Butch dynamited the rear shaft, the entrance was detonated and he was trapped with Lauri Beth, Dr. Middlestat, and me. That must have been one hell of a charge they set. It ended up blowing up the entire mountain."

"So, Saunders sent Butch back and then blew up the mine before he could get out and now, we find the other two guys killed when your house blows up. Strange coincidence, wouldn't you say?"

Donovan had been edging Lauri Beth and Kevin in the direction of his car and now, he suggested that they get inside and out of the rain so he could finish his questioning.

"Let's see, now," he continued. "Where were we?"

Kevin went through their ordeal and explained how he got involved, while Lauri Beth filled in some details and described her part in the affair. Ninety minutes later, Donovan folded his notepad.

"I think that just about does it," he said. "I've met this Saunders and I've heard some things about him. I'd be careful, if I were you, until we get some hard enough evidence to bring him in."

"Okay, Mr. Donovan," Kevin replied. "We're gonna put the horses out to pasture and check out the rest of the property then we'll be at Lauri Beth's apartment if you need us."

"You're lucky," Donovan said. "Nothing to the rear was affected by the explosion. Even the barn is still standing and that strange rig parked behind it seems to be okay. I think that ridge behind the house and the fact that the lot slopes to the rear protected that section."

"Thank God for small favors," Kevin said.

Lauri Beth gave Donovan her address and phone number. They got out of the car and shook hands with the FBI agent. No one noticed the glint of a pair of field glasses at the top of the ridge where the road made its final turn to Brian's driveway.

*

Sheriff Saunders was feeling pretty complacent. He had the TV on to a good sports show, a beer in his hand and seated in his favorite chair. He mentally congratulated himself on eliminating Butch, Jasper and Bubba as possible threats to his involvement. The phone rang and he took another slug of beer before lazily reaching for it.

"Saunders here," he said into the speaker. "Who?—yeah, sure, what's up? Yeah?—Yeah?—You're sure it was them?—What about Butch? Was he with them?——How about an old man? Was there an old man with them?"

"Thanks—You did real good—I owe ya one!"

By the time Saunders put the phone back in its cradle he was on the edge of his chair.

"Son of a bitch! Son of a bitch!" he swore as the TV was flicked off. "That's gotta be them. How in the hell did they ever get out of the mine? And what about Butch? If he's on the loose, he'll be comin' after me, and that goddammed doctor could ruin everything!"

He lifted the phone and dialed long distance, let it ring three times and hung up. Thirty minutes later, his phone rang again.

"Saunders," he said.

"One!" came the reply.

"General, we might have a problem."

"Go ahead. Tell me about it."

"I thought that everybody got trapped when we blew the mine, but now I'm not so sure. I just got a call from the bartender. He says that a guy and a girl came by his place in Tortilla Flat and he thinks that it could be that Kevin Stewart and the girl from the coroner's office."

"What about Butch and the doctor?"

"Don't know and that worries me!"

"Well, they can't do us much harm now. We kayo'd the IRS and that's what it was all about. You better get your ass up here. Can you cover yourself?"

"Yeah! No problem there! I'll be up in a couple of days. I gotta couple of things to take care of first."

Saunders sat back to consider his position. Maybe Butch and Middlestat hadn't made it out of the mine. If so, he only had the other two to worry about and maybe the bartender was mistaken. How the hell could anyone have survived that blast? But he couldn't take any chances. He had to assume that it was actually Kevin and Lauri Beth that the bartender had reported at the Tortilla Flat restaurant. He began to formulate a plan. If it was Kevin and Lauri Beth, then they had to be eliminated. He'd deal with Butch and Middlestat later if he was forced to. He turned on his police scanner and tuned it to cover both the FBI and the regular police channels. Then he called his deputy and told him that he was going to take some vacation time, maybe as much as two weeks. He'd call in when he got located. He was going up north to do a little fishing. That done, he went to his bedroom closet and opened a trap door in the floor. He lifted out a heavy wooden crate and pulled it into the room. He removed the lid and stood back to view the contents. Inside the box was a literal arsenal of weapons. Shotguns, automatic rifles and pistols, folding-stock terrorist and gang weapons, and single shot-miniature guns all were wrapped and stored in the crate. Saunders had painstakingly stolen or confiscated these weapons from various raids over the past ten years. They were unmarked and untraceable.

Saunders knelt down beside the box and extracted a pair of pearl-handled six-guns. He unwrapped them and lifted them with loving hands. These were his favorites but they wouldn't be selected today. He replaced them and drew out a Smith and Wesson automatic .38 caliber pistol. This would be the weapon of choice. He unwrapped it and examined it. He tested the action and satisfied himself that it was in working order. The clip was already in place and a spare had been wrapped with the gun. He covered the box and replaced it under the closet floor. Another box was lifted into view and from it he took a box of .38 caliber soft-nosed bullets. The second box was lowered and the trap door secured.

Saunders had just finished loading the spare clip, when he heard the scanner. He caught a routine message from Agent Donovan to his base stating that he was on his way to inspect the wreckage of the Nichols house and would be meeting with Kevin Stewart and Lauri Beth McCartney in the next couple of hours. That settled it for the sheriff. He packed his gear, including his fishing equipment as a last-minute addition, locked the door behind him and headed his car in the direction of Nichols' house.

As he turned off the paved highway and on to the dirt road to Brian's house, he slowed to a crawl and checked behind him. He didn't want anyone surprising him from the rear. He came to the final turn before the road straightened out and ran in a direct line to Brian's driveway. Before completing the turn, he pulled off to the side, uncapped his binoculars and made his way to a small berm that sheltered his car from view. What he saw both pleased and alarmed him. It was the first time that he had seen the devastation of the blast. There was no way that Jasper or Bubba could have survived. He swung his glasses to the vehicles that were clustered in the driveway. The doors opened on a car parked near a pickup truck. Saunders bit his lip as the passengers emerged. No doubt about it now. There stood Kevin Stewart and Lauri Beth McCartney and they were shaking hands with Joe Donovan.

It didn't matter anymore whether Butch and Middlestat had escaped from the mine. He had become a hunted man. He had money stashed away where he could get it and that thought comforted him but the overriding feeling was one of revenge. Those two had been a pain in the ass from the minute they came on the scene. He watched as Kevin and Lauri Beth drove to the rear of the property and released the horses. After checking for feed and water, they inspected the corral. Finding that secure, they turned their attention to the ultralight trailer behind the barn. A few minutes later, they entered the pickup and headed out of the driveway.

Saunders remembered a cut-off about a quarter of a mile back that would offer shelter for his car. He turned the vehicle around and proceeded to that turnoff. He parked out of sight and walked back to a spot where he could watch the pickup as it left. The flattened house was out of view, but the pickup was clearly visible as it sped by Saunders' hiding place. After he assured himself that no other vehicle had left the Nichols' property, Saunders returned to his car and followed the pickup. He kept well back, even though the weather obscured the rear vision of the driver ahead of him.

After his car was on the solid footing of asphalt, the task of following the pickup became relatively simple. Saunders was an expert at the art of shadowing and went undetected.

In the truck ahead, Kevin fought off the drowsiness that accompanied the letdown from the day's activities. Lauri Beth quickly lapsed into a deep sleep. She felt a gentle touch on her shoulder as Kevin nudged her into wakefulness.

"We're here, Sweetheart," he whispered.

"Where are we?" she mumbled.

"At your apartment. It's been a tough day. Let's get inside. I'm dead on my feet."

"I'm sorry! I should have done some of the driving. How long was I asleep?" she said as she became fully conscious.

"Man, you were out the minute I started the motor and you didn't wake up until just now."

"I'm sorry," she repeated. She was out of the truck and opening the door to the apartment lobby before Kevin had his door unlatched.

From a quarter-block down the street and parked on the other side, Pete Saunders watched them enter the apartment building. He saw the lights go on in the front unit on the second floor. He moved his car to a space opposite the front door and slouched down to wait. He'd give them a good hour after the lights went out, he thought as he checked the clip and the action of the .38 Smith and Wesson.

CHAPTER FORTY-EIGHT

Kevin followed Lauri Beth up the stairs and waited patiently as she fumbled for the key and finally got the front door unlocked.

"C'mon in," she urged. "I'll get the air turned on. It's hot and stuffy."

"You don't have to drag me in. Just show me the bedroom and I'll collapse."

Kevin double locked the front door and made straight for the bedroom. He threw his pack into the corner and started to take off his shirt. Lauri Beth came in right behind him, hurled the extra pillows onto a chair and pulled the spread off the bed.

"I'll be right back," she said and disappeared into the bathroom.

Kevin took off his shoes and lay down on top of the blanket. He was asleep by the time Lauri Beth came out of the bathroom. She lay down beside and pulled the blanket from her side over her and snuggled up to him. She laid her head on his chest and drooped her right arm over his body.

"Did you bring your piece with you?" he slurred without opening his eyes.

"Yeah, it's in my pack,"

"Do me a favor, will you, honey?"

"What?"

"Put it on my nightstand with your right hand, barrel pointing at the wall and make sure it's loaded and the safety is on. Okay?"

"Sure, honey. No problem. Why?"

"Mine's got a few tons of rock on it and Butch is guarding it, remember? And I don't want to take any chances as long as Saunders is still on the loose."

"All right." Lauri Beth got up and got her gun. She placed it on the nightstand next to Kevin's head and returned to bed.

"Thanks," Kevin said as she settled back into her original position.

She felt Kevin turn toward her and smiled as his right arm curled under her and his left lay gently across her back. They both fell into a deep but troubled sleep.

Saunders checked his watch. The lights had been out for just about an hour. He felt his shoulder holster for his regular weapon and picked up the .38 from the passenger seat beside him. He opened the glove compartment and removed a tubular object. This he affixed to the .38 above and in line with the barrel. He opened his window and pointed the gun at a tree across the street. He flicked on a switch at the rear of the tube and a red dot appeared on the tree about a half an inch above where he was aiming.

"That'll do," he whispered to himself as he rolled up the window and stepped out of the car. It was two o'clock in the morning and the street was deserted. Still, he looked in both directions before crossing over to the apartment building. He reached the outer door and found that it wasn't locked. That wasn't unusual, as passage to the inner hallway was blocked by a pair of doors that housed the bell and intercom system.

The first door fell easy prey to his lock picks and he allowed it to close behind him. He was now in a small anteroom that was lit by an overhead saucer-like fixture. He ran his finger down the list of tenants and stopped at L. McCartney, 2B. The number corresponded with the location that he had been watching and it would further verify the apartment if it appeared on or above the door.

The inner door was a little more difficult to force. The keying mechanism had been recently replaced with a modern "buglar proof" lock and it took Saunders a full five minutes to solve its intricacies. He wiped the handles and knobs clean and stepped inside. The hallways and stairs were brightly lit and stealth was abandoned. He walked up the stairs and turned toward the front of the building. There was a door on either side of hall. The one on the left had 2B in brass symbols just above the peephole. A quick scan of the area satisfied him that he was alone. The door had two locks, a regular type that prevented the knob from being turned when in the locked position and a deadbolt about six inches higher. He attacked the deadbolt first and with some effort was able to slide it back. The regular doorlock was easier and gave in without a whimper. He turned the doorknob and entered the apartment.

Lauri Beth and Kevin had been asleep for only a quarter of an hour, when it hit them. Kevin's reaction to the narrow escape in the mine produced a series of small shudders and his body broke out in heavy perspiration, but he remained relatively still. Lauri Beth, on the other hand, suffered dreams that bordered on hallucinations. She shivered violently and clung tightly to Kevin. At times she would call out either a warning or a muffled scream as she relived the terror of the mine heightened by the imagination of complete exhaustion. Lauri Beth's convulsive slumber and his own restlessness prevented Kevin from falling into a coma-like sleep. He was unconscious but his senses were alert.

The bedroom door was slightly ajar, and when Saunders slipped into the apartment, a small beam of light from the bright hallway penetrated the darkness and shown on the bedroom wall for a split second. It wasn't enough to awaken him, but Kevin's eyes flickered for an instant.

Saunders closed the entry door and waited inside for his pupils to dilate. The apartment was completely dark except for a backlit clock in the kitchen.

Saunders found that he was breathing heavily despite his efforts to control his excitement. He needed something to augment his sight. He couldn't afford the least bit of noise and was paranoid about proceeding before he could at least distinguish the outlines of room and its furnishings. Shapes began to take on a dim form as his eyes became accustomed to the extreme dark. He took a step forward and then another. He placed himself in about the center of the room and decided that he needed better vision. He turned on his laser beam and played it around the room. It gave him the help he needed. He found the door to the bedroom and inched toward it.

Lauri Beth was in the midst of reactionary nightmare. She imagined herself deep in the mine. She was being forced backward by Butch. He had a evil grin on his face and was frothing at the mouth. She stepped back and felt her foot slip on the edge of a bottomless shaft. Butch reached out to grab her. She extended her hand and felt his hand on hers. As he began to pull her to safety, she bent her knees, got both feet firmly against the rim and pushed backwards. She could feel Butch lose his balance as he was caught off guard by the unexpected force. He hurdled over her and they both began to plunge into the darkness. He was shouting obscenities and she was paralyzed with fear as they continued their fall. Suddenly from out of nowhere, she felt a rope alongside of her. She made a grab for it and missed. Then, she felt a strong hand grab hers and she was pulled against a firm body. It was Kevin. She felt his arms around her. She buried her head in his chest and began to cry.

Saunders slowly pushed open the door and quietly slipped inside.

Kevin felt Lauri Beth sobbing against his chest. He rolled toward her and tightened his arms around her.

Saunders detected the slight movement and focused on the bed. He was unable to make out any distinct shape as Lauri Beth and Kevin presented one target covered by the blanket that she had drawn around them.

Kevin opened his eyes to see if Lauri Beth was alright.

Saunders could see that Lauri Beth's head covered his line of sight to Kevin's.

He thought, "Oh, well," and lowered the gun.

Kevin saw a red dot slip down the wall, onto the headboard, across Lauri Beth's forehead and stop just above her right ear. His reaction was immediate. He rolled to his left carrying Lauri Beth and the bedding with him as a .38 caliber bullet tore into his pillow, crashed through the headboard and buried itself in the plaster wall behind. He was still in mid-turn as he stretched his right arm above his head, felt the night table and closed on Lauri Beth's pistol. Another round thudded into the mattress and a third smashed the lamp on the night stand as Kevin landed on top of Lauri Beth. As he continued to roll, he thumbed off the safety and fired two rounds in the direction of the last barrel flash. He heard them collide fruitlessly with the wall. Lauri Beth screamed in unknowing terror. They were hopelessly entangled in the bedding and she thrashed about in a vain attempt to get free. Two bullets imbedded themselves in the carpet as the red dot followed them across the floor. They came to a stop against the wall just as Kevin got off two more shots and felt a bullet enter the blanket. The succession of his discharges was so rapid that he couldn't tell which ended in the telltale thwump indicating that metal had struck flesh.

Saunders groaned as he felt a sharp pain in his left leg. He tried to put pressure on it and the pain increased. Another slug exploded next to his head and he decided that it was time to leave. He slammed the door behind him and dragged himself out of the apartment and down the stairs. His leg gave way five steps from the bottom and he tumbled the rest of the way down. He picked himself up from the floor and cursed his way to his car.

"You okay?" Kevin asked as they finally disentangled themselves from the covers.

"What happened?"

"Saunders! Who else?"

Kevin felt something wet on his fingers and checked his pants for a blood stain.

"Are you sure that you're okay?" he asked again.

"I think so," she said, brushing herself off. "Oh my God! I think I've been hit! Look!"

She winced as she raised her arm and revealed a red circle on her pajama top.

"Let me see," Kevin ordered.

"You are one very lucky girl," he continued after examining her wound. "Another inch and it could have been very serious. I'll have you patched up in no time."

"It's beginning to hurt," Lauri Beth said after Kevin had finished applying a gauze and tape bandage.

"What do we do now?"

"First we call the police. I'm sure the shots were heard and we don't want to become the fugitives. Then I'd better talk to Joe Donovan."

Kevin dialed 911, gave the requested information, hung up and began to dress and collect his gear.

"I thought that you were going to call Donovan," Lauri Beth said.

"It's two in the morning, Sweetheart. Let's get rid of the police first. They'll probably take down our statements and log it as just another break-in."

"But didn't you say that it was Saunders?"

"Did you see him? I didn't. I was just guessing and besides we can't accuse him without definite proof. If we mention Saunders, that's serious stuff, to accuse another cop. We could be tied up for days."

"Yeah, but don't you want to see him brought to justice?"

"I sure do!" Kevin said. "Do you feel up for a little trip?"

"I guess so," she answered as a small light began to dawn. "Where are we going?"

"Idaho!" he said.

CHAPTER FORTY-NINE

The first call came from Andover, Massachusetts. It was logged in at 8:17 a.m. Eastern Daylight Time by the executive secretary of Director of the Internal Revenue Service, Washington D.C. By the time Frank Edgar, the Director and long-time personal friend of the President, walked in the door, two similar messages had arrived. They were transcribed on paper that bore a bright-red border and marked "urgent."

"You'd better see these right away," Joannah Glascow said without even a "good morning, sir."

Edgar took the slips from her hand and disappeared through the door. Glascow saw the red light glow on her terminal and waited for her next order. It wasn't long in coming.

"Get me the Secretary of the Treasury, and I mean right now," the command echoed in her ear.

"Frank, Jason Brighter! What's up?"

"I've got a real problem here, Mr. Secretary," the formality of the answer caused Brighter to sit back rigid in his chair.

"I got a call from the Andover office and I just hung up on Atlanta to take your call. They were raided over the weekend. While we were sealing off the outside, somebody slipped in and erased all of our files and programs."

"Well, we've got backup don't we?"

"They got that, too!"

"Aren't we redundant at the other locations?" Secretary Brighter asked.

"Only about ten percent," Edgar replied. "But I got a bad feeling that they've been hit as well."

"I'll inform the President. Keep your day open," Brighter suggested as the phone went dead.

It wasn't dead for long as the calls came in following the time zones. By noon, all ten regional offices had reported in. The news was the same and it wasn't good. All of the electronic files and programs of the IRS had been sabotaged. The backup had been taken down at all locations, as well, and the IRS was left virtually without records or systems.

President Jefferson called a Cabinet meeting for three o'clock in the afternoon. Secretary Brighter called for a briefing at one. The Cabinet meeting began promptly at 3 p.m. EDT. President Jefferson addressed his appointees.

"Ladies and gentlemen," he began. "I have some good news and some bad news and that's not a joke. First the good news. I'm sure all of you are aware that we were saved from the forewarned riots in the inner cities by an act of God. Somehow, the weather pattern changed in an unprecedented manner. The ensuing rains washed out any organized threat to law and order. I will say, however, that we were prepared and even if the predicted rampages had occurred, they would have been brought under control. As it turned out, we weren't tested and for that I am thankful, for surely loss of property and even life would have been unavoidable.

"The second item of good fortune was the collapse of meat prices. This happened despite the warnings and forecasts of the most renowned economists in the country. Don't ask me to explain the workings of the free markets. Just be thankful that they worked in our favor. Secretary Harkens, would you care to comment?"

The Secretary of Agriculture literally rose to the occasion. "Mr. President," he said. "I have received word that the meat shortage and the ensuing high prices for meat and other foodstuffs was the result of an organized plot against the best interests of the population by a small group of ranchers." He stopped to allow for the exclamations and asides of those seated around the table.

"Yes!" he continued. "A virus was disseminated across the country that affected the reproductive ability of cattle and other large animals. This virus was artificially produced and was carried by wild animals, specifically coyotes, that had been injected and then released throughout the country. The virus was airborne. An antidote was developed at the same time and these ranchers inoculated their own herds. These ranchers have been identified and are now in custody.

"The operations were conducted in an abandoned mine in the Phoenix area of Arizona. The scientist who developed the virus and the antidote was held in virtual captivity and forced to oversee the production of the chemicals. I am happy to announce that the operation has been closed down, the mine destroyed and the scientist along with his supplies and formulas are in our possession. We will be in mass production of the antidote by the end of the week and inoculations should be completed by the end of the month.

"Ladies and gentlemen, the meat shortage is over! Of course, it will take some time for supplies to reach the grocery stores and butcher shops but, for all practical purposes, the meat shortage is over."

Harkens sat down amid the stunned silence of his fellow Cabinet members. Suddenly, the room erupted in a series of questions.

"I'm sorry," Harkens said as the room settled down. "But I've told you everything that I know. You will have further details as soon as I get them."

The President gaveled the room to silence. His countenance took on a serious look.

"I have some other news that is not so pleasant. Secretary Brighter, would you kindly report on the IRS situation?" he said as he yielded the floor to the Secretary of the Treasury. Brighter remained in his chair.

"We have a situation," he said. "It seems the someone has disabled the files of the IRS." He paused for the room to settle back to normal before he continued.

"Whether it was part of a plot that was coordinated with the defunct riots or not, we do not know. The facts are these: While the law enforcement agencies, government troops and the National Guard were concentrating and deploying for a physical attack on Government buildings and the core of the inner cities, some group, obviously organized, slipped into the Internal Revenue offices in our major districts and obliterated all of the files and operational programs of the IRS, including the backup systems."

"How could this be done?" was the unified question.

"First reports indicate that a powerful magnetic device was trained on the computers and their accessories. The hard drives and memories were completely erased. The backups were also completely destroyed. The trend has been to electronic filing and paying of income taxes. Oh! We still have about thirty-five percent using paper, but generally those are individuals and smaller corporations.

"This is a real problem. It will take years to reconstruct the tax programs and be in compliance to the volumes of tax laws that have been enacted, changed and modified over the decades. It's virtually an impossible task. And to rely on the honesty of the taxpayer to come forth with his past records is wishful thinking.

"Mr. President, it is my sad duty to report that of this moment the Government of the United States of America is out of business."

CHAPTER FIFTY

Pete Saunders was a fugitive from the law, the law that he had sworn to uphold. He knew it as soon as he had seen Kevin and Lauri Beth in front of the flattened house. Now he had failed to terminate them and there was no way out for him but to run. What had happened? Everything was going so well. The masses in the cities would riot and the IRS files would be destroyed and that would be that. There would be no connecting him with anything. He had covered his tracks perfectly. The coroner was dead, as were Jasper and Bubba. He had sealed the mine and seen it collapse. Butch, the professor and the other two should be dead, too. And the only ones who knew about him would be the general, Jimmy Ray Wheeler, and Charlie Whitfield, but they were in it as deep as he was. But damn it to hell, they weren't dead and he was in a mess. All of his plans to quit the force and take it easy had gone up in smoke and now he had to rely on

Plan B.

Plan B had sounded fine when he concocted it, but now he wasn't so sure. It was one thing to set up a plan for a contingency that you didn't expect to happen, but it was quite another when circumstances forced you to use it. Well, it was the only plan that he had and he had better get on with it. Damn, that leg was starting to hurt!

*

Kevin and Lauri Beth tried to sleep but were only able to lie awake and rest. They were up and dressed at the first sign of daybreak.

"We'll grab a quick breakfast on the road," Kevin suggested. "Now, let's pack every bit of gear that we can find."

"How about these?" she asked, holding up a small flashlight and a jackknife. He nodded assent.

"Your helmet and goggles didn't make it either," she said as she packed hers.

"I've still got my GPS. How about you?"

She held hers up for him to see.

"That should be about it," she said, more in the form of a question than a statement.

"We'll check out the truck when we get down there. How about food? Got anything to take along?"

Lauri Beth opened the refrigerator and pulled out a six-pack of water and one of pop. Kevin signaled to bring them along. She found a dozen cans of fruit, vegetables and meats in the cupboard and packed them as well.

"Let's go," they agreed and left the apartment.

Kevin drove the pickup out to Interstate Highway 17 and headed north.

"Just one more stop," he said. "Brian's house."

"Brian kept a couple of rifles and some ammunition in the barn in case he found any critters prowling around. I want to get them and I think we might as well tow the ultralight."

An hour later, they were back on the Interstate. Kevin picked up the cell phone.

"Time to talk to Donovan," he said.

*

Saunders pulled into his garage and closed the overhead door behind him. He hastily cleaned out his car, taking his phone, gun with the laser attached, box of ammo, sunglasses, maps, and anything else that he felt would be useful. He limped inside and went straight to the bathroom. He took off his shoes and removed his pants. He turned his upper body to the left and bent over to inspect his wound. The bullet had entered his thigh just below the buttocks. He searched for the exit hole.

"Damn!" he muttered to himself. "Goddam bullet is still in there. What kind of a pea shooter was he using? You'd think the son of a bitch would at least use a man's gun."

He probed about and located the lump of the spent slug. It had almost found its way completely through his leg but had stopped about a quarter of an inch short. No wonder it hurt most when he was seated in his car. He was sitting on the goddam bullet.

He took gauze and tape from the cabinet and put them on the sink top. He left for the kitchen and returned with a bottle of whiskey and a slicing knife. He poured a glassful of whiskey, flooded the wound with half of it and threw the other half into his mouth. His throat was burning from the alcohol, as he wiped the back of his leg with a whiskey-soaked rag, sliced an x across his skin and squeezed the bullet out. Another dousing of both ends of the wound was followed by a half-glass of whiskey, bandaging with gauze, tape and a double dose of painkiller.

Saunders sat on his living room couch sipping a glass of whiskey. The subdued pain kept him from succumbing to the effects of the alcohol. He still had more than an hour of darkness left and he knew that he had to take advantage of it. He forced himself to his feet and went back to the bathroom. There, he shaved off his mustache and dyed his hair a deep black. Satisfied, he dressed in jeans, T-shirt and work boots. Then, he made a round of all the rooms. In each he uncovered a secret trove and removed its contents. When he was finished, he had pocketed over $50,000 in cash and a new identity in the name of Sam Peters. From his closet floor he drew out his stash of weapons. He packed everything into a large soft duffel, including some clothes, making sure that he left enough to conceal the fact that he had gone. He made one final round through the house and went to the garage for the last time.

It was still dark when Saunders pulled up to the

police impound. He unlocked the padlocked gate and drove inside. He parked his car in the middle of the enclosure and began his search. He didn't have to look very far. About ten cars down and two rows back he found exactly what he wanted, a white Ford pickup truck with four-wheel drive. He changed the license plates with another white pickup three rows further back and then switched the plates from his car with a similar model at the far end of the enclosure. The impound office was empty. He unlocked the door and found the keys to the Ford. A few minutes later, he was on his way, his gear in his new wheels and the padlock back on the gate. He headed for I-17 North. His next stop would be Flagstaff and an RV dealer. He'd fit the pickup with a camper cap. That and the fact that white was by far the most popular color for vehicles in the Southwest, should get him to his destination without detection.

*

The reception was good and Donovan answered on the second ring.

"Joe Donovan."

"Mr. Donovan, this is Kevin Stewart"

"Make it, Joe, Kevin. Where are you?"

"Heading North on I-17. Lauri Beth is with me. Somebody broke into Lauri Beth's apartment this morning and tried to kill us. I think it was Saunders."

"I heard the police report. They're treating it like a random break-in. I'm putting out an APB on Saunders. He'll be pretty tough to catch. He knows about every trick in the books."

"Look, Joe! I think that he may be heading up to Idaho to hole up for a month or two, until the heat blows over. That's the headquarters for the New Revolutionary Militia. They're up in the Wilderness area some where. I could sure use some help in pinning them down."

"Maybe I can dig something up. I'll check out his phone records. With the technology now in place, the phone companies log cellular calls as well as land lines from point of origin to point of reception. Give me your cell number."

"Okay! Mine's 602-555-9584 and Lauri Beth has a beeper. Hers is 602-555-1463."

"Got it! If you stumble onto anything, for God's sake be careful and wait until we can get there," Donovan said as he snapped the cover on his cell phone feeling that his last statement had fallen on deaf ears.

*

Agent Donovan called his office and made his requests. He would need a search warrant for Sheriff Saunders' house and would expect it when he got there. He pulled up to Saunders' residence expecting to see the police still there. He only found Agent Noonan, a trainee from his office, with a piece of paper in his hand.

"Here's the warrant," Noonan greeted him.

"Thanks," Donovan answered and proceeded inside.

A careful search revealed nothing in particular. The condition of the interior failed to indicate whether the occupant had left for good or would be returning. Donovan didn't expect Saunders to make things easy for him. He spent over an hour inspecting the premises with Noonan dogging his every move. Finally, he gave up.

"Stake this place out until midnight," he said to Noonan. "I'm heading back to the office. Maybe they've had better luck with the phone records. If anyone shows up, call in immediately and don't do anything. Just keep track of whoever it might be."

"Got it!" Noonan replied and left to spent rest of his day in vain surveillance.

Donovan arrived at his office to find some mild excitement.

"We may have something," Sam Carver greeted him. "Looks like our friend has been in contact with somebody in Idaho. There's a rather strange sequence. First, he places a call, gets no answer and hangs up. Thirty minutes he gets a call from a cell phone and that conversation last for anywhere up to twenty minutes."

"Where's the cell phone located?"

"Can't pinpoint it, but I can get you within a ten-mile square."

"That's a hundred square miles."

"Yeah! And the area it's in is no bargain. I make it to be about twenty-five miles northwest of Salmon, Idaho. The north boundary looks to be the Salmon River. That's rough country. It'll be hard to find anyone up there, if that's where he went."

"Well, we'll try to pick him up around the Phoenix

area first, but my guess is that he'll try to lay low for a while and then get out of the country," Donovan concluded.

*

The cell phone rang just as Kevin and Lauri Beth had returned from a McDonald's road break. Lauri Beth handed him the phone.

"It's Joe Donovan," she said.

Kevin didn't say much after his "Hello." He simply nodded and traced his finger over a map of Idaho.

"Thanks, Joe," he said. "We'll keep in touch. Yeah, we'll be careful."

As they settled into the pickup, Kevin handed Lauri Beth the maps.

"Could you figure the best route and the approximate time that it will take us to get to Salmon, Idaho, Sweetheart?" he asked. "Figure that we'll drive straight through. We'll switch turns at the wheel every two hours. If we can get in tomorrow night, we'll rest up in Salmon and start to search for the militia headquarters the next morning."

*

The entire Cabinet room was in a state of shock. A few members tried to speak and then thought better of it. Fifteen minutes passed without a word. Finally, with his forehead resting on his crossed fingers, President Jefferson said, "I've been giving this some serious thought since I first learned of the problem a few hours ago. Drastic times require drastic actions.

Here's what I propose!"

The President outlined his plan in less than five minutes. It took more than the next two hours for discussion and the realization to set in that this was the only plausible solution.

"I'm going to meet with the leaders of both parties tomorrow morning," he announced. "If they're agreeable, duplicate bills will be introduced in the House and the Senate the following day and I'll sign it into law that evening. As you know it's very controversial and I've opposed it until now, but, frankly, I don't see any other way out."

Everyone nodded in agreement and began to leave the room.

"By the way," Jefferson said. "I'll be holding a press conference as soon as I get congressional approval."

CHAPTER FIFTY-ONE

Saunders roared northward paying cash for everything. He'd soon be at militia headquarters and safe. He'd wait at least a month before he headed for the islands. Once he was settled with a new identity, he'd simply disappear. He could transfer funds slowly and unnoticed from his other bank accounts. Thank God, he opened them all in different names. There would be nothing suspicious about small sums, all under ten thousand dollars moving from banks in different cities to an offshore account in his new name. It could take years. He had plenty of time and plenty of money.

*

Lauri Beth and Kevin had spelled each other from the driving chore since Flagstaff. It had been two hours on and two hours off. Each had noted the improving conditions as they assumed control. The rain had stopped at the Utah border and the roads were dry by the time they reached Idaho. The weather system that had caused the phenomenal downpours across the country had broken up and was being replaced by a series of highs and lows of more conventional character.

Lauri Beth pulled into the mom-and-pop motel in Salmon, Idaho. The vacancy sign was lit and the parking lot was almost empty. Kevin registered and returned with the key.

"It's around back," he instructed.

Lauri Beth drove behind the office and pulled alongside the room which had a freestanding kitchenette. The inside was clean but old. The furniture was cast-off fifties. The decorations consisted of two Marvel Cigarette posters and a smoky mirror served both the bathroom and the bedroom. The kitchen part of the kitchenette was a hot plate on top of an under-the-counter refrigerator.

"There's no home like this place," Lauri Beth said as she pulled the accordion door shut and claimed dibs on the bathroom.

Twenty minutes later, it was Kevin's turn. The water rattled off the walls of the metal shower stall and he emerged clothed in a towel eleven minutes after he had entered. Lauri Beth was already in bed and Kevin crashed beside her. The bed sagged like a hammock and rolled them to the center.

"Not bad," Kevin said.

"Not bad at all," she agreed as they collapsed into a deep sleep—the first either had had in over twenty-four hours.

*

Saunders pulled into militia headquarters, leaned on the horn and waited. Charlie Whitfield looked out the window and reported to his two cohorts.

"The party's over," he said. "Our good friend Sheriff Saunders has arrived."

General Boone pulled his bulk from a chair and lumbered to the door.

"Hey! Pete!" he shouted. "Get your ass in here!"

Saunders slowly extracted himself from his truck, reached back in and retrieved his pack and rifle and sauntered nonchalantly to the cabin.

"What's the big hurry?" he said. "I thought that the operation was a success and you all would be sittin' pretty."

"Yeah!" Boone answered as he let Saunders pass him in the doorway. "No thanks to you! And no thanks to the freakin' weather!"

Saunders looked around the austere cabin.

"Great spot you got here," he mumbled as he exchanged nods with Jimmy Ray Wheeler and Charlie Whitfield.

"Thanks!" the general snorted. "And to what do we owe the pleasure of your company?"

"You know goddam well why I'm here!" Saunders said as he turned to the general. They would have been in each other's face except that their bellies kept them apart.

"Tell me about it!" Boone demanded keeping the umpire-manager pose and refusing to be the first to back down.

"I'll tell ya all about it!" Saunders boomed back in his face. "You sit up here orderin' everyone around while you're safe in these woods and I'm down there doin' all the dirty work and stickin' my neck out a mile and a half."

"Well, it sure looks like you screwed up your end!" Boone retorted.

"It's that goddam Kevin guy and that broad from Blackwell's office. I can't figure out how they got out of the mine. I swear a scorpion couldn't a found daylight after the whole mountain came down on top of them. I'm tellin' ya, Dan'l, there's nothin' left but a pile of rubble."

"You're sure they got out?"

"I swear to God. I saw them with my own two eyes. After the call from Tortilla Flat, I went out to the house where I took care of Jasper and Bubba and there they was, plain as warts on a whore's nose, talkin' to th' G."

"What about Butch and the professor?"

"I already told ya! I don't know about either of them. Maybe they got out and maybe they didn't. I'll tell ya this. If Butch got out, we're all in deep shit!"

"We can handle Butch," the general said as the tension began to ease between them. "The main thing is that we got the damn government and we got 'em where it hurts."

"Yeah, Pete," Charlie said, feeling that it was now safe to enter the conversation. "You might not know, but we shut down the IRS just like we planned. The weather screwed up the riots and meat prices collapsed but, thanks to the general's foresight, the IRS teams went in the night before and got the job done."

"Well, that's somethin', anyway," Pete said. "What about the guys in the field? What are they doin' now?"

"The operation's over and they're disbanded. They've been told to disappear and wait until they hear from us. We're outta here tomorrow after we make sure that there's no trace of us left behind." Wheeler interjected. "You'd better hide that white truck first thing in the morning. Anyone snooping around would spot that in a minute, especially from a plane or chopper."

Everyone nodded in agreement. Pete walked over to the fridge and the others headed for their sacks.

*

Daylight began to filter through the window coverings as Kevin and Lauri Beth became conscious. The soft mattress had pulled their bodies together like a magnet and they awoke in each other's arms. They lay there unwilling to move, yet feeling the stimulation of their senses. Lauri Beth rolled on top of him and kissed him softly on the mouth and let the kiss linger.

"I'm afraid that we'd better get moving," Kevin said. "We've got a full day ahead of us."

An hour later, they were on the road, bill paid and a quick breakfast inside them. The queer rig that they were towing brought a few quizzical glances but nothing more. Folks in that part of the country were curious but not nosy. They left town northbound on highway 93, following the Salmon River. When the river turned westward, they left the road and followed a jeep trail for another mile. Kevin pulled off the dirt road and parked.

"We'll have to use the road as a runway," he said. "It's a little rough but we should be able to get airborne and over those pines without any trouble."

Lauri Beth wasn't so sure but she didn't comment. She waited for Kevin's instructions and together they assembled Brian's ultralight. The morning air was perfectly still and the overcast would provide a thermal-free ride.

"Couldn't be better," Kevin commented as he pushed the aircraft into position.

He helped Lauri Beth into the upper seat, buckled her seat belt and checked her gear. The trailer had contained two helmets fitted with an intercom system. Lauri Beth donned one helmet and pulled the face plate down to check for fit and comfort. Kevin put on the other helmet and did the same. He plugged the intercoms for both helmets into the central control and said, "How do you read me?"

"Loud and clear." came the response.

He pointed to her GPS.

"Are your waypoints in and corresponding to the map?"

"Checked them all as we were driving out," she assured him.

The GPS and map were strapped to her legs for hands-free access. A pair of binoculars hung around her neck and Kevin added a rifle to her equipment. He laid the gun across her lap and pushed her elbows down against it.

"How's that?" he asked.

"Fine!" she said and then added, "Just what the hell are you carrying?"

"I'm flying the plane," he answered. "I've got a GPS and a map and a sidearm but you'll be doing most of the spotting and recording. I plan to start on the east end of the box and fly west along the river. Then, we'll slowly make our way southward. We've got four hours of fuel in the ultralight's tanks and another four in the truck. All set?"

She nodded and gave him a thumbs-up. Kevin set the brake, braced his foot against the right main tires and pulled the recoil starter cord.

"That was just the prime," he said as the engine failed to start. Then he turned on the magneto switch, closed the choke, set the throttle to the starting position and pulled the cord. This time the engine jumped to life. He retarded the throttle, opened the choke and let the engine settle down to a smooth idle. Kevin eased himself into the front seat, swung his left leg over the center bar, and placed his foot on the brake pedal. He buckled his seat belt and pulled it tight. His right hand found the hand throttle bolted to the frame next to his hip and he pushed it forward. The little aircraft accelerated. Kevin pushed the control bar away from his body to arm's length. In what seemed to Lauri Beth only a few feet, the wheels left the ground and she felt herself propelled skyward.

The excitement was immediate. Lauri Beth felt a new exhilaration as Kevin guided the ultralight upward and safely over the towering pine trees. He leveled out fifty feet over the treetops and banked to the left. He found the Salmon River after a ninety-degree turn and traced it westward as he slowly gained altitude.

"Give me time and course to the first waypoint," he said into the intercom.

"Six miles. Heading 265 degrees. At present speed, we should be there in six minutes twenty-five seconds."

"That should put us at the curve in the river where it turns to the northwest. I think I'll head due west and form a triangle with the river. Then we'll search that area. I have a feeling that any buildings would be close to the river, anyhow. Can you compute the coordinates for the search pattern?"

"No problemo," Lauri Beth said. "As soon as I get my heart and stomach back into their regular positions! This country is so beautiful! And what a way to see it!"

Ten minutes later she said, "One minute to the check point. Then make a right one-eighty and head back to the river. At the river do a left one-eighty and I'll have the next check point ready for you. See anything yet?"

"Nope! These trees are so thick that we'll have to be right on top of them. Keep looking."

The ultralight was flying at an airspeed of fifty knots. That made for approximately ten-minute legs. The length of each leg decreased as they flew northward toward the point of the triangle and so did their corresponding time. They were now at the river and Kevin was beginning his fourth left one-hundred-eighty degree turn. As he swung around to the west, both he and Lauri Beth looked over their left shoulders.

"What was that?" she exclaimed. "Did you see that flash of white?"

*

Wheeler was the first up and his feet didn't hit the floor until after nine o'clock. Even in mid summer, the mornings were cool if not downright cold. He opened the door of the potbellied stove that occupied the center of the cabin. He stuffed in some newspaper and laid kindling over it. He poured half a cup of gasoline into a plastic container and spilled it over the kindling. He picked up a couple of small logs and laid them over the starter base. He took a kitchen match and scratched it on the stove. It sprang to life and he threw it into the open door. There was a small explosion as the newspaper and kindling ignited. In seconds there was a roaring fire in the belly of the stove. Wheeler warmed his hands in front of the open door then closed the door and climbed back in bed.

It took a half an hour before the warmth of the fire took the chill off the room. Wheeler lay in his bed fighting off the urge to use the privy. Finally, the warmth of his bed and the sound of the rushing waters of the North Fork of the Salmon River were too much for him. He slipped on his pants, stuck his feet into his boots and left the cabin.

Twenty minutes later, he returned to find the general and Charlie stumbling around the cabin, shaking off the night's sleep.

"Hey, Charlie!" Wheeler said. "I thought Pete was

supposed to move his truck last night!"

"You mean it's still out there?" Boone stormed. "Goddam you, Pete, get your ass outta bed and move your truck."

He walked over to the sheriff's bunk and yanked the covers off the prostrate body and threw them on the floor.

"In a minute! In a minute!" Saunders mumbled.

"Right now!" the general fumed. "And I mean right this goddammed second!"

Saunders swiveled out of the bed, swung his feet to the floor and into his boots. He fished the keys out of his pants pocket and left the cabin in his skivvies. In a few seconds, the truck engine roared to life and Pete drove it under some tall cover. The initial sound of the truck almost drowned out the noise of another engine.

"What's that?" Boone asked no one in particular.

Wheeler shrugged his shoulders.

"Dunno," he answered.

*

"Where?" Kevin asked.

"Right there in that opening," Lauri Beth pointed.

"I see it now! It looks like a pickup and it's moving."

"Yeah! Can you circle that spot? I think I caught a glimpse of a building under the trees."

Kevin swung the ultralight around in a tight left turn and lost some altitude. He reentered the small clearing at no more than twenty-five feet above the treetops.

"There it is! There it is!" Lauri Beth shouted and

pointed at the same time. "I can barely see the truck and there's a man running from it to the cabin. I can see the cabin plainly now! Circle! Circle!"

*

"It's sounds like one of those damn ultralights," Charlie answered.

He ran to the door and looked up. "There it is!" he pointed. "It looks like the one that was flying around the mine!"

Just then, Saunders burst through the door, colliding with Charlie and knocking him against the door frame.

"It's them! Ain't it?" he screamed. "It's that goddammed Kevin and the broad! Ain't it?"

"Well, it sure looks like the same ultralight and there's two people in it."

"I knew it! I knew it," Saunders yelled. "Gimme a gun! Gimme a fuckin' gun!"

He grabbed a twelve-gauge shotgun from a makeshift gun rack, along with a box of number two shells, and raged out the door into the clearing, clad only in his underwear and boots. He loaded the shotgun and pointed it skyward.

*

When Kevin saw the man running across the clearing he began to climb. He had only risen a few feet when Saunders burst into the opening and pointed the shotgun at the ultralight.

"He's gotta gun!" Lauri Beth screamed.

"I see it! I see it!" Kevin yelled back as he tried to maneuver. He decided that his best escape was to lose altitude and disappear behind the pines. Lauri Beth lifted the rifle from her lap and tried to bring it to bear. Kevin pulled the control bar back into his chest and swung it hard to his right. The ultralight made a diving left turn. Lauri Beth pointed the rifle down and pulled the trigger. A puff of dirt appeared about ten feet from the gunman on the ground just as the barrel of the shotgun discharged a load of number two shot. The pellets tore through the right wing and left a gaping hole without doing any structural damage. Kevin was now flying directly away from the cabin and was almost out of sight from below. Lauri Beth tried to bring the rifle around but couldn't find her target. She sighted the pickup truck and squeezed off a shot just as Saunders fired another round. Lauri Beth's bullet found the gas tank of Saunders truck and the woods erupted in a flash of exploding gasoline. The noise hid the sound of the shotgun pellets striking the tip of the Rotex's propeller. Kevin knew that they'd been hit. The engine began to vibrate as the now-eccentric propeller transmitted its unbalanced condition to the drive shaft and then through the engine to the frame. Three of Saunders pellets' had struck the end of the spinning propeller and taken a ragged inch off of the end.

Kevin throttled back and pushed the bar forward. The ultralight slowed and maintained a tenuous altitude above the trees. The river was fifty yards straight ahead and the treeline sloped downward as it approached the shore. Kevin applied just enough power to keep the ultralight above the trees. The engine was shaking badly and the trike felt as if it would fall apart at any moment. The little aircraft sheared off the last treetop as it soared into the open air above the water. Kevin banked to his right and felt the tension slip enough to ask Lauri Beth,

"Did you get a waypoint fix on the cabin before we left?"

"You bet, I did," she answered. "But we shouldn't need it. You can see the smoke five miles away."

"I want to call Donovan as soon as we get to the truck. We're gonna need a chopper and some firefighting gear."

"You mean 'if' we get back to the truck, don't you?" Lauri Beth said fighting to get her words out as she hung on to the convulsing airframe.

The ultralight was now ten feet over the river and Kevin was exerting all of his strength to hold direction and altitude.

"I think the truck is around the next bend and about a quarter mile in from the river!" he shouted.

He was searching for some kind of smooth area to set down and was edging toward the south shoreline. The river made a slow bend to the left and the current had deposited silt along the shore. The resulting area was relatively rock free and looked to be about thirty yards long and an irregular four yards wide. Kevin made for the spot. He nursed the ultralight along until they were twenty yards from the silt. His right hand found the magneto toggle switches and he clicked them off. The engine and the vibrations ceased immediately. Kevin still had seven or eight feet in altitude. He pushed the bar forward and slowed the aircraft to just over twenty knots. The ultralight sank and its wheels touched the silt about five feet from the end. The silt deposit sloped up from the water and the right wheel hit first. The left wheel dug in at the same time as the nosewheel and the angle of the trike caused it to turn left. Kevin turned the nosewheel to the right but it sank into the soft silt and acted more like a brake than a directional control. The resulting left turn combined with the jammed nosewheel caused the trike to tilt to the left and capsize into the water. The wing prevented the trike from turning completely over on its side and held it to a sixty-degree angle.

Kevin unbuckled his seatbelt and dropped into the water.

"Are you all right?" he asked Lauri Beth.

"I think so," she answered. "This is my first landing in an ultralight. Would you consider it a normal one?"

"Very funny," he said as he undid her seatbelt and lowered her into the shallow water. "Help me tip this thing upright and then let's see if we can't pull it up onto shore a little bit."

*

"I think I hit him," Saunders shouted as he danced about in his underwear. "That'll teach the son of a bitch!"

"I think that he might have got you, too," Boone said as he pointed to the burning pickup. "And, by the way, I didn't hear a crash. You may have hit him but I don't think you stopped him."

Wheeler rushed out of the cabin with a fire extinguisher in his hand. He foamed the pickup and soon had the fire under control.

"Lucky we had that downpour. I didn't think the trees were still that wet. I'm surprised they didn't go up like tinder," he said to no one in particular. Then addressing the general, "What're we gonna do, now, General Boone?"

"We're gonna get our collective asses outta here. That's what we're gonna do. That ultralight wasn't here by accident. You can bet your ass that he's got help on the way. Jimmy Ray, pack up all your computer stuff. Charlie, shut off the generator and load it on my pickup. Pete, see if you can make yourself useful without burning down the cabin."

CHAPTER FIFTY-TWO

Kevin and Lauri Beth struggled with the ultralight but finally got it facing the shore. They managed to pull it a few feet up into the silt. Kevin unbolted the pylon and lowered the sail to the ground. There he took out the batons and released the tension. The wing sagged and Kevin folded it together like an accordion fan. He pulled it across the silt and into the trees. Without the weight and the awkwardness of the wing, the trike moved easier and Kevin and Lauri Beth huffed and puffed it out of sight next to the sail.

"Let's see if we can find the pickup," he said.

"I think our best bet would be to walk the shoreline and then cut inland," she offered.

"Agreed," Kevin said as he checked the trike for anything they shouldn't leave behind.

He packed his GPS and maps and indicated that Lauri Beth should do the same. He picked up the rifle, motioned for her to follow and began walking. The going was tough, for the shoreline was littered with rocks and fallen trees and once they left the bend in the river, the silt disappeared. Forty-five minutes after they had begun, Kevin pulled up.

"What do you think?" he asked. "I figure that this should be about the place to start inland."

"See that pile of rocks with the two trees criss-crossed on top of them," Lauri Beth pointed across the river. "I marked them when we took off and you made that first turn to the river. From the air, they looked like a skull and crossbones. The truck should be a hundred yards or so straight in."

Kevin put his arm around her shoulders and gave a little squeeze. She looked up at him feeling very much a full partner in the team. Without a word they turned inland and began picking their way through the overgrown woods. They arrived at the far end of the take-off opening and took a moment to catch their breath. The truck was at the other end of the clearing and they walked to it without talking. Kevin broke the silence.

"I hope the cell phone will work out here," he said. "I'd sure like to know that backup was on the way."

He turned on the phone and nodded an okay to Lauri Beth, indicating that the LCD display showed a cell connection. He dialed and waited for an answer.

"Joe Donovan," he heard.

"Joe, this is Kevin Stewart. We've found Saunders and probably the headquarters of the New Revolutionary Militia as well."

"Where are you?" Donovan asked.

"Idaho!" Kevin replied. "We're on the north fork of the Salmon River. Here's the coordinates of the cabin that they used for headquarters."

"Thanks! What's your situation?"

"We're on the ground. They spotted us and shot up the ultralight. We think that they'll be pulling out as soon as they can. We could use some backup."

"Okay!" Donovan said. "We've got a chopper in Boise. That's only about a hundred miles from you. They should be able to scramble in about ten minutes. They should be there in an hour or less."

"Listen, Joe! Lauri Beth shot up a truck and it exploded. I hope there's firefighting equipment aboard."

"Standard!"

"Gotta go," Kevin said. "Anything else you need?"

He closed the cell phone and turned to Lauri Beth.

"Now to find the cabin," he said. "Any idea where we can pick up that jeep trail?"

"Well, the river took a turn to the northwest and the cabin should be in that direction from here. I think if we can head directly west, we should come across it and still be south of the cabin."

Kevin unhooked the trailer from the pickup and pulled it into the woods.

"Toss your gear in the bed and we'll cruise this clearing," he said as he threw his pack into the back of the truck in obedience to his own order. "But bring your GPS and map with you."

Lauri Beth emptied her pack into the bed of the pickup, held up her GPS and map for Kevin to see, and climbed into the passenger side of the cab. Kevin made sure that the vehicle was in four-wheel low before he put it in gear and drove to the other end of the clearing.

*

Boone was standing just outside of the cabin. He had his hands on his hips and was issuing orders in rapid succession. Wheeler and Charlie were scampering about in compliance. Saunders was operating in slow motion. His face reflected the surliness of his disposition. He had lost his wheels and had been humiliated by the general in front of Wheeler and Charlie, both of whom he considered his inferior. He blamed everything on Kevin and Lauri Beth. One part of him hoped that they had crashed and burned, another part hoped that they had survived and that he would see them again and personally terminate them with a slow and painful death.

"All right, men!" Boone boomed. "Final inspection!"

Wheeler and Charlie snapped to on either side of the door to the cabin. Saunders sat down on the log that served as an entry step and leaned back against the cabin wall. Boone gave him a scornful look and marched into the cabin. He walked every inch of the inside, opened every drawer and searched every cabinet and closet. Only when he was sure that nothing had been left behind, did he say, "Well done, men!"

"Sir!" Wheeler said as the general emerged from the doorway. "What about the truck?"

"The truck," Boone said. "That could pose a problem. I was thinking about sinking it in the river but that bright white would show up even if it was ten feet under. I'll tell you what! Push it deeper into the woods and cover it with branches."

"Saunders!" he shouted at the sheriff. "Make sure that your goddamned truck is cleaned out and then help hide it!"

Pete painstakingly got to his feet, gave the general a look of insolence and ambled toward his burned-out truck. It took a full half hour to camouflage the pick-up. As the three emerged from the woods, they found the general standing by his SUV.

"Saddle up, men," he said. "It's time to move out. Major Wheeler will drive me. Charlie, you and Pete take the pickup."

Charlie and Saunders started for the left side of the pickup at the same time. Charlie got there first and opened the driver's door. He was about to step in when Saunders stepped in front of him and grabbed the steering wheel.

"I'll drive," he said and seated himself in the left front seat.

Charlie walked around the rear of the truck and got in the passenger seat without objection. He mouthed the words, "What a real pain in the ass!"

Saunders pulled up along side the general's SUV and rolled down his window. "Where to?" he asked.

"First we gotta get outta here," the general answered. "Then we'll head for Northern California. I know a spot where we can hole out. Follow me."

The general nodded to Wheeler and they started down the rutted excuse for a road. Saunders and Charlie fell in behind.

*

"Why don't you tune in your GPS," Kevin suggested to Lauri Beth. "At least that way, we'll have an idea as to the location and distance to the cabin.

"We're headed 270 degrees and I make the cabin to be 4.76 miles at 287 degrees," Lauri Beth said after she had set up her GPS. "Are you sure that this is a driveable trail we're on?"

Kevin spotted a path near the west end of the clearing that appeared to lead mostly westward. He didn't hesitate for an instant and drove the four-wheeled pickup into the forest. Since they had entered the overgrowth, he had been crawling over small boulders and fallen trees. They were making slow, steady and extremely hazardous progress. Suddenly, they crossed a somewhat better trail and Kevin pulled to a stop.

"How does this look?" he asked Lauri Beth, referring to her GPS readout.

"This has got to be the trail to the cabin," she said. "The heading and course match and it shows that we're about four and a quarter miles away. Let's take it."

Kevin made a forty-five-degree turn to the right and lined his tires up to the ruts. He paused for an instant and was just about to apply power to the engine when Lauri Beth held up her hand.

"Did you hear something?" she asked.

Kevin let the engine idle down and put the gear selector in neutral.

"Yeah," he said. "Sounds like a car or truck coming towards us. It's got to be them."

"What'll we do?"

Kevin had already made up his mind. Up ahead the road narrowed even further and passed between two giant pine trees. The forest on either side of the pines was impenetrable. Kevin pulled just ahead of the two towering sentinels and worked his way back and forth until his pickup was perpendicular to the road. The front bumper was touching one pine and the rear bumper was touching the other. He put the gears in park and turned off the engine.

"This is where we get off," he said as he dropped to the ground and leaned over the truck bed. Lauri Beth did the same on her side.

"What should we take?" she asked.

"Guns, GPS, phone, and some rope," he said as he grabbed the rifle and a coil of rope.

Lauri Beth held up the GPS and phone. Kevin rounded the rear of the pickup, took Lauri Beth by the arm and led her into the woods. Fifteen yards into the thicket, he turned toward the sound of the approaching vehicles.

*

The two-vehicle caravan had been proceeding slowly down the trail from the cabin. The passengers were tossed back and forth and side to side as the SUV and the pickup crept over the uneven ground. The lead vehicle, driven by Wheeler, rounded a rutted corner at a speed of five miles per hour and drew to a halt. Fifteen yards ahead, a pickup truck blocked the road.

"What the hell is that?" Boone growled.

Wheeler didn't answer. Instead, he opened his door

and got out of the SUV with the intention of inspecting the obstructing vehicle. He was immediately knocked to the ground as a burly, cursing Saunders charged by with his weapon drawn.

"That goddam, no good, son of a bitchin' bastard," he swore. "I'll kill 'im! I swear to God, I'll kill 'im!"

He began firing at the pickup when he got to within ten feet of it. Bullets smashed the windows and body of the truck. He blew out the two nearest tires and pumped four or five rounds into the cab.

"Where in the hell are ya?" he yelled, completely out of control.

He yanked the passenger door open and jammed his gun into the empty space. He fired a shot into the upholstery and began throwing anything that wasn't nailed down onto the ground behind him. With his fury still unspent, he turned his attention to the bed of the pickup. He climbed into the cargo space in one leap and resumed his unloading tirade. Everything that Kevin and Lauri Beth hadn't taken with them was tossed unceremoniously to the ground. With the truck bed completely empty, Saunders stomped around and fired two shots into the decking, one narrowly missing the fuel tank. He then vaulted to the ground, ran to the front of the truck and shot out the headlights.

Wheeler used the door of his vehicle as a shield as he tried to avoid a stray bullet. The general did likewise. Charlie lay across the seat, using the entire vehicle as barrier. When the firing ceased and Saunders stood triumphantly in front of the blind, lame truck, Wheeler and Boone cautiously left their positions of safety and ventured a step or two into the open.

"Take it easy! Take it easy!" the general soothed as they walked toward a still fuming Saunders. "That won't do any good. Just calm down and we'll pull this thing out of the way and get out of here."

Charlie raised himself off of the seat and peered over the dashboard. His eyes were transfixed on the scene in front of him. The general and major were now in a huddle with Saunders and were calming him down. Charlie felt that it was safe to leave the pickup. He opened the door and began to get out, never letting his gaze drift from the three in front of him. His feet touched the ground and as he straightened up, he felt an odd sensation against his skull. His head had encountered something hard and cold. He instinctively froze and heard a voice whisper, "One word and you're a dead man!"

His face was pushed down on the seat and his arms were yanked behind him. He could feel a rope tying his wrists together. His mouth contorted as a gag was tied around his neck.

"Move!" he was directed. "And quietly!"

He was pushed to the rear of the truck and then off the road on the far side. He stumbled and fell on his face in a damp ditch. Before he could move, his feet were bound and he was rolled over to face his assailants. He looked up at two very angry faces. Kevin and Lauri Beth!

Kevin held a finger to his lips and whispered, "If you make even one little sound, Lauri Beth will come back and kill you."

He looked at Lauri Beth and shivered. Her eyes convinced him that it was no idle threat. He closed his
eyes and nodded in subjection. Kevin and Lauri Beth
crouched low and used the two militia trucks as a
screen. The general and the major were still calming
Saunders and all three were focused within their
group. The doors of the general's SUV were open and
Kevin and Lauri Beth slid behind them on either side.
Kevin cradled his rifle in the crotch formed by the driver's side door and the body of the car. Lauri Beth took
up a position on the other side. Her armament was a
pistol which she held in two hands, arms stretched out
in front of her.

The general and Wheeler were standing with their
backs to Kevin and Lauri Beth. Saunders was facing
them, his pistol pointed at the ground. Kevin squeezed
off a shot that whistled between the general's ear and
Saunders' head and splattered against the pickup's
right windshield post. The roar of the rifle drowned out
the trio's conversation.

Boone and Wheeler turned so that all three were
facing the source of the discharge.

"Throw down your weapons and place your hands
over your heads!" Kevin ordered. It took an instant for
the words to sink in and for the three men to become
aware of their situation.

"Throw down your weapons and place your hands
over your heads!" Kevin repeated. "NOW!" he added for
emphasis.

The three looked at each other and then at the pair
behind the open doors of the SUV. Wheeler was the

449 • T LURE OF THE DUTCHMAN

first to comply. He raised his hands skyward, palms out and empty. The general unholstered his sidearm and followed Wheeler's example. Saunders was still behind the other two and was thinking about his options. He still had his pistol in his hand.

"I said NOW, Sheriff!"

Kevin brought his rifle to bear on the side-view mirror of the truck.

"NOW!"

Saunders hesitated for millisecond and Kevin fired. The sideview mirror exploded with fragments of glass peppering the sheriff.

"Okay! Okay!" Saunders shouted. The gun was tossed onto the ground in front of the militiamen.

"One at a time, you may lower your left hand and toss out any other weapons. I mean knives, tools and any other thing you might be carrying. Don't let me find anything on you later." Kevin instructed. "You, first, old man."

A hunting knife and a Swiss Army knife were thrown alongside Saunders' pistol.

"You next," he said, pointing the rifle at Wheeler.

Wheeler pulled a knife from his boot and produced a small pistol from his rear belt.

"Sheriff?" Kevin said.

Another knife and a nightstick joined the growing pile.

"Now back up," Kevin ordered as he stepped out from behind the SUV's door.

"Lauri Beth, would you bring those weapons over here?"

She stood up, tucked her gun in her belt, walked around the SUV's door and advanced on the stockpile. As she got closer, she inadvertently stepped between Kevin and his prisoners.

"Don't!" he began.

Lauri Beth made her second mistake. She turned her head toward Kevin.

It happened in a flash! Saunders shoved the general into Wheeler and leaped toward Lauri Beth. He grabbed her in a bear hug with his left arm and circled her neck with his right.

"All right! Smart ass! Drop your gun right now or I break her neck!"

The general and Wheeler were disentangling themselves from Saunders' push and were now advancing on Kevin.

"Get his gun!" Saunders ordered.

Kevin had no choice. He couldn't risk a shot at Saunders without the fear of hitting Lauri Beth. He lowered his rifle and was instantly pinned by Boone and Wheeler.

"He's all mine!" Saunders yelled. "Just hold him! He's all mine!"

Without warning, Saunders swung Lauri Beth around and held her by the neck with his left hand. He drew back his right fist and punched her squarely in the face with all of his might. Lauri Beth's head snapped back as she was propelled backward by the blow. She hit the side of the pickup truck with her shoulders and sank slowly to the ground. Kevin strained but his arms were pinned behind him.

"I'll get back to you in a little while, sweetheart!" Saunders salivated at Lauri Beth as he turned to face Kevin.

"Now, let's see how tough you really are!" he said. "When I get through with you, you'll be just conscious enough to see what I do to your girlfriend!"

He began to move toward Kevin.

Lauri Beth sat on the ground in a daze. Her face was bleeding from every pore. Blood ran into her mouth and the sensation jarred her into semi-consciousness. She shook her head and rolled from her sitting position to her hands and knees. As her right hand touched the ground she felt an object under her palm and her fingers automatically closed around it.

Saunders had closed half of the distance between himself and Kevin. Kevin strained to see past him to Lauri Beth but his view was blocked by Saunders' bulk.

Lauri Beth picked up the object and raised it shoulder high and recognized one of the hand axes that Saunders had thrown from the pickup to the ground in his initial rage.

Saunders was two steps from Kevin with a knife in his right hand and a sadistic grin on his face.

Lauri Beth spun around on her knees and squared her body. She raised her left knee and let the pickax drop behind her head. Then, almost falling forward, she brought her arm up and over. She released the handle at the top of the arc and let her hand follow through to her target. She fell on her face. The weight of the head of the pickax acted like an axis and the lighter handle rotated around it. The spinning pickax traveled a slightly curved path. The handle completed one full revolution and was pointing straight downward when the sharpened tip of the ax head struck Saunders in the back directly between his shoulders.

The force of the blow pushed Saunders forward and the knife tip penetrated Kevin's skin. Saunders reacted against the pressure on his back and jerked up and back. He pulled the knife away from Kevin's neck and tried to speak. The words gurgled up in his throat as blood filled his mouth and the tip of the pickax emerged from his chest.

Saunders looked down at his sternum in disbelief as blood oozed onto his shirt and dripped from the tip of the pickax. The knife dropped from his hand and his eyes locked onto Kevin's in pure hatred. His knees began to buckle and he sank to the ground in a breathless heap.

Boone and Wheeler widened their eyes in unison and stared at a limp Saunders at their feet. They eased their grip on Kevin. Wheeler felt himself spun inward and a crushing blow landed on his nose as Kevin's elbow smashed into his face. The blackness that followed was a blessing.

Boone viewed the two comrades at his feet and threw up his hands.

"On the ground! Feet spread! Hands behind your back!" Kevin ordered.

The general complied and soon found himself hogtied and seated beside his equally incapacitated major. Kevin rushed to Lauri Beth, who was just rolling onto her back.

"What happened?" she asked with blinking eyes.

"You just took out one of the most vicious criminals in the world and saved our lives as well! That's what happened."

Kevin helped her to her feet and cleaned up her face with his shirt.

"You look better," he said. "I hope you feel better."

"I don't feel all that great," she said. "But I bet I feel a whole lot better than those guys."

They had been back at the cabin for over a half an hour, prisoners secure and Kevin was examining a deep cut on Lauri Beth's face when they heard the welcome sound of the chopper blades.

CHAPTER FIFTY-THREE

Lauri Beth held her left hand out in front of her with her palm facing away. "Oh! Kevin! It's just beautiful!" she exclaimed as she viewed the solitary diamond set in a plain platinum ring. "And the rest of it? It's all true, as well? When did you decide? Oh, I really love you!"

"I love you, too!" Kevin said. "It was in the mine, when it was caving in all around us. I thought that if we ever got out of there alive, I'd ask you to marry me and if you said, 'yes', then I'd retire from the military, rebuild Brian's house and raise our family on the ranch. That is if that's what you wanted, too."

"Sounds like a dream come true," she said as she kissed him lovingly on the lips.

They were in her apartment lying on the bed with the television turned on, waiting for President Jefferson to address the nation.

"Be right back," she said as she left the bedroom and

went to the small alcove that housed a clothes washer, dryer and a small laundry sink.

"Com'on back," Kevin yelled. "It's starting. What are you doing in there, anyway?"

"Just soaking some of our equipment. I want to get it clean before we put it away," she answered as she lay down next to him and focused on the TV.

"Ladies and gentlemen! The President of the United States!"

President Branden David Jefferson strode to the dais and stood erect before the cameras.

"Four years ago," he began. "I promised you, the voters, that I would get to the bottom of the meat shortage and the terrible rise in food prices that it was causing. I am happy to announce that this goal has been accomplished.

"As you know, three weeks ago, meat prices suddenly dropped dramatically and supplies have been growing ever since. This was no accident! This administration dedicated itself to that one campaign promise and, thanks to our diligence and resourcefulness, we have solved the problem.

"The solution was not a simple one. Our investigation revealed that the shortage was not an ordinary event. Indeed, the shortage was the result of a conspiracy. A conspiracy contrived by a few greedy men. These men, cattle ranchers from the great state of Texas, had discovered a virus that when contacted by cattle and other large four-legged animals, would affect their ability to breed. These same despicable men developed a serum—an antidote, if you will, that allowed them to protect their own herds. The result was that they were able to make huge and unconscionable profits at the expense of the American people.

"I am pleased to announce to you, at this time, that these men have been brought to justice. They will be tried and, I hope, convicted and sent to prison for the rest of their lives. We have in our possession, at this time, samples of the virus and antidote along with the formulas for their production. We have every reason to believe that our scientists will be able use these chemicals to increase production of meat products, thereby insuring us of ample supplies for ourselves and for our children.

"In our relentless pursuit of these culprits, we also discovered that these men had made a covenant with the devil in the form of a dissident group who called themselves The New Revolutionary Militia. This militia was bent on the destruction of your government. They were headquartered in the wilds of Idaho and were the main source of the distribution of the virus. The leaders of this group have been apprehended and full disclosures and confessions have been obtained, thanks to the turning of state's evidence by one of their leaders."

"Charlie?" Lauri Beth whispered.

"My guess," Kevin answered.

"Full details will be released to the media at the conclusion of this address," the President continued. "Now I have a very special announcement to make."

President Jefferson paused for effect and used the

moment to raise a glass of water to his lips.

"As you know, for the past three years, I have opposed any changes to our tax codes. This opposition has been based on the fairness to all of our people in the resulting changes. Not just the special interests! I have been working diligently with the leaders of both parties to find a fair and equitable solution.

"We have reached an agreement. A bill will be introduced in both chambers tomorrow morning. This bill is essentially the same for both the Senate and the Congress. I expect immediate passage and I will sign it into law. This bill calls for the establishment of a fixed rate income tax. The rate is set at 15% and there are no deductions. The tax will be retroactive to the first of the year. The volumes of tax codes presently in force will be replaced by a single fifty page document. All of our present tax programs will disappear, to be superseded by the new simple regulations. Our computer experts inform me the conversion will be in place before Thanksgiving. All past records will be committed to the archives and we will, in effect, start over as of last January first. Again, all details of the new tax codes will be released to the media as soon as possible.

"This administration has proved, once again, that it has the best interests of the American people at heart and I pledge to you that it will continue to respond to the needs of every man, woman and child in this great country of ours.

"May God bless you! Thank you and good night!"

Every hand in the room shot up begging to be heard. The President ignored them all. He turned and, with great dignity, left the room.

Kevin and Lauri Beth stared at the screen as the commentators began to make their assessment of the startling speech. Finally, he got up and turned off the set.

"What do you think?" he asked.

"Talk about taking credit where credit is due!" Lauri Beth said. "Not one mention of the mine, Dr. Middlestat or Brian. Do you think that he didn't even know?"

"Oh! He knew! My guess is that it's all become classified information and will be buried somewhere in the tombs of Washington."

"And what's all the tax stuff about?" she persisted.

"Oh, that!" Kevin said. "It'll take about ten years but you can bet that the fifty-page document will become fifty volumes."

"I guess you're right," Lauri Beth said as she went back to the laundry alcove.

Kevin followed her.

"I'll give you a hand," he said.

"Okay! you clean up the jumars and I'll do this pick."

Kevin began wiping the jumars and Lauri Beth took the pickax out of the water and dried the iron head. Then she began rubbing the wooden handle with a dish towel. She stopped the drying and began to run her hand over the wood. She held it up to the light and the took a scouring pad and gently rubbed it over the surface of the handle.

"What are you doing?" Kevin asked.

Lauri Beth dipped the handle in the water, took it

out, rubbed the pad over it and repeated the process.

"Look at this! Can you make it out?" she said, holding the pickax up to the light and rotating the handle.

"Yeah! I see it!" Kevin agreed. "I'll be damned."

She laid the pickax on top of the dryer and they both stared as the handle began to dry and the lettering stood out in etched relief.

They mouthed the words in unison, "J. WALTZ"